PRAISE FOR MARY STRAND

For *Sunsets on Catfish Bar*:

"Emotionally complex and deeply involving, this is the story of a woman dealing with impossible challenges—and finding grace and humanity in the journey." —SUSAN WIGGS, #1 New York Times Bestselling Author

For *Pride, Prejudice, and Push-Up Bras*:

Listed among "the best indie *Pride and Prejudice* books the IP staff has seen..." —*Independent Publisher*

"This Minnesota-set rom-com hits the ground running and never draws breath until its satisfyingly foregone conclusion." —*Jane Austen's Regency World* magazine

SUNSETS ON CATFISH BAR
A PENDULUM NOVEL

MARY STRAND

This book is a work of fiction. Names, characters, places, and incidents are either the product of the author's imagination or are used fictitiously. Any resemblance to actual persons, living or dead, business establishments, events, or locales is entirely coincidental.

Triple Berry Press P.O. Box 24733 Minneapolis, Minnesota 55424

Copyright © 2022 Mary Strand

Cover Credits
Cover design: LB Hayden
Pier on a Calm River @ Givaga

Logo Credit: LB Hayden

All rights reserved. This book is licensed for your personal enjoyment only. No part of this book may be used, reproduced, stored in a retrieval system, or transmitted in any form or by any means whatsoever without the author's express written permission, except in the case of brief quotations embodied in critical articles and reviews.

Electronic ISBN: 978-1-944949-10-5
Paperback ISBN: 978-1-944949-16-7

Printed in the United States of America

For Miriam Seltzer,
without whom the St. Croix has never been the same.

With all my thanks to:

Don and Arvonne Fraser, who owned and loved our St. Croix River house before Tom and I inherited it. I'm still grateful despite the fact that Arvonne painted everything red, and I loathe red, and HELLO, my life would've been much easier if you'd painted everything blue! Ha ha!

Bonnie Skelton, who still hangs out with us at the St. Croix house, and who waterskied in her eighties and went tubing with me in her nineties. Bonnie first showed me the beautiful hikes up the hill at the St. Croix River that I describe in this novel, and she used to always leave all of us in her dust.

My mom, Betty Strand, who taught me more than I ever wanted to know about brain cancer.

So many good friends who provided critiques, edits, beta reads, or brainstorming help along the way (some of it a million years ago), including Connie Brockway, Susan Kay Law, Carol Prescott, Jennifer Crusie, our Maui writers group, Just Cherry Writers, Romex, Ann Barry Burns, and Tom Fraser.

Michael Bodine, who knows everything and occasionally tells me some of it.

Mariam AlAdsani, my daughter Kate's friend at Boston University, who came up with the "Pendulum" name after many of my Facebook friends took a shot at it. (Thank you all!)

Keely Thrall, who (along with the Washington Capitals) saved my writer butt just as this book was about to go out into the world.

Several wise published writers (and adorable friends) who gave me much-needed advice when it was time to bring this book into the world, including Judith Arnold, Brenda Hiatt, Lori Matthews, Cathy Maxwell, and Melissa McClone.

Laura Hayden and Pam McCutcheon, collectively also known as Parker Hayden Media, LLC, who patiently answer some of the most anal-compulsive and/or wildly ignorant questions in the world on a routine basis, all of them from me.

CHAPTER 1

Swans and fairies twirled and leaped across the stage in frenetic glee, spinning and turning and—

Damn. Liz Tanner cringed when Jenna nailed another dancer, her third so far, and the other little girl skidded on her butt, landing against a fake tree. Miss Sam came running out, a horrified smile frozen on her face, and scooped up the sobbing girl. Jenna, utterly oblivious, continued to twirl. The other five-year-olds now kept their distance, leaving Jenna to dance an impromptu solo.

The spring recital program called it Swan Lake, but it looked more like the dance of a lethal sugarplum fairy.

Biting back an embarrassed grin, Liz resisted the urge to slink down in her seat. Jenna had improved since her first dance recital last December, when she'd frozen in place, sucking her index finger for the entire routine. But the other parents might not agree.

Paul wasn't here to agree or not. Liz checked her watch, then glanced back at the doors for at least the fortieth time this afternoon. The woman behind her nodded at the empty seat next to Liz and smiled sympathetically.

A flush crept up her cheeks, but Liz didn't need sympathy. She needed Paul. No, *Jenna* needed Paul. He'd promised a dozen times that he wouldn't miss the recital, or forget it, or come up with yet another excuse. Mr. Hotshot Junior Partner at Brennan & Locke, the third-largest law firm in Washington, D.C., had a lot of them.

And he'd blown it. Again.

As she turned back to watch the finale, a sudden pain stabbed her. She pressed a hand against her stomach, feeling the ugly raised scar from the last surgery. She still had one ovary, as if it mattered. As if a baby could save her marriage.

Wild applause, whistles, and bright lights brought her focus back to the stage just in time to see the class bow and file off the stage—except for Jenna, who tumbled forward into the front row, landing in Liz's lap and slamming against her stomach.

Oof. Liz sucked in a breath at the shooting pain. Another breath, this time slow and calm. A tiny "Mom?" from Jenna, who jiggled in Liz's arms as her short white-blond hair sprang out at odd angles. "Where's Daddy?"

"Um, still at work?" Biting her lip, Liz tilted Jenna's trembling chin upward and planted a kiss on her forehead. "Hey, you were fantastic, sweetie." The woman behind Liz snorted. Liz whispered in Jenna's ear. "The best one out there."

"I hit Virginia." And two others, but who was counting? Jenna looked past Liz, scanning the audience. "Maybe Daddy's in the back. He said he'd come, 'cause it's Sunday and I was dancing and he—he promised."

A tear formed at the corner of Jenna's eye, and Liz touched her thumb to it before it could trickle down her cheek.

"I guess he got busy."

How could she explain Paul to a five-year-old when, at thirty-seven and after eleven years of marriage, Liz didn't understand him? Her brain churned, trying to offer excuses. Finding none, she shook her head and hugged Jenna.

After a quick trip backstage to pick up Jenna's dance bag and whisper an apology to Jenna's teacher, they headed out into the bright sunshine of the May afternoon, hand in hand, walking up Connecticut Avenue toward the zoo. A little girl who'd survived her recital and whose father was missing in action deserved a reward.

She reached into her purse for her cell phone, then shrugged and withdrew her hand. If she called Paul, she'd only yell and upset Jenna, and what was the point? He wouldn't change.

As she walked with Jenna, Liz pondered the riddle of Paul—and how to solve the riddle without ruining everyone's life. Jenna squeezed her hand, an instant reminder of the one precious thing she'd gained from marrying Paul.

But Jenna couldn't fix what ailed her parents' marriage.

A bus honked its horn, jarring Liz as a blast of exhaust hit her. She glanced at a street sign and realized they were almost at the zoo. The walk hadn't done much for her abdominal region, but resting for the last four weeks hadn't, either. Luckily, deals were light at her investment-banking house, and Peabody McBain didn't miss her. Much.

Bottom line, she needed to do something about Paul. He barely knew his daughter and no longer knew Liz at all. Had he ever? What had happened to the thoughtful man she'd married? The guy who'd left work early so many times just to surprise her with a picnic in Rock Creek Park or tickets to a concert at Wolf Trap? Had he been faking it?

She didn't have a clue. But today's recital had been the last straw—and the last time she'd let Paul disappoint Jenna.

With new determination, she hopped up onto a curb, blinking at the sudden jolt. Gripping Jenna's hand as they waded into the crowd near the zoo entrance, she tried to ignore the pain. She was going to take action—finally—and she'd make it work. For Jenna's sake and for hers.

Her cell phone rang. Paul, undoubtedly, begging forgiveness for sins he'd never admit to committing. She let it ring again, then pulled it out of her purse and glanced at the screen. Her eyebrows rose, even though she shouldn't be surprised.

"Diana?"

A pause. "Is that how they greet people in the big city these days? How's my little dancer?"

Liz caught herself smiling. Her stepmom had probably calculated the precise moment the recital would end.

Liz rubbed Jenna's shoulder and mouthed the word "Gram" in response to the question in her daughter's eyes. "Hi, Diana. You missed quite a performance. I'll let Jenna tell you all about it." Jenna tugged on her sleeve, begging to talk, and Liz nodded as she held up a hand. "But last time I checked, Minneapolis was a big city, too."

"With drafty old houses."

Liz pictured the elegant mansion in Wayzata, the wealthy suburb where Liz's dad and Diana had moved a few years after Liz left for college. "What are you up to these days? You've retired now, right?"

"In theory." Diana sighed, loudly, which only drew another smile. "But that's a subject for another day."

"Oh? And what's today's subject?"

Another slight pause. "It's . . . your father, dear."

———

MONDAY MORNING, after a restless night in which Paul slept on the living-room sofa and left the house before dawn, Liz promised Jenna lunch downtown—a special treat in honor of her first dance recital at which she'd actually danced—and a trip to her daddy's office.

Why Jenna wanted to see Paul, Liz couldn't imagine. Maybe she just wanted to remember what he looked like.

In Liz's current mood—overcast with a chance of lightning—she debated the wisdom of visiting Paul, especially with Jenna in tow. After she filled him in on the latest news, not to mention her big decision, she was pretty sure Paul would agree.

Leaving the kid-friendly eatery nestled amid a cluster of banks and high-powered restaurants, she squinted at the blinding sun, clutched Jenna's hand, and hurried past a little boy and his earbud-wearing mom—or nanny, more likely.

Fifty yards later, she rounded the corner onto K Street and reached the heavy glass door to Paul's building. Tugging it open, she hustled an already-tired Jenna inside. As Liz blinked against the cool air and dim lighting, Jenna pointed to the far corner of the marble lobby, where a teenage girl scooped out ice cream from a makeshift stand. Jenna's eyes, wide as saucers, went from exhaustion to delight in the space of a heartbeat.

"Ice cream! Can I?" Tugging free of Liz's light grasp, Jenna didn't wait for a reply. With one stride for every three churned out by Jenna's little legs, Liz caught her a moment before she pressed her face inside a large tub of ice cream.

"Just one scoop, Jenna." Liz eyed her daughter's pink-and-orange tank top and matching shorts, still remarkably intact after their pizza lunch. "Strawberry?"

After ten minutes, two spills, and five rounds of Jenna's giggle fits, she pushed the elevator button for Paul's floor. Two tight-lipped young lawyers joined them, nodding once before checking their phones.

The elevator lurched at the sixth floor. Catching Jenna's sticky hand, Liz hoped Paul could squeeze in a quick break. She couldn't have this conversation on the phone or in the middle of the night. That didn't leave many options.

She pushed open the solid wood doors to his firm.

"Paul Worthington, please." Smiling at the receptionist, Liz tapped her nails on the marble-topped counter while she waited for Margo to buzz Paul.

She glanced around the reception area, realizing she hadn't set foot in Paul's office since Christmas, when she and Jenna had forcibly kidnapped him for an hour of shopping.

Buzz. "Mr. Worthington, your wife and daughter are here to see you." Pause. "Send them back? Yes, sir."

Margo held up a hand as Liz started down the hall to Paul's office. "Ms. Tanner, his office is—"

"Thanks, but I remember the way."

Margo coughed, loudly, causing Liz's head to swivel. "He moved to a new office." She pointed left. Liz had headed right. "Down that hall. I can have someone show you."

"I'll find it, thanks." Shaking her head, Liz wondered what else Paul hadn't mentioned. Thank God he hadn't switched firms. He'd tell her a year later, or maybe send a memo.

Four doors down the left-hand hallway, she found him, hunched over a stack of papers at eye level, swilling a cup of coffee as if it held the key to eternal life.

When he didn't look up, she sighed. Jenna skipped around Paul's desk to his chair. She squeezed his arm and a handful of his shirt, getting an absentminded pat on the head in return.

"Jenna's here to see you, Paul." She watched his eyelids flicker as he flipped a coffee-stained page and still didn't look up. Exasperated, she turned to leave.

"Liz." Gazing through her, he forced a smile before offering Jenna a wider, more genuine one. "Hey, peanut." He wouldn't smile when he noticed that Jenna's sticky pink fingers had left their mark on his white shirt. "What brings you guys here?"

Liz gritted her teeth, having expected a different reaction from a man who'd just spent a night on the sofa. She nodded at Jenna, who was now prancing around Paul's office. "She didn't see you all weekend."

He flinched. "She wasn't around this weekend."

"Oh?" She raised one eyebrow. Had he always been so defensive? "You're right. She had a dance recital yesterday."

No reaction. Unbelievable.

His gaze skittered from her to Jenna to the stack of paper. The stack won. She hadn't made him salivate like that since they were dating.

"I can see you're busy, so I'll be quick. Carrie gave notice today. She's done as of Friday."

"Carrie? Friday?" Frowning, he pushed his wire-rim glasses higher on his nose.

"Our nanny." She hoped he knew that, but she wasn't sure of anything anymore. "Friday. Just in time for Memorial Day weekend."

Paul straightened in his chair. "Our contract with her requires thirty days' notice."

"Tell it to a judge. In the meantime, we have a problem." She dropped into the ugly burgundy-plaid chair across from him.

"Won't you—"

She waved away his question, which she knew from experience required her to "fix" the nanny problem. She'd hoped that cutting back her work hours would give her time to heal from the surgery. Time to think. She hadn't anticipated being the only parent on duty until they somehow found a new nanny.

"Diana called me yesterday." She took a deep breath. "Dad isn't doing well."

Paul's eyes glazed over the way they did whenever she mentioned something that didn't directly affect him.

Jenna plopped herself down on the carpeting with a few sheets of hopefully blank paper she'd grabbed from Paul's desk and a crayon she'd found in Liz's purse.

"He has brain cancer."

Paul stared at her, silent. She'd stunned the mighty deal lawyer with two words: brain cancer. Come to think of it, Diana had done the same thing to her when they'd talked, and most of Diana's remaining words had blurred together.

When Carrie gave notice five minutes after she walked in the door this morning, something Diana said made its way through the haze. *Come home.*

"I'm going back there. To the house on the St. Croix River. Next week." Liz glanced from Jenna, oblivious to the conversation, to Paul. "Don't worry. I'll take Jenna."

Paul squinted at her. "How long?"

"If I can swing it with work—" She crossed her fingers; she still had to ask her boss. "I'll take three months off and help Diana take care of Dad. He might not have much time left."

Paul's voice rose, surprising her. "You're kidding, right?"

"It's also good timing for—" The word *separation* lodged itself in her throat. "Time apart. Time to think."

Paul nearly ground his glasses into his nose. "Don't you think we should talk about this?"

"That's the problem." Liz rose, ignoring her trembling knees, and held out a hand for Jenna. "We never *do* talk."

"LIZ IS COMING to see you, dear." Diana Carruthers-Tanner peered over the top of her reading glasses at her husband of twenty-seven years and awaited his reaction.

Frank blinked.

Turning away, she bent her head, pretended to read the fine print on a cereal box, and tried very hard not to chew her lip or commit the grievous sin of showing her disappointment.

It got more difficult every day.

She pushed back her chair from the kitchen table. The last few mouthfuls of whatever she'd eaten had gone down hard, and everything tasted like cardboard.

"She's arriving on Tuesday. With Jenna." After Frank's radiation session tomorrow, they'd finish packing and move out to the River for the summer.

The St. Croix, an hour's drive from their Wayzata home, felt so much more remote. Secluded on a tree-covered hill above a stretch of sand called Catfish Bar on the River's Wisconsin side, the summer house couldn't be reached by car —at least, not within a half mile, and from there it was a somewhat steep hike. Instead, they drove to tiny Afton, Minnesota, and ferried across the River in one of their boats. She'd always considered the trip an adventure and the summer house a refuge.

This summer, she wondered how they'd manage it.

"I can't wait to see how much Jenna has grown. Can you imagine? Five already. She'll start kindergarten this fall." Moving past Frank's wheelchair, she paused, smiling brightly as she patted his arm. His head tilted sideways. She pursed her lips and helped him straighten his shoulders.

Continuing her chatter as she walked to the first-floor

study and pulled together a box of reading material, she wondered whether she'd ever again get a normal response from Frank. Ever again have a normal conversation.

Beyond her other worries, the silence was driving her crazy.

She picked up the box, straining under its weight, and made it as far as the hallway. David and his boys could carry it to the car tomorrow with the rest of their things.

That task completed, she returned to Frank. As she pulled out a chair beside him, wondering what else she needed to pack and what else she could talk about until his morning nap, he opened his mouth. Startled, she held her breath.

His pale blue eyes widened. "Liz?"

———

LIZ WAS COMING HOME. Finally. And too soon.

Piper Jamison stared at her computer screen, twisting a strand of her bangs around one finger as she reread Liz's latest email. Frazzled, she tugged at the hair, almost yanking it out before the head-splitting pain drew her attention away from the screen and the smoldering piles of work in front of her.

Even this dilemma wasn't worth losing hair over.

She'd enjoyed another weekend of bliss with her new man, hidden away from prying eyes and probing questions they weren't ready to answer. She knew him, and yet—somehow—she didn't, not really. They'd spent every spare moment of the last three months exploring each other.

And not just in bed ... although that was fantastic, too.

She thought back to the bouquet he'd sent from a "secret admirer" on Valentine's Day. She, in turn, had spent half the day racking her brain, trying to figure out who on earth it could be. She'd dated more men in the last few years than she'd admit to Tracy or Liz, each possibility fizzling faster than the Vikings often did.

Then *he* appeared, as if for the first time. She should've known all along. She wasn't ready, though, to reveal her heart to the rest of the world. She wanted to savor this time with him.

With Liz around, that would be almost impossible.

Sighing, Piper glanced at the top file on her desk. She should've worked this weekend, even for a few hours, and she'd paid for it all morning. The client wasn't happy. She shuffled through all the notes she'd taken as the client's CFO ranted for over an hour, until finally Tracy had sailed into Piper's office and saved her lazy butt with this file. Thank God for Tracy.

Thank God for friends. She had to remember that.

Her stomach rumbled as she glanced at the small gold clock on her desk. Twelve-thirty. Liz had probably arrived. They'd always been best friends, closer than sisters, but too many years apart had left too much room for secrets—or not enough time to share them. She couldn't just blurt it out. She'd have to juggle her new relationship with finding time for Liz, too. And work. Definitely work. Picturing it all made her head spin.

The phone rang. Despite the headache taking root between her eyes, she chirped her name into the mouthpiece. Her friend—and love, although they both still stuttered over the word—greeted her with a deep, rumbling chuckle, prompting a smile.

Startled, she realized something. As best friends went, Liz had dropped into second place.

Their luggage stowed in the rental car, Liz checked Jenna's car seat before climbing into the front seat. She adjusted her seatbelt, then the rearview mirror, and dropped her cell phone back in her purse after a quick "we're here" message on Paul's voicemail, which was as close as she got to him these days.

Turning the radio to rock, she blasted the air conditioning and rolled down the front windows before heading out onto the maze of roads leading away from the airport. She caught the Highway 494 turnoff, then glanced into the back seat. Jenna. Already sound asleep.

Humming along to an old Soul Asylum hit, Liz found Bailey Road and zipped the final fifteen minutes to the River. The wind whipped her as they passed farms and scattered houses, then a golf course, followed by a cluster of designer-gray houses.

Almost there. She turned right onto the main street of Afton and hung a quick left into the marina. The St. Croix. Diana had emailed precise directions—just in case Liz had forgotten the way home—and told her that someone would pick her up in one of their boats for the short ride across the River to Wisconsin. To the summer house.

She hoped she'd recognize her chauffeur.

She arrived ten minutes early. Pulling into a parking space set back from the deserted city docks, she climbed out and unfastened Jenna, who didn't stir. While Jenna snoozed, she could get her bearings and maybe spot the boat as it crossed the River toward her. Pebbles crunched under her feet as she approached the steps to the city docks.

A speedboat idled below her, rocking in time with the waves slapping the docks. A man, familiar from pictures, idled in the boat. The breeze fanned the ends of his longish brown hair streaked with coppery gold. His bare chest, already surprisingly tan in late May, left her mind blank. As it always had.

David. The boy, now a man, she'd wasted too many teenage nights dreaming about. Wishing, always in vain, that he'd been dreaming about her. Wishing he hadn't been off-limits. Wishing he'd drop off the face of the earth.

Why couldn't it have been someone—anyone—else?

CHAPTER 2

"Lizzie? Is that you?" Tipping back the brim of his baseball cap, David grinned as he held the boat against the dock with his other hand.

She hadn't been Lizzie in too many years to count.

Almost everyone at work called her Elizabeth, friends shortening it to Liz, a few people she'd outmaneuvered on deals opting for Barracuda. Not even Paul called her Lizzie. She'd earned a tough reputation in the sludge pits of mergers and acquisitions. No one fucked with her.

People might fuck with a Lizzie.

"It's Liz now." She didn't stutter, the way she always had around David, but her stomach churned as she offered a hesitant wave. Not like herself at all. But, then, she hadn't seen David—except in Diana's photos—in ages.

Nineteen years, to be precise.

David being David, he just shrugged. "Need a hand?"

Moving closer to the steps, she rested a hand gingerly on the rusted iron railing. "Looks like you've already got your hands full with the boat." The teenager hired to watch the docks slouched against a far pole, staying as far as he could from both the boat and Liz's cargo. "I can make a few trips."

David nodded, glancing at the teenage slacker.

With another wave in David's general direction, Liz returned to the car. Jenna rubbed her eyes and peered around while Liz unbuckled her.

"This is the River?"

No squeals or claps or bright eyes. Nothing. Even at five, Jenna had already spent too many years in D.C.

"Yep. The St. Croix River, otherwise known as the River to us natives." Could she still call herself one? Maybe not in front of the natives. "Let's get moving, cutie. David is waiting for us at the dock. He brought a speedboat."

Jenna climbed out of the back seat in record time. "A real speedboat? Will he go fast?"

"Not unless you say so." Laughing at Jenna's wary look, Liz nodded. "Check it out. And meet your ... well, David."

Jenna hesitated, her steps slow.

"He's not a stranger. David is one of Gram's boys. Like his brother Brandon." She gave Jenna a tiny push. "Go ahead, but be careful on the steps."

Liz watched as Jenna increased her speed. At the top of the stairs, Jenna paused a moment, then raced downward, her little legs flying.

Rolling her eyes, Liz unloaded a summer's worth of gear from the trunk and followed Jenna with the first round of baggage.

By the time Liz reached the boat, Jenna had a new friend.

The girl who shrank from all "strangers"—the mail carrier, the clerk at their neighborhood grocery, and her preschool teacher for the first week each year—sat on David's lap, frantically steering a boat that wasn't going anywhere.

With David's cap now perched on Jenna's head, tufts of her short hair peeked out from underneath. Jenna's instant rapport with David, the guy who'd always turned Liz into a stammering idiot, provoked a ridiculous twinge of envy. She brushed it off, wishing she could brush off David as easily.

She dumped two bags on the boat's back seat, then turned back to grab the rest.

"Wait!" David called out to her, his voice deeper and a little harder than when they'd been teenagers. "Hop in. Let me get the rest of your stuff."

Feeling her spine stiffen—with nerves or disappointment, she wasn't sure which—she almost refused. She wished Diana or Brandon had come to pick her up, but seeing Jenna's smiling face, she didn't argue. "Thanks."

As David trotted up the steps, her unwilling gaze followed. His body, although still slim, had filled out. He'd grown up and then some. The boy she'd secretly idolized as perfect in her teens now had the rugged grace and burnished charm of a man who knew himself.

The thought annoyed the hell out of her.

Glancing down, she skimmed her hands over hips no longer boyish, across a waist now soft. The skinny days were ancient history. Pregnancy, and depression over the endless rounds of infertility treatments, had taken care of that.

"Is this the last of it?" With two totes slung from one shoulder, Jenna's backpack over the other, and his hands gripping suitcases, David paused at the top of the steps.

Feeling stupid, Liz nodded. "We came prepared."

"I always liked that in a woman." His lopsided grin triggered something bordering on heartburn—she hoped—but Jenna giggled as he edged down the steps.

After setting the luggage in the back of the boat, David stepped around the engine cover in the boat's center and tapped Liz's shoulder. "Do you remember how to drive, or should Jenna and I handle it?"

"It's been a while." Her first trip behind the wheel wouldn't be in front of David. "I'll let you guys do it."

"Aye-aye, ma'am." With a jaunty salute, he settled Jenna on his lap. "Could you do me a favor and untie the bow line?"

She hesitated, then squeezed past him into the bow. Holding her breath, she wondered how fat she looked. Whatever. He'd see her soon enough in a swimsuit.

She'd spent too much time worrying about spending a summer with Dad after all these years, but she should've worried about David.

He scared her to death.

ONE EYE ON JENNA, another on Liz—who hadn't uttered a word since they left the marina—David wondered whether Liz was oblivious to the world, or just ignoring him. As usual.

Might as well find out. "Is that a rental car?"

She reeled from her watchdog position in the bow and looked back at him, busy wrestling Jenna while the little girl steered the boat with more enthusiasm than skill. Nudging the wheel discreetly from time to time, he kept them headed —mostly—toward the summer house, Jenna none the wiser.

He nodded toward the marina.

"Uh, yes." She frowned. "They didn't have convertibles."

"Your dad does. A couple, last time I checked." He tickled Jenna's hand to distract her while he steered away from the cabin cruiser bearing down on them in the no-wake zone. "Aren't you here for the summer? You could've borrowed a car."

Ignoring his question, she just gazed along the shore. His eyes traced the same path.

Boat waves lapped rhythmically against the sandy beach.

Between the winter's snow and recent rains, the beach was only half its usual size. In some spots, high water rose almost to the base of the trees that started where the beach left off, blanketing the lush hills above them and hiding from the River's view the few houses tucked up in those hills.

Silent beauty. He never got tired of the sight.

Liz had been away almost twenty years. He wondered if she still felt, or even saw, the River's magic. If she ever had.

Or if she'd ever answer his question. "I said, why didn't you borrow a car? Hell of a lot cheaper."

She bit out an answer. "I can afford it."

"No doubt." Frank and Mom had given her stock in Carruthers Medical, and she and her husband both made the big bucks. That wasn't the point. "Then I'm surprised you're staying with them." He waved at a passing boat and tried without success to tamp his irritation. "Can't you afford the Afton Inn?"

She flinched. Good.

"Actually, I considered it." Her back straightened, as if someone had jammed a steel rod along her spine. "I'm not, uh, exactly sure if this is going to work. With Dad and all."

"I was just kidding." Okay, half-kidding. She squirmed, looking everywhere but at him. He didn't need her baring her soul or anything. He wasn't sure he was up to it.

She glanced at a distant hill, then half-turned to face him. "I wanted Jenna to have somewhere safe to play and not worry whether some big-city bad guy would snatch her off the sidewalk. One of her pre-school friends—" She broke off and looked meaningfully at Jenna, who was busy watching all the boats. "Anyway, you know how it is with kids."

"I guess." Reading between the lines, he couldn't blame her. He'd do anything for Pete or Billy. Obviously, she hadn't come home—after nearly two decades away—to see Mom,

Frank, or anyone else. She'd brought Jenna to the River for a vacation from Washington.

He glanced at Jenna. Her tongue hung out one corner of her mouth as she navigated around the sandbar and past an intrepid swimmer. Pointing, he drew Jenna's attention to an eagle gliding on a thermal above them. As her hands flew up to shield her eyes against the sun, he steered wide of the swimmer and maneuvered behind a sailboat, slicing across its wake.

Three hundred yards farther, the beach beckoned, strewn with all the beach toys he hadn't gotten around to picking up yet.

Liz leaned over the bow, then quickly sat again, turning away from the beach and toward him. "Where are your kids? Pete and Billy?"

"In school. Three more weeks." Frowning, David slowed the boat, shifting from forward to neutral several times as he navigated to the dock. "No offense, but I haven't seen you in twenty years. How do you keep up with the family grapevine?"

She rolled her eyes. "It's my family, too."

After all these years away? She could've fooled him.

THEY'D BE HERE any minute. Wiping her wet hands on a beach towel that hung over the railing, Diana scanned the River while she pressed a hand against her topsy-turvy stomach. She'd barely swallowed a fraction of her normal lunch, and it felt like it might bubble back up to greet her.

David had helped her settle Frank in bed for his afternoon nap before running down and leaping into his boat. In his excitement, which he only halfway tried to hide behind his usual blasé mask, he probably raced through the no-wake zone at top speed. She cocked one ear for the sound of the sheriff's siren, sighing when she heard only blessed silence.

He'd gotten lucky again.

Of course, that was David. Her golden boy, now a golden man who shrugged off worries the way most people shed their wet clothes after a storm. Life had—mostly—been kind to him.

Life hadn't been as kind to Liz. Difficult early years that Diana still struggled to understand. Difficult teenage years. Now, in adulthood, Liz hid her difficulties under a mantle of work and family.

But Diana knew about Liz's struggles to get pregnant, her miscarriages, her surgeries. She had her suspicions about Liz's marriage. Career success didn't make up for unhappiness.

Unfortunately, Liz's unhappiness started with Frank and had never ended. Diana hoped the summer house wouldn't witness another round of battles between Liz and her dad. This time, it wouldn't be a fair fight—and with Diana's luck of late, she'd be the one who wound up with a black eye.

Sighing, she started down the steps, watching as David eased the boat toward the dock. She hadn't spent much time talking to God over the years. Maybe it was time to start.

She prayed for a miracle.

THE BOAT NUDGED THE DOCK, jarring Liz. She felt a sudden, insane urge to turn around and go back across the River. No, she couldn't. She'd promised Diana.

"Hop out." David set two suitcases on the dock. With a

sweep of his arm, he pointed toward the beach and the steps leading up to the house. "And welcome home."

Home? Not in this lifetime.

Her parents had bought the house, with Mom's money, the year she'd been born. During summers, she'd grown up in it. Mom had more or less died in it.

Liz eyed the battered white plastic chairs and tables, the waterskis and toys, the driftwood and assorted junk littering the beach. The concrete steps. Above, peeking through gaps in the leafy trees, she saw the crusty-gray stone façade of the hundred-year-old house. Nothing had changed. Yet, somehow, everything had.

"Are you staying out here, too?" Slinging her purse and carry-on bag over her shoulder, she grabbed the handle of a suitcase—and, weighed down and off-kilter, had no idea how she'd make it off the boat.

After reclaiming his baseball cap from Jenna, who stood on the dock, David picked up the suitcases Liz hadn't grabbed. "We have our own summer place here now." He nodded at the small, luxurious house adjacent to the family's big summer house. "Suzy and I wanted to be close to Mom and your dad, and the McIntyres sold us their house a couple years ago."

Suzy and David. David and Suzy.

Undoubtedly still madly in love, ever since high school. Suzy had always worshipped David. David liked being worshipped. A perfect match.

She had to see Piper. Her best friend always put Liz's idiotic, unrequited crush on David in perspective, if not on ice. Ice sounded positively refreshing right now.

"Where's Suzy?" Struggling under the weight of the bags more than she'd ever admit, Liz inched along the dock, disappointed at the lack of a welcoming party.

"In town." At the end of the dock, David shifted his load before stepping barefoot onto the sand. "We moved out here for the summer on Friday, but during the week she and the boys are staying in our Edina house until school is done. They'll be back this weekend."

"Is Brandon out?"

"He probably won't be here much until July. He hates cold water, and he'd rather work." Reaching the bottom of the concrete steps, David waited for Liz and Jenna to trudge across the sand. "He still stays in the big house, by the way."

With six bedrooms and a cottage in back, the house could shelter a small army. Brandon probably still slept in the kids' porch upstairs, which looked out over the River and had inspired countless battles in their teen years. Jenna might have to fight him for it.

"Liz? Jenna? Welcome!" Diana's voice called from above as Liz and Jenna started up the steps, right behind David. Liz's head whipped up. Diana waved, smiling.

She still looked great. Slender, vibrant, and seemingly a decade younger than age sixty-five. Her silvery blond hair, cut in a sleek bob, shimmered in the sunlight that poked its way through the trees. Even in faded khakis with turned-up cuffs and one of Dad's old Brooks Brothers button-downs, she managed to look perfect.

"Diana!" Liz grinned, feeling the first trace of being home since arriving at the airport.

A small hand tugged on Liz's shirt. "Is that Gram?" Peering up at Liz, Jenna whispered just loud enough for anyone within ten miles to hear. It had been almost a year since Diana's last trip to Washington. In a five-year-old's world, a year felt like a decade.

Diana's bare feet padded down the wooden steps from the house and paused at the top of the concrete steps.

Jenna had stopped, halting Liz's progress, but now she raced up the steps. She ran into the open arms of her grandmother—stepgrandmother, but Jenna didn't cling to details the way Liz did—and gave Diana a breath-choking squeeze.

"Oh, Gram! Is this your house? You live here? And you have a boat, and Unc' David drives it, and now I drive it, too?"

Diana nodded yes to the stream of questions, ruffling Jenna's hair as she bent to hug her. Liz reached the top step and hung back, wanting a hug, too.

Diana's eyes flashed briefly at David, who exchanged his cargo for Jenna, hoisting her on his shoulders as she wriggled and kicked. He yelped when Jenna's foot connected with his face.

Dropping her bags, Liz hugged Diana, awkwardly at first, then rocking back and forth in an embrace that felt . . . wonderful.

Diana drew back, holding Liz at arm's length while she gave her the once-over. "Hmmm. You're still too thin." Obviously, she needed glasses. Diana winked. "We'll work on that."

Not with her cooking, unless absolutely everything had changed. Liz grinned, remembering Diana's penchant for takeout.

"By the way, I sent Piper an email on Friday, letting her know we'd be getting here today. I never heard back."

"We had the best Memorial Day in years. The water is still chilly, but no clouds all weekend. If I know Piper—" Diana smiled. "She took the weekend off."

Liz shook her head. Piper and Paul had both graduated from Harvard Law School, but they couldn't be more different. She'd joined a boutique Minneapolis law firm after graduation, practicing health law and saving doctors from themselves and their crazy business schemes. Or trying to.

She also had a life. Paul couldn't grasp the concept.

"I thought I'd call or text her today, see if she wants to come out. Do you mind?" Wincing, she realized she should've checked on Dad before throwing parties at the River. Not that Piper, and maybe Tracy, constituted a party. Just a trio of friends.

"Of course not. I'd love to see Piper." From what Liz heard, Diana already did. A lot. After Piper lost her parents in tenth grade, Diana had unofficially adopted Piper, giving Diana the daughter she'd always wanted in Liz.

Liz understood Diana, and liked Piper, too well to mind.

"Okay if I invite Tracy out, too?"

"The more, the merrier." Diana opened the screen door to the porch and held it for Liz, who paused on the threshold before stepping inside. "Give them both a call. I haven't seen Tracy in ages. How's she doing?"

Liz dropped onto a glider strewn with mismatched cushions. The same rusty glider, the same crazy fabric, they'd always had. Liz glanced around, soaking in details, absorbing changes she couldn't quite pinpoint. Wooden rockers with musty cushions that matched the fabric on the two gliders. Walls with peeling paint from constant humidity. Weathered chairs around the long blue table at the far end of the porch.

"One of Tracy's daughters is starting college this fall; the other is two years younger. I think Tracy's finally over the divorce." When Diana clucked in sympathy, Liz nodded. "She's dating a guy she met at Piper's firm. Hopefully not a client."

"Doctors aren't all bad." Diana's eyes twinkled.

"I didn't mean Brandon." Before joining the family's medical-device business, he'd graduated from med school, then opted out of a residency, preferring labs over people. "I'd love to see him. David says he won't be out until July."

Diana jotted a note on her legendary to-do list, then joined Liz on the glider. She plumped a pillow behind her back.

"He's been caught up in clinical trials on one of his devices, and it's difficult dragging him away. Maybe you girls will have better luck." Turning her head, Diana scanned *The Wall Street Journal* on the wicker table next to her. "Hmmm. Slytherby Labs looks interesting." Semi-retired or not, her mind never stopped. "Excuse me a moment."

Crossing the room, Diana punched in a number on her cell phone, her foot tapping softly on the floor. While she waited, she called to David. She murmured something into the phone, listened, murmured again, hung up. David soon appeared and shared a few words with his mom in low tones. Then he grabbed his own cell phone, mirroring Diana's actions.

Liz glanced around the room, trying not to care. Diana couldn't drop everything just because Liz had arrived, even if she'd been here only five minutes. Naturally, Diana had to consult David, who'd taken over as Chairman when Diana retired. Diana didn't need Liz's help, even though she knew a thing or two about deals.

Besides, she'd taken a break from deals and work. She'd come home to see Dad, enjoy her time with Jenna, recuperate. Maybe start writing the novel that had lurked in her mind for years. And decide what to do about Paul.

She had a full plate. She didn't need to worry about Carruthers Medical, Slytherby Labs, or anything resembling work.

While Diana and David wheeled and dealed, she could either go find Dad or give Piper a call.

She whipped out her cell phone.

"That didn't take long." Disconnecting after a short conversation with Charlie Moore, his head of acquisitions, David eyed Liz. She'd been quick, calling her pal before the twenty-seven bags she brought hit the floor. "Can we expect Piper within the hour? Or are you waiting until dinner?"

Liz dropped her cell phone into a purse big enough to hold a laptop and toolbox. "Why? Should I tell her to rush?"

"Not on my account."

David bit his lip. He'd hoped to spend time with Liz before the hordes descended. She'd left at dawn the morning after her high school graduation party and hadn't been back since. She hadn't even stayed for his wedding, claiming she forgot about it when she lined up a summer job in New York.

He'd never understood her.

He tried picturing the tomboy she'd been when they met. A skinny nine-year-old with a chip on her shoulder bigger than his. Her dad joined Carruthers Medical after David's dad died. Frank had lost his wife a year earlier, and Liz hadn't dealt well with it. Mom, reeling with her own troubles—at work and at home—had invited them over. Way too soon, Mom and Frank were tight.

David wanted to escape everyone that summer. He'd also been thirteen—too old to hang out with a nine-year-old who hated the world, especially her dad, for reasons he'd never understood.

By the time he'd finally dealt with Dad's death, Liz and Brandon were pals. And Liz had stopped following him around, asking him to play. She avoided him like the plague.

From the looks of it, she still did.

"Unc' David!" Jenna scampered up to him, having changed into polka-dot shorts and a striped shirt that didn't begin to match. Pitching herself at him, her arms gripped his knees like they held candy.

He missed those days. Sixteen and the proud holder of a driver's license, Pete hung out with his buddies, escaping the River whenever he could. At eleven, Billy still loved the River and spending time with his dad, but it wasn't like this. Total worship. He'd lost that a couple years ago, about the same time he'd lost the slobbery kisses.

Jenna planted one on him.

"Jenna, don't bother David too much. He's a—" Liz bit her lip. "He's a busy man."

Jenna looked up at him, cross-eyed and upside-down. "I wanna drive the boat."

"Maybe in a bit. I was hoping I could talk to your mom before her friends come out." Flipping Jenna backward in a somersault, he glanced at Liz, who stared at the worn rug. "If that's okay?"

She ran a hand through her shoulder-length hair, still blond, and probably not from a bottle. Jenna was her clone, from her light-blond hair and blue eyes to the pert little nose.

Mom sighed, loudly, and left the room.

"They won't be out until tomorrow night." Leaning back on the couch, Liz closed her eyes, then opened one to look at him. "So no rush. You guys can take a boat ride while I unpack."

"There's plenty of time to unpack. Want to ride along?"

Looking oddly nervous, she lurched to her feet. "I'm sorry. I really do want to unpack, but I didn't mean to dump her on you." She grabbed Jenna's hand, but the kid squirmed out of her grasp. "Jenna, we can go in the boat later. I'll bet I remember how to drive it."

"No! Unc' David was gonna let me drive."

He didn't utter a peep.

Liz ran a ringless left hand through Jenna's hair. "First, we'll go see your room. It's the best in the house."

Jenna's lower lip quivered. "Unc' David showed me."

"He's not your uncle!"

Stung, David crossed his arms and glared at her. She drew a deep breath, then gentled her tone. "Anyway, we still need to unpack. C'mon, Jenn. Upstairs."

"No." Eyes wide, Jenna looked at David for help.

He was no fool. "Sorry, kid. Your mom's the boss." Something flashed in Liz's eyes as he turned to her. "Do you know which room you're in? I could show you."

She looked at the ceiling. "I think I can find my way."

He dogged her heels all the way up the stairs.

CHAPTER 3

She'd had hopes for David and Liz. Ridiculous hopes. That they'd finally get along.

It didn't look promising.

Diana closed the door to Frank's bedroom, softly, after making sure he was asleep. His afternoon naps usually lasted from just after lunch until just before dinner, but she worried that the thrum of tension in the house would wake him up.

Asking Liz to come home might've been a mistake.

She didn't make many. And, really, Liz needed to see her dad. Needed to bury the hatchet—hopefully not in him—while she still had time. While Frank still had time and understanding.

When Frank first appeared in Diana's life, he'd been a savior. He'd helped her hang onto the business, then grow it, and he knew when to back off and let her make decisions. So different from George. George worked, she stayed home. He didn't consult her or want her to "worry." She hadn't minded, much, until she woke up one day with a company she knew nothing about.

A couple of George's top men had left within weeks of his death, shocked that Mrs. Carruthers would be running the ship. Not wanting to answer to a woman. Expecting the ship to sink.

It hadn't. Her boys depended on her.

She climbed the steps to her own room, remembering.

She'd gotten to know Frank, first in a work context, then—after he told her about Liz—as another parent. She hadn't known much about Meredith or how she died until later, when it mattered. Frank knew he had issues and worked with therapists to resolve them. She made sure of that. But Liz never forgave him, and she'd escaped at the first opportunity.

It didn't explain why she'd avoided David all these years.

Upstairs, Diana brushed her hair, staring at the tired eyes reflected in her bedroom mirror. No time for a nap. She moved into the hall just as Liz's door opened. Liz tipped her head toward Diana's room, her eyes questioning.

"He's downstairs. Asleep." Frank couldn't manage stairs, and they'd put his hospital bed in the first-floor bedroom. "He'll be up in time for dinner."

They walked down the stairs, Liz a step ahead.

"How . . . is he?" At the bottom of the stairs, Liz paused before heading into the great room, which spanned the width of the house. "I mean, what is it? A brain tumor? Can he talk?"

"It keeps changing." Diana shrugged. "He finished five weeks of radiation on Friday. He's pretty weak and can't say much. He makes a little more sense, though."

Liz's brow furrowed. "I don't understand."

"We have some catching up to do." Diana pointed to the porch. "Is Jenna napping?"

"She's too big for naps." Liz winked. "But she curled up on my bed while I unpacked. The rest is history."

"Did David head back to his house?"

"No idea." Liz's grin faded, leaving her face blank.

Diana had heard the front screen door slam fifteen minutes ago and almost hadn't bothered asking.

They crossed to the porch gliders, squeaky old iron things covered with patchwork fabric and minimal padding.

"How long has Dad been sick?" Liz's voice held a note of reproach, and Diana couldn't blame her. She'd first noticed a few symptoms last Thanksgiving. True to form, Frank had stonewalled her and insisted she tell no one. Even Liz. Perhaps especially Liz.

They couldn't have kept it from David and Brandon if they'd tried. Both boys saw too much of Frank not to notice. Brandon had dinner with them at least once a week. Suzy and the boys kept David occupied, but he found excuses to drop by every few days. Here at the River, daily. His work schedule—or lack thereof—allowed it.

Lost in her thoughts, she jumped when Liz touched her arm.

"Sorry. Just thinking." She collected herself, something she didn't often need to do with family. She loved Liz dearly, but the distance from Minneapolis to Washington didn't allow a normal closeness. Liz didn't always, either.

"How long?" Liz fiddled with the bottom of her T-shirt, staring at it. "I first noticed something when I called at Christmas. It was a lot worse a couple months ago."

"You never said anything?"

Liz just looked at her. No wonder she did so well negotiating billion-dollar deals.

"You're right." Diana blew a breath upward. "I should've told you. But you know your father—"

Liz shook her head. "Actually, I don't."

"Fair point. I hope we can fix that this summer." She patted Liz's hand. "But he's not . . . the same as he once was."

Liz pursed her lips on a retort. Knowing the likely gist of it, Diana admired her control. Liz had always had control.

"I think I mentioned at Christmas that he'd been a little off." Diana glanced at Liz, who was biting her lip. Hard. "He talked about old times. Until then, he'd mostly buried his earlier memories—of his parents, your mom, you as a little girl—in the past."

"I can imagine." Bouncing her leg against the glider in a frenetic rhythm, Liz stared blankly at the far wall.

"He also talked about our early days together, when he first joined the company. But he'd mix things up. A little at first, when he awoke in the morning or after a nap. Then more often. He confused David with Brandon, sometimes mixed them up with Pete and Billy. I didn't know what to make of it."

"So you took him to the doctor?"

Diana sighed. "Not right away. He found excuses or just refused to go. We'd fight about it, and he'd be as lucid as you or I." She shrugged. "I know—I can run Carruthers Medical but can't get a stubborn seventy-two-year-old to go to the doctor."

"Running the company would be easier than running Dad."

"You'd think I'd know that by now." Relaxing, Diana ran a hand through her hair, wishing again that she'd forced the issue sooner. Wondering if it would've made a difference. "It got worse after Christmas. Finally, in February, it happened."

"What happened?" Liz gripped Diana's forearm.

"At first they thought it was a stroke."

"He had a stroke and no one told me?" Springing to her feet, Liz paced, hands on narrow hips. "I can't believe it!"

"It wasn't a stroke." Holding up a hand, Diana watched

the storm cloud cross Liz's face. "I didn't tell Brandon or David either." Not at the time. "You and I had just talked."

Liz spoke slowly. "I remember. Dad sounded... off."

"He was." Diana glanced at her hands, noting the chipped nail polish. "A gung-ho intern figured he'd had a stroke. When the neurologist saw your dad, he apologized. It hadn't been a stroke. At that point, they didn't know much else."

Liz's footsteps slowed. "And then what?"

"We had a long wait."

As Liz listened, alternately pacing and perching on the edge of a chair, Diana recounted the three months they'd just survived. The weeks Frank spent in and out of the hospital, enduring tests that only raised questions. The two-week stint at Mayo Clinic, where a team of neurologists finally reached a conclusion. They called the tumor B-cell lymphoma.

She had a few other choice names for it.

George had died of a heart attack at age thirty-nine, surrounded by his closest buddies on a golf course in July. She hadn't had a chance to say goodbye.

Frank was seventy-two. They'd shared twenty-seven good years. She had time to say goodbye. Time to say all the things she wished she could've said to George.

Part of her wondered if a heart attack would've been better.

Frank now spoke slowly, sparingly. His soft whispers were a distant shadow of the booming voice she'd heard, twenty-eight years ago, greeting her in their first interview.

Everything had changed.

After the weeks at Mayo, she brought Frank to their Wayzata home, where she hired a part-time nurse and arranged radiation treatments. The nurse hadn't followed them to the River. Frank didn't want a nurse and Diana longed for a summer with just family.

The latest MRI showed that the tumor had shrunk. In many ways, so had Frank. When he walked, which wasn't often, his shoulders stooped and he clung to his cane or walker. He needed help eating and dressing. Using the bathroom. He was an invalid, and that wouldn't change.

Their golden retirement years? She'd spend them alone.

She shook her head, blinking away tears. Liz, almost forgotten, held her hand as they rocked together now on the glider.

"I'm so sorry, Diana. I wish I'd known."

The guilt stabbed again. She brushed at her eyes, patted Liz's knee. "I wanted to tell you. It's just been hard."

Liz nodded. "I can't imagine hashing through such awful news over and over again."

Unpleasant, yes. The hard part had been fighting Frank's demands that she not tell Liz. Stubborn, foolish man. She forced a smile. "Enough moping. Let's explore the beach while Frank and Jenna are both napping."

Liz helped Diana to her feet. "I guess that won't happen often."

Diana laughed. She hadn't done enough of that lately. "You're right. For Jenna, naps are probably a hard sell."

They weren't for Frank.

———

THE WATER CLIMBED HIGH, shrinking the beach, and the sun's warmth danced on Liz's skin. Cool sand crunched under her toes as she walked with Diana across the beach in front of David's house toward Catfish Bar. Too soon, the tiny sandbar called the "point" would be crammed with a few dozen cruisers and houseboats.

Summer weekends drew masses of boats and people to the River. Weekdays had always brought peace. In May, mornings were crisp, evenings chilly, but a bright sun often broke through. They'd have too much rain in June, but late May gave them cool, hard sunshine.

Perfection.

She dipped a toe in the water and shivered. David and Brandon swam in water like this—Brandon grumbling—but it left Liz gasping and chilled for hours. She hated to swim, period, and definitely not in ice cubes. A wetsuit eased the sting, but wetsuits meant waterskiing, and she'd left those days behind.

She'd grown up.

Sudden footsteps raced behind her. Diana turned, letting out a startled cry just as Liz felt the air leave her lungs. Tackled at the waist, she fell onto the beach, face down. Her assailant landed on top of her, his head somewhere near her butt. Diana stifled a laugh into her hand.

David.

Not everyone had grown up in the last nineteen years.

He started to roll off her, a low rumble of laughter against her thighs, but her foot kicked out, connecting somewhere in his midsection and spraying sand. Turning, she slugged his upper arm for good measure. The blow stung her hand as it glanced off him. Figured. He was six feet to her five-six, and she'd never landed a blow that affected him.

She wished she'd been equally immune.

"What was that for?" Liz brushed the sand off her legs, rising with the help of Diana's outstretched hand.

David grinned from a sitting position, his arms stretched

across his knees. He'd pulled a T-shirt over his head since she last saw him. She liked him better this way. Covered.

"Just my usual welcome. You had too many suitcases in your hands when we arrived, and Mom would've killed me."

Diana arched one eyebrow. "You think I won't?" She shook her head. "No wonder we get so many complaints at the office."

"Not to mention workers' comp claims." David grinned.

Liz hugged herself, feeling awkward. She'd never been comfortable bantering with David. Or talking to him. Or existing in the same room, or stretch of sand, with him.

David turned to her. "Do you want that boat ride now? Or is Mom too busy talking your ear off?"

Not in the last twenty minutes. She and Diana had walked in silence, skipping an occasional rock across the water and closing their eyes against the slight breeze. After sharing the blow-by-blow details of Dad's illness, Diana clearly needed the break.

"Jenna's still asleep. Maybe when she wakes up?"

David shrugged. "Whatever. Give me a shout." Leaping to his feet, he strode to the wooden walkway leading up to his house.

"His social skills leave something to be desired." Diana gazed after her son, then rubbed her hands briskly. "Let's go up, too. Frank will be awake soon. Jenna might already be jumping on his bed and introducing herself."

Liz shuddered, telling herself it wouldn't happen. "Living in Washington, Jenna isn't like other kids. She's, uh, pretty afraid of strangers."

And Dad was a stranger. He'd never met his granddaughter. Until now, Liz hadn't seen that as a problem.

Diana gazed down the beach toward the neighbors' house on the north. She knew some of what he'd done, and he'd gotten counseling before Diana married him. He'd never hit Diana; she would've slugged him back. Picturing it, Liz felt keenly all the differences between Diana and Liz's mom. And Liz.

They'd never stopped him. They'd never fought back.

"It's tough for kids today." Diana wrapped an arm around Liz. "Growing up in a city. Being afraid of strangers whisking you off a street—hurting you, maybe killing you. I suppose parents have to warn their kids about almost everything."

Liz looked sideways at Diana. "You're a big-city girl. How did you handle the streets of Chicago?"

"The streets of Chicago?" Diana hooted. "We lived in a wealthy suburb, and my parents sent me to boarding school when I was thirteen. During school breaks we traveled."

Liz whistled. "Doesn't sound like much of a home."

"I wanted something different for my boys. And for you." Stopping, Diana tilted Liz's chin up. "When your dad brought you into my life, I wanted you to feel safe. And loved."

"I know you did." Too many years of bitterness clogged Liz's throat. Turning away, she squeezed her eyes shut. "My mom loved me."

It hadn't been enough to save her. Desperate to escape her life with Dad, Mom had coped—or not—with alcohol. She'd mostly kept her secret from friends and relatives, but she hadn't been able to hide it from her own daughter. A month after Liz turned eight, Mom died of liver failure.

Liz and her grandparents had been with her at the hospital in her last moments. Dad stayed away, playing cards with friends. When Liz's grandparents dropped her off at her house that night, hours after Mom died, Dad was waiting for her in the living room. Angry at the world, he'd punished her one last time.

She hadn't run. Hadn't hidden. Hadn't even cried.

By the grace of God, he'd never hit her again.

Diana's hand touched her shoulder. "You're lucky, Liz."

Luck had never entered into the equation. Not in her life.

Head down, she stubbed her toe in the sand. "How do you figure? I lost my mom."

"You've had two moms who've loved you. Yes, your first mom is gone—" Grabbing Liz's hand, Diana tugged her toward the steps. "But I'm still here. You're stuck with me."

———

"Mom! Mom!" Crying out, the trembling voice startled David as he tiptoed down the hall, trying not to disturb naps.

He looked around. Listened. After a moment, he heard a whimper. Knocking, he opened the door to the sleeping porch.

His old room, shared with Brandon when they'd first spent their summers with Liz and her dad. A couple years later, he and Brandon lost the room to Liz and her girlfriends. When Liz left for her summer job before college, he'd been two weeks shy of his wedding. He'd never slept here again.

Scanning the room, he didn't see Jenna. The most obvious choices—two twin beds adjacent to the window overlooking the River—were empty. He swung left, where a small form huddled on the farthest bed from the window. Under the quilt. Shaking.

"Jenna?" The shaking paused. "Looking for your mom?"

No answer.

"She's probably in the boat. I'll bet she's trying to drive it all by herself." The shaking resumed. "It's a problem."

A head emerged. "Wha's a problem?"

"Your mom." David shrugged. "She doesn't know how to handle a boat the way you do. I wish you'd help her out."

Jenna sat up but made no effort to leave the bed. She looked way too cautious for a five-year-old. "You're teasing."

It was more a question than a statement. "Scouts' honor." He held up two fingers, then three, then two again. Whatever.

"I-I couldn't find her."

"No wonder." When she looked up, he laughed gently. "It's hard finding anyone under that quilt." Bending, he patted the bed. "Nope. I don't think she's under there."

Jenna giggled, a tiny sound accompanied by a shy smile.

"Is she really in the boat?"

Doubtful. "You never know. If you want, we can go look for her."

She thumped onto the floor and offered her hand. An odd combination of shy and trusting.

Ten minutes later, they found Liz in the back house—the one-room cottage that Mom and Frank rebuilt a few years ago. Liz hunched forward as she peered at her laptop screen and typed in a flurry.

She didn't look up when the screen door banged.

"Missing work already?" David frowned, thinking of the little girl clinging to his hand as she'd searched for her mom.

Liz held up a hand to ward off the interruption. Jenna skipped to her, ignoring the command.

"Mom?" Jenna poked at the keyboard, causing Liz to whirl and hold her at arm's length while saving her work. "What'cha doin'? Writin' to Daddy?"

"I was just—" Liz sounded distracted, but she quickly stood up and offered Jenna a genuine smile. "Finishing. So I could see you."

She didn't glance at David.

He smiled, pretending not to be pissed off. "Ready for a boat ride? Jenna hoped she'd find you hiding in the boat."

Liz raised her eyebrows. "Oh?"

He cleared his throat. "I, uh, might've suggested the possibility. She didn't know where you were."

Rising, Liz headed for the door, hoisting Jenna in her arms with a slight wince. "Okay, sweetie. I can give you a boat ride now."

"With David?"

She glanced over her shoulder at him. "If you insist."

He'd had better offers. But he'd take it.

THE BOAT RIDE had been a good idea. Starting to write the Novel of the Century on the first day of vacation hadn't been a hot one. The hero looked like David, acted like David, smelled like David.

He also irritated the hell out of her. Like David.

Liz ran a hand through her hair, a tangle of wind and Jenna she'd acquired during the fastest boat ride on record. Jenna's bravado evaporated on David's first turn, and she'd clung to Liz the rest of the ride. They didn't make ski boats like they used to. These days, they made them like turbo jets.

Liz concentrated on the small bundle in her arms as she crossed the sand. David trailed behind, probably wondering how her butt had gotten so wide in nineteen years.

She shrugged, inadvertently bouncing Jenna. He'd married Suzy the twerp. She'd married Paul. Her childhood crush was safely stowed away with her old softball cleats.

"Are you joining us for dinner?" She could be polite. He was Diana's son, after all. A relative of sorts. Not a crush. Not even, really, a former crush. Separated by four years and a thousand miles. And, this summer, every other obstacle she could throw in their respective paths.

Not that he knew or understood or cared. David had always been David. Untouchable. Unconcerned. Perfect.

"Yeah, if that's all right." David drew next to her. "When Suzy and the boys are in town, I usually eat at the big house."

She set Jenna down, grabbed her hand, and raced her up the concrete steps.

Hearing voices, she stopped on the path that connected the nine houses along the beach. Forgetting David and Jenna, she took the remaining steps two at a time, pausing at the wooden half-step on the top landing. She peered through the screen door. Saw Diana, standing on the rug. Saw . . . Dad.

Opened the door anyway.

He sat in a porch glider, the same as he always had late on a summer afternoon. Looking twenty years older than the last time she'd seen him, eight years ago.

Diana hadn't prepared her for this.

Her hand flew to her mouth before she dropped it back to her side. Feeling her dad's and Diana's eyes on her, Liz tried to hide her reaction. For someone who'd learned to negotiate deals with a poker face, she did a lousy job.

The only thing unchanged was the porch glider—sagging cushions, rusted iron, and all. She hardly recognized her dad.

Diana had offered a few details, but she'd obviously skipped some major ones. Dad's thick hair, recently turned white, hung in scraggly clumps. Dark stains from broken blood vessels marred his skin. She couldn't pull her gaze away from his bloated face.

He looked thinner, weak. Not like Dad at all.

His head leaned to one side as if his neck couldn't handle the strain of holding it upright. One hand lay on his lap and the other hung to one side. Against a cushion. Unnatural. His legs bent awkwardly. His walker stood before him.

She felt someone move, felt Diana's hand on her arm. Numb, she somehow had to pretend her dad wasn't dying. That the sight of him didn't make her sick to her stomach.

Diana's elbow jabbed her ribs. "Uh, hi, Dad."

He blinked. "Hi." The voice, soft as Jenna's, barely carried. He didn't smile. Looked right through her.

Maybe everything hadn't changed.

Diana moved closer to him, nudging Liz along. She stumbled, regained her balance, tried to smile.

She hadn't smiled at Dad in more than thirty years.

"Liz is here, Frank. Isn't that nice?" Diana nodded her own answer, then leaned down and pecked Dad's cheek.

Maybe she should go home. On the next available flight. She could flag down a helicopter flying over the River. Or she could swim across. Walk back to Washington. Barefoot.

Diana grabbed her hand and nodded at Liz to keep trying.

"I, uh, brought Jenna. Your granddaughter."

Still no reaction. She gazed into blue eyes as pale as the faded sailboat curtains in her bedroom upstairs.

She clenched and unclenched one fist, losing herself in the mindless rhythm. The man she'd feared and loathed most of her life no longer existed. The thin, stooped, scraggly-haired man in front of her wasn't Dad. She didn't know who he was.

The screen door banged.

"Dinnertime?" Turning, she caught David's wide grin as he strode across the porch and dropped onto the glider next to Dad.

Jenna, following David, stopped behind Diana and clung to her. She peeked around one thigh at her grandfather.

David's arm swung around Dad's stooped shoulder. "How's it going, Frank? Nice nap?" He peered into Frank's eyes, unafraid of the man who'd terrorized Liz. Casual, friendly, loving.

Like a son. The son Dad had always wanted.

She hated them both.

IF HE DIDN'T COUNT the awkward silences, Jenna's fearful glances at Frank, and Liz not uttering a peep . . . all in all, it had been another good family dinner.

Hanging the damp dishtowel on the rack, David gave the kitchen a final visual sweep. Chrome gleamed, counters no longer hosted ants, and the floor—well, he'd picked up the biggest chunks and swept the rest into the back hall.

By the time someone discovered it tomorrow, he'd be across the River for his twice-a-week meeting at company headquarters in Lakeville. He'd pay good money for a shorter commute.

He'd pay bigger money to avoid the company altogether.

Unfortunately, it wasn't in the cards. He couldn't do it to Mom, and—especially next to Brandon—he already looked like an ungrateful jerk. His kid brother worked ungodly hours, traveled to Timbuktu at the drop of a hat if Mom asked, and kept coming up with new and better medical devices to grow their profits and save the world. And not even in that order.

David spent his life avoiding work and long silences with Suzy. His kids claimed his time and his love.

He turned off the light and left the kitchen after snagging a glance at the clock over the sink. Almost nine. They'd eaten late, then Liz headed outside. Without explanation. Jenna had slid down from her wooden chair and stood at the door, obviously wanting to follow but unsure about the night and, probably, her mom.

He couldn't blame her.

He'd always loved the River, but he'd been thirteen when he first came here. The dark woods and strange sounds could scare the hell out of a timid five-year-old.

The great room was empty as he crossed it to the porch. Liz had been gone a half hour. Frank was already settled in for the night, and Diana was probably putting Jenna to bed.

He opened the screen door and made a quiet getaway.

At the path, he paused, listening to the silence. A cold wind blew through his shirt. Shivering, he jammed his hands in the pockets of his shorts. Maybe a quick stroll along the beach, then back upstairs to his house and a good book.

He found Liz on the beach. In an old, beat-up plastic beach chair pulled to the edge of the water, hunched against the evening breeze, shivering. She didn't turn, and half of him considered sticking to his original plan, only with lighter footsteps. Actually, no. Ninety percent of him voted for running like hell up to his house.

A man stayed alive, and warm, doing things that way.

He paused a moment longer, studying her. She'd grabbed a decrepit old windbreaker that could've held someone twice her size. It didn't stop the shaking. Her arms wrapped around her knees, and her head pressed against them.

The hairs on his arms stood on end. Seeing her like this, braced against the cold, he wanted to reach for her. Hug her until she warmed up.

Not being a complete idiot, he didn't act on that thought.

He cleared his throat. A mild flinch betrayed her, but she didn't turn.

"Hey." He whistled softly, off-tune.

She brushed a hand across her eyes. "What's up?" Like nothing had happened. Like she hadn't run from dinner. Like she hadn't run from the whole damn family for the last twenty years.

He grabbed a beach chair, as much of a wreck as hers, and pulled it up beside her. "I thought I might walk down to the point before heading to bed." He perched on the edge of his chair. "Cold?"

"Hmmm?" Arms wrapped around her knees, she stared out over the water. "Not really. I was just thinking."

"Thinking about what?"

"Stuff."

She turned to him, her smile brittle against the wind.

"It must be rough seeing your dad like that. After—" He shot her a quick glance. "After all these years."

"You have no idea."

Nope. He didn't. And, based on the frost in her voice, she wouldn't illuminate his understanding anytime soon.

"Okay." He groaned to his feet. "G'night, then."

He took a step, not expecting an answer. "David?" His name floated to him on the breeze, startling him. "I—"

When she didn't continue, he turned back. "Yes?"

She shivered and shook her head. "Maybe we could, uh, talk. Sometime."

Yeah. Probably the same day that hell froze over.

CHAPTER 4

The sun dazzled Wednesday morning, enough to tempt someone who didn't know better to venture back to the beach, the scene of last night's painful, worthless musings.

Liz knew better.

Seven a.m. Despite the sun, it would still be cold out. She'd stay indoors and under the covers. Maybe forever.

Jenna had cried out twice during the night, each time prompting Liz's mad dash down the cold wooden floor to the sleeping porch. She hadn't heard a peep since three. She should soon, though, when Jenna arrived like clockwork for their daily snuggle.

Her door creaked open. Sure enough, a sleepy-faced Jenna scooted across the floor and crawled onto her bed. Lifting the comforter, Liz smiled, then tucked the little body up next to her. Jenna. The absolute best thing ever to have happened to her.

She prayed she didn't screw this one up.

Diana adjusted the comforter over Frank, smoothing it needlessly while she contemplated life. Her life. Frank's.

The one they'd intended to have.

Frank dozed, eyes clamped shut, mouth open, forehead shiny and pale. She could hardly bear to look at the man who'd once been so handsome. Her husband, now her patient.

A scuffle of feet pattered behind her. Jenna. With Liz in the back house and David next door, the little girl followed Diana everywhere, like a quiet shadow. If it weren't for the wooden floors, a person could almost forget she were here.

She felt hands clamp onto her thighs, and Jenna's head poked around one hip. Jenna stared at Frank, eyes wide.

Diana motioned her out of the room.

"He's sleeping, dear. Let's not wake him."

Just outside the door, Jenna continued to stare in at Frank. She tugged on the hem of Diana's shirt and whispered. "He takes naps 'cause he's sick? When will he get better?"

"I'm not sure. Maybe someday." Or not.

"He looks scary." Jenna moved closer to Diana.

Diana closed the door to Frank's room. "Well, he's not. He's just sick." She couldn't bear the thought of Liz's fears passing to Jenna. "He loves you."

Jenna frowned. "He looks at me kinda mean. I get scared."

"You shouldn't." Easy for Diana to say. Jenna was afraid of everything. "He's not mean. Maybe *he's* a little scared."

A tiny crease marred Jenna's forehead. "Why?"

"It's no fun being sick." Diana ran a hand through Jenna's baby-soft hair. "I'll bet he'd like a friend right now. Maybe a little girl just like you."

Jenna's eyes grew wide. "I better go see my mom."

She scurried outside as fast as her legs would take her.

———

ELEVEN-THIRTY. Liz stared at her laptop screen, trying to recall the books she loved and wondering why her own writing didn't remotely resemble any of them. Her novel looked more like the diary entries she'd scribbled in her teens, late at night under a flashlight's glare.

Then, as now, she wrote about David.

She didn't mean to. The hero's name was Chance, even if she kept spelling it "D-a-v-i-d" before hitting the backspace key. Chance lived in Montana. He drove a Chevy pickup, not a sports car. Sure, he had hazel eyes and longish brown hair, streaked with coppery gold, but Chance worked for a living. He didn't sit on his butt and—

The whole damn book reeked of David.

She closed her laptop. She'd confided in Diana her secret desire to write a novel, and Diana offered to watch Jenna while Dad napped. Almost lunchtime. Time to get Jenna.

Jenna found her first.

The screen door to the back house creaked open. Head down, Jenna tiptoed into the room. Ten microscopic footsteps into the back house, she finally looked up. Liz smiled at her.

"Mom? Are you done writing?"

"Done." Jenna skipped to her, smelling of shampoo and the unmistakable scent of the River. "Did you and Gram have fun?"

Violent nod.

"What did you do all morning?" Hoisting Jenna onto her lap, she felt a slight stab of pain. Pursing her lips, she tugged on a short blond lock. "Did Gram go waterskiing?"

Jenna giggled. "She doesn't waterski."

"Every year, just once, so she can say she still does."

"No way."

"Way. But not until the water's warmer." Letting Jenna slide off her lap, Liz groaned to her feet. "Race you to the kitchen?"

Jenna charged outside, squealing. Liz followed more slowly, reminding herself to call Paul. Maybe send him an email.

Or a card on his birthday.

GOD, he missed them.

Liz had taken Jenna yesterday for a summer in Minnesota—land of lakes and mosquitos, and not in that order—and didn't even say goodbye.

Not that he remembered, at least.

Paul sipped his coffee, which had grown cold somewhere between the merger agreement and the antitrust filing. His head throbbed. He'd worked late last night, using Liz's absence as an excuse to log more hours before heading home.

His body felt it today. He'd be forty in October. Forty going on sixty, his secretary liked to joke. Liz didn't joke about it. Lately, she didn't joke about anything at all.

Maybe if he got ahead on work in the next few weeks, he could squeeze in a week at the St. Croix with Liz and Jenna and Liz's assorted friends and quasi-relatives.

Maybe just a long weekend.

He shuffled through the antitrust file and sighed, running a hand over his face. Another long night ahead.

"Piper!" Trying to hold the speedboat against the city dock in choppy waves, Liz realized it wasn't as easy as David made it look yesterday. Nothing ever was.

Piper stood on the stairs, shielding her eyes against the late-afternoon sun. A baseball cap covered her short auburn hair. Spotting Liz, she waved, then trotted down the steps. She breathed hard as she stepped onto the back end of the boat.

"Aren't health lawyers supposed to be in good shape?" Liz's grin slipped as she lost her grip on the dock. "Damn."

"That's what you get." Dropping her beach bag, Piper grabbed a mooring and strained to pull the boat back to the dock. "Besides, someone with a pasty-white face shouldn't talk."

"Busted." But Liz laughed. She definitely wasn't tan, and she also usually skipped makeup at the River. No one noticed or cared.

After Piper tied up the boat and they shared a quick hug, Liz surrendered the driver's seat without a word. Piper bit down on a grin.

Piper had always paid attention to every scrap of boat information Brandon imparted during their teenage joyrides up and down the River. Liz focused on sun and sand. As a result, Liz could start, drive, and dock a boat with only minor damage to the boat and/or the dock. Piper could probably overhaul the boat's engine.

"Where's Tracy? Still coming?"

Piper shrugged. "I thought so. She left work when I did." She jumped out of the boat and onto the dock. "I'll go check."

Piper sprinted back up the stairs, scanned the parking lot for a moment, then returned to the boat. "Maybe she's busy kissing her boyfriend goodbye."

Liz grinned. "I can't remember what that's like. Can you?"

Piper hopped back in the boat, perching on top of the driver's seat as she stared up at the parking lot for an awkward minute or two. Weird.

"Hey, there she is." Piper waved at Tracy.

Tracy gave a quick wave before grabbing the railing and proceeding down the steps to the dock. Since the last time Liz had seen her—three years ago?—she'd lost twenty pounds, the last of the weight she'd gained from two pregnancies and the strain of a bitter divorce.

In capris and a short-sleeved V-neck that showed off curves her two friends could only envy, Tracy looked happy. Finally.

Liz held out a hand as Tracy took a cautious step onto the back seat. Gripping Liz's hand, she tottered a moment before sliding gracefully into a sitting position. She smiled at Liz. "I'm so glad you're here for the summer."

"Actually, I'm taking it week by week." After untying the boat, Liz sat next to Tracy, wrapping an arm around her shoulders.

"It sounds more like day by day." Hooting, Piper backed the boat out of the slip, then cruised slowly across the channel. "David will be the death of you."

"David?" A crease split Tracy's forehead. "Your brother?"

"Stepbrother." Piper's and Liz's voices joined in harmony.

Tracy swished a hand in the air. "Whatever. Are you two still fighting? I didn't think you ever saw him."

"I try not to." Liz leaned back, savoring the sun and the breeze. "It's not so easy when he's next door."

Piper glanced back at them. "I heard about that. I—" She

broke off as she maneuvered around a fishing boat anchored in the channel. After they passed it, she didn't continue.

Liz frowned, feeling unwanted prickles of envy. "You must see a lot of Diana."

"Hmm." Her head swiveling, Piper eyed the buoys marking the channel. Another twenty yards and they'd reach the end of the no-wake zone. Knowing what came next, Liz gripped the rail. Tracy sucked in a breath and grabbed the other rail.

Piper slammed the throttle forward, and they took off.

With a roar, the bow rose out of the water. Piper accelerated as she swept the wheel from side to side. Liz laughed, looking sideways at Tracy, who looked green. Minutes later, Piper made a final slashing turn, almost losing Tracy. At Liz's shout, she killed the engine and turned around, innocence itself.

"Nothing like a good boat ride." Dimples edged her cheeks. "Wanna go fast now?"

"Funny." Tracy sniffed. "If Brandon saw you—"

Piper glared at her. After a moment, though, she laughed. She'd always been two steps short of reckless. And Brandon would never know or care. It wasn't his boat, and he wasn't here.

Finally, Piper headed for their beach. At the dock, Liz breathed a sigh of relief. At least they hadn't rammed it.

———

DAVID REACHED for another slice of banana bread. When Jenna's wide-eyed gaze followed his hand, he leaned all the way across the table to give her one.

"David!"

Grinning at his mom, he pointed at Jenna. "She was hungry."

"Someone else could've helped her."

"Yeah, right." Seated between his mom and Liz, Jenna might as well be invisible. His mom was busy with Frank, helping him eat and cleaning his frequent spills. Liz gave all her attention to her pals—except for an occasional grimace aimed at her dad.

Piper leaped to her feet.

"We'll take care of the dishes, Diana." She grabbed David's plate, his fork halfway to his mouth. Startled, he tried to get it back but wasn't fast enough. "C'mon, guys. If we hustle, we might catch the sunset."

"Doubtful." David pointed at the darkening sky.

She thrust her chin out as she held his plate aloft. His mom chuckled. "Children."

"Yes, Gram?" Jenna's droopy head bobbed.

His mom patted her hand. "I didn't mean you, dear. Some grownups act like children."

"Oh." Her head drooped even more.

"Hey, squirt." David circled the table and held a hand out to Jenna. "Since they swiped my dinner—" David's eyes flashed at Piper. "Wanna go get your pajamas on? We can read stories with a flashlight, just like Brandon and I used to do."

"Brandon?"

He tapped her nose. "You'll meet him. He's my brother."

"And Mom's brother?"

"Kinda." Shrugging, he looked at Liz.

She put her arm around Jenna. "Thanks for offering, but the beach can wait. Jenna always wants me to—"

"I want David to put me to bed!" Shrieking, Jenna

squirmed out of Liz's embrace and lurched to her feet, knocking down her chair in the process.

As he watched Liz's discomfort, David's lips twitched.

"Fine." Liz turned away from him. "I'll come up and kiss you goodnight in a little bit, sweetie."

"An' David?"

Grinning at Liz, he waggled his eyebrows.

She snorted. "He has boy germs."

LIZ CAUGHT a glimpse of the setting sun's dusty pink glow flickering over the water as they started the dishes. By the time she stepped outside, the sky had faded to deep purple and was on the run toward black. She sighed.

Next to her, Piper and Tracy echoed their disappointment. They'd missed catching a first sunset together.

Piper grabbed her hand. Impulsively, she grabbed Tracy's. They raced down the steps, whooping the way they had the first time Piper and Tracy had come out—and every time since.

Barefoot, they raced to the water's edge, Piper leading them in a few steps. Tracy broke hands first, shrieking as the cold water hit their shins. Liz, who'd always gone head-to-head with Piper, backed out a second later.

As she shivered, her gaze swept the beach for something warmer than her T-shirt. Spying towels piled on a beach chair, she grabbed one and tossed another to Tracy. Piper, still dancing knee-deep in the water, could fend for herself.

Tracy scrunched her nose as she debated aloud the wisdom of wrapping a sandy, filthy object of unknown origin around her pristine outfit.

When Piper finally rejoined them, all three dropped to

the sand. Liz huddled under her towel, Tracy on top of hers but with her feet wrapped inside, Piper without anything.

"I can't stay outside long. It's too cold." Liz rested her chin on her raised knees.

Tracy nodded. "Fine by me. I have an early day, and—"

"—Kevin's waiting up." Piper hooted, stopping when Tracy pushed her into the sand. Liz's and Piper's jaws both dropped.

"Kevin? Is that your new man's name?" Liz had heard only that he worked at Piper's firm. "What's the scoop?"

Tracy beamed. "Nothing to tell. We've only dated a month."

"Isn't it more like five weeks, three days, and two hours?" Piper grinned as she edged away from Tracy, who jabbed a finger at her.

"You should talk. You and—" Tracy clapped a hand over her mouth.

Liz looked at Piper, feeling left out. "What don't I know?"

When Piper just poked at the sand with a stick, Tracy cleared her throat. "Speaking of nice, David seemed better than I remembered."

Liz waved her off. "I'd rather hear about Piper's love life. Or yours. At least you guys seem to have one."

Tracy frowned. "What do you mean? Isn't Paul—"

At Piper's quick head shake, Tracy gave an embarrassed laugh. "So much for safe conversation topics. How's the weather, anyway?"

"Cold, last time I checked." Liz stared up at the blackness above her. A few stars twinkled. In the vast sky, they looked as lonely as she felt. "Do you guys have any plans this weekend?"

Tracy and Piper glanced at each other before Tracy

spoke. "Um, yes. With . . . the kids. And Kevin." She let out a breath in a rush. "But next weekend is free."

Tracy must know that her kids and Kevin were welcome at the River, but maybe it meant Liz could catch up with Piper. Somehow, the three friends had faltered tonight. Talking one-on-one, especially with Piper, might fix that.

But then Piper spoke. "Next weekend looks good. I can't this weekend, either."

She'd been gone nineteen years. She shouldn't have expected them to pick up where they'd left off. But she had.

Flushing, she felt grateful for the darkness.

DAVID ENDED his fourth call of the day with Charlie Moore. He rubbed the back of his neck, wishing again he hadn't taken over as Chairman. Monitoring investments on his laptop had been less stressful.

More suited to the David everyone knew.

He wondered what Liz was doing. She'd arrived two days ago, but—except at dinner, when she glared at Frank and fidgeted in silence—he hadn't caught more than glimpses of her, usually with Jenna. This morning, out for a solo hike, he'd approached her near the end of the path. When she veered left into a tree, he left her to pick the bark out of her skin and went back to his beach house. His sanctuary. From Liz, at least.

It wasn't the big house, but he liked it. A spacious, modern kitchen with enough gadgets to satisfy Suzy, which said a lot. Gorgeous views of the River from the porch and the bedrooms downstairs. A basement workshop for tinkering.

The light rap on the door startled him. Jenna had already

visited five times today, but she'd stopped knocking at some point yesterday.

At a second faint rap, he whirled around. Liz.

Wonders never ceased.

"Come in." Folding his newspaper, he set it on the desk.

"I'm not interrupting?" At his wave, she opened the door. So tentative. As if they hadn't been stepsiblings—or some mutant form of them—for almost thirty years.

He moved to the other end of the porch, waving at her to join him on the wicker couches Suzy had just bought.

Liz stayed just inside the door. "Diana asked if you had a bottle of wine she could borrow. For dinner."

His eyebrows rose. "She did?"

A small nod, almost imperceptible.

He headed toward the kitchen. "Sure. Wanna see the place?" He motioned to her to follow, even though she probably wouldn't. "White or red?"

"White." At her voice right behind him, he jumped.

She backed up a step. Eyes lowered, she stopped at the threshold between the porch and kitchen, then slowly padded into the kitchen as if on a stealth mission.

Shaking his head, he opened the fridge and stooped to examine the bottom shelf. Mom loved pinot grigio. This weekend, he'd carried a case of it up from the dock for her. He grabbed a bottle. "Here you go. Tell Mom there's plenty more."

Liz peered into the fridge. "It doesn't look like it."

"Not in here. We'd have to try a different fridge."

She turned in a half-circle. "Where?"

"Not here." He winked. "The big house."

"I don't understand." She propped her hands on her almost-nonexistent hips. Liz and Suzy couldn't look more different.

He didn't know why he thought of that.

He shrugged. "That makes two of us. Mom bought a case this weekend. Better label. She doesn't need my wine. I'd bet—"

"Dad's dementia is contagious?" Laughing softly, she reached past him to grab a can of Diet Coke. Popping the top, she took a long gulp. "Thanks. I mean, sorry. I was thirsty."

"Apparently." He frowned, trying to figure her out. Liz was even more complex than she'd been as a teenager. Angry, shy, nervous, bold. With her friends, surprisingly fun.

With him? He wouldn't know.

Head down, she scuffed her bare toe against the floor. "I'd better head back—with the wine and all."

"Yeah. I'll bet she needs it right away."

Her back went rigid. "Look, I have no idea why Diana sent me over here if she doesn't need wine."

"Because she always wants to fix what's broken. Same old." He reached for a bottle of beer, shaking his head at the label. Suzy didn't drink it, and she'd gotten the wrong brand. Again. Twisting the cap, he kicked the refrigerator door closed.

Liz spoke, her voice wary. "What's broken?"

"You. Me. Us." Taking a swig, he almost choked on it. He'd have to start making the liquor runs himself—which was probably Suzy's point.

The knuckles on Liz's hand that gripped the wine bottle had turned white.

"It doesn't have to be like this." At his words, she stopped but didn't turn around. Faintly encouraged, he kept going. "We're family. My mom, your dad . . ."

She stuck her nose in the air. "I like Diana."

"Who wouldn't?" Liz had always liked Brandon, too. That left just him.

She took an intense interest in the vase of flowers on the counter. "Suzy's good at arranging flowers."

"Thanks, but I did that."

She blinked.

"I like to garden, okay?" He took a swig before slamming the bottle on the counter. "Look. You don't know me, and I don't know you. I've always wondered why we never got along, but we can change that."

Looking everywhere but at him, she crossed the kitchen and stopped five feet short of him. He flinched, expecting a slap. Her words came out on a squeak. "It's not you. It's . . . me."

"Hey, it's probably no one's fault. Like I said, we really don't know each other." He watched her hands twist, almost painfully. Whatever demons she wrestled had to be more significant than him. "But you're here all summer. You said maybe we could talk."

"Maybe." She tilted her head, adding nothing more.

He propped on a stool. "What do you think of the River?"

"The same. Different. I don't know."

"How is it different?"

Her finger traced the hole at the top of her soda can. "Dad."

It was like asking his boys about school. Monosyllables. He took another swig, wondering how many bottles he'd drink before she actually said anything. Maybe a case. "I know what you mean. He's changed a lot."

She shook her head. "I'd hoped we could talk."

"You can still talk to him. He just can't say much back—or have it make sense. If the tumor keeps shrinking, though, he might regain more of himself."

"God, I hope not." Looking down, Liz took another sip.

"What do you mean? Don't you want your dad back?"

"I never had one." She smiled ruefully. "Didn't anyone ever tell you? Why my mom died? Why I always hated him?"

Seeing her wide eyes, he wasn't sure he wanted to know. Cautiously, he shook his head.

"He . . . hit me. Hit my mom. A lot." She drew a few shallow breaths and stared down at her sandals. Birks. Not that it mattered. "He let my mom die and didn't do anything."

The beer drilled a hole in his gut. "No."

Mom wouldn't have married a man like that. Frank had played baseball with him. Grilled burgers. Taught him to drive. He'd never replaced Dad, but he'd made an effort.

"Yes." She crushed the can and tossed it blindly at the recycling bin, missing it by a mile. "That's my dad. Now you know."

Leaving the wine on the counter, she fled.

THE SCREEN DOOR SLAMMED, jolting Diana as she curled up on the glider with Jenna, reading *Green Eggs and Ham*. Liz tore through the porch, her sandals clattering all the way up the stairs. Another door slammed moments later.

She hadn't brought the wine. Or David.

Foiled again.

Resisting the urge to follow, Diana readjusted Jenna on her lap and finished reading the last page. She closed the book with a snap just as the screen door banged again.

"Tell me it's not true." In a wide-legged stance, hands jammed in his pockets, David looked fit to be tied.

Obviously, her ruse had been a mistake. "The wine? You're right. I suppose I already had a bottle."

"No shit." He clenched and unclenched one hand, then ran it through his hair, leaving cockeyed tufts at all angles.

"I thought you two should talk." She stroked Jenna's hair, trying to soothe her. Jenna held the book in a death grip, and Diana patted her hand. "Jenna, dear, could you please get me a Kleenex? For my allergies."

Jenna wrinkled her tiny nose.

She nudged her. "In the upstairs bathroom? Please?"

Jenna slid off her lap and scurried out of the room.

"I can't blame you." David's fists returned to his pockets. "Why should Jenna have to hear what you never told me?"

Diana caught her breath. "What didn't I tell you?"

"Guess."

"I really couldn't." She had no idea. Actually, no, she had the faintest smidgeon of an idea, but it wasn't her story to tell. Except for Liz, it was long ago and best forgotten. And Liz wouldn't say anything. She barely said hello to David.

"Is that why she hates me? Why she always has?"

Now she really had no idea.

"Hate you?" She took off her reading glasses, setting them on the wicker table. "That's a bit strong, isn't it? I know you two have never been close . . ."

Anger positively shimmered from him. "Close? She runs when she sees me coming. What does she think I am? Like Frank?"

Oh. Dear.

Perhaps she should've told the boys. After they'd grown comfortable with Frank. Certainly when Liz left after high school and never returned.

From David's glower, it might be too late.

"Sit down." He didn't move. She patted the space next to her, her smile commanding. "Please, David."

Arms crossed, he stayed standing.

"What did Liz say to you about Frank?"

She waited as he drew a breath, held it, blew it out. She'd rarely seen David so angry. He'd always been almost too relaxed about everything, a quality that made him both good and bad as Chairman of a large company.

He didn't meet her eyes. "He actually hit her? When she was a little kid? Is that true?"

She nodded. Awake or not, Frank couldn't be part of this conversation, and he needed to be. He'd lost his daughter years ago. He couldn't afford to lose the boys, too.

"Does Brandon know?" His eyes, more naked and vulnerable than she'd seen them since George died, pierced her. "Why did you keep this from me?"

Sighing, she folded her hands in her lap. "Brandon doesn't know, either, unless Liz told him. I doubt it."

He waited.

She studied the ancient white hooks in the ceiling. "I didn't know right away. The violence happened when he drank, and he'd already quit when we met. Later, before Frank and I married, he got counseling. Yes, he had issues. But they're his issues, and Liz's. They didn't affect you."

She thought back to those early days. Her worries that Frank could harm David or Brandon. Or her. Or Liz again. Her constant fears for Liz, which had never gone away.

His quiet question startled her. "What makes you think they didn't?"

CHAPTER 5

Mid-morning on Friday, Liz stared at her blank screen, tempted to play Spider Solitaire—anything to break the tedium of trying to write the damn novel. Maybe she'd call it "Impossible" and leave it at that.

David had skipped dinner last night, both irritating and relieving her. Liz choked down her own silent dinner, leaving the table with Jenna in record time. Diana's eyes had held a mild reproach, but Dad's held nothing.

She should've moved on by now, but she didn't have Diana's strength, Piper's nonchalance, Tracy's faith. Or the unquestioning love of anyone but Jenna.

Not to be self-pitying or anything.

She should start a different novel. The hero wouldn't have David's eyes, David's hair, David's anything. The heroine would be strong and loving.

Utter fiction.

She checked email for the tenth time since she'd logged on. Paul hadn't called or replied to the few emails or texts she'd sent since she'd arrived, and it was up to him. This summer would make or break their marriage, if the damage wasn't already irreversible.

A message! Seeing the name, she blinked. Blinked again. David Carruthers.

Jenna wants you to come out and play. She can't type. I can't either, but she doesn't know. Don't tell. If you do, I'll beat you up. Oops. No, you can beat ME up. It's your turn. :-)

Sucking in her breath, she gripped the mouse, sending the cursor running for cover. After confessing something she'd held inside all these years to a man she hardly knew, she wasn't sure what she'd expected. But it hadn't been this.

Then . . . she laughed. The rumbles started low in her stomach and shot up her throat, ending with tears pooled in her eyes.

The creep. Smiling as a tear dribbled down her cheek, she closed the laptop. No writing today. No return email to David, either.

He deserved a sneak attack.

———

HOLED up in the back house, pecking away at that novel of hers, Liz probably didn't even check email.

Everyone wanted to be an author.

David watched as Jenna tried on his smallest waterskis at the edge of the beach. It was more like one big ski, shaped like a horseshoe at the front tip. He'd bought it the summer Pete turned four. Not appreciating his role in history, Pete didn't even attempt to ski until he turned eight.

Jenna was five. With a little over a month to learn, she might be able to show off for everyone on the Fourth of July.

Splash! A shower of ice-cold water hit him in the back, and he recoiled in shock. Chilled and ready to kill, he whirled on his attacker. A pail in her hands and a gleam in her eye, Liz backed up a step.

So this was what he'd missed, with her, all these years.

Lunging, he tackled her head-on, laughing when she screeched in fake pain and landed on her skinny little butt. Actually, he'd never noticed her butt, or any other body parts, or the way they hung together. Guys didn't notice their kid stepsisters. Kinda, sorta stepsisters.

Rolling off Liz, he got a face full of sand just as Jenna took a flying leap and landed on him. *Ouch.* He curled into a fetal position, his mouth twisted in pain. He had two kids. After that blow, he wouldn't have any more.

Suzy might send Jenna a thank-you note.

"What was that for?" He and Liz spoke in unison.

"I asked you first." Ditto.

"You sent me that stupid, insensitive—did I mention moronic?—email. I was just responding." Brushing sand off her shins, Liz looked like the calm, cool acquisition shark he'd expected to see after twenty years away.

"Glad you liked it." He waggled his eyebrows. "That's what brothers are for."

She glared at him. "You're not my brother. At all."

"Get over it." Figuring Jenna might land another blow, he sat up. "I'm not like your dad."

"Like Dad?" She stopped scraping sand off her knee and looked at him. "You've got to be kidding."

A long-held breath escaped him.

"Thanks." He drew his knees in tight and rocked on the sand. "I always wondered. Why you stayed away. Why we never became friends."

Jenna, now curled up in Liz's arms, twisted her head to look at him. Hugging Jenna, Liz didn't speak. She pointed at the hot-air balloon floating over the River at a distance, probably close to Hudson. Jenna's eyes went wide.

The breeze fanned David's hair and neck, chilling the

skin under his damp shirt. Standing up again, he watched the rapt mother-daughter duo, then headed for his house.

"David?" Liz turned her head slightly. "Maybe we could talk. Over a... a lemonade sometime?"

Whistling, he headed upstairs to change into dry clothes.

LIZ WATCHED from the path above as Suzy Carruthers leaned over the side of the speedboat. When she lifted her weekend tote onto the dock, her butt rose in the air like Mount Vesuvius.

David tied up the boat before helping her out. A couple of skinny boys, an older one with spiked blond hair and the younger with reddish-brown hair in his eyes, slouched against the diving board at the end of the dock.

Besides the fact that Suzy had always loved David, and he'd always loved her, Liz didn't know why she couldn't stand Suzy.

She jogged down the steps, mostly to show Suzy that not everyone was as unathletic as a chunk of cookie dough.

"Suzy." She waved a greeting. "It's been a long time."

Suzy flushed, halting everyone's movement along the dock to watch Liz approach. "Oh. Liz. I almost didn't recognize you."

Two steps behind her, David frowned.

Liz stepped onto the dock. "I know what you mean." Suzy had either just returned from a spa or bought a tanning bed. Her skin looked orange.

"Won't your office miss you this summer?"

"They'll get over it." She extended a hand to Suzy. "Can I take your bag?"

David hauled three bags of groceries and his boys each

carried an industrial-size backpack over their shoulders. In contrast, Suzy's weekend tote wasn't much bigger than Liz's briefcase.

David broke in. "Sorry, Suz. D'you need help?"

"I'm great as is." She flashed her dimples.

Suzy didn't actually look too bad. A little extra weight, sure, and the slightest hint of gray in her dark hair, but her designer duds molded themselves to her figure.

She didn't look much different from how Tracy looked until her recent weight loss, except that Suzy's flat brown eyes didn't match the newfound sparkle in Tracy's green ones.

And except that Liz liked Tracy.

That made all the difference in the world.

———

"Is that all you ever talk about? Medical devices?"

Suzy tossed her napkin on her plate.

Flinching inwardly at Suzy's words, blurted when Liz asked Mom another question about the family business, David shared Suzy's sentiment, if not her manner or timing.

"You're right, Suzy." Mom smiled. "I forget how dull it sounds to most people. Liz and I can talk shop another time."

David cleared his throat. "Suzy, tell Liz about that new restaurant. What was the name? Something Fruitie?"

"Tootie Fruitie." Suzy glanced at everyone but Liz. "But I doubt anyone wants to hear about it." She sniffed, loudly. "It's not exactly like medical devices."

Mom smiled even more brightly. "We all like to eat."

Except Frank, who couldn't even feed himself, and maybe Liz, who must've chewed the same piece of meat the entire meal.

Pushing back from the table, Liz excused herself and walked outside.

David wished he hadn't said a word.

"YOUR DAD LOOKED BETTER TONIGHT." Startled, Liz turned at the sound of David's voice behind her.

The last rays of purplish pink smoldered over the trees on the Minnesota side of the River, half a mile away from her chilly spot on the beach. Her stomach churned and the shivers were starting to become spasms.

She tensed, wondering what David wanted. Not to talk seriously about Dad, and she needed to. With someone. Watching Dad at dinner, she wasn't sure she had the heart for the conversation she'd planned for twenty-five years.

"What brings you outside?" She looked up as David jammed his hands in his pockets. "I figured you'd be curled up by a roaring fire with Suzy."

He bent to pick up a few twigs. "What makes you think that?"

His keen gaze erased her smirk. She patted the sandy towel next to her but jumped when he landed on it.

David leaned back on his hands, oblivious to the breeze. Shivering under her fleece pullover, Liz tucked her knees inside it.

"Cold?" He sat up, crossing his arms. "You come down here every night, but you're freezing to death."

"Freezing has its merits."

"Such as?"

She sighed. "I come to escape the demons. The house gets a little crowded with them."

"He can't do anything to you anymore." Rising, David

picked up a few stones from the beach, examining one before he skipped it over the water. "Frank can barely pick up a fork."

Staring across the water, she burrowed deeper into her fleece. "I wouldn't expect you to understand."

He skipped another rock. It bounced twice and sank. "I probably don't, but my beach house is right there whenever you need a break." He looked at the speedboat, bobbing at the buoy. "Or to warm up. Maybe we could get to know each other this summer."

Dead silence.

Giving him props for trying, she finally broke the silence. "What's in it for me?"

He laughed. "My undying gratitude. You'd save me from boredom. As a bonus, I could help you write your novel."

The so-called novel that, despite herself, still starred David.

She'd rather freeze.

DIANA AWOKE Sunday morning with a small warm body cuddled under her arm. Baby-fine hairs tickled her nose, and a gob of—ew—something stuck to her elbow. Against her better judgment, she ventured a taste. As she'd suspected, grape jelly.

Jenna.

Her first early-morning visit from a grandchild. Or from any child since Brandon turned seven. Strike that. Brandon resumed the ritual the summer George died, when he'd crept into her bed nearly every night between midnight and dawn. It ended when school began again that fall.

Even when David and Suzy had shared the big house, Pete and Billy hadn't followed the custom. Diana missed it.

She wondered when Jenna had joined her. Glancing over her shoulder, she squinted at the digital clock. Seven-thirty.

"Where's your mom?"

As the child stirred beside her, Diana ran a hand through Jenna's silky hair, then drew a squeal when she rubbed her tummy.

"Dunno." Jenna squirmed. "You're tickling, Gram!"

Her hand stopped. Immediately. "I'm sorry, honey. I didn't mean to tickle."

When she'd learned about Frank's past, she'd devoured books on abuse—to help Frank, find hope for Liz, protect her boys. Even tickling could be a no-no, because it often went too far.

She wished she'd do something right. Nothing had gone quite right since Frank got sick. Absolutely nothing since Liz arrived.

Jenna giggled. "I liked it."

Diana laughed. "Hmmm. Then I might have to—" She paused as Jenna's eyes widened to saucers. "Tickle your belly button!"

Shrieking, Jenna tumbled out of bed and raced for the door.

Following more slowly, Diana pulled her flannel robe off its hanger. Another day. Time to face it.

"Sun's up, sleepyhead!"

The voice greeting Liz was too husky for Jenna and too close to be outside her bedroom. She must still be dreaming.

Her eyes refused to open. Was it Monday? Cobwebs

covered her brain, echoing her tangle of dreams last night. What happened last night? Oh, yeah. Suzy had left the minute dinner ended, sticking Liz with the dishes. David drove her and the boys across in the speedboat and hadn't returned.

David. The voice belonged to him. He shook her shoulder, gently at first, now more urgently.

She wasn't dreaming.

Rubbing her eyes, she sat up, belatedly looking down to see what she'd worn to bed. A large, wrinkled Washington Capitals jersey. She wiggled her legs under the covers. No pants or underwear. She pulled the comforter tight around her waist.

"Don't worry." David chuckled. "I made sure you were decent when I poked my head in the door."

He obviously hadn't gotten a glimpse under the covers. Thank God.

David pointed at the window, where sunlight peeked through gaps in the curtains. "I thought you might want to go for a hike."

Fumbling, Liz reached for her glasses and leaned back to read the clock behind her head. Six-fifteen.

"Are you nuts?"

His smile faltered. "You used to do that in high school. With Brandon. And Piper."

Not with Tracy, who'd always predicted—or hoped— they'd break their necks tripping over fallen tree trunks, land in poison ivy, and be eaten alive by wild dogs.

She also hadn't hiked with David, who'd usually been at Suzy's house, especially when Suzy's parents weren't there.

"Do you ever knock?"

He shrugged. "I forget. I think of you like my sis—"

"I'm not."

She hadn't worked out much since her surgery. Understatement, and she missed it. Among other things, exercise kept her halfway sane.

"Give me a minute, okay?" She shooed him out the door. "I need to get dressed."

He raised one eyebrow. "Looks like you're already dressed. You wouldn't try to dodge me, would you?"

"You never know."

THE NEXT MORNING, David woke up at six. Grinning as he jumped out of bed and headed for the big house, he thought about the day before. The first perfect day in months.

He'd prodded Liz up the hill, enjoying her grumbles and avoiding the fake punches she'd aimed at his midsection. Afterward, he'd made blueberry pancakes—succeeding Frank this summer in the family tradition. The rest of Monday had flown by in calls with the office, playing with Jenna, a comfortable dinner.

Time for a repeat.

He rapped on her door, turning the handle when she didn't respond. Her bed was already made, or she hadn't slept in it. He tiptoed down the hall toward the sleeping porch.

Peeking in, his gaze moved to Jenna's bed, where she lay curled up with her stuffed monkey. No Liz.

He padded downstairs, grabbed a bagel, and stuffed it in his mouth as he opened the back door. Liz must be writing.

He stepped lightly along the crooked cement walkway, then peered through the screen into the back house. Liz, hunched over her laptop, was oblivious as she pounded the keys. Her hair stuck straight up in blond tufts.

He shouldn't bother her. He pulled open the door anyway.

"That must be some book."

She rubbed a kink out of her neck, then absentmindedly tilted her head toward the door, where he leaned against the jamb.

She shrieked.

Her eyes flashed a furious blue. "Can't you knock?"

Stepping forward, he laughed as she stabbed at keys in a desperate attempt to close the laptop before he reached her.

"I knocked." On her bedroom door. "Sorry to startle you, but you're pretty intent."

She opened her mouth, then shut it. Shaking her head, she stood up, brushing off the black sweatpants she wore with a blue sweatshirt.

A minute later, he clomped up the hill toward the woods, watching Liz's narrow butt and ratty sneakers while he contemplated the myriad differences between Liz and Suzy, his always-pristine wife, and wondered why he even noticed.

Liz hugged herself against the cold as she maneuvered around assorted rocks and tree branches. Watching the trail, David realized too late that she'd picked up her pace and was suddenly way ahead of him.

"Aren't you going too fast? I thought you just had surgery." Female stuff, Mom had told him, as if he were twelve and didn't run a large medical-device company.

"What's the matter? Can't keep up?" She glanced over her shoulder at him—and almost tripped over a large rock. As she caught her balance, he jogged closer, wishing he hadn't. The hitch in his side doubled him over.

Liz wasn't doing much better. One hand pressed against her stomach, she leaned over, breathing hard.

"Can we stop a minute?" He spied two logs nestled on top of each other. "Let an old man take a break?"

Snorting, she examined the logs before perching gingerly on top of them. "If I get ants up my butt, you'll—"

"There are limits to what I'll do."

Her eyes grew wide as her mouth closed on a squeak.

He sat beside her. One minute stretched into five, the silence of the woods broken only by their rasping breaths.

"We should probably start moving again." His knees creaked as he rose. "Before my butt attaches itself to this log."

She brushed off her own butt. "Don't worry. I'd send for help."

"Yeah, but only after a couple days."

They moved at a slower pace now, side by side despite the narrow path. He glanced sideways. Her cheeks reddened, but no perspiration dotted her face or neck.

Sweat poured down his forehead, stinging his eyes.

After half a mile, they reached the top, where a clearing opened into a dirt road and two different paths. One led to an old stone fireplace—a crumbling altar to the gods of summer —and the other to a crusty bench overlooking the River.

"This way?" She pointed at the path to the stone fireplace, which was more like tire tracks than a real trail. They'd taken the dirt road yesterday for a mile before turning back.

His feet matched the rhythm of hers. "I was thinking . . ."

Her head snapped back, as if she'd forgotten him.

". . . maybe we could, uh, do more together."

She stopped, staring at him. "Like?"

"I don't know. Sail, play tennis, rollerblade."

She sped up, her voice strained. "You don't have to babysit me, if that's what you mean. Jenna and I are doing okay."

"That's not why I wanted to hike."

Her feet slowed. "You just thought I needed exercise?"

"Obviously not." He picked up his own pace, making her catch up for once. "I want to get to know you better."

She rolled her eyes. "Oh, right. Your sudden dream of us being brother and sister. But we're not. I'm not Brandon's sister, either."

True, but she and Brandon had always been tight.

"I know." As she lengthened her stride, he slowed. "I want us to be more than siblings."

She tripped on a rock.

He caught up to her, making sure she was okay. "I'd like to be friends."

EXHAUSTED from her third crack-of-dawn hike in a row, Liz ran into the kitchen and snagged her cell phone on the third ring.

"Liz?"

Surprised, she glanced at the clock over the sink. "Paul? Are you already at work?"

"Not yet." He sounded distracted, as if she'd caught him in the middle of a merger agreement. But he'd called *her*. "I can't find my blue suit."

No wonder he'd called. "You have five of them."

"Huh." His teeth clicked. "I can't find it, and I have a big meeting today. You know—blue with pinstripes?"

"You have three of those." She sighed. They hadn't spoken in a week, and all he cared about was a stupid suit. "I dropped one off at the cleaners before I left town."

"Where?"

"The cleaners. The one on Connecticut near the zoo."

"Uh-huh." From the scratching sound, he was writing it down. "But that's not why I called."

"Right." Irritated, Liz almost didn't notice the tugs on the bottom of her sweatshirt. Jenna, in pajamas and tousled hair. "What else? Can't match your socks?"

"No. I mean, yes." Paul blew a breath into the phone. "I miss you guys. Is Jenna up yet?"

Jenna. He missed Jenna, not her.

"She's right here." Jenna's arms hugged Liz's right leg. She held the phone down to her. "It's Daddy."

Jenna held the phone to her ear. "Daddy? Where are you?"

Liz listened to their conversation while she moved to the refrigerator, pulling out a carton of juice and a bag of coffee.

Diana appeared. As Liz measured scoops of a medium roast, she whispered a greeting, then prompted a nodding Jenna to say "yes" into the phone.

At last the coffee maker bubbled, and Liz grabbed her phone a split second before Jenna dropped it on the floor.

"Paul? Are you still there?"

"I miss you guys."

She didn't really miss him, and she couldn't lie, and Diana didn't need to hear this. "Let's talk later, okay?"

"Wait!" He caught her as she almost hung up. "I was thinking about flying out there sometime. Work's pretty busy, but—"

"I figured, or you might've called before now." But she'd only left him a couple of quick voicemail messages. Plus emails and texts. "Let's talk sometime soon. When you're not busy getting ready for work."

With a shaking hand, she ended the call, then washed down her disappointment with a glass of juice.

"Where . . . is she?"

Carrying a breakfast tray into Frank's room, Diana paused at his question, asked with a feathery quaver. Her hands jiggled, sloshing coffee over the rim of the travel mug.

Since the brain cancer did its damage, "she" could mean anyone, from his grandmother, long deceased, to little Jenna.

But Diana had a good guess. As she took in his wide eyes and clenched fists, she remembered Liz's pointed words at dinner last night. He might want to tell Liz something—or hide from her. Not knowing which, she opted for the direct approach.

"Liz is on the beach with Jenna." She set the tray on the bed. "After that she'll probably work on her book." His eyes flickered, questioning. "She's writing a book."

She wiped off his coffee mug, then held it out to him, but he just stared at his hands, trembling in his lap. His voice rose slightly above his usual whisper. "Writing . . . about me?"

"Oh, no, dear. It's just a novel."

She hadn't considered anything else. With sudden horror, she hoped Liz hadn't, either.

AFTER A WILD GAME of horseshoes on the beach—proving that five-year-olds couldn't be trusted with heavy metal objects—Liz left Jenna with Diana and trudged up to the back house.

The novel wasn't going well. Her hero, Chance, still looked, smelled, and—she didn't want to think about it—probably tasted like David. He'd also started asking for a convertible.

Deleting another paragraph, she banished it into the computer's netherworld.

Ten-fifteen. She'd been at it for an hour already and nearly every day since arriving last Tuesday.

Maybe she should do something else. Stretching her neck, she studied the back house. Its cedar walls and clear new windows gave it a freshness the big house lacked after all these years.

Maybe a remodeling project? Something small to start? As she pondered, her right forefinger tapped the keys without leaving letters on the screen. Just like—

Just like her. Never leaving a mark. Story of her life.

The story of her—

She gazed at the ceiling, wondering if she could do it. If she should.

After opening a new document, she started typing.

———

DAVID WIPED HIS FOREHEAD, wishing Liz would take pity on him and slow down.

She'd been banging away on her laptop early again today. The hours she spent on her novel kept growing. Now, she worked before and after their morning hike and during Jenna's afternoon nap—or while Liz thought Jenna was napping. The kid was usually hanging out at his house, acting like she owned the place.

During last night's storm, Liz had even returned to the back house after she'd wrestled Jenna into bed, leaving David to clean up, figuratively speaking, after a tense dinner. The more time she spent writing her novel, the more frustrated she seemed to get with Frank.

Mom had written "TUMS" in large caps on her shopping list.

"Are you okay?" Liz called out without slowing her pace.

"I'm—" He wheezed. "Fine." Stopping, he rested his hands on his knees.

She tilted her head, studying him. "Are you sure? The bench is just another couple hundred yards."

"I'll take your word for it."

"Come on." Closing the distance between them, she grabbed his hand, then jerked free as if he held a live wire.

She jogged ahead a few yards. "You're probably sick of me racing like this. I'm just trying to get back in shape."

"Like you need it."

"I also figure that with Suzy and the boys here, you won't be able to . . ." As the sentence trailed into nothing, she looked away.

Shit.

Suzy and the boys arrived tonight. After next week, they'd be out here permanently. He'd looked forward to having the boys at the River full-time, even though Pete would disappear every chance he got and Billy would go into town for tennis.

But Liz was right. With Suzy at the River, the morning hikes ended. Suzy wouldn't allow them. After twenty years together, he knew that much. He just didn't know why.

He nudged Liz, then raced ahead, trotting backward as he called out. "You never know, Lizzie." At the hated nickname, she sprang forward, and he didn't turn fast enough to avoid her light punch. "We Carruthers boys like our hikes, even if they're with *girls*." He sneered, imitating the boy he'd been when they first met. "Girls who can't keep up."

Charging past him, she left him grinning in her dust.

CHAPTER 6

"A slight change of plans, honey."

Suzy hadn't called David "honey"—without wanting money or an unscheduled vacation—in at least five years. Maybe ten.

Friday night, she bustled around the kitchen, cleaning up the remains of dinner. "It's just that Billy really enjoys tennis."

News flash. He ate, slept, and read tennis. "Yeah?"

"And he'd like to play more this summer." Head down, she scrubbed at an imaginary spot on her pristine counter.

David lifted one eyebrow. "I'm not sure that's physically possible." Last summer, Billy played six hours a day, his chief obstacle the lack of viable opponents. Even Liz hadn't done that until high school. "At some point, he's got to sleep."

Her giggle startled him. "Listen to you!" She'd given up that pet expression about the same time their flirting had cooled to kid-focused topics. "But really. I think he's serious."

"As serious as Pete is about Nicole Jenkins." Or Amanda Vaughn, his dream girl three weeks ago. "It'll pass."

"It's all he talks about." Not to David, which probably

meant they should spend more time together. "He wants—" Her words flew out in a rush. "To go to tennis camp."

"Tennis camp?" Billy barely survived his first overnight camp last summer. "Where? When? How long?"

Suzy's eyes flickered on a glossy brochure on the counter. "Um, Vail. A week from Monday. For two weeks."

As if on cue, Billy cut through the kitchen, half-dragging a boy who looked two or three years younger than him. "Hey, Dad. Mom."

David caught him by the shirttail. "Just a second, sport. What's this I hear about tennis camp?"

Billy's gaze skittered to Suzy. "Uh . . ."

Suzy pursed her lips. "We can talk to Billy about that later, David. He has company right now. Mark, right?"

From behind Billy, a timid voice squeaked. "Max."

"Max." She shooed them away. "You can go now, boys."

Billy shot a nervous glance at David before going downstairs, Max trailing in his wake.

"Anyway." Suzy folded the dishrag, setting it on the edge of the sink. "We'll fly out that morning. Camp starts that afternoon and runs for two weeks."

"I don't understand." Grabbing the dishrag, David swiped at a spot she'd somehow missed and threw the balled-up rag in the sink. "He finishes school next week. When did you decide this?"

"Billy's been wanting to—"

"Go to Vail. Right. He's eleven. If he wants it that bad, I'm sure there are camps in Minnesota." He crossed his arms. "Who found out about this camp—Billy or you?"

Suzy retrieved the dishrag and folded it again. "I don't know what you mean. Billy loves tennis."

"And you want to get away from the River." He watched as she turned the smelly dishrag into an origami masterpiece.

She pursed her lips. "It always rains in June. And there's Liz. And it's *your* family's—"

"What about Liz?" He grabbed a beer from the fridge, then ransacked two drawers before he found an opener. "You've hardly seen her long enough to have an opinion."

"She hasn't shown up in twenty years, and I'm supposed to welcome her? Liz, the girl who used to drool all over you?" She spat, stared at the floor in horror, then wiped up her mess. "I don't think so."

He felt the beginnings of a headache.

"What are you talking about?" Liz would sooner spit on him than drool. She hardly even spoke to him. "I barely knew her even in high school. Still don't."

Suzy rolled her eyes. "Liz had a mile-wide crush on you. If you never saw it, you were the only one."

He choked on his beer, dribbling it down the front of his shirt. Maybe Liz didn't hate him the way she hated Frank—please, God—but there'd never been any love lost there. Sipping the beer more slowly, he drummed his fingers on the counter.

"It sounds like you need a vacation, Suz." Because she'd clearly gone off the deep end. "So go to Vail. Rest. Relax. I'll hold down the fort."

"Really?" She searched his face, then clapped her hands in delight. Her mood swings gave him whiplash.

"Sure." He'd have a couple more weeks getting to know Liz, who sure as hell didn't have a crush on him. "It'll give Pete and me a chance to hang out together."

"You're forgetting about Nicole." She batted her eyelashes.

He laughed, surprised but relieved at Suzy's sudden return to her old self. Her long-ago self. Vail might actually be just what the doctor ordered.

And Billy could go along for the ride.

THE SHRIEKS DIDN'T COME from Liz and weren't aimed at Frank.

Clearing the table of lunch debris, Diana thanked the heavens for small miracles.

Brandon and Piper had arrived mid-morning and almost immediately took off with Liz in the speedboat for a five-mile, windblown cruise to Hudson. David trudged up the steps minutes later. He hadn't been part of the gang in high school. He still wasn't.

Seeing his disappointment, Diana had invited him to join her for lunch. His "yes" surprised her until he confessed that Suzy had driven to Stillwater for a massage.

So David stayed for lunch, amusing Jenna while Diana pulled together an assortment of fruits, breads, and meats from the refrigerator, and awaited the trio's return.

They rushed in, chattering a mile a minute. And, for the most part, leaving David out. He wasn't part of their shared history and memories. Even Brandon hadn't spent much time with David after David settled on Suzy so early and then headed off to college.

Even with the trio, she heard the awkward pauses, sensed the thoughts they didn't share. Liz had been away so long. Piper and Brandon didn't see each other much more, but Diana had invited Piper for occasional dinners, lending the pair a casual familiarity that Liz couldn't capture in a mere two weeks' time—let alone instantaneously.

Diana was glad she'd talked Brandon into coming out this weekend. Busy with Frank, she hadn't spent as much time or energy on him in recent months. With Piper and Liz, and out of the lab, he looked happier than he'd been in too long.

Having him as an additional buffer between Liz and her dad was just a bonus.

SATURDAY AFTERNOON, Liz tapped the number scratched on the kitchen whiteboard into her cell phone. Feeling about thirteen years old, she held her breath until he answered.

"David?" Too late to claim a wrong number. "It's Liz. Do you guys want to come over and play bridge?"

The odds of Suzy unshackling him for a hand of bridge were slim to none, but Brandon had suggested it. The beach was cold and wet today, they needed a fourth, and Diana refused to play.

"Hang on a sec." His voice low, David murmured something, presumably to Suzy. "Uh, I can. Suzy's watching TV."

"Cool. We'll get the table set up."

He arrived before they'd even found a deck of cards.

"Who's my partner?" He looked from Piper to Brandon to Liz. "Not much choice, unless you've all improved. The only other time you guys let me play, Piper kept messing up the cards, Brandon couldn't remember the rules, and Liz cheated."

"I did not!"

Three pairs of eyes stared at her.

"It wasn't cheating. I just like to win the bid."

"With reckless disregard for your cards." Brandon shook his head. "Give it up, Liz. You bid six no-trump with only twelve points in your hand. We all thought David was going to climb over the table and choke you."

"But he didn't, did he?" She'd wanted to impress David, which hadn't happened when he saw her hand.

"I was too polite."

Three pairs of eyes shifted to David.

"Hey! You were lucky I played. I was probably busy—"

"—with Suzy." Brandon and Piper grinned at each other.

"Children!" Diana, curled up on the porch glider, stopped pretending to read. "I'd hoped you'd all improved more than your bridge game. No wonder no one wants to play with you."

Piper winked. "No offense, Diana, but you never like to play any game you can't win." At Diana's startled look, Piper shrugged. "Who around here does?"

LIZ SQUEEZED her eyes shut against the sunlight and tried to ignore the finger tapping her shoulder. What was it with Minnesotans and rude awakenings?

It was . . . Sunday. Her mind struggled to clear its haze. With Suzy here, she hadn't hiked with David yesterday, but she was pretty sure she hadn't missed a day without realizing it. So Suzy was still here and David still wasn't hiking.

Hands started shaking both her shoulders. After the first day, David knocked—or found her in the back house. Assuming he'd skip a hike today, she let herself sleep in.

She opened one eye. Piper, with Brandon right behind her.

"Isn't anyone safe in their own bed anymore?"

"Nope." Piper tugged on her arm. "You didn't used to be this difficult to get out of bed."

She glared at her friend, who laughed. "You didn't used to be so obnoxious first thing in the morning."

"Yes, I did." "Yes, she did."

Brandon, his cheeks flushed, looked as if he'd questioned the merits of waking her up. At least one person around here had a little sense.

Not Piper. She started dragging Liz out from under the covers.

"I'm coming, I'm coming." She swung her legs over the side of the bed. "Not that anyone told me where we're going."

"Pajama raid on David and Suzy?" Piper smirked.

Liz's legs swung back into bed.

"She's kidding." Brandon shuddered, but his eyebrows were dancing. "David looks like hell in the morning. I wouldn't risk it."

Even Liz laughed. The guy had million-dollar looks, but the first fifteen minutes after David woke up were brutal.

"Come on." Brandon held out a hand to Liz, pulling her to her feet. "David said you've been hiking with him."

Piper snorted. "If I'd known you were that desperate for exercise, I'd have been here sooner."

"No, you wouldn't." Liz stretched the kinks out of her neck. "I keep begging, but you've been too busy."

Piper glanced at Brandon before turning back to Liz with a laugh. "Get over it. Not all of us are on summer vacation." She moved toward the door, tugging on Brandon's hand. "So get dressed, or I'll invite David along."

The door shut, and Liz scrambled into hiking clothes.

Her friends never gave up. Except, on weekends, David.

DAVID HEARD the bang of the big house's screen door and sprang out of bed to peer out his window. Brandon, Liz,

Piper. Jenna, straining to go along, held back by Mom's firm hug.

They hadn't bothered waking him, even after David suggested a hike to Brandon last night.

"Are you coming back to bed?" Suzy's sleepy voice floated to him, and he looked over his shoulder at her. Her hair fanned across the pillow in the way he used to find intoxicating. But at some point, years ago, he'd become a teetotaler.

He took one last look as the three started out, Liz in the lead, Brandon behind her, Piper in third. With a sigh, he lay down again. On his side of the bed, leaving Suzy on hers.

Like always.

"Liz?"

Silence. Paul frowned.

"Sorry, it's Diana. Liz left her phone in the kitchen. Is this Paul? I'll get her."

"Wait!" Trembling, he shouted, then regretted it an instant later. "Could— Could I talk to Jenna first? If she's around?"

More silence. "Sure. I think she's coming up from the beach now."

He heard a door bang and running footsteps. It couldn't be Jenna. His daughter was well behaved and nearly silent.

Were other kids around? Liz hadn't told him. He hadn't thought to ask what Jenna would do this summer, cooped up on a tiny, cold, stretch of sand with no other kids around. She usually played with other kids. Actually, he wasn't completely sure what she did when he wasn't around.

He just knew he loved her. And missed her.

"Daddy?" Jenna's small, sweet voice. "What'cha doin'? Are you workin', like Mom says? So you can't come see me?"

The questions came in rapid-fire sequence, like the ones from his senior partners, only in a higher pitch.

"It's Sunday. I'm reading the paper and missing you." And working on some files, but that would only confirm Liz's opinion.

Late yesterday, he'd walked down an empty corridor at work on his way to the vending machine. A few offices had lights on, but he hadn't seen anyone. He wondered if other lawyers came in on weekends, turned on their lights, then left. He'd never noticed before.

He never made it to the vending machine. Grabbing files, he'd headed home and spent the evening in Liz's upstairs office. Smelled her candles. Noticed the photos of Jenna that lined her bookcases. Most of them were of Jenna alone, a few with Liz. None of him.

Today, he'd work at the dining room table.

Jenna babbled into the phone, chirping about things he didn't understand. But she sounded alive, alert, happy. And she shared more than Liz did, at least lately. He worked, Liz worked, they tried to spend time with Jenna. They'd also tried to have another baby, but they hadn't tried for a while. Liz hated in vitro, hated needles, had hated being pregnant.

Sometimes, he wondered if she hated him, too.

"Daddy!" He held the phone out from his ear, trying to avoid her shrieks. "Don'cha wanna?"

He hadn't been paying attention. "Don't I want to what?"

She sighed the way Liz did. "Weren't you listening?"

Caught between a rock and a hard place, he tried flattery. Jenna was still young. "I was just thinking about all the fun things you're telling me."

A giggle. "Oh, Daddy. It's so nice here. If you come out, you can watch me waterski. David is showing me how."

Waterski? Jenna was five, for God's sake. She didn't even know how to swim.

"Could you find your mom? I'd like to talk to her."

"You're not gonna yell at her, are you?"

Before he could answer, the phone clunked on something.

"Paul?" Liz's voice was layered with frost, probably from the cold Minnesota summer.

"Hey, Liz. How are things going?"

He already knew too much from Jenna, who was being forced to waterski before she could swim, in water that was probably frigid with a strong current, after being dragged away from her father to spend three months with virtual strangers.

Liz hesitated. "Things are fine."

"What's new? What are you guys doing?"

"Not much. Hanging out. Water and beach, beach and water. Hiking. Wild games of gin rummy and horseshoes."

It sounded like a nightmare.

"I've missed you guys." There. He said it. Liz always claimed he didn't express his feelings.

Another screen door slammed somewhere at the River, the only reply he received after sharing those feelings.

He tried something else. "Is it going okay with— with your dad?"

"Yeah. I mean, okay, I guess." She chewed on something as she spoke. She'd forgotten her manners since arriving in Minnesota, which wasn't odd considering that she seemed to have forgotten him, too. "Paul, did you just call to say hi? Or did you really want to talk?"

He'd woken up this morning feeling more alone than he

ever had. Every day stretched before him in a mindless chasm of work and nothing more. None of his socks matched. The green things in the refrigerator weren't vegetables.

"I miss you guys. I miss Jenna and . . . you." He hadn't really thought about it until this morning in the middle of a large, empty bed, but he loved Liz. At least, he loved the old Liz. The new one sounded a little brusque.

"Is that all? I've been waiting for you to—"

She paused mid-sentence, and the hairs on the back of his neck prickled. "To what?"

She dropped her voice to a murmur. "Jenna's right here, so I can't talk now. But you need to think, Paul, like I talked about before I left. Please. I hope you're thinking."

About what? As he debated exactly how to ask that, the phone clicked in his ear.

Frowning, he wandered into Liz's office, pulled a small photo of her with Jenna out of its frame, and stared at it for a long moment before tucking it into his wallet.

She hadn't expected to write today. The opportunity, engineered by Diana, left Liz feeling . . . a million things.

Piper and Brandon ran an errand for Diana while she watched Jenna, Dad napped, and David and Suzy did their thing. She had no idea what Pete and Billy were doing. In a few years, Jenna would be the same.

Meanwhile, Liz wrote. Words flowed from her fingertips, appearing by magic on the screen. Surprising her. Sentences, even paragraphs, ripped themselves out of her, scattering pieces of her soul on the floor of the back house.

A range of emotions flooded her, some—rage, mortification, hurt—like old friends she'd had since childhood. She understood them. She felt rage when she looked at Dad, mortified every time she almost told Piper, hurt when she remembered Mom.

She'd gone through one box of tissues and could barely see the screen for the tears. She'd held it together all these years in front of family and friends and strangers. Now she sat in front of an inanimate computer screen that sucked her dry.

Her stomach growled. The old clock radio on Diana's desk read eleven-thirty. Almost lunchtime. Piper and Brandon would be back soon, if they weren't already, and Diana would need a reprieve from Jenna.

She saved her work and headed out to rescue Diana.

Her mind still churning, she walked in the back door of the big house into an empty kitchen. Grabbing a bagel, she headed through the house on the way to the beach.

As she crossed the porch to the screen door, intent on Jenna's high-pitched voice on the beach below and Diana's lower-pitched calm, she almost didn't notice the person sitting on the glider on the far end of the porch. Dad. Alone.

Faltering, she held her breath and nearly kept going.

She'd been here almost two weeks and hadn't yet been alone with him. It worked better for both of them that way.

The morning's writing flooded through her as she watched the man who'd provoked the bitter words inside her computer. He stared at her, unmoving, not speaking.

No big surprise on either count. The difficulty of forming words that made sense to anyone else probably ate at him. He could hardly walk. She wondered how he'd made it on his own from his bedroom to the porch.

She rocked back and forth on her heels, wishing she could escape. She'd always wanted to, and never had—

despite moving out at eighteen, first to New York and then to Washington.

The River offered no escape, period.

"Hi, Dad." She'd stopped calling him Daddy the first time he hit her—at age four, when she'd gotten too excited on the playground and wet her pants. It hadn't been the last time she'd wet her pants, but it'd been the last time he knew about it.

Staring blankly at her, his watery eyes blinked twice, as if in code, and one hand kneaded the bottom of his shirt.

She couldn't help hating him, and hating herself for never crushing the monster of her childhood the way she'd crushed all her opponents in negotiations. The monster in front of her had killed Mom, then moved on to a new family.

"Mom!" Jenna's voice preceded the banging of the screen door by a split second, rescuing Liz. "I missed you!"

One thing she'd never say to Dad. No matter what.

"YOU'RE sure you don't need help?" Diana frowned, watching Frank struggle with his walker as he shuffled to the bathroom. "David will be back soon. He's taking Suzy and the boys across."

She could help him, but it always left her once-dynamic husband sullen and embarrassed until his next nap, at which point he'd forget it, as he'd forgotten so many things. Like Billy's name, just yesterday.

Besides, from a practical standpoint, it strained her back, and her weekly massages were no longer a luxury she could afford. She couldn't leave Frank alone with Liz. She also couldn't ask David all the time. She already depended on him too much, and she knew how much she'd have to lean on him in the coming months.

Diana sucked in a quick breath, grateful that David hadn't turned on Frank since learning about Liz's childhood. He'd helped Frank into his chair at dinner, as usual, ignoring a toe-tapping Suzy as she waited beside hers.

The bathroom door clicked shut. Her ear pressed against it, attuned to the slightest sound of distress.

Her other ear picked up the low rumble of the speedboat returning from its nocturnal run, followed by the clunk of the boat hitting the dock. She blinked, surprised. David, whose sometimes lackadaisical attitude didn't extend to his boats or cars, would never risk a dent or scratch. He didn't bang into docks. Ever.

Leaving the bathroom door, Diana crossed to the porch and peered out at the darkening sky. She heard voices below. No, just one voice, chattering a mile a minute. Liz? Diana couldn't hear David at all. Odd. With David and Liz, it was always the other way around.

LIZ'S HEAD, buried against her knees, had jerked at the harsh grind of boat against dock. David. For the first time in his life, doing something less than perfectly.

She almost smiled.

In the growing darkness, he secured the speedboat to the dock with steady precision, turned off the running lights, and stowed the debris accumulated during the day. He leaned over the side of the boat, softly cursing. His haphazard docking had probably left a tiny scratch that no one else would ever see without a magnifying glass.

Liz curled tighter against her knees, warding off the chill and David's bad mood. She hoped he didn't see her.

His pounding footsteps punctuated the night as he strode along the dock toward the beach. He'd soon veer right, headed for his house. Thirty feet down the beach in the opposite direction, Liz's heart pounded for reasons she couldn't explain.

When he jumped off the dock and onto the sand, her ears strained to hear him. To know when it was safe to lift her head. Much like, as a girl, she'd hidden in her room at night, listening for the sound of her dad's drunken snoring.

Lost in that thought, she didn't hear David until he landed on the beach next to her.

She tensed, waiting for him to do some dumb-ass thing like tackling her or kicking sand all over her.

When he didn't, she surprised herself by speaking. "Are you bummed about Suzy and Billy going to Vail?"

No response. Had she sounded sarcastic? She didn't mean to. Besides, Brandon had already given David enough crap about the tennis camp. She didn't need to pile on.

She glanced sideways, but he was staring at his feet, grinding his bare heels into the sand. "You'll see them next weekend. Maybe even sooner?"

"Huh."

She forced a laugh. "Hey, usually you're the one trying to get *me* to talk. Did we trade places and nobody told me?"

He finally looked up. His eyes, dark against the night, darted from her face to the sand between them. Suddenly uncomfortable, she tucked herself even further inside her fleece.

"David? What is it?"

He reached down and she flinched, but he came up with a flat rock. Moving to one knee, he skimmed it across the water, his gaze glued to the rock's path long after it sank to the bottom.

He paid as much attention to her as Paul did.

Springing to her feet so fast that she stumbled, Liz caught her balance, brushed off her jeans, and walked away. Away from the water, away from David. Toward the big house.

He didn't follow, which figured. He must already miss Suzy. The stupid, selfish, big-assed love of his life.

"Sorry." The word rumbled behind her. "I'm sorry, Liz."

Despite herself, she turned back to face him. But when he just jammed his fists in the front pockets of his jeans, muttering, she headed again for the big house.

She was too tired to deal with cranky men tonight.

When she reached the steps, his hand caught her upper arm. "Wait."

"Why?" Her arm tingled in a way she found . . . odd. "I already get the silent treatment from Paul and, for that matter, my dad. I don't need it from anyone else, thanks."

He let go. Taking it as a sign to leave, she sprinted up the steps.

"Do you always have to be a damn track star?" But he caught up to her, surprisingly enough. "Suzy says . . ."

When he trailed off, Liz waited another moment, then headed up the steps again. He kept talking to her back. "She says you used to have a crush on me."

Oh. My. God.

David's voice was soft. "Crazy, right?"

Thank God for the darkness. As she forced a hollow laugh, hot tears flooded her eyes. "I wouldn't know. You're the one who married her."

This time, when she trudged up the steps, he didn't follow.

CHAPTER 7

"What? You're not ready to hike? Or writing your novel?"

Bending over the bed, David kept tapping Liz's shoulder. Still sleeping, or she faked it well.

She groaned and rolled over, wrapping her arms around her head. Caught off guard, he took a step backward. The rumpled sheets covered her up to the waist, revealing her Capitals hockey jersey, size XXL. If he thought at all about Liz, which he hadn't until Suzy brought up that bizarre crush nonsense, he might try to imagine her in something different.

But he still didn't want to think that way about Liz.

Groaning, she finally opened one eye. He'd let her sleep in, but from what little he could see of her fresh-scrubbed face, she didn't look grateful.

"What are you doing here?" Her low-pitched rumble sounded like it came out of a throat soaked with whiskey. Definitely not like Liz. "Not snoozing with Suzy?"

"Uh, she's not here." He flushed as he hadn't since high school. "She and the boys left last night, remember?"

She pulled the pillow over her face, her fists clenching the ends. With a yank, he snatched it from her.

"C'mon. Time to hike." His sports watch read six thirty-two, not that he was counting. "We're usually halfway up the hill by now."

His chuckle stuck in his throat when she ran a hand through her hair.

Her tangled, snarled blond hair that looked like it had spent the night testing blenders. As in, not attractive. Except maybe at six thirty-two in the morning. On Liz.

He was dwelling on her way too much.

Lucky thing, like she always said, at least she wasn't actually his stepsister.

She rolled over, her hands tugging beneath the covers at the bottom of her jersey. He tried looking away. Mostly.

"You win." She sat up, her first genuinely hopeful movement so far. "But give me a minute so I can get dressed."

"You're dressed already." Pointing to the jersey that clung to her like a pup tent, he wondered if she ever wore any of that filmy, clingy, Victoria's Secret stuff.

Jesus. If she knew what he was thinking, she'd slug him.

From the glacial stare she gave him, she might. "Out. Now."

"I'll wait outside."

"How thrilling."

Suzy was an idiot. Liz didn't have a crush. Even when he'd ogled her this morning—surreptitiously and against his will—she didn't give him the time of day.

Like always.

———

"PIPER? IT'S LIZ TANNER." As her secretary's voice came through the intercom, Piper frowned at her calendar.

It wasn't a surprise she needed today. She'd spent Friday

night and last night with the love of her life—which still sounded pretty funny—sandwiched around her time at the River. Another weekend she hadn't worked. Another Monday paying the price.

The intercom buzzed again. "Piper? She's in the lobby."

Quarter to twelve. Damn. She didn't have time for lunch. She'd planned to choke something down at her desk.

She sighed. "Could you bring her back? I'm crunched."

A minute later, Liz poked her head into Piper's office. "Am I interrupting?"

"No problem." She waved her inside. "What's up? I'm actually buried in work, but you're a good excuse for avoiding it."

"Glad to help." Liz stood an inch inside the door. "Can you do lunch? I needed to come downtown and was hoping you might be free."

"Yikes. Not an ideal day for it."

"Twenty minutes?" Staring at the carpet, Liz didn't see Piper's raised eyebrows. "Something close and fast? I saw a Five Guys." She finally looked at Piper, a rare plea in her eyes. "I need to talk, and I was afraid you'd turn me down if I called."

They knew each other too well. She would've.

Piper looked at her watch. "Okay, but I can't believe you asked for a twenty-minute lunch with a straight face. You can't do it in less than sixty."

"Forty-five." Liz's face curved into a grin. "I've gotten efficient in my old age."

"Tell me about it." With a last look at her computer and cluttered desk, Piper grabbed her purse and sailed out the door.

"YOU CALL THIS FAST FOOD?" Liz glanced around the bar, dimly lit even at noon. Between the Patsy Cline blaring from the jukebox in the corner, where a woman's hips swayed in time to the music, and the large lunch crowd, it'd be tough to have a conversation.

Of course, it'd be tough to have this conversation anywhere.

Piper sipped her lemonade, then picked up her hamburger. "It's fairly fast if you sit at the bar, especially if you know the owner." She smiled at Liz. "And we do. Besides, you can't beat these burgers."

"We know the owner?" The odds of getting through this conversation just got even worse, if that was possible. Liz's stomach clenched, but it could be from the aromas wafting past her. Her fries smelled like they'd been cooked in motor oil.

They were actually pretty good.

"Jake Trevor. Remember him from high school?" Piper glanced at the far end of the bar. "He and Victoria—Vic—Carlyle used to be inseparable?"

Twisting slightly, Liz frowned. "That's Jake? Didn't he used to be really cute?"

"He still is. Gorgeous, in fact." Piper laughed into her napkin. "But you're looking at the bartender. Jake is sitting at the end of the bar talking to—" Her jaw dropped. "Omigod. Isn't that Tess? You know, Vic's bestie? Before Vic disappeared senior year?"

"Dance school." Checking out the couple—were they a couple?—at the end of the bar, both of them looking good enough to make her feel self-conscious, Liz tried to remember. But it'd been nineteen years, and she'd skipped all of their reunions. She turned back to Piper. "Didn't Vic go away to dance school, or with a touring company? Something like that. But what are the odds of seeing two of our Southwest classmates after all these years?"

Annoyingly high, as it turned out.

"Hey, Pendulum is the most popular place in downtown Minneapolis." Piper waved a hand at the crowd. "It's packed."

"Maybe, but they have to dim the lights so people won't notice the food."

Piper wiped her mouth as the juice from her burger trickled down her chin. "I realize it's not the sort of swank restaurant you find in *Washington*, but you said you wanted to talk, and you haven't said a word yet."

Liz eyed her own untouched salad, wilted lettuce and all, and reached for more fries.

Piper leaned forward. "It's about your dad, isn't it?"

"Not today, at least." Picking up her Diet Coke, she drained half of it. "It's—"

"Brandon." Piper shrugged. "What's there to talk about?"

Liz scrunched her nose, wishing Piper would let her finish a sentence. Just once. "Brandon? What's the matter with him?"

"You're right." Piper nodded briskly. "Not Brandon, and it can't be Diana, and we hardly ever see David, so—" She tapped her plate once, twice, then blurted another guess. "Paul."

That would be another conversation, but she'd promised Piper twenty minutes. A half hour ago.

"It's not Paul. At least, not right now. It's David."

"David. Crap." Startled, Piper dropped the rest of her hamburger, quickly attempting a search-and-rescue mission on her pink blouse.

Mission accomplished—somewhat—Piper stuffed a last bite in her mouth. "I always hated what he did to you. Even before Suzy entered the picture, he had a swelled head and treated you like nothing. Like dirt."

"Like an ugly stepsister." Liz offered a rueful smile.

"Not even remotely. On either count." Piper leaned toward Liz, touching her arm. "I was glad he was older. Part of me didn't want him to steal you away from Tracy and me, and part of me was pissed he never tried."

"He was four years older, so he would've been robbing the cradle." Liz shrugged, even though she'd never felt nonchalant about it. "But Brandon didn't exactly slobber over any of us, either."

Head down, Piper dabbed at her blouse. The stain, which had begun the size of a quarter, was now at least five times larger. Finally stopping mid-swipe, she glanced at Liz. "Brandon? I thought we were talking about David. Is he being a jerk?"

"No, nothing like that. It's . . . Suzy."

Flattening her palm over her chest, Piper sucked in a breath. "What? She's actually being *nice* to you?"

"Only if hell froze over. Suzy told David—"

"She wants a divorce? Finally." Piper smirked as she picked up the dessert menu.

Liz rolled her eyes. She couldn't imagine eating another bite. Okay, maybe a few more fries. "She told David I had a crush on him in high school. She probably told him I still do."

"Do you?" Piper leaned in, her blouse pressed against a glob of ketchup on the bar. "And does he believe her?"

Liz had asked herself both of those questions all morning.

"I don't think he does." She ran a hand through her hair. "That crush is ancient history—no different from the crush you had on Brandon for all of about fifteen minutes."

Piper looked oddly annoyed. But she *did* have a crush on Brandon. A million years ago.

Liz glanced down at her salad. Ew. "I have no idea what David thinks. He just asked me. Casually, like he was asking how often I watch TV."

"Hmmm." Piper set her purse on her lap, rummaging through it before pulling out a tube of lipstick and applying a fresh coat. The way her blouse looked, the effort seemed futile.

"What should I do?"

"Nothing." Piper glanced at her watch, then picked up the check. "You've got Paul."

Liz rolled her eyes, prompting Piper's frown.

"At least, you're married to him—which sounds like another conversation. But I have to get back to work." She looked down her front. And cringed. "Thank God I picked up my blouses at the cleaners this morning."

Liz followed, hurrying to keep up with Piper. "But I don't know what to do about David. He's—"

"Married, too, last time I checked. And you said you don't have a crush anymore." Turning back to Liz as the crowd jostled them, she nodded. "I do know how you feel—or I've got a clue, at least. Life's a bitch, sweetie." She laughed. "And so is Suzy."

"But David?"

Outside, Piper moved at a brisk pace. "Seriously, Liz, there's not much you can do, but hang out with the guy. That's one thing you never tried. Maybe if you got to know him, you'd be rid of the crush for good. Or maybe you'll wind up with a great friendship."

"What if I wind up with something more complicated?"

Stopping mid-stride, Piper threw an arm around Liz's shoulders. "Don't even go there. Suzy will eat you for lunch."

———

DIANA BENT TO pick up coloring books from the porch rug, scattered along with a handful of crayons when Jenna screeched out David's return. He'd spent the morning at the office after roaring off at the crack of dawn.

She rubbed her back, wishing the ache would go away. Wishing, for a moment, that everyone would go away. David, who'd been missing since yesterday's hike with Liz. Liz, who kept leaving Jenna with Diana for longer stretches. Even Frank, who couldn't help it, who wasn't her husband in the way he'd been.

Actually, she'd keep Jenna. The child was polite, cuddly, and as thoughtful as a five-year-old got. Still too quiet, but that screech five minutes ago rang all the bells.

The screen door banged. Diana glanced up, expecting David at last.

It was Jenna. Alone.

"Isn't David home, dear?" She set the coloring books on a wicker table and sat on one of the gliders, knowing Jenna would seek out her lap.

Jenna sat in a different chair, little arms folded, bottom lip protruding an inch. "He didn't want to see me."

She patted the space on the glider next to her. "Come here. I can't believe David didn't want to see you. He must be busy." Or something.

Jenna's lower lip quivered. "He's not busy. He doesn't wanna play with me."

Shades of her mother. At age nine—and older—Liz had uttered almost the same exact words about David.

As adults, David now said it about Liz.

Sighing, Diana patted her lap and opened her arms. After a moment's hesitation, Jenna climbed down from her chair and skipped to Diana, crawling into her lap. Diana held her, stroking her hair.

"David loves playing with you." She got Jenna's upturned face in response. "Cross my heart."

"Oh, Gram. You're funny." Jenna giggled, grabbing Diana's fingers.

She cuddled Jenna, loving the sweet-smelling softness of her hair, the way she alternately squirmed and held still when Diana sprinkled kisses on the top of her head.

"So tell me." At Diana's gentle command, Jenna stopped squirming. "What's David doing? What did he say?"

"Nothing. He was busy. I could tell."

Jenna wouldn't make much of a detective. Obviously, David and Liz had had some sort of falling out, and she'd have to patch it up. Again. This time she'd have to be more direct than sending Liz for a bottle of wine.

Even Jenna would've caught on by now.

Bottom line, she needed David back, and she needed Liz to make more frequent appearances. Diana had her hands full. She didn't think Liz meant to do a dump-and-run with Jenna, but she had, and now David wasn't helping, either. He'd also been rude to Jenna, who didn't deserve it.

"Is David in his house?"

A slight nod.

"Did he say what he was doing this afternoon?"

Jenna shook her head. He was probably avoiding Liz and pouting.

Straining, she tried to lift Jenna off her lap. Ugh. Not without breaking her back. It'd already been a long week, and she'd only made it to Wednesday.

She had to put her foot down—one on David, one on Liz. The only question: which problem to fix first?

LEANING BACK in lazy splendor against the hard cushions of Suzy's floral-print chair, David congratulated himself on being free of all irritations. Like Liz, for starters.

He twisted, slugging the cushion, trying to make it feel like something that didn't resemble cement.

Liz bugged him, annoyed him, riled him. She had a way of wrecking the perfection of a sky-blue June day. Just when they'd started to be civilized—even talking on their hikes, when he wasn't too winded—she'd gotten pissed off and stormed away. As if he'd done something horrible just by asking her again about her so-called crush.

Fine. He hadn't missed her all these years. He didn't now. And he wouldn't babysit her daughter just because she didn't feel like doing it herself. Especially when her daughter looked so much like Liz as a kid. Only a lot nicer.

But with Liz in hiding and Jenna off somewhere, probably also hiding from him, he didn't have anything to do. This morning he'd visited headquarters for the third time this week, and his secretary, Crystal, had nearly fainted.

He glanced around the upper floor of his beach house. Nothing needed fixing. Except for a dirty plate and glass in the sink, the house still looked the same as when Suzy left Sunday after her manic fit of housecleaning.

A book? He'd already read everything in sight. Before Liz and Jenna arrived a couple weeks ago, he'd spent hours online, monitoring his investments and trading with his usual profitable abandon.

Since they'd been here, though, he'd rarely logged on. He didn't miss it. He'd spent his time hiking with Liz, playing with Jenna, talking to Frank and Mom—and trying to talk to Liz while she sanded and painted the entire second floor of the big house, room by room, without anyone's help.

The knock on his door wasn't tentative, like Liz, or angry,

again like Liz, or nonexistent, like Jenna. It had all the command of a Chairman of the Board. Or a former one.

Peering in, Mom didn't look happy to see him.

"C'mon in." He crossed the porch to open the door. "When was the last time you stood on ceremony around here?"

"Ever since the last time I walked in without knocking."

He winced. Suzy wasn't a fan of drop-ins, especially his family. Mom sailed past him into the porch, surveying the room and his idle state, her hands on her trim hips.

"You're not doing a damn thing, are you?" As she shook her head, her sleek hair swished a couple times, then fell back into place. "And you're avoiding Jenna, who—I might remind you—is five years old? Who, for lack of sense, adores you?"

"You might remind Liz. I think she forgot she has a daughter." Shoving his hands in his pockets, he pretended a nonchalance his mom would see through in a heartbeat.

"Are you also avoiding Liz?" Her eyes glittered emerald as her gaze nailed him. Damn the way a mom could do that to a guy.

He dropped into the big flowery chair in the corner. Maybe he'd buy new chairs while Suzy was gone. More masculine ones. Maybe with pictures of cars and trucks on them.

"Who could blame me? She's a piece of work."

"You're not so perfect." She waved a hand in the air. "In any case, Liz is part of your family. Maybe you had a fight—"

"Understatement."

Just because he'd mentioned Suzy's nonsense about the crush again. Liz obviously didn't have one, but some part of his male ego just wanted to know. He certainly didn't care.

He also couldn't ask his mom about it.

"Even so—" Mom was nothing if not dogged, a valuable

business trait that rubbed him like sandpaper. "You need to get over it. Both of you. I'll talk to Liz."

"Good luck."

"David, I'm tired of it." She sagged, glancing around the room before claiming a pale yellow chair. The only piece of furniture Suzy hadn't picked out.

God, Suzy's furniture was ugly. He *would* go shopping for something new. Maybe with Mom, if that wasn't too dumb for a forty-one-year-old guy to do.

Her sigh made him turn back to her.

She stared at her hands, which suddenly held the same age spots he'd seen in Frank's weathered hands years ago but which—stupidly—he'd never expected in his mother's hands. Hands that, he noticed, could use a manicure.

"I'm so tired." As her gaze met his, he saw the dark circles. "Physically, yes, but more than that. I'd hoped for a nice summer. Having Liz come home—"

"—wasn't an easy way to achieve that."

"No, but it was the right thing to do. I've missed her, and Frank has missed her in his own way. He has terrible memories of what he did. Of course, she also reminds him every day, without even saying a word. Even though he's . . . sick."

"Dying."

Despite the cancer diagnosis, despite all the treatments, the hospital stays, the way he looked—no one said it. Frank wasn't going to be around much longer.

He was going to die, and his last summer here at the River would suck. For Frank *and* for Mom. Because Mom had Liz and Jenna and even David to deal with, when she'd rather spend as much time as she could with Frank.

"We don't know that." Mom said the words, but her eyes didn't deny the truth. "We have to hope he'll get better." She ignored David's raised eyebrows. "In the meantime, I need a break. Help. Peace. Conversation."

He dropped into the chair next to Mom's. "I don't know how you're going to get both peace and conversation—" He grinned, drawing a faint smile in return. "But I'll give it a shot. Even if I have to be nice to Liz."

"I thought you two were finally getting along." She shook her head. "She must like you. Lord knows I wouldn't get out of bed at six a.m. for just anyone."

"You wouldn't do it, period."

She rose, heading to the kitchen. Opening the refrigerator, she wrinkled her nose. "I'm not too sure about this wine."

He pulled a bottle of Glenlivet from the cabinet above the sink. "No wonder. Suzy bought it."

She bypassed the wine in favor of water. "I don't have a problem with Suzy. I also don't like to interfere."

Suzy thought Mom interfered just by living next door all summer.

"I'll talk to Liz." Rummaging through the cupboards, he came up with a plastic cup, added ice, and splashed scotch into it.

He glanced up to find his mom sipping her water and looking bewildered. "About what? Suzy's taste in wine?"

"No, about helping you out. But you're right. The wine sucks, just like the furniture Suzy picked out." His whole damned life sucked right now. Except for the boys. But Pete would rather hang with his friends, and Suzy was kidnapping Billy just for an excuse to escape the River.

He linked arms with Mom, heading for the door. A sip of scotch fortified his resolve.

At the threshold, Mom hesitated. "But . . . I was going to talk to Liz."

"No need." He nudged open the door with his elbow.

"We've been dumping on you. I'll go yell at Liz—" He winked when Mom gasped. "And then we'll relieve you of Jenna."

"Frank and Jenna are both napping." She took his arm as they went down the steps, then walked single-file ahead of him along the path to the big house.

"Even better. You can rest, relax, get some of that peace you've been craving." He lifted her hand. "Or make an appointment for a manicure. Your nails are a mess."

"Oh, you!" She smiled, looking years younger. Looking like Mom again.

Whistling as he headed up the sidewalk, he aimed for the back house. And Liz.

"Have you read today's paper?" Tracy dropped the business section of the Minneapolis paper on Piper's cluttered desk and sat down across from her.

Piper glanced at a large headline about the biggest medical device company in town, busy gobbling up another early-stage company, then scanned the first few paragraphs. Neither company was her client and, therefore, not her problem.

She had enough problems with her own clients.

"No, no, no." Her eyes widened as she skimmed down the page. After discussing the pending acquisition of a tiny R&D company, the article mentioned other rumored deals.

"Yes." Tracy waited while Piper reread the same paragraph for the fourth time. *Industry insiders speculate that Carruthers Medical will soon approach Slytherby Labs.*

Tossing the paper aside, Piper drummed her fingers on the only bare patch on her desk. "No one would acquire

Slytherby right now, God knows, with the FDA investigation going on. Especially Carruthers."

As Slytherby's chief outside legal counsel, she'd have been one of the first to hear. And it was news to Piper. Tina Franklin, Slytherby's CEO, had complained in recent weeks about how Piper had handled the FDA probe—as if she could miraculously fix a faulty product and questionable advertising—but she'd called Piper about a tough issue just yesterday.

And hadn't mentioned an acquisition.

If Carruthers was indeed the suitor, maybe it had slipped Brandon's mind as well. Someone in product development wouldn't typically know about an acquisition unless it involved his product area—or unless his family owned a majority of the stock and his brother ran the company.

"Brandon hasn't said anything?" Tracy read her mind too well. Most of the time, it was a good thing. "By the way, have you told Liz that you two are going out?"

Piper grimaced. "It's complicated."

Brandon hadn't even told Diana or David yet. She'd wanted to tell Liz this weekend, but it never seemed like the right time—especially when Liz kept referring to their happy trio.

Tracy got up, retrieved the newspaper, and left.

Closing the door, Piper picked up her phone.

CHAPTER 8

"Knock, knock." David's relaxed baritone called out, accompanying his rap on the screen door to the back house and prompting Liz to dump coffee all over her lap.

He stepped inside without waiting for a response.

The coffee had long since cooled, thank God. Liz swabbed at her lap with one hand while the fingers of her other hand desperately tried to hit "save." Nothing. The screen froze as David moved behind her. In a last-ditch effort, she flung herself at the laptop, arms and torso and sloshing coffee cup and everything.

"Need help?" Perched on the arm of the only other chair in the room, out of easy view of her computer screen, he crossed his arms and looked smug.

She slid a horrified glance at him. "No, thanks. I've got it covered."

"I can see that." A grin split his face as she realized, too late, what she'd said.

She ran a hand through her hair—sticky now, thanks to coffee and the gargantuan bag of Hershey's Nuggets she'd inhaled as she typed.

David watched her in silence, a rarity for him except

when they trekked up a hill on those crack-of-dawn hikes she hated and wouldn't miss for a moment. He hadn't shown up this morning. She'd waited in bed until seven, listening to every creak that might be David's footstep. All she'd gotten was a sore neck and the knowledge, which twisted her heart, that Jenna scampered down the hall to Diana's bed in the morning now, not to hers.

She couldn't blame Jenna. She'd gotten in the habit of getting up early and cranking out a few pages before David appeared for their hike, so Jenna had found another bed.

Oddly, she wondered whether Paul had, too.

"What brings you here?" She tried to look relaxed, hampered slightly by the fact that her sweatshirt caught on the laptop, leaving the keyboard brown and gooey. "I, uh, missed you on my morning hike."

"Huh?" Startled, he stood up, then sat down hard on the chair's arm, wincing.

"I was surprised I didn't run into you. Didn't you hike?" She knew he hadn't. When she heard the speedboat's engine roar at seven, she assumed he'd headed into town to see Suzy and his boys.

"I went to the office." Dropping down into his chair, he stared at the floor, which held more than a few of her little silver Hershey's wrappers. "You hiked? I figured you might've given up on that after yesterday."

Mortified by the curious look on David's face when he'd asked her *again* about her so-called crush, she'd outrun David and a thousand laughing demons, sprinted up the steps to the big house, and raced past a startled Diana and Jenna.

"I lied." She turned back to her laptop, which had snagged a bright-red thread from her sweatshirt, a chocolate smudge, and unidentifiable crumbs. The screen was now a black rectangle of death. Crap. She slammed it shut. "And I didn't miss it. Freezing my butt on a way-too-early hike while we argue? Life's too short."

David ran a hand through his hair, which needed a haircut. "It's time we talked."

Legs spread wide, elbows on his knees, he hunched forward in the chair as if he owned it. As if he owned the whole damn room.

She lurched to her feet. "We talked yesterday. It didn't go too well."

"Can we try again?" His hand stopped her before she'd taken two steps. "I talked to Mom."

Oh, no. Diana must be upset, and justifiably. Brushing past David, Liz headed for the door. "I didn't realize what time it was. I left Jenna with her too long."

She'd been engrossed in writing, yes, but it wasn't just that. The deeper her memoir delved into her horrible childhood, the more intense she felt. It also triggered all her old fears that she'd turn out even remotely like Dad. A monster.

Had she left Jenna with Diana to keep her safe from herself?

And Diana, as usual, kept doing her favors and getting zilch in return. Maybe nothing *had* changed since high school. Her throat went dry. Spying the cup in David's hand, she pried it from his hands.

"Oh!" Feeling the burn of liquor, she wished she'd asked.

"Not a big drinker?" He laughed as he retrieved his cup. "And you forgot boy germs. I'm loaded with 'em."

"I'm immune." Not. She took a step back, trying to reach a safe distance. A thousand miles sounded pretty good. "I have to go find Jenna."

"She's napping now, but you're right. Mom is getting tired of all the work. And everything else."

She heard the pause. Knew "everything" was probably

spelled "L-i-z." Feeling a few tears in her eyes, she turned her back on David.

She wished Diana would've told her directly, rather than send her golden boy to do the job. More tears clustered, a few traitorous ones trickling south.

She heard David moving toward the door, almost as if he realized she was on the verge of a meltdown and needed space. Almost as if he weren't completely clueless about her.

But he didn't leave. Unfortunately. "I can't help noticing that you keep running away every time I try to talk. It's killing my ego."

"You'll get over it." Clearing her throat, she prayed he didn't hear her sniffle. "Even if Jenna's napping, I should go talk to Diana."

"But not to me."

"What do you want, David?" She blew a breath upward, making her bangs dance. "You want to make fun of me? Ask me yet again if I ever had a crush on you? Maybe throw in a few slams about what a lousy mom I am?"

"Whoa." He held up a hand. "You're not a bad mom, and you already told me what you thought of Suzy's crush scenario. I believe you."

He believed her. Idiot. Self-absorbed, clueless idiot.

She crossed her arms. "Then what do we need to talk about?"

David took a slug from his plastic cup. "You and me."

"Seriously? Again?"

"Not that. Mom thinks we don't get along well." *Smart woman, Diana.* David tugged on the collar of his T-shirt. "She needs a little peace and quiet. And, uh, conversation."

Liz raised her eyebrows at the contradiction.

"And . . . I really would like to be friends." He eyed her cautiously. "I know I keep saying that."

"But only until Suzy comes back, right?" At her question, his gaze dropped to the floor again. Probably to the candy wrappers. "Since Suzy doesn't speak to me, or let you come near me, I guess we could—what—attempt a two-week friendship?"

He stared at her, mute.

"I think I'll pass." She turned to open the door. "But don't worry. I'll take Jenna off everyone's hands."

He grabbed for the door but missed, stumbling after her down the steps. At the bottom of the steps, he touched her arm.

"You've really got to stop grabbing me." She faked a grin, as if the contact didn't affect her. "Or I might start wondering if *you* were the one with the crush."

His hand dropped as if scalded, and he looked everywhere but at her.

"Yeah? As it turns out, Lizzie—" She cringed at the old nickname. "I'm a little worried about that, too."

PAUSING halfway up the steps to the second floor, her breathing a little unsteady, Diana cocked an ear, half-expecting to hear yelling. Or running footsteps. Or slamming doors.

She wasn't thinking of the five-year-old in the house.

David had gone up to the back house half an hour ago. He hadn't reported back to her about his talk with Liz or stormed back to his own house. He didn't do anything quietly.

"Diana?" A faint voice called to her from downstairs.

She turned, hurried back down, and approached Frank's bedroom as his voice floated softly again. "Diana?"

Her heart racing, she opened the door.

Frank lay back, his head on two pillows, one arm across his chest and the other limp at his side. Much as she'd left him two hours ago. Perhaps he'd been dreaming, calling her name from the depth of unconsciousness, where he was still Frank. She stepped into the room, debating whether to wake him and spoil the dream.

His dream, and hers.

His face, still swollen from the steroids that had been part of his treatment, turned toward her. "Diana?"

"Frank." She sat on the edge of the bed and clasped his hand. Like old times, and not at all. "Did you sleep well?"

His tongue worked to wet his lips. She reached for a foam swab to moisten them.

"Liz. David." Names sprang out of him like popcorn.

She patted his hand. "Liz is up in the back house, working on her novel. And David—" She smoothed her face over the frown that threatened. "He was at the office this morning."

"They never . . . got along." Frank's voice dropped back to a whisper, and Diana bent to catch the words. "My . . . fault."

She rubbed his hands, which felt cold against her skin. "That's not true. David and Liz may have issues—" And they'd work through those issues this summer if she had anything to say about it. "But they're not your fault. They're both headstrong." She saw the question in Frank's eyes. "Yes, even David."

He nodded, acknowledging the truth of it, his thin, parched lips looking strange on his once-handsome face.

"And neither one got that from the neighbors." She smiled, thinking about their patched-together family. Warts and all.

Frank shared a shadow of her smile. She wished they

could share everything again. Opinionated discussions, laughter, even tears. Comfortable sex that was sometimes, ahem, more than that.

After all, she wasn't dead yet.

But David might be by now, even though Diana hadn't heard any shouts from the back house. If anyone could soothe whatever ailed Liz, she'd pick David, her silver-tongued son—except that he'd never achieved it when they were young.

She should've talked to Liz first, as she'd done with David. She'd had a few good conversations with Liz when Liz hadn't been closeted in the back house or fighting with David.

She'd better check on those two.

DAVID RAN a hand over his face, wishing he could find a large solid object and club himself to death.

Could a grown man even *have* a crush?

Liz's mouth hung open, eliminating the faint possibility that he hadn't really voiced his fear out loud. That he hadn't really been a total freaking idiot.

"Hey, I was kidding, okay?" He tried to laugh, but it failed when he started choking. Maybe he'd choke to death. It would solve any number of problems.

Hell. Liz wasn't even his type. He'd always been attracted to Suzy—at least, the Suzy he'd known in her teens and twenties. Lush, curvy, easy to talk to.

In high school, Liz had gone from being a twig to a twig with muscles. From afar, he'd admired what she could do with her body. Waterski hard through a slalom course, bomb the slopes, take a basketball to the hoop.

Other guys might've noticed her long, lean legs, but he'd

had Suzy. Besides, Liz was Frank's daughter. Family of sorts. And much younger.

Not to mention a pain in the butt.

He touched a hand to the small of her back. Just to keep her upright, really, since his big, fat, stupid announcement seemed to have left her wobbly. Not because her shirt had crept up, baring smooth, warm skin he had no business touching.

She brushed off his hand.

"I can't believe you said that." She stared past the big house, out through the trees, toward the River below. "What a joke."

"Funny, huh?" A guy could hope.

"Not particularly." She took a step toward the big house, stopped abruptly, then looked down, scuffing the toe of her sneaker on a broken patch of sidewalk. "Look, it's not like I can't take a joke. But sometimes I get a little tired of it."

"I wasn't joking—"

Her head snapped up. Great. Blow the whole thing.

"Okay, I was, but, uh, about myself." At his stammered words, her eyes flashed. Maybe if he dug his grave deep enough, he'd reach China. "I mean, what self-respecting woman would want *me* to have a crush on her? Ha, ha."

He'd started at idiotic, raced past pathetic, and—if this latest try didn't work—would soon be groveling.

Silent, she tilted her head, probably trying to figure out when he'd turned into such an ass.

"Anyway." He couldn't stop himself from studying her, noticing the way the sun danced like fire on her blond hair. And the way her blue eyes hardened to steel when she was pissed or upset—which was often, thanks to him—but sometimes softened to a smoky hue. Like now. She met his gaze for a fraction of a second before looking away.

"Good. I found you two." Letting the back door bang shut the way she harped at everyone else not to, Mom clapped her hands—prompting Liz to jump half a foot in the air.

"Shoot." David grinned at Mom. "And here we thought we'd found the perfect hiding place, and you'd never find us."

Hands on her hips, she looked from him to Liz. "Funny boy."

Liz rushed past them up the back steps to the big house.

Mom watched her escape, then turned back to him. "I see you two had a good conversation."

He nodded, smiling brightly.

Shaking her head, she ruffled his hair the same way she'd done for forty years. "Did you two talk?"

Yeah, if he counted a hundred words, max, in the last half hour.

"I told her you wanted some help, and some peace and quiet, and maybe she could stop yelling at me all the time."

"Charmer." She sighed. "I knew I should've talked to Liz myself." At the distant sound of Jenna's voice, she looked over her shoulder, then back at him. "The next time I feel the need to upset someone, I'll call you."

"Happy to help."

He started to walk around the house rather than cut through. No point taking more chances today. Any moment now, he might confess his lifelong aversion to medical devices.

"Are you joining us for dinner?"

Already on the path, he hesitated. "Are alcoholic beverages included in your offer?"

"Definitely." Mom sounded more anxious than usual. He couldn't blame her. "For me, at least, if your conversation with Liz went as well as I suspect."

"Worse." The ice had long since melted in his plastic cup.

He tossed the liquid on the grass. "Dinner should be quite a treat."

"Mom?" Jenna rubbed her eyes, sitting up quickly. Liz didn't move from the end of Jenna's bed, where she'd curled up for the last few minutes, watching her daughter sleep. Jenna hung her head. "I'm sorry I took a nap."

Liz flinched. She'd been so tense about David in the last few days—and with Dad, thanks to pouring so many hard memories into her memoir—and now Jenna must somehow be afraid that even taking naps might upset her.

"No, no, sweetie. I'm the one who's sorry." For so many things, many of which Jenna would never understand. "Did you have a nice nap?"

Jenna nodded, all seriousness. "David didn't wanna play with me, an' Gram said a nap would make me big and strong."

Liz tried not to smile as she ran a hand through Jenna's baby-soft hair. "I'd love to play with you. Whatever you like." She poked Jenna's lower lip, which thrust out far enough to land a plane. "But David likes you, too. Everyone does."

"No." A determined head shake didn't retract the lip. "David thinks I'm a dumb little kid. He's grumpy."

As Jenna dropped back on the pillow, Liz lay next to her, thinking how much she missed their morning snuggles. Giving them up to write the memoir wasn't a fair trade.

She drew her daughter close. "He's not usually grumpy." She heard a tiny sniffle, felt the little body shaking. "And I know he doesn't think you're a dumb little kid."

Jenna's body stopped quivering. "He doesn't?"

"Not one bit." She hugged Jenna. "If he did, Gram might hit him with a canoe paddle."

Ouch. Probably not the right thing for her father's daughter to say, all things considered, but it produced a tiny giggle.

"Mom?" Jenna snuggled closer. "Would you ever . . ."

Liz held her breath, waiting.

"Hit me?" Trembling again, Jenna's body reminded Liz of another little body, so many years ago. "If I was really bad?"

"Never." She gave Jenna a tight squeeze, kissing her head. "Moms and dads should never do that."

And Liz's own mom should've protected her, or at least tried to stop Dad, rather than reach for a bottle. Liz sighed, missing her mom but wishing Mom had stood up to Dad. If she had, maybe she'd still be alive. And then Liz might've never met David.

She just didn't know which way that cut.

―――

"Jenna? Jenna, where are you?"

Liz poked her head into the kitchen just as Diana pulled a pan of steaming lasagna from the oven.

She sniffed appreciatively. "Mmm. Have you seen Jenna?"

"Not since lunch." Diana set the pan on the counter and straightened, rubbing the small of her back. In uncharacteristic fashion, she'd spent the afternoon baking. She told herself she was just thankful that David and Liz had made peace and taken Jenna off her hands.

But perhaps she'd been premature. They'd lost the child.

Liz wrinkled her nose. "Have you seen David?"

"I think he went across the River to Afton." She felt a slight niggle of concern before dismissing it. Jenna wouldn't try swimming—

Echoing her thoughts, Liz sprinted toward the porch. "I'll check the beach."

The screen door slammed as a tiny giggle caught Diana's ear. By the time Diana reached the screen door, Liz was already on the beach and running toward the water, calling Jenna's name frantically, her head swinging left and right.

"Liz!" Diana stepped outside and waved until Liz looked up. "She's in the house."

Liz's shoulders sagged as her feet trudged up the steps. Relieved, Diana went in search of Jenna. Silence. Moving through the porch and into the great room, Diana strained to listen. A soft voice greeted her, followed by a high-pitched one and a symphony of giggles.

Jenna. In Frank's room.

The child didn't go near Frank. She separated herself from him at meals by at least two chairs, watching him with wide eyes but never speaking.

A sliver of light peeked through his bedroom door. Diana opened the door wider, staring in amazement. Jenna sat on Frank's bed, close to his knees, chattering and showing him her doll. Frank was awake. And smiling.

The screen door banged. Breathing hard, Liz came up behind Diana. "Where is she?"

When Diana pointed, they bumped heads as they both peered inside Frank's room. Diana smiled, glad for Frank's opportunity to get to know Jenna.

The sight drew a different reaction from Liz. With a gasp, she bolted, her feet pounding loudly up the stairs. Jenna and Frank, fortunately, didn't look up.

Sighing, Diana closed the door. She'd barely begun

patching Liz's rift with David. Liz and Frank would take much more work.

"Good news, Liz. I'm flying to Minnesota."

With her cell phone pressed to her ear, Liz clutched her glass of lemonade, loosening her grip only when Diana tapped her shoulder and pointed at the glass. Another minute and she'd have shards of glass embedded in her fingertips.

"What do you mean, Paul? Don't you have to work?" For once, she didn't even mind. She'd found herself forgetting him, and feeling better when she did.

"That's just it. I'm coming there for work." He laughed, self-consciously. "Isn't it funny? My first deal in Minnesota is when you're there."

Hilarious.

Taking a gulp of lemonade, she smiled through moist eyes. "When do you arrive?"

"In two days. Saturday." He cleared his throat. "Can you pick me up?"

He wasn't renting a car. He wasn't arriving two minutes before work required him to be here. He wasn't her husband.

"So early?"

Diana frowned at her, but this was Paul, and Diana obviously didn't understand. The man who'd ignored Liz for the last five years, if not longer, wanted to rain on her summer. June in Minnesota, at least lately, already offered enough of that.

She peered out the kitchen's large picture window toward the side yard. Gray drizzle. Three days in a row.

"It'll be late morning." Paul spoke again, quickly, when she didn't respond. "I—I've missed you guys."

"But you're probably bringing a trunk full of work."

"Just a briefcase. You know, for down moments."

To Paul, every nonbillable minute between dawn and bedtime was a down moment. Liz wondered how he'd ever found the time to date her. Or to get her pregnant—which had been no small feat.

A voice in the back of her head told her that Paul was making an effort. That Jenna should see her father. She told the voice to shut up.

A minute later, after handing the phone to Jenna and avoiding Diana's raised eyebrows, Liz asked herself why she felt so . . . annoyed? Disappointed? Confused? She'd been the one who asked Paul to make an effort on their marriage, after all.

And after all these years of asking him, maybe he actually would.

For better or worse.

"Rise and shine!" David stood next to Liz's bed, watching her sleep. He knew the moment she woke up, even though her eyes didn't open and—to a casual observer—her breathing didn't change. He bent down, passing his palm back and forth over her nose. Flinching, she opened one eye.

She shut her eye again and rolled over, pretending to snore. Loudly. Her grade for faking it slipped a notch, but she had chutzpah. So, overall, maybe a B minus.

When he grabbed her pillow, she yelped.

He grinned. "Sorry. But the sun's up. It's gorgeous out."

He couldn't quite hear her response. He caught the word "rain" and an anatomical suggestion that sounded more than a little painful.

But he didn't plan to give up. "You know you want to."

She turned her head sideways. "Another thing you don't know about me."

"I'll hold my breath until you say yes." Sucking in a huge breath, he tried to ignore what this conversation was doing to his ego.

Liz finally rolled over, her jersey scrunching up while she tugged it down and twisted it around, squirming in a way that shouldn't be even remotely sexy. "So what should I wear? A down parka or a rain poncho? I can't decide."

He walked around the end of her bed and flung open the window.

"Hey! I said I'd hike." She yanked the comforter up to her neck. "But I'd rather be bundled up before I freeze to death."

He pointed outside, drawing her skeptical gaze. "See? Sunshine. It's supposed to hit seventy-five today."

"Where? In Florida?"

"Cute." She was. More than he liked. "Right here on the St. Croix. I thought we'd try to get Jenna up skiing today so she can show off for her dad tomorrow."

"There might be a few problems with that idea, starting with the fact that she doesn't know how to swim."

"That only proves you've been spending too much time up in the back house, banging away—" The words drew the wrong picture, but he kept going. "On your great American novel."

"That must be it." Her face went blank. "But you know the rules as well as I do. She can't waterski if she can't swim. Tell me you haven't had her out waterskiing."

"I haven't had her out waterskiing." Yet. "But I've got the perfect skis for her. Pete and Billy used them."

"When they were eight or ten, probably."

A prickle of irritation crept up his neck. She was taking the fun out of his big news.

"So your only objection is that she can't swim?"

She shrugged. "While I'm at it, she's also five."

"No way."

She nodded, completely serious. "I've never seen anyone ski that young. Her legs aren't strong enough."

"Billy skied when he was six. And I have a waterski boom on the boat, guaranteed to get the smallest kid or the biggest adult up out of the water. After our hike, I'll—"

She brushed away the rest of his sentence. "I need to write after our hike, then play with Jenna. Besides, last time I checked, all she could do in the water was splash her arms."

"Like I said, you haven't checked recently. She's skipped a few naps in order to learn how to swim."

"Or she just wanted to skip a few naps." She rolled her eyes, then suddenly frowned. "Wait, are you kidding? Jenna? She can swim?"

Without waiting for his answer, she threw off the comforter and leaped out of bed. Her Capitals jersey had come up around her waist, revealing a pair of yellow cotton bikini undies.

He tried not to notice.

"Out!" After yanking the bottom of her jersey down, she hopped around, waving wildly. "You did that on purpose!"

Damn. Mom thought this was a difficult summer.

She had no idea.

CHAPTER 9

"Mom-meeee!" Several hours later, outfitted in a tiny wetsuit with a bright-yellow life jacket and—leave it to David—matching gloves, and standing in a strange pair of U-shaped waterskis, Jenna squealed and clapped her hands.

She'd also called Liz "Mommy." A first. Walking down the steps to the beach, Liz cringed but waved to Jenna, who whooped as only a five-year-old could.

"Smile for the camera!" Diana's voice rang out.

"Cheese!" As she screamed the word, Jenna's natural grin contorted into the worst smile Liz had seen since the picture of herself at David's high school graduation.

David picked up Jenna and carried her into the water. The speedboat idled nearby. Its bow nosed into the beach and an odd-looking black contraption—the boom?—jutted out the port side of the boat.

"Stay right here, Jenn." David kept one eye on Jenna as he waded to the bow of the boat, nudging it away from shore. "Who's joining me for Jenna's maiden voyage?"

Diana moved closer as Liz felt the first niggle of apprehension. Too late, she recognized her fear as it shot into her stomach. Pressing a hand against it, Liz didn't budge.

"I haven't seen her swim."

David claimed Jenna could swim, and Diana had told her—a bit belatedly—that David had worked with Jenna for the last two weeks, but she hadn't seen it herself. The acid churning in her gut told her she had to.

Jenna's eyes flooded with tears. "Mom, I can swim! Please can I waterski, please?"

"I'm sorry, sweetie. I need to know you can swim before you waterski. That's the rule at the River."

"David said I can." She bit her lip. "I swim real good."

David looked irritated. Even if Jenna took off the waterskis, she couldn't show Liz how she swam without also taking off her life jacket. For all Liz knew, the wetsuit might be buoyant, too.

As Jenna grew hysterical, Liz felt a flush creep up her neck. She'd ruined the day. Again. She'd hoped for a good summer with Jenna—without work, without nannies, without Paul. So far, she'd spent too much of it working on the stupid book or arguing with David.

"You're absolutely right, Liz." At the gentle sound of Diana's voice, Liz's eyes filled. Diana touched her arm, comforting her, then took a step toward David.

David nosed the boat back toward the beach and started to say something, stopping only when Diana shushed him.

Diana rolled up her capris to just above her knees. "I'm sorry, Jenna, but your mom is keeping you safe, and I'm very proud of her. I did the same thing when David and Brandon were your age." She waded out to Jenna. "And they didn't like it a bit better than you do."

Jenna's lower lip quivered. "No way."

"Yes way, dear."

Liz headed for the edge of the beach as memories of her childhood terror of the water washed through her. She'd always hidden that terror behind bravado when she water-skied, but it had never really left. Now, Jenna looked away from her, fiercely, and Liz took a step backward. Diana helped Jenna out of the skis and carried them to the edge of the beach, then waded back to Jenna and unfastened the clips on her little life jacket.

In that moment Liz decided—in what might be her first rational decision all week—not to make an issue of the wetsuit. Even though she hadn't seen it, she already knew that Jenna must be able to swim. David said so. The guy was irritating and cocky and a million other things that drove her crazy, but he didn't lie.

Free of the life jacket, Jenna stood in the water, shivering despite the warm day.

Liz knew exactly how she felt.

"Jenna?" As Liz spoke, the little chin jutted out. "Won't you swim for me? I need to make sure you know how."

Jenna looked at the speedboat. "I know how. Ask David."

David wasn't saying anything. He wasn't stupid.

"I'm asking you, sweetie." Bracing herself against the cold water, Liz waded in. "Please swim for me? Then we can all watch you waterski."

Jenna swung back toward her, defiant. "I don't want you to watch. Go away."

Diana tossed Jenna's life jacket on the beach. "That's not nice, Jenna. You're going to make your mom sad." She brushed a stray lock of hair off Jenna's forehead. "I'll bet you're pretty good."

Jenna puffed out her chest. "I'm really good. Like this." Bending over, she showed Diana—without glancing in Liz's direction—a fair imitation of a front crawl, considering that her chest never touched the water.

Diana clapped. "I bet you can't do that in the water."

After a slight hesitation, Jenna splashed down into the water, sinking for a horrible moment before coming up to the surface sputtering in a wild dog paddle that evolved into some sort of front crawl. Ten, fifteen, twenty feet, two or three breaths for every sputter.

Whooping and clapping, Liz waded in farther.

"Jenna!" She called until the little girl turned, bobbing in the water. "You did great!"

Jenna smiled quickly, delighted, before burying it in an afterthought of a pout. David turned back to the boat, rubbing an imaginary spot. Diana nodded at Jenna, who'd started paddling again, this time more dog paddle than crawl. But good enough to ski.

Her shoulders tense from the cold water, Liz moved past Diana until she was almost waist deep. She grabbed Jenna before she could try to escape.

"I'm so proud of you, sweetie." Awkwardly, with Jenna struggling to get away, Liz pulled Jenna into her arms. Despite the cold water soaking through her skin, she'd never felt happier.

"Was I good, Mom? Huh? Was I good?"

"Until the part where you got me all wet—" She winked. "You were great. The best."

Diana quietly moved backward onto dry land. Picking up the life jacket, she tossed it into the water in the general direction of no one.

David retrieved the life jacket a few feet from the beach. "Okay, kid. Ready to waterski?"

Despite his question, his eyes were on Liz.

So she answered. "You're asking me?"

He laughed as he helped Jenna into the skis. "Wait your turn, hotshot. Unless you've forgotten everything you know."

Her answer came out on a choked sputter.

IT PROVED the importance of checking conflicts.

Paul sat back in his leather chair, trying to put a better spin on his mistake. He didn't need more work. He had enough to keep himself and four other lawyers busy. Enough to avoid the pinprick of his conscience—or intuition or whatever had nagged him ever since Liz left—that kept telling him to fly out to Minnesota.

But he'd blown it. Yesterday he'd called Liz and told her he'd be coming out tomorrow. Today he lost the client. More precisely, he had a conflict that wouldn't allow him to represent the client.

Groaning, he felt like an idiot. The conflict? Carruthers Medical, the company Liz's family ran. Liz even owned stock. He'd had to tell the client he couldn't work on the deal. He didn't relish calling Liz, but he couldn't justify a flight to Minnesota right now just for pleasure. He also didn't mind skipping the sunburn, mosquitos, and all those Norwegians.

Maybe he could make it for the Fourth of July.

He picked up the phone, drumming his fingers as it rang. When his call went to voicemail, something told him this was the sort of news she'd want to hear directly, so he hung up.

He'd call again later. As he jotted a note to himself, he dreaded the conversation.

THROUGH FINGERS SPREAD over her eyes, Diana peeked at the scene before her.

Her heart had jumped into her throat when Jenna's head bobbed underwater and her arms thrashed in that little swimming demonstration a few minutes ago. Yes, the child swam. Barely. Liz had been right to insist on seeing it, and brave to face the childish scorn. Diana applauded her for having the stomach to stick around for the waterskiing.

From her perch in the back of the boat, Diana had a perfect view of whatever disaster awaited them. She hoped there wouldn't be one. They needed something to go right.

Climbing in and out of the speedboat with the ease of a younger man, David checked the lines connecting his boom to the boat. He'd already checked them twice, but Diana knew he'd do anything to ensure Jenna's safety.

Liz sat in the bow, chewing her fingernails. Diana had shared the same fears when she and her two boys had first spent a summer at the River. Water, water everywhere and no lifeguard in sight.

Jenna, though, was the picture of unfettered joy as she stood in chest-high water and tried to peer down at her waterskis.

Finally, David pushed the boat away from the beach, then hauled himself up. Stepping over the engine cover, he propped himself on the driver's seat. He stayed there, oh, five seconds before jumping up again. Leaning over the side of the speedboat, he gave Jenna the same instructions he'd given her three times already. With the moment of truth upon her, she didn't seem to comprehend a single word.

David leaned farther over the side, pushing down on the boom to drop it closer to the water. Jenna's fingertips barely touched it before she gave up. And tried again. And again. David looked from Liz to Diana.

"Someone needs to get into the water with Jenna."

The suggestion didn't fit Diana's job description.

"What should I do?" Liz looked quizzically at David.

"Drive the boat." When she seemed unsure, he pointed at Jenna. "One of us needs to stand in the water and hoist her up so she can grab the boom. She's too short."

"Maybe she's too young to do this."

"I'm not too young! I'm a big girl!"

Diana hid a smile, remembering all the times Liz had encouraged Jenna by calling her a big girl. She was probably regretting it right now.

"Don't worry, kid. You'll do it." David landed with a splash next to Jenna, who nearly toppled. Catching Liz's gaze, he pointed up the River. "Start when Jenna yells 'hit it' and go straight. Ten miles an hour."

Liz knelt on the driver's seat. "That slow?" David nodded. "What if she gets up? What do I do?"

He grinned. "Keep going 'til she drops."

At last David counted "three—two—one" and then, in unison, he and Jenna shouted "hit it!" The boat lurched, then chugged forward as Jenna shrieked loudly and clung to the boom. A few yards later, she fell, face flat in the water.

She came up sputtering. "I wanna do it again!"

First, they needed to restart Liz's heart. Leaping out of the driver's seat when Jenna fell, she leaned over the side and repeatedly asked Jenna if she was okay.

Diana glanced at her watch. Almost two-thirty. She could stay for one more waterski attempt, two at the most, but then she needed to check on Frank.

Despite her intentions, she sat through four more attempts, each of them not much different from the first. Time to call it a day, even if the others stayed out until dusk or collapse, whichever came first. David and Liz, together, could handle Jenna.

David and Liz. Together.

The tension of helping Jenna learn to ski wasn't exactly an easy route to a better relationship. But Suzy would arrive tonight and Paul tomorrow. Diana wasn't entirely sure if that was good or bad, but it would change the dynamics, and change might be good.

Crossing her fingers, she waved at Jenna, wishing her luck. Privately, she wished David and Liz even more luck—with Jenna's waterskiing and with themselves.

———

"Jenna almost skied today, Suz. You should've seen it."

Sitting ramrod straight in the passenger seat of the speedboat, Suzy yawned.

"Really, Dad?" Billy leaned forward from his perch on the engine cover. "How old is she, anyway?"

"Five. A lot younger than you, but she *is* your cousin." Feeling Suzy's gaze skewer him, he shrugged. "Sort of. She's a cute kid."

"Like her mother." Suzy practically meowed the words, and David looked at her with raised eyebrows.

"How old was I, Dad?"

"Six. I'll never forget." In the process of teaching Billy to ski, he'd been sure several times that he must be having a heart attack.

Pete, who hadn't skied until age eight, maintained a silent vigil in the bow.

"Liz's husband arrives tomorrow?" Suzy must've talked to Mom in the last day or two. Strange.

"Yeah. Paul. Late morning, I hear."

"That should liven things up." Digging through her weekend bag, Suzy pulled out a lipstick and reapplied it. "I might have to run into town most of the day tomorrow." When David stared at her, she giggled uncomfortably. "Too much to do before Vail."

"You're leaving Sunday and you'll be gone for two weeks." He gritted his teeth as he heard his voice rise. "What is it, Suz? Can't you spend a couple days at the River?"

She glanced pointedly at the boys, who'd both taken an avid interest in the water. David ran a hand through his hair. Yeah, he'd lost it. They'd danced around this topic too often, though, and they needed to tackle it head-on. But maybe not right this moment.

"I have things to do." Suzy hunted again in her bag, this time finding a nail file. "Maybe next summer, when Liz is back in Washington, I won't be so busy."

Feeling a sudden chill, David stared over the windshield at the horizon. By next summer, maybe he'd be busy, too.

THERE WAS nothing like standing in an airport on a bright Saturday in June, waiting an hour for someone who must've missed his flight.

Watching the baggage-claim area for Paul, Liz glanced at her watch and wondered again if she'd gotten the flight wrong. No. He'd said late morning, and this was the only Delta flight from Washington to Minneapolis between ten and noon.

The carousel continued to revolve, offering a handful of unclaimed bags. She moved closer, checking the bags again. None of them looked like anything Paul owned.

It was her own stupid fault. She must've left her cell

phone in her bedroom. Weird. It had been practically attached to her ear when she'd arrived this summer, and only three weeks later she'd almost forgotten she owned one.

After a last look at the carousel, she headed back to the parking garage.

Paul could take a taxi or Lyft to the River. Or walk.

———

DAVID WAS RAKING debris on the beach when the little boat chugged slowly up to the dock, an obviously upset Liz at the tiller. He couldn't blame her.

No one could. Not even Suzy.

He helped Liz tie up the boat. "Are you okay? Did Paul reach you?"

Dead silence. But at least she wasn't pissed at *him*, right?

His unreasonable elation at the earlier news surged again. He wasn't the only husband to pull a bonehead move. Paul was at two and counting, and it was barely past noon.

Finally, she spoke, her voice small and not at all like her. "I must've left my cell phone up in my room. So Paul called? Did he say which flight he's on?"

"He's not coming." David smothered a strange urge to laugh.

"What do you mean? Is he coming tomorrow?"

"Nope. His trip got cancelled."

"When?"

"No clue." Paul hadn't told Mom, who'd heard Liz's phone ring not long after Liz left for the airport, and Mom hadn't asked.

But Liz was Paul's problem, or vice versa, and they'd have to sort it out themselves.

"Liz?"

She stared into space, but at least she quit grinding her teeth. "Yes?"

"Look on the bright side. Now Jenna has more time to learn how to waterski for her dad, and that would be way more fun than watching you throw something through a window."

Rolling her eyes, she headed up to the big house. But she smiled. Faintly.

"You didn't bother calling to tell me you weren't coming." Pacing the wooden floor of the back house, her cell phone pressed to her ear, Liz considered pitching the damn thing in the wastebasket. Or against the wall. But not through a window.

"I told you, Liz. I called. You didn't answer."

"When?" Leave it to Paul to call and not leave a message. Or wait until she'd already driven all the way to the airport.

"Yesterday. But I didn't want to leave a message."

"Apparently not." She didn't completely believe him, which told her something. "Why didn't you call back? Or text and ask me to call you? Like, before I left for the airport."

Without her cell phone, sure, but that didn't excuse him.

"Huh. That would've been a good idea." He blew out an exasperated breath. "I'm sorry, okay?"

Liz nearly dropped the phone. He hadn't been gracious or even remotely sincere, but Paul had actually apologized, maybe for the first time in his life.

"I guess that's a start." More and more each day, she saw them splitting up at the end of the summer—or sooner. If Paul made an effort, he actually might confuse the issue. Would she start to remember what she'd loved about him in the first place? "So . . . tell me again why your trip got cancelled?"

He cleared his throat. "I told you—it's confidential."

"We're married, in case you forgot."

"Really, Liz, I can't. Just this once." He laughed, in a fake kind of way. "It's something you'll hear about soon, if you haven't already."

She never heard anything at the River. No radio, no TV —except David's, which she wouldn't ever see—and no one seemed to spend much time on internet news. It was a lucky day when someone remembered to go to Afton for a newspaper.

"No news here. We just lie on the beach."

Actually, she'd done that only once since arriving. It'd never been her thing.

"Must be nice." Paul wasn't envious. He was even less likely to lie on a beach.

"Yep." No point quizzing him further. Jenna was probably the only one who wouldn't consider it good news that Paul wasn't coming, but it'd be good practice for the rest of her life. "Anyway, I guess I'll talk to you whenever."

"Can I talk to Jenna?"

"She's taking a nap." She actually was. "If you *really* want to talk to her, maybe you should hop on a plane. She misses you, Paul."

"Is that my fault? Who dragged her away for the summer?"

Liz sucked in a breath at Paul's flash of anger. She'd gotten so used to being ignored.

"I did. But maybe you were supposed to follow us."

"SHE ALREADY TRIED SKIING YESTERDAY. Don't push her so much, David."

Jenna's lower lip curled, and David knew the feeling. Pissed off after her call with Paul, Liz's lousy mood was affecting all of them. He almost wished Paul had shown up today.

Not really.

Suzy had already headed into town, and Pete was missing in action. At least Piper was here, thanks to a frantic call from Mom. She handled the boat well and didn't panic at the thought of five-year-olds skiing.

"The first try doesn't count." Or the first ten or fifteen tries. He laughed, erasing Jenna's pout. "Jenna's the best little waterskier I've seen in way too long." Billy scowled from the back seat of the speedboat. "Since Billy."

Jenna piped in. "See, Mom? David thinks I'm good."

"She'll be fine, Liz." Propped on top of the driver's seat, Piper looked over the aviator sunglasses she'd stolen from David.

Liz sat hunched in the bow. Mom hadn't ventured outside yet, although she'd promised Jenna she'd watch her ski. She probably wasn't betting on it happening soon.

"Ready, Jenna?" Piper looked over at her, bobbing in the water in David's arms, and smiled her encouragement.

Jenna nodded, more cautious than yesterday. He couldn't blame her. The kid had taken more falls without complaint than anyone he'd ever seen, both of his boys included.

The boat didn't go anywhere. David nodded his approval at Piper, who snorted and called out again. "Whaddaya say?"

The tiny voice yelped. "Hit it!"

The boat took off, nothing like the nervous lurches by yesterday's driver. Piper was a pro, seamlessly glancing from Jenna to the water and back again. Jenna struggled to hang on, struggled to press the skis against the water. Five feet, ten feet, fif— Not quite. Another face plant.

Jenna rolled in the water, one leg still in the skis and the other caught behind her. David waded over to her, the water nearly up to his neck. She'd gone a little farther this time. He'd have to pull her backwards in order to start over.

"C'mon, kid. I'll carry you back."

"No! I can do it, David. All by myself."

Minutes crawled by while she bobbed in the water, treading water in a circle while her errant foot chased after her ski. Finally, he waded toward the boat.

Climbing up on the swim platform on the stern, he turned to Jenna, who'd somehow connected her foot and ski and was now paddling slowly in the direction of the boom. "Sure you're okay?" She nodded quickly, looking doubtful.

Climbing over the back seat and Billy, who watched in silence, David moved to the boom. Ignoring Liz, who held a cushion against her stomach, he pressed down with all his weight to tilt the boom toward the water. Toward Jenna, who jumped up and caught it. Even Billy clapped.

"Ready, kid?"

An audible swallow and gritted teeth. "Hit it!"

They took off. Again.

And . . . Jenna hung on. Fifteen feet, her previous world record, then thirty feet, and David quit counting.

"Straight arms! Bend your knees!" A cacophony of shouts prompted Jenna to do the opposite. She stayed up anyway, somehow, with her butt tilted up and her back parallel to the water. Whooping, Piper bounced on the driver's seat, and it was a miracle that she kept the boat headed in a straight line. Billy leaned so far over the side that David had to grab the back of his shorts, and Liz almost fell off the bow.

Only Jenna maintained her dignity. Even if it sprang from stark terror, the kid kept her cool.

As they approached the cove, Piper shouted. "Jenn!" Piper's hand made a large circle. "We're going to turn."

Jenna's eyes grew wide, and she shook her head furiously. Piper nodded, laughing. "You're fine! Just hold on."

Against all odds, she did. David glanced into the bow, where Liz had stuffed a towel in her mouth. Jenna still bent at the waist but kept her gaze locked on the shore. As they approached their beach, David spied his mom standing there, alone. Either she had a great sixth sense or she hadn't lost her ever-remarkable hearing.

She started clapping when they got within fifty yards.

"Wave, Jenna! Wave at Gram!" Liz called out, the first discernable words she'd uttered in ten minutes of screaming.

Jenna glanced at Liz, then David. He nodded, waving at her. Tentatively, one of her hands let go of the boom long enough to wave at his mom before she clutched the boom again with an even tighter grip.

The catcalls were deafening.

They drew closer to shore. "Let go, Jenn!" Piper's command drew only a frown.

David wagged a finger at Jenna. "If you don't let go, you'll ski right up on the beach and slam into Gram."

Horrified, she yanked her arms off the boom, her legs slid forward, and she landed on her back in the water.

David did a wolf whistle—stopping only when fists started pummeling him. "Ouch! Hey!"

Liz flung herself at him, trying to strangle him. "You jerk! Why'd you say that to her? You scared her!"

Billy sank into the back seat, eyes wide, and Piper steered the boat around the dock and the swim raft before chugging back to pick up Jenna, who floundered in the water. The whole time, Mom just kept clapping.

The pounding continued, and David felt another pair of fists slugging him now. He grinned at Billy and covered his head to fend off the blows. "Hey, no fair! Two against one."

Piper started laughing, and then Liz did, too. And Billy and, finally, Jenna.

What a day. Paul hadn't shown up, Jenna skied for the first time, and two cute women attacked him in a boat.

It didn't get much better.

CHAPTER 10

Diana watched their approach, silently urging them closer.

She'd tripped down the cement steps and watched Jenna's big moment almost from its start. She was so proud of Jenna.

The child just didn't have good timing.

She hugged Jenna, who was the first one off the speedboat, hoping to stop the chatter that threatened to drown out the panic inside her. She didn't want to scare anyone. The moment had passed, but another could be happening as she stood here, a dripping-wet Jenna plastered against her. She looked meaningfully at David, hoping he'd know what to do. Finally, following Liz and Billy over the side of the boat, he met her wide-eyed gaze.

He landed in knee-deep water. "Mom, what is it?"

She trembled. "It's—" Her hand fluttered, trying to finish the sentence.

"Frank?" "Dad?" David and Liz spoke almost in unison.

"Yes. No. I don't know." She tilted her head meaningfully at Jenna and Billy, who both tensed.

Piper, bless her, hopped out of the boat and headed for

Jenna and Billy, helping Jenna out of her life jacket before the trio raced down the beach toward the point.

"Is Dad okay?" Her eyes clouded with concern, Liz started upstairs.

David took Diana's arm. "What happened?"

"He . . . he fell."

"He fell?" Liz took off at a run.

David urged Diana to go faster, but her knees felt weak. Frank had fallen, and she'd been alone with him, unable to help him up. Her greatest fear. Well, one of several.

At the top of the steps, Liz stopped, not venturing inside.

Diana knew how she felt. Fifteen minutes ago, as she finished loading the dishwasher, she'd heard Frank calling. Not sensing any urgency, she'd loaded a few more glasses and was drying her hands on a towel when his voice came again, stronger, almost shouting.

Frank hadn't shouted since before the radiation. She'd thrown the dishtowel on the floor and run, only to find Frank lying on the woven rug in the center of the porch. The stark image sprang back into her mind as she and David reached Liz and, together, entered the house. Frank still lay on the floor where she'd left him, a pillow under his head and a blanket over him. Her pathetic attempt to do something useful.

"Diana?" Frank turned his head.

Moving to his side, she tucked the blanket tighter around him.

"I'm right here, Frank." She smiled at him as he craned his neck to look past her. "How are you feeling?"

On Diana's left, Liz drew closer. Frank's gaze followed Liz's footsteps until she stopped and bent down. David joined them, but Frank continued to stare at Liz.

Diana patted Frank's shoulder. Once they got him

comfortable, they could make sure he hadn't hurt anything. She'd done a cursory check before racing to the beach, but any medical knowledge she'd ever possessed flew out the window when she saw his prone body.

"Frank?" He blinked in response. "We need to get you onto a glider or into bed. David and Liz can lift you."

He moved his arm, wincing. Proud, stubborn man. He wanted to get up by himself, even though his pride had landed him on the floor in the first place.

As she nodded at David to help, Frank pointed a shaky finger at Liz. Unfortunately, his weak voice could be heard only too well.

"I don't . . . want her here."

LIZ DIDN'T HAVE much choice. She could yell or cry—or run, as usual—but Dad would still be lying on the floor. She couldn't help him. He didn't want her.

Same as always.

She froze, watching his faded blue eyes stare through her, striking her heart. Hating her. As if she was five years old again, or six or seven or eight. Bile rose up her throat, choking off the scream that drummed inside. With a silent plea to Diana or David, she turned and fled. From all of them.

As tears filled her eyes, she stumbled up the stairs. At the top, her stomach slammed into the wooden post. Sucking in a breath, she pressed her hand against the pain.

She'd come home because Dad was dying. To find the missing piece she'd sought since childhood. To understand what had made him hit her. Why he'd let Mom die.

With his words, she'd finally gotten her answer. He hated her. His own daughter.

Blindly, she found her room, slamming the door behind her. She'd brought enough suitcases, enough clothes and toys and books, to spend several months here.

She hadn't even made it three weeks.

Stuffing everything she could find into the suitcases, she did a visual sweep, then moved to the sleeping porch. Jenna's clothes were easy to pack. Another five minutes and she'd be done. The sooner she left this hellhole, the sooner she could start the rest of her life. With Jenna and Paul.

Paul. God. From one disaster to another.

She collapsed on Jenna's bed for another round of tears.

FRANK WAS OKAY. No broken bones, no cuts, no apparent trauma—except the trauma he'd just caused Liz.

Sonofabitch.

David sat with Frank while Mom disappeared into the kitchen. Nothing seemed to be wrong with him that a good, swift kick wouldn't fix. He shook his head, remembering Liz's halting, stammered description of how he used to hit her. At the time, he'd hardly believed it. Not Frank, who'd stepped into Dad's shoes all those years ago. The shoes hadn't fit perfectly, but he'd managed, despite all the hell David gave him, especially that first summer.

If he'd had even a clue how much hell Frank had put Liz through, he would've done some serious damage.

Liz. Damn. From the thumping he heard above him, she wasn't taking a nap.

Mom called out. "David, could you come here?"

In the kitchen, Mom looked frantic. "Should we call a doctor?"

"Naaa." He crossed his arms. "He's just too stupid to know better than to stand up by himself."

Her eyebrows rose. He hadn't called Frank stupid since he was fourteen and itching for a fight.

"I should talk to Liz. But—" She bit her lip. "I should also sit with Frank."

"My money's with Liz. I bet she's packing."

"No!" She grabbed his arm, startling him. "I'll go upstairs if you'll sit with Frank."

He shook his head. "If I have to sit with Frank much longer, I'll probably slug him."

"Don't talk that way. He's sick!"

"Like I said." He pried her hand loose. "The guy can barely talk, and he still treats her like dirt."

"He didn't mean it."

"Tell Liz that. Better yet, don't. I'll talk to her."

She moved with him to the foot of the stairs. "Are you sure that's a good idea? You two don't always get along."

"Maybe it's time we started." He took the stairs at a dead run.

Ten seconds later, he poked his head into Liz's room. "Liz—"

Empty, but all twenty-six bags were packed. Hearing a noise from the direction of the sleeping porch, he headed there and barged inside. Liz jumped, dropping an armload of shorts and shirts.

"Christ! Can't you—"

"—knock?" He knocked on the doorjamb. "There you go."

Turning away from him, she curled up on Jenna's bed. "Go away. Please?"

As she faced the wall, shaking, Liz reminded him of Jenna that first day, huddled under the quilt. He took a step closer. "Sorry, but it's my job to rescue women and small children. And possibly the occasional goldfish."

She finally looked at him, wiping her hand across a face devoid of makeup. Suzy would've had rivers of mascara running down her cheeks right now. Actually, no. Suzy wouldn't give a crap what anyone in this family said to her.

"He hates me. I—" She hiccupped. "I wasn't lying."

"You may be any number of annoying things—" He grinned to soften his words. "But you don't lie."

She slid off the bed, stooping to pick up the clothes she'd scattered, and he bent to help.

"You're that desperate to get rid of me?" She snatched a shirt away from him as a tear splattered on her hand.

"Hardly." He grabbed the shirt back before sitting awkwardly, cross-legged on the floor. It killed his knees. "If I wanted you out of here, I wouldn't wait for you to pack."

"Ha ha." She stared blankly at a pair of shorts in her hand for a long moment before tossing them aside and sitting next to him. "At least you won't have to hike anymore."

"I live for that shit." Groaning to his feet, he yanked her up from the floor. "Come on. Let's go find Jenna and do something fun. Maybe she'd like to try hiking up the hill."

She struggled a moment. "I need to pack."

"You're not going anywhere. Your dad didn't—" He choked on the words. "Mean it."

She just stared at him.

"Hey, I'm not defending him." Not in a million years. "But you've waded through half the sloppy days of June. You can't miss an Afton Fourth of July."

"If you blink, you can." Sniffles gone, she followed him.

"You forgot waterskiing."

"That goes without saying."

She sighed, glancing at her bedroom as they walked past it. "Like everything else around here."

THEY'D DODGED A BULLET YESTERDAY. A couple, at least.

Wiping her hands on a dishtowel, Diana wondered if she'd ever find the peace she craved so desperately this summer. Right now, she'd settle for five minutes.

A shuffle of footsteps came from behind her. "Mom!" Brandon landed a loud smack on her cheek. "I love this new domestic side of yours."

She twisted the towel and snapped it at him, catching his shoulder with a glancing blow. Cheeky kids. She'd messed up and produced two of them. Three, counting Liz.

Her proudest accomplishments.

Brandon grabbed another dishtowel and snapped her back.

"Good." She pointed to the stack of freshly washed dishes in the drying rack. "You're just in time to help."

Rolling his eyes, he picked up a plate. "What's the point of a dishwasher if you don't use it?"

What was the point, indeed? Frank had suggested a few improvements last summer, but she'd resisted. The River needed to stay as it was. Unspoiled, old-fashioned, simple. She'd caved in, though, on the microwave and the brand-new bathroom.

Liz had higher standards. Yesterday, she'd finished painting the upstairs and started on the porch. Her frenetic pace left Diana puzzled.

"I use the dishwasher." She wiped a glass. "For large parties."

Brandon pretended to toss a plate in the air, making her

shriek and grab the plate back. "Don't look now, but I think you've got a large one. Ten, including me."

"If you're counting David and his family, don't. Suzy and Billy are leaving tonight, and I don't know when I last saw Pete."

"I just saw him getting dropped off in a boat." Brandon wiped another plate, then set it on the counter in the center of a large juice spill.

Sighing, Diana picked up the plate, set it back in the sudsy water, and wiped off the counter. All while Brandon watched, unperturbed. But, somehow, troubled.

"What's the matter? Didn't you want to spend time on the beach? Isn't everyone down there?" She hurried her movements, not wanting to delay Brandon. And secretly wanting the kitchen to herself. "It's a beautiful day."

"I came to see you, too, and Dad."

Early on, he'd begun calling Frank "Dad," irritating Liz and pleasing Frank to no end. Diana had always wondered, for some reason, what Brandon's own father would think.

"I'm not that old and infirm yet." Frank was, but she chose not to mention it. "You don't have to worry."

Lines bracketed his mouth, giving him the appearance—to his ever-watchful mother—of a much older man. "I do worry."

"Good. One less thing for me to do." She grabbed his dishtowel. "Now scoot, and go enjoy yourself. There's plenty of time later to chat."

Time for everyone but Frank.

BRANDON COULD BE a total prick sometimes.

He'd disappeared into the house the minute he arrived,

alone, even though she'd asked him to bring Tracy out, and he hadn't bothered. He also hadn't bothered to say hello to her—let alone pounce on her in the sand.

Okay, scratch that. But he could at least say hi.

Alone on a towel on a lonely patch of sand, Piper ran a hand through her short hair. She wondered whether Brandon found it even remotely sexy. He'd returned to the beach ten minutes ago. She watched as he finished burying Jenna in the sand and picked up a Frisbee, tossing it to David.

"Piper! Want to ski?"

Liz ran up, spraying sand and dripping water, in the same frenzy she'd exhibited since returning to the beach yesterday with David. Looking surprisingly comfortable with him.

Glancing up, Piper shaded her eyes with one hand. "Not really." She jabbed a thumb at Brandon and David, now joined by Billy and Pete. "I don't think the macho studs plan to quit anytime soon, and we need a spotter."

Liz headed toward Jenna, still buried in the sand.

"Don't even think about it." But Piper got up and followed Liz. "I've seen you drive, and you need a decent spotter. Minimum."

"I always drove just fine. No complaints."

"Twenty years ago, I didn't have the guts to tell you." She bent down, brushing sand away from Jenna's knees. "But don't worry. You were good at everything else."

Liz's face clouded over. "Not everything."

"Everything that mattered." She uncovered Jenna's legs while Liz freed her arms. "C'mon, you. Time to waterski."

The squeals drew the guys' attention. "Okay, let's go. Before those morons find out what we're doing and beg to join us. We don't want their cooties, do we?"

Jenna's mouth twisted as if she'd sucked on a lemon. "Ew!"

Piper wished she could always get rid of guys so easily. And wondered why she just had.

"THEY'RE GOING WATERSKIING." In between Frisbee tosses, David watched Liz, Piper, and Jenna every step of the way.

Brandon shrugged. "Uh-huh."

"Don't you want to join them?" He dropped the Frisbee on the ground. "Let's go."

Brandon didn't budge. "Doesn't look like they need us."

"They're desperate for our help." David grinned, throwing an arm around Brandon's shoulders. "You haven't seen Jenna ski."

"If you've been teaching her, I'm not sure I want to."

"I'm not that bad." While David tried to talk Brandon into joining him, Pete and Billy ran over and climbed into the boat. "She got up for the first time yesterday."

Brandon snorted. "With all the gizmos you've got, you could get a baby up. Which is basically what you did."

When they reached the boat, Piper was fighting Pete for the driver's seat, Billy sprawled on the engine cover, Jenna hung off the boom, and Liz gripped the handrail. Everyone in position.

Before David could reach them, Jenna shrieked "hit it!" and Piper took off, leaving a disappointed David in her wake. But only for ten seconds, until another fall. He waded over to Jenna, whose lower lip was hanging out.

"I skied yesterday."

"Beautifully." He tapped her nose. "But skiing isn't easy. You've got to keep at it."

"You get up every time. An' Mom. An' everybody."

"Not every time." He'd fallen once this summer.

Driving, Liz had panicked when he jumped off the dock to start his run. The lurching start snapped the rope out of his hands, leaving him in four feet of water, going nowhere fast.

Brandon climbed onto the swim platform, then into the boat, leaving David waist deep in the water to help Jenna. He hoisted her in the air.

The boat took off, and Jenna with it. The hoots and clapping almost drowned out the roar of the motor. Fifteen minutes and three falls later, the boaters returned. Jenna was dragging, but Piper looked furious and Brandon like he'd rather be anywhere else.

Brandon jumped over the side of the boat as David held out a hand to help Liz. She looked at it before jumping over the side, too. Pete and Billy scrambled after them.

"Want me to tie up the boat for you, Piper?"

She raced the engine in neutral. "No." After making sure everyone was out of her way, she blasted off with a roar—not toward the dock, but north toward the cove.

"What the—?" David looked from Brandon to Liz. Brandon ignored him, and Liz shook her head.

She glared at Brandon. "What did you say to her? I haven't seen Piper that angry in ages."

Brandon shrugged. "That's only because you haven't seen her in ages. It's not the first time I've seen her like that."

Mystified, David followed them onto the beach, where Brandon took off running.

David turned to Liz. "What's up with him? And Piper?"

"No idea." Her gaze followed Brandon as he sprinted toward the big house. "Piper's been pissed since he arrived. He said something in the boat."

He looked at Brandon's retreating back, then out at the water. Piper was heading toward them now. He breathed a sigh of relief when the boat slowed on its approach, then coasted to an easy landing.

"She wouldn't have hit the dock." Despite her words, Liz looked worried.

"You never know. It's my boat."

Their gazes caught, and she grinned. "Good point."

He looked at Piper, whose stony gaze swept the beach. "You don't think . . ."

Liz glanced at him before heading toward Piper. "Those two? No way. We've always just been friends."

But a lot changed in twenty years. Maybe, for once, Liz didn't know everything.

SITTING between Piper and Brandon at dinner, Liz glanced at her two friends. Brandon had scarfed down a huge plate of food before anyone else made it through the salad. Piper, busy taking verbal swipes at Brandon, hadn't touched a bite.

Suzy seemed almost pleasant in comparison. Sure, she didn't say much, especially to Liz, but she fussed sweetly over Billy. Billy ignored her.

Jenna, equally independent in her own mind, knelt on her chair and tried cutting her chicken with a spoon. She finally peered up at Liz's dad. "Gramps? Help me?"

He couldn't even help himself. Choking on a broccoli spear, Liz jumped up from the table. In her rush to help Jenna, she knocked over her own chair. Finally, she pried the spoon from Jenna's grasp and cut the chicken before setting her chair upright again.

She shot Diana an apologetic grimace, which Diana waved away.

Suzy's smile was even sharper. Like, say, a machete. "It's

hard watching out for a child, isn't it? Lucky thing you decided to have just one."

The table fell silent. Flushing, Liz bent her head over her plate—until David slammed back his chair and stormed outside.

"That's actually not true, Suzy." Pausing as she helped Dad with his dinner, Diana smiled gently at Liz. "Liz wanted—"

Liz shook her head, furiously, cutting off Diana's words but catching her eye and offering a mental apology. They were all family—counting Piper, which Liz did—so Liz's struggles to get pregnant shouldn't be a big secret. But damned if Suzy had to know.

Billy piped up. "What's for dessert?"

Everyone except Suzy laughed.

"Your favorite." Diana, next to him, rubbed his shoulder and drew a self-conscious squirm. "Caramel apple pie."

"We don't have time for dessert, Billy."

"Aw, Mom. Please?"

Suzy dragged herself to her feet, as if she couldn't bear the thought of leaving, but she couldn't hide that triumphant grin. "Time to leave."

"I'm sure he can stay for pie, Suzy." Diana held Billy in place. "I'll get it."

Bristling, Suzy plunked herself back down. The screen door banged, and David returned, calmer. He stood in the center of the porch, eying the scene at the far end.

Brandon cleared his throat and stood up. "I guess this is as good a time as any."

"To speak to me?" Piper shot back. "Finally."

Laughing nervously, he moved to stand behind Piper. "No. I, uh—"

He dug into his pocket and fished something from it. Liz turned to see a small box in his hand.

"Everyone's here." Brandon's knee cracked as he knelt.

Head down, Piper covered her face. "No!"

"Piper—"

"No! No! No!" Piper shook her head frantically as she kept screaming.

"Would you marry me?"

Shaking convulsively, Piper actually giggled. And sobbed. What the hell? Frowning at Brandon, who had never been so insensitive in his life, Liz leaned over to hug Piper.

She got her arm slapped.

"Yes." Piper looked at Brandon and grinned, nodding, running her hand over her wet face, smearing her mascara. She sniffed. "But that was a pretty stupid-ass way to do it."

Brandon threw both arms around Piper, squeezing the life out of her. Diana smiled and patted Dad's hand. David looked confused for a moment before muttering something about champagne as he headed for the kitchen.

Suzy frowned. "Shouldn't you guys at least date first?"

Liz sucked in a breath. For the first time in her life, she agreed with Suzy.

"Sure you want to leave for two whole weeks?" Docking the boat in the marina, David ruffled Billy's hair for a split second before Billy pulled away in alarm.

"I don't wanna spend my whole summer around dopey little kids like Max, okay?" He slung his duffle bag over his shoulder, the weight of it nearly propelling him into the water before he grabbed onto the dock.

Suzy waited in the boat. Knowing the drill, David

hoisted her bag onto the dock before holding out his hand for her. She let go as soon as she set foot on the dock. David followed behind as she climbed the steps to the parking area, where she'd parked her new Mercedes convertible.

"We'll miss you guys." After loading the trunk, David tried to hug Suzy. Her arms hung down, and she turned her face away. His kiss landed on her cheek. "Come back soon."

She pulled from his grasp. "To cook? I think Diana can take care of that. Or Liz, when she's not yelling at her dad."

"She doesn't yell at him, but she also doesn't cook. And neither does Mom, if she can help it."

"No wonder you married me." Opening her door, Suzy offered a thin smile. "You needed a woman who cooked."

"That's not fair." He glanced at Billy, who hunched over in his seat. "We used to cook *together*, and you didn't do much cooking on your own until you started taking all those cooking classes. You booted me out of the kitchen."

"So you're saying I'm fat."

"Not at all." He hadn't, and he wouldn't. Ever. If Suzy wanted to lose weight, she would. "Look, don't leave like this." She fiddled with something in her purse. "I know you hate having dinner with everyone, but Mom asked. She's not going to see Billy for two weeks. Or you."

"She has Liz. And her precious Jenna." She rolled her eyes. "If I have to hear about her snuggles one more time, I think I'll throw up. She's five. Of course she cuddles."

David frowned. "Jenna was pretty quiet when she first got here. She's changed."

"So?" Suzy snorted. "I'll bet she lives in a big house with every toy she wants and nannies watching her every hour."

"So did our boys."

"But I stayed home! I could've had a great job, just like

Liz, and make everyone hang on every word I say." She chewed her lip. "I don't know why she has to be here."

"She came out because of her dad."

"Well, I can't stand her. I never could." Folding herself into the driver's seat, she turned on the ignition.

David crouched down to speak before she could slam the door in his face.

"Wait. Don't go yet." He didn't want to fight with Suzy, and certainly not here. He also didn't want Suzy so pissed off that she drove the car off the road. He sprinted behind her car —preventing her quick exit in reverse—and over to Billy's door, which was still open. One leg hung out, as if he was debating whether to stay at the River.

David crouched down by him. "Sure you want to go, Billy? It's not too late to change your mind, and I'd love to have you here. Always."

"I-I—" Billy looked at his hands. "I guess I—"

Suzy revved the engine. "Of course he wants to go." She ran a hand through Billy's hair. "It'll be fine, Billy. Dad is just upset that we're going to have more fun than he will."

At Billy's confused look, David put his hand on his son's arm. "You don't have to go. But if you want to whip a bunch of kids' butts while I slave away here, go for it."

A shadow of a smile touched Billy's face. "Yeah, right. You're gonna be so busy working—" He elbowed David. "I guess I can play tennis." He flicked a nervous glance at Suzy before turning back to David. "But, uh, maybe next time I don't have to go so far?"

David ruffled his hair again, earning a swat and a grin. "Sounds good, sport. Knock 'em dead."

CHAPTER 11

Wednesday. Halfway through another week, halfway through June. She'd intended to stay the whole summer?

Liz stretched her arms over her head in the creaky wooden chair, a back-house relic that should've hit the dump years ago. Wincing, she rubbed the small of her back right where the chair nailed it. After she finished scraping, puttying, and painting the big house, maybe she'd buy some new furniture. Not that any of it would make the place feel like hers.

Tapping her fingers on the desk, she reread the words on the computer screen.

Utter dreck.

Hitting a little kid wasn't funny, and she kept trying to make it sound like *Saturday Night Live*. She didn't want to scare anyone the way she'd been scared, nearly every night of her life until her mom died, and a long time after that.

She floated the cursor over the block of text she'd just spent an hour writing, then hit "delete." She might never show this to anyone, but she had to tell the real story. Without jokes. Without turning Mom into a saint.

To think she'd wasted so much time on this when she could've spent it with Jenna or Diana or even David.

Or Dad. He hadn't said anything horrible to her again, but what was the point of having a meaningless, one-sided conversation with a vegetable? Staring at his blank face, wondering whether any wheels were turning? She couldn't imagine how Diana did it.

After deleting even more words, she hit "save." But seriously, she couldn't write. She couldn't pick husbands, either. Yes, she was good at sports, she negotiated lucrative deals for her clients, and she loved Jenna to the moon and back.

But none of it made her happy.

No, Jenna did. Every single day.

She closed her laptop. Time to rejoin the world.

"You're just in time."

Liz stepped onto the porch, met David's eyes, and took a step backward. "For what?"

He held out a tennis racquet.

"If you're making spaghetti, the strainer is in the cupboard under the microwave. You might try using that instead of—" She snatched the racquet out of his hand. "My tennis racquet? Where'd you find it? I buried this in my closet."

He nodded. "I found it behind your forty-nine suitcases."

"Funny." She tossed the racquet on the nearest glider, and her body followed. "What's the matter, David? Are you bored?"

"I don't—"

"No offense, honestly, but you don't seem to spend much

time working." Not bothering to look at him, she picked up the racquet and spun it in her hand.

"Medical devices don't exactly thrill me." He watched as her jaw dropped and the racquet stopped spinning. "But feel free to jump to conclusions. Everyone else does."

"Does Diana know?"

"It's a little hard telling her. At least right now." As he counted all the times he'd avoided the conversation, starting with the day Mom had asked him to join the company, he pointed at Liz's racquet. "But I thought we could play tennis."

"Whew." She ran her hand along the length of her racquet, sending annoying shivers down his spine. "If you wanted to play *football* with my racquet, I'd be worried."

He blew out an exasperated breath. He was married but pursuing a relationship—a completely harmless one—with a woman who barely seemed to care that he existed.

"Where would we play?" She kept spinning the racquet and avoiding his gaze. If he didn't know her better, he'd almost think she seemed nervous. "Not the court on the hill, right? The balls would hit the cracks or the weeds growing out of them."

"A friend of mine has a court in Afton."

She glanced upstairs, as if expecting Jenna to appear.

"Jenna's napping. I took her up fifteen minutes ago."

She flushed. "I'm sorry. I was working on my . . ." She trailed off as her hand circled in the air.

"Your novel. Yeah, I know."

She flushed brighter.

"Hey, no prob." He waved his own racquet. "C'mon. The sun's shining, and you have nothing better to do. Let's hit a few balls."

"I don't think . . ."

In a leap of faith, he'd already put her tennis shoes in the boat. "Don't think. We don't get that many beautiful days."

She lifted one eyebrow. "We don't?"

He winked. "Not in January."

———

Liz looked each way, then held the lemonade carton to her mouth, pouring it down her dry throat and adding a few spills to the sweat stains dotting the front of her T-shirt.

"What do you think you're doing?"

She wiped her mouth with the back of her hand, mostly for effect, before turning to face Diana—who stared at her in disbelief.

"Hot day." She offered the carton to Diana. "Want some?"

"Of course not. What have I always told you kids? Drinking out of cartons isn't just disgusting—it's bad hygiene."

Diana held out her hand for the carton. Shaking her head, she screwed on the top and put the lemonade in the fridge.

Crossing her arms, Liz waited, but that was all Diana said. "What's the matter? You always gave the guys at least a five-minute lecture. Don't I rate?"

Diana rolled her eyes. "They were teenagers. I still had some control."

Liz raised her eyebrows, drawing a laugh from Diana.

"But when did you start drinking out of cartons? I've never seen you do that before."

"I was thirsty?" She bit her lip. "And I, uh, never tried it before. When the guys did. Back then."

Diana nodded as if she actually understood. "By the way, I saw David and you sneak off in the boat. Sly dogs."

Liz blinked. "Wh— Why? We just—"

Diana laughed. "He told me. You actually went to play tennis, together, and David didn't have your hands tied behind your back. Almost as if you were becoming friends."

"Don't bet on it." She thought back to the hard-fought tennis match, which had started with easy volleys and turned into something else. War? Or foreplay? "It's hard to imagine us as friends."

"Try harder." Diana scanned the counters, cleaning a juice spill with an efficient swipe of the dishrag. "Believe it or not, I have hopes for you two."

Unfortunately, lately, so did Liz.

———

"Liz, I'm coming out there next weekend."

"Hello to you, too, Paul." Her voice was calm and cool, something he'd always admired until this summer.

"Did you hear me?" Boats or mosquitos, he wasn't sure which, roared in his ear. She must be on the beach. "I said I'm coming to visit next weekend."

"Yes, but are you sure this time?"

His heart skipped a beat, as if he'd lost her. But he hadn't. She was still Liz, right? The woman he'd loved and married. His wife. Jenna's mom.

Nothing changed that quickly.

He blew out a frustrated breath. "I can come. I mean, I will. I've cleared my calendar."

Most of it, anyway, and he could tie up the loose ends with phone calls and emails. He'd bring his laptop. He wondered if they had wireless at the River, but this probably wasn't a good time to ask.

"Is Jenna there?"

He caught an odd sound. Like a snort or cough or something. Maybe it was the phone line, or someone passing by.

"Is that all you ever want? To talk to Jenna?"

"Shouldn't I?" He missed Jenna. He missed Liz, too, but in a more complicated way. "Does she have enough books? You didn't take many."

"I had enough luggage to carry as it was." She laughed, unexpectedly. "But she's fine, and this house is filled with books. She has everything she needs."

"Except me, and I shouldn't have to beg to talk to her." An ache tugged at him. If he'd known Liz would yank Jenna away for the summer, he would've spent more time with her. He might've spent more time with Liz, too. But right now, he wasn't as sure about that.

When she paused for a moment, he held his breath, expecting her to hang up on him. Again. "I'll get Jenna for you."

———

TIPTOEING across the wooden floor at dawn—actually, past dawn, but only because dawn came so early these days—David approached a slumbering Liz. A snuffling Liz, face down, head twisted to one side.

"Hey." Leaning over, he tapped her shoulder. "Wake up."

Nothing moved except her lips. "I hiked yesterday. I played tennis. Wasn't that enough?"

He nudged her again. "Nice try. Time to get up."

Rolling over, she clutched the pillow against her chest.

Until that moment, focused on their hike, he hadn't noticed that she wasn't wearing her standard-issue Capitals jersey.

She wore a tiny yellow camisole.

He turned away, whistling off-key. Trying not to look like a stalker or, worse, a pathetic jackass. "C'mon. Hop to it, sport."

She hugged the pillow tighter and blinked several times. "Give me a minute?"

"Yeah, yeah." He took a step toward the door and ran a hand through his hair, hoping he looked nonchalant, which was tough when his hand shook. "But don't take all day."

Despite everything, he wanted to be with her as soon as possible.

Damn him all to hell.

"Tell me again why you woke me up for this?" Sucking in the cool morning air, Liz stood on the path in front of the big house and stretched her arms, trying to work the kinks out.

David chuckled. Annoying guy. He looked way too happy for six-thirty in the morning and too damn good, period. She knew exactly what she looked like.

Warmed-over garbage.

She moved on to leg stretches. Ouch. A sharp pain shot up her right leg to her knee.

David hopped in place a few times and bent his neck to one side, then the other. As if yesterday's tennis hadn't killed every muscle he owned.

She turned away, partly to stretch her other leg, but also because she was too aware of him. Feeling flustered and confused, she took off hiking. Without any warning to David.

He called out from behind her. "Hey! Wait up."

Head down, she increased her pace. She heard him running, then a crash and a loud "fuck!" as he hit the fallen log she'd barely avoided.

Then his hand caught her shoulder.

After stopping her, he doubled over, wheezing and rubbing his shin. That's what he got for trying to catch a woman who shouldn't be caught—by him or anyone. She was married, and so was he. End of story. *Right?*

"Hang on a sec, will you?"

As David pried a sliver out of his shin, Liz felt horrible. She should've warned him, like they'd normally do for each other. Spinning in a slow circle, she looked for a place to sit and spotted another fallen log. She swept her hand over it, checking for bugs or other gross things before sitting down. Gingerly.

"Are you okay?" Elbows propped on her knees, she watched David, who winced as he rubbed his knee.

It was totally her fault.

"Not really. I didn't see the log, because I was running after you, because you took off without telling me. Geez. You could've warned me."

She patted a spot next to her and tried not to feel guilty. "You're right, and I'm sorry. I was in a hurry." Or something. But David didn't sit down, which bugged her more than it should. "Have a seat."

Hands on his hips, he frowned. "Why should I?"

She shrugged, feeling stupid. She kept acting like the teenage girl she'd been, madly in love with David and damned if she'd show it. It was time to grow up. "Does your leg hurt? I thought you might want to rest it."

When he still didn't move, she started to get up. He nudged her back down—okay, *shoved* was more accurate—

before sitting down himself, muttering something that probably wasn't a compliment to her.

Liz didn't want to sit another minute, though. For one thing, the sharp bark was killing her butt. For another, some disgusting, slimy, eight-legged creature was probably crawling up her shirt or into her shorts.

But David's hand on her arm held her in place.

She stood up anyway. "I don't want to get tight."

With a wry grimace, he let go of her. She bent over, stretching, while self-consciously tugging at the bottom of her shirt. Not that David hadn't ever seen her shirt ride up on her, or would care if he did. It was the principle.

He stood up, his knees creaking, and immediately bent over to rub them. His own shirt rode up, revealing abs so tight he obviously didn't do a damn thing except work out.

She accidentally whistled—not under her breath, but loud in the early-morning silence. Oops. Talk about embarrassing! She took off at a brisk clip but this time glanced back over her shoulder. David stayed on the log, his gaze following her.

She waved at him to join her. "Aren't you coming?" As he trudged toward her, not exactly eager, she wondered why he'd wanted to hike in the first place.

Finally, he caught up to her. "Can we hike at a normal pace, or did you have a few more logs picked out?"

"None in mind, but maybe one will catch my eye as we go." At his frown, she grinned and landed a fake punch on his bicep. "Oh, don't be a grouch. That's my job."

"Yeah." It got his feet moving. "I almost forgot."

They kept hiking uphill, Liz in the lead, starting slow and gradually working up to a pace that winded her. At the top, she pointed at the path that ran to the bench overlooking the River. She always loved the way the early-morning sunlight danced on the water, shimmering. As if life, and everything in it, were perfect. A beautiful fiction.

Nodding, David took the lead this time. His head down, he almost ran into the bench.

"Da—"

He gave her a less-than-enthusiastic thumbs up. "Thanks for the warning."

"Anytime."

He moved to one end of the bench, she the other, leaving a huge gap between them. A few cruisers dotted the water below, as expected, all but one or two of them still anchored or on shore. A speedboat zoomed, pulling a kid on a wakeboard.

She glanced sideways at David, feeling shy and tongue-tied and thirteen years old. She put her feet up on the bench and wrapped her arms around her knees. "Paul's coming out next weekend."

"Yeah?" He stared at his fingers, spread wide on his thighs.

"Friday night." She laughed nervously. "Or so he says."

David laid an arm across the back of the bench, then crossed an ankle over his knee and played with his shoelace. "I still can't believe he didn't even bother making up a decent excuse. I would've at least invented an accident, if not a natural disaster."

"Smooth operator. I suppose I should be grateful."

"Oh? There's actually something you like about me?"

"At least a couple things." She ticked them off on her fingers. "One, you're not Paul." He smiled in that cocky way that had made her heart flutter in high school. "Two—"

When she paused, his eyes lit up. "Yeah?"

She hugged her knees to her chest. "I'm not married to you."

"Funny." Dropping his arm off the back of the bench, he stared out over the water. "I'm not like Paul, you know."

"You don't even know Paul. You've never met."

He shrugged. "He stood you up last weekend. You were right to be pissed."

"True, but you can't judge anyone's marriage by isolated events." Paul's own "isolated events" had become a pattern for a long time now, but she didn't need to discuss it with David. Besides, he wasn't exactly Mr. Loquacious when it came to his own problems. "Have you talked to Diana? About wanting to leave the company?"

When he stood up and stretched, not answering her, she dropped her feet back on the ground. "I'll take that as a no."

"It's complicated."

She patted the bench. "Talk to me. Did you say anything? What was her reaction?"

Snorting, David plunked back down on the bench, right next to her. Liz felt an urge to move away, even an inch, but she was already hugging the end of the bench. Another inch and she'd be on the ground.

Twisting to look at him, she tried to act as if she didn't even notice how close they were sitting. He was staring at her neck. Heat stole up her cheeks, but she blamed it on the exercise. "So? What happened with Diana?"

He blinked. "My mom?"

"Did you talk to her?"

He ran his hand through his long hair, then dropped his arm onto the top of the bench, just barely brushing her back. Feeling a slight tickle, Liz couldn't help shuddering.

"Liz, I—" Breaking off, he shook his head and gazed out over the River.

"What? Tell me." She leaned into him, casually, trying to act exactly the way she acted around Brandon.

He flinched as if she'd dropped a lit match on him.

"Sorry." She chewed on her lower lip. "I never know how to act with you. It's just—"

"Different. Always has been."

Feeling heat creep up her neck, Liz smoothed her shorts. "But we're trying to work on that, right? Tell me about Diana."

David sighed. "We talked. She asked me to wait."

"How long?"

"Probably until retirement age." He slid her a rueful grin. "Maybe not literally. It just feels like it. But, with Frank's health and all..."

Liz nodded. "So we'll have to work on that, too."

"We?"

"Sure. You and me. If you promise not to call me Lizzie." On an impulse, she reached up and ruffled his hair. Guessing his likely reaction, she jumped up and ran. She made it ten feet before his hands grabbed her arms, then yanked her backward. Laughing, she pulled away and got yanked again. "Brute! Just wait until I—"

He twisted her to face him as she pushed, still laughing, against his chest. Shaking his head, he held her, closer than before, pulling her into something that didn't feel at all like the wrestling matches Liz and Brandon used to have. It felt like—

Oh.

Leaning down, he cupped her face and kissed her. Softly, pressing his lips against hers, holding her so close that she almost couldn't breathe.

It felt... perfect.

She pushed hard against his chest, breaking his hold, and ran blindly down the path.

This time, he didn't follow.

"Piper, what a nice surprise!"

Diana held the door open, and Piper happily accepted her surrogate mom's and future mother-in-law's hug. The first person in Brandon's family to hug her, or even acknowledge her, since the Big Engagement. The big, moronic engagement at an awful moment to a terrific man who made her heart soar.

She supposed she'd have to forgive him for proposing like that. Maybe in ten years.

"Where is everyone?" Piper glanced around the porch and into the great room. No movement, no sound, at ten o'clock on a Friday morning. All the boats were docked or buoyed. "By the way, I helped myself to your only boat in the marina. I hope no one needs it."

She hadn't talked to Liz since Sunday night, when Piper and Brandon left soon after his slipshod proposal. But she'd taken today off, an impulsive decision she'd spent the week planning, and wanted to see Liz.

"We're not expecting anyone, and I'm glad you're here." Diana took Piper's overnight bag and set it on a chair. "It appears David and Liz had another fight."

"Oh?" Last weekend, they'd actually looking surprisingly comfortable with each other. Finally. After all these years.

"I'd hoped they were getting over it. She's in the back house, he's at his house, and I think Jenna's shuttling back and forth between them."

"I should—" "You should—"

They laughed as their voices blended. "—see Liz."

"Is she working on her novel?"

Diana held up her hands. "She ran through the kitchen

after she came back, alone, from their morning hike. I don't think she even saw Jenna here on the porch."

"Weird." Piper followed Diana into the kitchen on her way to the back house. "She's having a tough summer. Her dad's sick, and you're so busy, leaving David as the only adult to hang out with."

"He's not so bad." Diana's eyes twinkled. "Although I'm sure he can't compare to my *other* son."

"You got that right." Reaching into the fridge, Piper pulled out a bag containing two bagels. Stuffing one bagel in her mouth, she grabbed the bag and headed out the back door. "I'll see what's up, and then we'll take Jenna off your hands."

"I've already sent Jenna over to David, but good luck with Liz."

Piper nodded. She had a feeling she might need it.

DAVID ALMOST DIDN'T ANSWER the hesitant knock, figuring it had to be Liz. Or Mom, anxious for an explanation of something he'd spent half the morning trying to explain to himself. So far, he was clinging to temporary insanity.

Jenna appeared just inside the door. "Is my mom here?"

"Nope. Did you look in the back house?"

"It's dark. I was scared to go in."

"Don't be. Want me to take you there?" Part of him would rather chew nails. Another part felt a flicker of completely unreasonable excitement at the idea.

He wanted to strangle that part. Fortunately or not, so would Liz.

Jenna shook her head. "Can Pete play?"

"Sorry, kiddo." Pete limited his conquests to girls who had ten years on Jenna. "He's working over at the marina."

Pete had told him about the job, in great detail, last weekend. He'd started on Monday—which was the last time David had seen the kid for more than thirty seconds at a time.

"Gram said he likes girls. I'm a girl, so maybe he'd like me?" Jenna's question ended on a hopeful note that David couldn't bear to crush.

"Everyone likes you, Jenna. You're the best."

Her lower lip stuck out. "My daddy doesn't come see me."

Poor kid. "He's flying out here next weekend."

She shook her head, making her short hair dance. "He didn't come last time." She crooked a little finger at David. "Just like you don't go see Billy. Or . . . or me."

He flinched. "I'm just busy working this morning."

"Like my daddy." She crossed her arms, recrossing them when she didn't quite get it right, and looked impossibly cute.

Bending down, he met her troubled gaze. "If it's okay with your mom, we can take a boat across the River and get some ice cream at Selma's. What do you say?"

"Yes." A smile lit her face as she grabbed his hand and dragged him out the door. "But we don't hafta ask Mom. Gram said it was okay when she sent me here."

Rolling his eyes, he grabbed his wallet and Jenna's hand. Between Jenna, Liz, and Mom, he didn't stand a chance.

He just didn't know if that was good or bad.

CHAPTER 12

Still chewing her bagel, Piper rapped on the door to the back house. "Any famous writers here?"

After another rap, Piper opened the screen door. "Liz?"

She glanced around the dark, slightly musty room. Liz must've headed over to David's house to collect Jenna, or make up, or both.

"Piper, is that you?"

At the muffled voice, her head jerked. She fumbled for the light switch and flipped it on.

A screech followed. "You didn't need to do that."

"If we're playing hide-and-seek, I do." Scanning the room, she caught sight of Liz, curled up in a ball on a sketchy-looking bed in the far corner. "Nap time already?"

Liz didn't answer, let alone get up. Puzzled, Piper hurried to the bed. Liz's arms were wrapped around her legs, cocoon fashion, and she faced the wall.

"What's the matter, Liz?"

"Nothing. Everything. I'm not sure."

"That pretty much covers it." She propped on the edge of the bed, both concerned and frustrated, half of her wishing she'd gone to the office and worked today. Or at least brought Tracy out here for reinforcements.

More silence.

"Hey, you. It's me, Piper. Your old friend. What's wrong?"

A sniffle. "David."

"Don't tell me. He's trying to act like your brother."

"Worse." Rolling onto her other side, Liz faced Piper. Tear tracks streaked down her face, and the mascara she almost never wore had turned her cheeks into a puddle of black.

"Am I going to have to drag it out of you?" Piper glanced around until she spied a box of Kleenex on the nightstand, then pulled out a few tissues and handed them to Liz. "Here. You're a complete mess, by the way."

Liz balled the tissues in her fist. "Thanks."

"Don't mention it. Hey, why don't we—"

"He kissed me."

Piper felt her jaw hit the floor. "You're kidding."

"Would I joke about that?"

"When we were teenagers? Only several hundred times."

Piper grabbed another tissue and dabbed at Liz's eyes. Short of a washcloth or fire hose, she couldn't do much about the black cheeks. The back house needed a sink.

"It's what I always wanted. All those . . . those years." The sniffle morphed into a groan.

"But you're married now, and so is he." Another groan, which almost tempted Piper to slap some sense into Liz. "To Suzy. When is she coming home?"

"Next Friday. Same as Paul."

"She'll kill you, you know. She might just sit on you and crush you to death."

"She's not that big." But a tiny glimmer of a smile flickered on Liz's face. "And I didn't kiss him. He kissed me."

"Yeah, and I'll bet you slapped him real hard afterward."

"I pushed him away. And the kiss didn't last very long." The dreamy look on Liz's face said otherwise.

"Right. Ten minutes? Or are we talking world record?"

Liz sat up, still hugging herself. "More like five seconds. Then I ran."

"Hmmm." Piper studied her for a long moment. Yeah, she was way more remorseful than dreamy. But maybe a little bit dreamy. "It's not exactly the scenario we always envisioned. What did David do?"

"He didn't follow, thank God. Maybe he threw himself off the cliff."

"No such luck." Piper smoothed a tuft of Liz's hair, which looked like a five-year-old's right now. Like Jenna's. "Diana said he's at his house. She thought you had a fight."

"Actually, we did." A puzzled frown darkened Liz's face. "I didn't warn him about a log on the path, so he tripped over it, and then we argued about Paul and whether David is leaving the company, and then he kissed me."

"Busy morning." Liz's words belatedly hit Piper. "David's leaving the company?"

Liz rocked back and forth on the bed. "Diana isn't exactly encouraging about it, to say the least, so please don't tell anyone. On top of everything else, I don't need her mad at me."

"She adores you, in case you hadn't noticed."

"She's nice to everyone. And I'm her husband's daughter."

"No, you're Liz. *Her* daughter, as far as Diana's concerned. You're the only one who doesn't realize it."

Diana had done everything but adopt Liz. She'd tried to

do that, too, but Liz had refused. She'd only been ten, but Diana hadn't forced the issue. She didn't do cram-downs.

"Look, I don't need any lectures, okay?" Liz jumped off the bed and headed for the door. "Especially from someone with a perfect life."

A lightbulb flashed in Piper's head.

"So that's why you haven't called? Haven't even wished me, I don't know, luck?"

"With Brandon? Who needs luck? You found the perfect guy." Liz stopped at her desk but just stood there, clenching her fists as she stared at her laptop.

Piper stood up, planning to follow her, but sagged back down on the bed. The springs protested, and the bagel she'd inhaled was now wreaking havoc with her gut. "Tell me you're not jealous."

Dead silence. Her back to Piper, Liz hugged herself.

Piper called softly to her. "Whatever it is, just tell me. Let's get it over with."

Finally, Liz turned to meet her gaze, smiling even though more tears fell. "You're kidding, right? You know I've never been interested in Brandon. *You* were, even if you pretended it was old news when I brought it up this summer. Brandon's a great guy, but he's all yours." She shrugged, her gaze locked on the floor. "Not that you bothered telling me."

"It was complicated."

"Where have I heard that before?"

Piper laughed as the tightness eased in her chest. "You haven't exactly been forthcoming, either. And we don't see each other much, but I wish we did. When you showed up this summer, how could I tell you about Brandon when you kept telling me what a jerk his brother was?"

"By blurting it out while I plied you with liquor?"

"Unlikely, of course, since you don't drink."

Liz bit her lip. "My mom and dad both drank more than their share. I've always been terrified it might be genetic." She glanced up at the ceiling, her eyes unfocused. "But that isn't the point. I *am* happy for you, but I just want what you have. Not with Brandon, but with the right guy."

Piper's breath caught. "Tell me David isn't the right guy."

"He's not. Or I don't think so." The vertical groove in Liz's forehead deepened. "In any case, it doesn't matter. Like you said, he's married."

"And so are you. How *is* Paul, anyway?"

"Apathetic and in denial most of the time, but he suddenly seems to be snapping out of it." Liz hesitated. "I thought *I* was the only one who was angry, but I'm starting to piss him off. He misses Jenna."

"He probably misses you, too." Leaving the creaking bed, Piper crossed the room and put an arm around Liz's shoulders, then led her outside. The back house was dark and depressing. How did Liz spend so much time up here? "Do you miss him at all? Or is it too late?"

"When I left for the summer, I told myself it wasn't. But now I'm not sure." She looked so lost, so unlike Liz. "I've spent too much time being pissed."

They walked down the narrow sidewalk along the side of the big house, stopping for a quick detour at the outdoor shower, where Piper grabbed a washcloth and wiped the rest of the mascara off Liz's cheeks. Then they headed toward the steps to the beach. Piper thought about Brandon, and the stupid arguments they'd had even on the day he proposed, and wondered if this could ever happen to them, too. No, she'd fake-slug him or yell at him, and they'd wrestle on the rug and be done with it. She hoped.

"Do you still remember what you first saw in Paul?"

Liz tripped as she started down the steps. "Paul? I—I'm

not sure." She stared out over the River below them. "He wasn't Dad, to be honest."

"And he probably wasn't David."

Liz tilted her head, thinking. "True. But I'm not sure I compared him with David. He was sweet and dependable and, believe it or not, sometimes even fun."

Piper frowned. "Only sometimes?"

"A lot of our friends were workaholics, too, so it felt normal. Okay, I was an idiot." They reached the bottom step and strolled together across the beach. "It's not the first stupid thing I've done in my life, and it's not like *you're* so perfect." She slid a sideways grin at Piper. "After all, you're marrying the brother of the moron who kissed me this morning."

Piper snorted. "Fine. I guess we both have too many secrets and too many complications. Let's take a fast spin in the boat while we discuss them."

"Deal."

"But only if I get to drive."

They raced each other, laughing and shrieking, to the speedboat.

AVOIDING David was easier than avoiding his emails.

And why didn't he just text her? Or even call? Or walk a few dozen yards?

Sighing, Liz double-clicked on his message and felt a tingle race up her spine.

Subject: Truce

You tripped me. I kissed you. Call it even? Jenna and I can make only so many trips to Selma's before she'll start missing you. :-)

Selma's. She'd practically lived at Afton's ice-cream shop in her teens. And everyone she knew still loved it.

That settled it. She'd cooped herself up here in the back house for almost a month. All she had to show for it were cramped fingers, an aching back, and a memoir that brought pain without eloquence. She slammed the laptop's lid and headed to David's house.

Halfway there, she ran into him. Literally. Breaking his loose grip on Jenna.

She bent to hug her daughter, who was remarkably tan for someone who was always slathered in mega-sunblock. Paul wouldn't be pleased. "Hi, sweetie. What are you and David doing? I hoped you might want to play on the beach?"

"He's taking me to Selma's again." She covered her mouth. "Oops. Maybe I wasn't s'posed to say that."

"Do you want to join us?" David's eyebrows rose.

Blushing, Liz stared at her feet. His feet. Both were barefoot, and it somehow felt too intimate.

Jenna's flowered sandals, tapping an excited beat, brought Liz back to reality. "Mom? Do you wanna go to Selma's?"

"I don't have a purse. Or sandals. Or—"

"I've got money." David pulled a hand from behind his back, dangling a pair of her Birks. "And footwear. Just in case."

Liz squinted at him. "You've thought of everything."

"Not beyond Selma's." He offered a grimace that seemed to cover more apologies than just a trip for ice cream.

She glanced around, possibly for an excuse to get out of this, wishing she could spend time with Jenna alone. "Where's Piper?"

"Probably with Brandon, planning the big shindig." The three walked down the steps, then across the beach to the dock. "I guess I'll have to wear a tux. Why couldn't he get some other sucker for best man?"

"Poor baby." She'd spent most of yesterday with Piper, and Piper hadn't asked her to be in the wedding. Liz felt a pang in her stomach that had nothing to do with her surgeries. "Maybe he thought you'd look better in a tux than I would."

"Hmmm." Stopping on the end of the dock, he looked her over, head to toe, while she tried not to flinch. "Maybe you're right. I'll wear the tux, and you wear something short. And slinky."

Her mouth hung open as Jenna tugged on their hands.

"Can I drive? Huh? Can I?"

Jenna hopped into the boat, claiming the driver's seat. Liz tapped David's arm. "I just wanted to say, um, I thought yesterday was a mistake."

"I sure hope so." He smiled, his eyes glittering, making her heart thud. "You mean the part about tripping me, right?" He put an arm around her but quickly let go. Before she could throw him over the side of the boat. "I figured it had to be."

She glanced at Jenna, whose hand pumped the throttle, probably flooding the engine. "I meant the other part."

"It might've been a mistake. Not to mention impulsive, insane, and a million other things." He, too, glanced at Jenna. "But I still liked it."

Her head spinning, Liz dropped into the passenger seat.

Ten minutes later, David coasted up to the gas dock at the marina. He leaped over the engine cover and onto the dock, where a teenage attendant in low-slung shorts and an orange shirt shuffled over to greet him.

"Hey, Mr. Carruthers. Need some gas?"

"Not today, Tommy." David leaned against the pump,

casual and way too good looking. "I just wanted to say hi to Pete."

The teen glanced behind him at the marina office. "Pete? I haven't seen him this week."

"What do you mean?"

"Uh, I haven't seen him. But I don't really, uh, do the party scene. Too busy working."

David frowned. "Isn't he working, too?"

"Here?" Tommy took a step backward, running a nervous hand through his short hair. "Not that I know. I could, uh, check in the office. Or something."

Shaking his head, David gave Tommy an apologetic smile before climbing back into the speedboat and taking off slowly toward his slip.

Trying not to get involved, Liz tapped Jenna on the knee. "What are you going to get at Selma's, Jenn? Ice cream? Or chocolate-covered toenails?"

"Yuck!" Jenna scrunched her nose. "Do they sell them?"

David glared straight ahead as he maneuvered the boat into his slip and hit the front of the dock.

Jenna jumped. "You banged it! Just like Mom does!"

Liz coughed into her hand, feeling her face flush. "Only on special occasions, Jenna. Nothing worth mentioning."

"This must be a special occasion, kid." He tied up the boat, not bothering to check whether his landing had done any damage. "It's not every day I find out my son's a liar."

"Isn't that a bit harsh?" Unconsciously, Liz touched David's arm. "What about the other marina? Maybe he meant that one."

"Yeah, maybe." He tweaked Jenna's nose, then carried her piggyback along the dock. "I guess I overreacted. Sorry."

"I understand. It's been a week of overreactions."

"A whole damn summer, if you ask me."

He ran up the steps to the parking lot, unfazed by hauling Jenna on his back, while Liz followed at a slower pace. In silence, they walked the two blocks to Selma's, where they ran into—

"Pete?" David lost his grip on Jenna, who slid into Liz's arms. "What are you doing here?"

"Oh, hey, Dad." Dropping his arm from around a teenage girl in short shorts, too much makeup, and what looked like a stuffed bikini top, Pete slouched on his stool. "What's up?"

David glanced from the girl, who wet her lips, back to Pete. "How's work? Quite a strain?"

Shrugging, Pete ran a hand through his spiked blond hair.

David turned to the girl. "I'm Pete's dad." She batted her eyelashes, and Liz tightened her grip on Jenna's hand. "You must be . . . Amanda?"

"Nicole." Crossing her arms, the girl shot Pete an icy look. "You're not still seeing her, are you?"

Wild-eyed, Pete mouthed a "no" to Nicole, then glared at David. "Dad, you know it's—"

"Nicole." David smiled at Nicole. "It's hard to keep track of Pete's love life. You know how that goes."

Liz moved to the other end of the counter, pulling Jenna with her over Jenna's loud pleas to see Pete. She glanced at Pete, who couldn't slouch lower without hitting the floor.

"Well, it's great meeting you—Nicole." David's white teeth dazzled from across the room. "Come to dinner sometime. Maybe we'd see Pete then, too."

Liz ordered a small cone for Jenna and debated whether to get another one to throw at David. As he headed toward her, she glanced past him at Pete, who had his arm around Nicole, obviously trying frantically to mop up his dad's well-aimed mess.

"I hope you're proud of yourself." Liz handed Jenna the

cone, then shook a finger at David. "You don't even know that girl. I can understand being mad at Pete, but it's not the girl's fault. Why did you act so horribly to her?"

"No clue." He shook his head, chastised. "It wasn't like me. I just erupted."

Liz shuddered. "Try not to erupt around me, then."

"I already did. Yesterday, in case you forgot."

Flushing, she turned to order some ice cream her hips didn't need.

He tapped her on the shoulder. "Getting that for me?"

"You or your lap?" She nodded in Pete's direction. "Tell you what. You make up with Pete, and I'll spring for ice cream all around."

"That's my wallet you've got."

"And that's your son. Sounds like a fair trade."

Turning, he inched through the crowd toward Pete, who looked away. Finally, David's arm came around his shoulder and they talked. Quietly. David gave Pete a typical guy's half-hug and bowed gallantly to Nicole, obviously charming her.

He hadn't lost his touch.

That was the whole problem.

"Liz?" Approaching the bench overlooking the River—which now held a lot of new memories, many of them awkward, after yesterday morning—David slowed his frantic pace.

Head on her upturned knees, she didn't look up.

"I'm glad I found you."

When he stopped in front of the bench, she finally lifted her head. One blue eye peeked at him through a tangle of bangs.

He sat next to her. "I wanted to thank you."

She scooted farther down the bench. "This isn't about that kiss..."

"Nope." He held up his hands, the picture of innocence. In his own mind, at least. "Unless you want it to be."

"I don't."

"I meant Pete. Thanks for Pete." He leaned back against the bench and tilted the brim of his baseball cap over his eyes, trying to block the mid-afternoon sun. "I lost it yesterday, and you were right to make me apologize to him."

"No kidding."

"I know. But wait until Jenna's sixteen, hanging out in some joint with a slacker draped all over her."

"Does Selma's qualify as a joint?" Turning toward him, Liz tipped up the brim of his cap. "Hopefully, Jenna won't be wearing so much makeup or have her bra, uh . . ."

"Stuffed like that?" He grinned when she swatted him, then used it as an excuse to move an inch closer to her, dropping his arm onto the back of the bench. Liz wasn't wearing a bra under her black tank top, probably thinking nothing showed. Ha. As her nipples caught his attention, he closed his eyes and tried to remember what he'd been talking about. Oh, yeah. Pete. "Man, he gave me a boatload of grief."

"In front of Nicole?"

Liz didn't seem to notice him touching the ends of her hair. Soft, silky hair with just the slightest wave on the ends. "Uh, yeah. I mean, no." He lost track of everything when he breathed in her scent—a mix of raspberries and sunshine. "He showed up for lunch. First time all week. Solo."

"What happened to Nicole?"

He grinned. "Probably off getting implants."

She rolled her eyes.

"So tell me about Pete." Leaning toward him, she seemed oblivious to the direction his thoughts were going. Fortunately or not. He couldn't help noticing her lips and thought she glanced at his. "Did you guys make up?"

"As much as guys ever do." Forcing himself to look away from her, David stared out over the River, watching speedboats and cruisers, the occasional sailboat. "I offered him a summer job at the company, which should be enough incentive for him to find something else to do. He doesn't need to spend the whole summer with girls."

"Why not? At sixteen, as I recall, you did."

"That's my whole point." Remembering the early days with Suzy, he grimaced. "But I'm not sure I can explain the facts of life to a sixteen-year-old."

Liz stretched out her legs, drawing his gaze. "I think it helps to admit your mistakes."

He scoffed. "Guys don't do that."

"That's why guys keep making the same mistakes."

"And you don't?" He turned toward Liz, still resting his arm along the top of the bench, not touching her but thinking about it. Thinking way too much about it.

She tensed as his arm dropped onto her shoulders—but she didn't move away. "I make a lot of them."

"Maybe, but . . . I like your style."

"Right." She looked at her hands. "I pick on you, fight with you, sometimes don't even speak to you."

"Okay. Except for that."

As they both laughed, he moved an inch closer, wrapping his arm tighter around her shoulders. "Liz, I—"

She leaned in and kissed him, startling the hell out of him. Her arm snaked around his waist and held on. He felt her lips, her breasts pressed against him, her leg brushing his. Damn it, he couldn't stop himself. His free hand sneaked under her tank top, sliding upward while he waited for a protest that didn't come. Her eyes widened, but her lips kept kissing him. Tentatively. God, he wanted her.

They were both married.

They pulled back at the same instant. David stared at her, seeing his own emotions race across her face—excited and nervous and terrified out of her mind. Halfway to heaven and halfway to hell, and landing somewhere smack-dab in the middle of purgatory. Where he'd spent most of his adult life. With Suzy.

Liz looked embarrassed. "I'm sorry."

"Don't be." Please. He wanted to do it again. Like, right now.

She shook her head. "No, I mean . . . I just always wanted to do that. Even just once. When I was in high school, I had it all planned."

"You did?" In high school, in college, he'd thought only about Suzy. Damn. She'd been right all along about Liz but probably wouldn't appreciate knowing just how right.

She nodded, not meeting his eye, but when his hand went under her tank top again, not hesitating this time, she sucked in a breath. It totally worked for him.

She closed her eyes for a moment. "Stupid, huh? I always dreamed we'd meet at the end of the point, and you'd tell me how much you—well, you know."

She'd dreamed of him telling her how much he loved her? Wow.

Right now, he was still working on getting to know her and flirting wildly with lust, but love took a while. Except for the boys, he'd felt it only once in his life, with Suzy. And he wasn't even sure about that. He wasn't in a position to make Liz any promises—understatement—but he felt things with her that he hadn't felt in years, if ever, with Suzy. In many ways, Suzy was still the teenage girl he'd known: hung up on him and fashion and money. Okay, no longer hung up on him. She'd never even asked, not once, how he felt about working in the family business.

"David, I—"

He pulled away from her, reluctantly, but held her hand. He might've left his Boy Scout days behind, but guilty thoughts about Suzy kept intruding. "I know what you mean. It's probably not the smartest thing in the world, but I . . . want to explore this. Whatever that means."

"I can't do this again."

Breaking free of him, she smiled sadly, stood up, and slowly walked away.

Oh. So they *didn't* feel the same way. At all.

"LIZ? YOU SOUND DIFFERENT."

"Different?" She cleared her throat. "I don't think so. What's new, Paul?"

Everything. Nothing. He worked, he ate, he slept. He'd even gone to church this morning, probably for the first time since Jenna's baptism. He'd gotten lost finding the place.

He'd felt lost all summer.

"I just wanted to check on next weekend. If it's still okay, I'm flying out Friday night."

Sitting at his desk at work, where—unlike everyone else in his firm—he spent most Sundays this summer, he flipped through his calendar. Next week looked rough, but he couldn't postpone this trip. He had a feeling his marriage depended on it.

"I already told you it was okay."

"I just wanted to make sure. I want to see you and Jenna. My two girls. I miss you." There. He'd said it. Uttered a declarative sentence, as Liz would say, although she hardly said much of anything anymore. At least not to him.

She sighed. "We might come home early."

"Early?" He sucked in a hopeful breath.

"Maybe in a week or so." She paused for a moment when someone called her name. "Look, I should run. But maybe you should cancel your trip, or delay it a week. Afton will be all decked out for the Fourth of July."

Whoopee. Paul blew out a breath. She wasn't coming home; she just didn't want to see him.

"Liz, I want to see you."

"Why? Have you been doing any thinking?"

"Of course." He was thinking almost nonstop about a deal for his biggest client that the Justice Department had pounced on last week. He wasn't exactly sure what Liz wanted him to think about, but he'd thought about her, too. And Jenna. Jenna was easy; he loved her and missed her. Liz? She'd changed so much this summer, he wasn't sure what to think.

"What have you decided?" Liz sounded muffled, unsure, just like she had when she'd first answered her phone.

Did it even matter? "I don't want to lose you guys."

"You'll see us soon. Maybe we could all go home after the Fourth." She hesitated. "Together."

"I guess it's okay to wait until the Fourth." It would actually help his schedule. He could spend more time putting out his clients' biggest fires, then have a relaxing holiday and see some fireworks. "Is Jenna around? Or is she napping?"

"She's down on the beach. We were about to take out the canoe when you called."

Damn it, he'd missed her again. "On the beach? Is she alone?"

"She's fine. Piper and Brandon are down there, and she knows not to go in boats by herself."

"She's five, Liz."

"You haven't seen her lately." Was that his fault? "She follows all the water-safety rules. Wear a life jacket. Don't swim alone. Don't take a boat out until you're—well, older."

"And she's safe?"

"Safer than she'll ever be in Washington."

Somehow, the thought didn't comfort him.

———

SUNDAY NIGHT, Piper looked around the sprawling porch table as dishes clattered, everyone talked at once, David stole a dinner roll off Liz's plate, and Jenna spilled milk on the floor.

Diana patted Piper's hand. "Would you please pass the spaghetti sauce? I'm afraid I missed it when the bowl went by."

She reached past Brandon for the spaghetti sauce, which now held a broccoli spear. Diana didn't bat an eyelash. Across the table, Liz swatted David's hand, blushing as she did. On the other side of Liz, Jenna sat beside Frank, offering to cut his food with a sharp knife that Pete handed her and Liz quickly took away.

No one asked about the wedding. Except for Tracy, no one had all week.

"So, Piper and Brandon." Diana leaned forward to smile at both of them. "Tell us everything. Have you set a date? Is it a spring wedding? Or next summer?"

"Uh, summer." Piper caught Brandon's eye. "This summer."

Conversation screeched to a halt.

Diana's brow wrinkled. "Oh? How soon?"

Brandon cleared his throat. "July twenty-six?"

Diana choked on something, and Piper thumped her back. The woman owned a medical-device company and was getting whacked on the back while she choked to death.

Liz stared at her plate, and Piper couldn't guess her problem, except maybe the fact that Piper had sprung another surprise on her and Liz hated surprises. But she and Brandon had just picked the date this morning, while snuggled in bed, before Brandon slipped back to his own room to avoid pissing off his mom. As if Diana would give a rip. Piper frowned, wondering whether Brandon was thirty-eight or sixteen.

In any case, they'd picked the date for Liz, while she was still here. While Frank was still here, too. To the extent he was.

"So. July twenty-six." Diana dabbed her napkin on the corner of her mouth. "We'll have to get busy."

David winked at Piper. "I've already reserved the beach and picked out my swimsuit."

Liz caught Piper's eye. "So soon?"

"We wanted to do it while you were here." She didn't dare look at Frank, or even Diana.

"Jenna and I might be heading home soon. After the Fourth." She gave Piper an embarrassed smile, ignoring David, who looked stunned. "We'd come back for the wedding, of course, so you don't need to rush it on my account."

Under the table, Piper's hands clenched. She told herself she hadn't mentioned the wedding date to Liz only because the day had slipped by in a blur of waterskiing, volleyball, and a glorious, high-speed cruise up to Stillwater in the speedboat. The truth? She had to pick a bridesmaid and couldn't decide between Liz, her oldest friend, and Tracy, who'd been closer in recent times. But Liz hadn't told her she was leaving. They'd spent the day together on Friday, but recapturing the casual intimacy of their old friendship wasn't always easy.

They needed another boat ride. Or she needed one. Alone.

"What? You guys don't like my beach idea?"

"Shut up, David." Piper, Liz, and Brandon spoke in unison.

Diana frowned. "A wedding at the River would be nice." She smiled at Frank, who struggled to swallow a bite of spaghetti. "But I think we can come up with something better than swimsuits."

"T-shirts?" David held up his arms, shielding himself, as four napkins flew at him. Pete's napkin nailed him in the face.

"Good work, Pete." Piper gave him a thumbs up.

"Speaking of which—" David cleared his throat. "Pete needs a summer job. Does anyone happen to know of a good one?"

"Dad . . ."

"I said I was sorry." David stared intently at Pete as an unspoken understanding passed between them. "And you can invite Nicole over sometime, but you do need a job."

"Why should I be any different from you?"

Open-mouthed, David didn't answer. And Pete stalked out of the house, soon trailed at a slower pace by David.

When Piper had dreamed about planning her wedding, it definitely hadn't been like this.

CHAPTER 13

"Are you really leaving?" Monday morning, Diana poked her head inside the back house, where Liz had hidden all morning.

"I'm not sure. Just considering it." Liz closed the game of Spider Solitaire that had helped her avoid her memoir for the last half hour. "Nothing is working out the way I hoped."

"Nothing ever does." Diana dragged a chair next to Liz and sat down. "What's wrong?"

Nothing she wanted to tell the mother of the man she'd kissed this weekend. A man she couldn't have. Ever.

"Is it David?"

Liz's gaze flew to Diana's face. "What?"

"It doesn't take a rocket scientist to see what's wrong." Diana pointed at Liz's laptop. "I'm proud of you for writing a novel, but I suspect you're using it as an excuse to avoid David and your father. I so hoped you could patch things up with both of them this summer."

The so-called novel didn't exist—something else she couldn't admit to Diana—but the thought of talking to David or Dad was even more overwhelming. Liz shook her head, feeling hopeless. "Easier said than done."

"True, but it would be worth it." Diana took Liz's hand. "In any case, I need your help, and I'm hoping you'll stick it out for the summer. I have a project."

She'd already painted the entire second floor of the big house and half the first floor, and no one noticed. Except her.

"Can't David do it? He practically lives here. Or Brandon and Piper. They're—"

She couldn't say it. Dad bought the house with Mom's money, even her life, and he'd moved on. Liz could knock down every wall and rebuild the house from scratch, and it would still belong to Diana. David and Brandon. Soon, Piper.

But not Liz. The thought pierced her, but she loved Diana too much to say it.

"They're getting married. But isn't that wonderful?" Diana peered into Liz's eyes. "A month is too soon for my taste, but I know why they're doing it. For you, and also for Frank. The trouble is, I'm not sure how much Frank will understand or appreciate."

Twisting her hands in her lap, Diana sighed.

So did Liz. "What do you want me to do? Replaster the bathroom? Change a lightbulb?"

Diana smiled with watery eyes. "You've done enough on the house already. I can get someone else for that."

Someone who'd own the house someday. Liz's face fell.

"Fine. Change a lightbulb or two. Go wild." Diana tilted her head, studying Liz. "But that's not the project I have in mind. This one is right up your alley."

Liz groaned. "Maybe I should hide."

"No, that's my job." Diana reached for a blank notepad next to the laptop, found a pen, and started a list. As always. "If I stay busy, maybe I won't think about it too much."

Looking upside-down at the notepad, Liz tried to see what Diana was writing. "So what's the project?"

Diana set down the pen. "David doesn't want to stay with the company. I hate to say it, but I think our only option is to sell it."

"DOES SHE HAVE TO TAG ALONG?" Pete jerked his head at Jenna, who fumbled with the buckles on her life jacket.

Frowning, David touched a finger to his lips. "She's five. Not deaf."

"Ready!" One buckle fastened, one not, Jenna climbed into the speedboat. "Can I drive, David?"

"I'm driving, squirt." Pete slid into the driver's seat.

Jenna stopped at David's side, grabbing the bottom edge of his T-shirt with one hand. Staring at Pete, she sucked the thumb of her other hand—something she rarely did.

"You can drive on the way back, Jenn." He patted her shoulder. "We're just giving Pete a ride to the marina."

"What's he gonna do?"

"Get a job."

Scowling, Pete revved the engine.

"It's a no-wake zone, last time I checked." David took the passenger seat next to Pete and settled Jenna on his lap.

"Yeah? We could move the white buoys at midnight, like you used to do." Pete ran a hand through his hair, sending the spikes higher.

David cringed, remembering only too well all the pranks he and Brandon—and sometimes Liz and her friends—used to do, like moving the no-wake-zone buoys to expand their waterskiing territory. "Where'd you hear that?"

"Mom." Pete shot David a sly look. "She told me a lot of stuff."

His gut clenched as images of what he and Suzy used to

do flooded back. His stupid hormones had led to marriage too young to the wrong woman. "I have higher hopes for you."

Pete's knee bobbed up and down. Nervously? "What about you, Dad? All you do is ski and hike. And hang out with Liz and Brandon. And the kid."

The kid—Jenna—whipped her head in Pete's direction, nailing David in the jaw.

He had a feeling Pete wanted to do the same thing. "Hey, you forgot swimming and canoeing. And sometimes tennis."

"Funny. Don't you work?"

"Yes." But his CEO ran Carruthers Medical better than David could in his wildest dreams. "But I might be leaving the company."

If he wanted Pete to be honest, he had to set an example by discussing things. Life. Dreams. Fears. Realities. Truth.

He wouldn't mention Liz.

David bounced Jenna on his lap as they neared the marina. "I'm not happy, Pete. Not that life has to be fun and games—"

"It is for you." Ever defiant, Pete glared out across the water.

"No, it's not. You need to work, and so do I. It's not the money. It's doing something you feel good about."

"I don't get it." When Pete turned to David, frowning, he almost didn't see a cruiser heading straight at them.

"Pete!"

"I got it." With a sharp turn and more gas than the no-wake zone permitted, he missed the cruiser. Slowing again, Pete coasted to a smooth landing at the gas dock. "We're here."

Thank God. He'd rather trust Jenna behind the wheel. "Need any help?"

"Naa." Hopping out, Pete pushed the boat off the dock,

and David leaped to grab the steering wheel. "The guys at the marina are cool." Pete stared down at his orange Converse Chucks. "Thanks, uh, for getting me the job."

"Anything for you, kid."

With a wave, David settled Jenna behind the wheel and headed back across the River to the summer house. He wondered how much Jenna had picked up from his tense talk with Pete. Or if Pete had picked up anything.

"I DON'T KNOW what to do, Brandon."

"Simple. Ask them both."

Piper sighed into the phone as she pondered the dilemma.

"You just have David. I can't have two."

Brandon chuckled. "Okay, pick Tracy. I'll pick Liz."

Piper played with the photo of Brandon on her desk. "Smart. David would give an indecent toast."

"He will anyway. By the way, I think Mom's right. I hadn't thought about doing the wedding at the River, but—"

"I agree."

"You do?" He didn't know she'd always wanted a wedding at the River, and she could use the brownie points. "Really? You're the best."

"Isn't that why you're marrying me?"

"Nope, it's the sex. Sorry."

"Forgiven." She fiddled with her top button. Remembering exactly what she'd been doing with Brandon just a few short hours ago in bed, her office started to feel a little warm. "But help me. I need solutions."

Tracy walked in with a stack of files. "Pick Liz."

Piper covered the phone's mouthpiece. "Excuse me?"

"Pick Liz." Tracy smiled as she set the stack on Piper's desk. "Liz. Your best friend."

Piper put the phone back to her ear. "Brandon? Gotta run."

"No prob. Let me know what you decide. Love you."

"Love you more." Hanging up, she frowned. "First, how do you know what we were talking about? Or who I was talking to?"

"Whenever you talk to Brandon, you get this dreamy look that you don't get with clients." She winked at Piper. "Been there."

"Doing that."

Tracy blushed. "And you said Brandon asked David. I figured out the rest."

"I'm not sure if I should give you a raise—or fire you." Piper grabbed the top file on her desk and groaned. "Shoot. I can't fire you. I'd have to fix this all by myself."

"Then I guess it's a raise." Tracy leaned over Piper's desk and pulled out the second file, then flipped through the pages. "Good timing. I'll need more cash for that wedding gift I spotted."

Piper jotted a note in the file. "I don't need gifts."

"But pick Liz, really. You two have been best friends since forever." When Piper started to object, Tracy waved it away. "We're all friends, and I love you both, but everyone has a best friend."

"I think mine might be Brandon now."

Tracy grinned. "Unless he's doing double-duty, that doesn't help your bridesmaid decision."

Brandon in pink taffeta. Nice. "But you're—"

"—happy not to be in another wedding. No offense, but I've worn enough butt-ugly bridesmaid dresses for one lifetime." As Tracy scrunched her nose, they both laughed.

"That's not my point. Everything is going well for me right now, but Liz seems to be struggling."

"The summer isn't what she'd expected."

"So do it for her." Tracy snapped her finger. "Consider it my wedding present."

"Nice try. Get shopping." Piper laughed as she picked up the phone. "But I'm not sure we'll be doing Liz a favor. After all, David is best man."

"You're kidding. Sell the company?" Liz stared at Diana in horrified amazement.

"I rarely joke, dear, about something so important."

As Diana started to jot another note on her list, Liz snatched the pen and set it on the desk. "Enough lists. Why do you want to sell the company?"

"Want to?" A cloud darkened Diana's face. "I don't. In fact, the timing is poor, because we'd need to suspend some pending acquisitions. I just don't see any alternative."

"Why not? David said he picked a great CEO."

Diana tapped her freshly manicured nails on the desk. A recent gift to her from David. "Theo Bennett is wonderful. A good man, a good executive with vision, and he knows medical devices. But—"

"He sounds perfect."

"He's not family. It's a family business, Liz. George started it." She ran a hand through her hair. "I managed to hang on to it after he died—"

"Hang on? You built it far beyond what he'd done."

Diana pursed her lips. "With the help of a few good people, including your father."

Liz stared down at a floor that needed to be swept as she

tried not to think about Dad. She swallowed past a lump in her throat. Yes, she owned stock in Carruthers Medical, but she'd never paid much attention to the business. It would've only made her feel like even more of an outsider in her so-called family.

Even sharp-eyed Diana obviously didn't have a clue how Liz felt. She just ticked off names on her fingers. "David started right out of college, although he's moved in and out over the years. And Brandon has been with us since med school. He's a wonderful scientist, but he's not interested in business."

"Have you asked?"

"Yes and no. I've broached the topic, but I didn't want to push. I'm told I can be formidable, and I want Brandon to be happy."

"How happy will he be when you sell the company?"

Diana tilted her head. "Now that you ask, I'm not sure. I'm not particularly happy myself. But I have Frank to think of, and my own health, and—"

"You're the healthiest person I know."

"I'm sixty-five. I retired, Liz, and I wanted to have a comfortable retirement. We may not have Frank much longer—" She gazed out the door for a long moment. "But I don't want to keep running the company. I'm tired."

For the first time, Liz noticed the lines on Diana's face, the slump of shoulders she'd always held straight, the pallor of her skin. Impulsively, Liz grabbed her hand.

"I'm here, Diana. What do you need?"

"You." Diana laughed. "Well, it's a big company. I was thinking your investment-banking firm."

Liz swallowed hard. "My firm?"

"Isn't it one of the best?"

"Sure." She glanced at her laptop, tempted to send David an email asking for help. A weird impulse. "It's just—"

Diana laughed. "Don't worry. We can afford their fees."

"But I—"

"I understand." Diana waved a hand. "If you don't feel comfortable working on the sale, you can choose other people to do it."

"I guess it's settled, then." Liz couldn't bear to look at Diana, who hadn't even considered asking her to join the family business. Even when Diana needed investment-banking expertise, she didn't want Liz: she just wanted her firm. The lump in her throat became a boulder, and she pushed back her chair and headed for the door. No wonder she'd spent her life preparing for worst-case scenarios. She *lived* them. "I'll give you names and phone numbers."

"Liz?" Diana rose to follow. "I'm sorry. I suppose this is upsetting to all of us."

Liz glanced over her shoulder at Diana. "You have no idea."

———

DIANA RAN a finger down her to-do list, which she'd left yesterday in the back house—and which, when she'd gone back to retrieve it, had somehow landed in the wastebasket.

She'd called Brandon last night, hinted at the idea, and gotten no reaction. Strange. Perhaps she'd been too vague—but she'd been direct with Liz, and that hadn't gone well. Liz and Jenna had disappeared in a boat in mid-afternoon, not returning until past Jenna's usual bedtime.

Diana had also mentioned it to Frank, who nodded absently and probably forgot the conversation within minutes.

That left David.

She walked the thirty yards from her house to his.

"David?" She knocked, peered through the screen door, and cautiously grasped the knob. Suzy wasn't here to object to her intrusion, but there was nothing wrong with wanting privacy. She only wished *she* ever got any. "Hello? Are you here?"

"C'mon in." His hair damp and tousled from a recent shower or swim, David strolled upstairs from the lower level.

Walking over to Suzy's flowered chairs on the porch, he cleared them of a few days' newspapers. "Have a seat, Madam Chairman."

"Too late. I lost that title." She eyed the chairs, brushed a small mound of sand off of one, then decided to keep standing.

"That's not what I hear." Moving to the floor-to-ceiling windows overlooking the River, David gazed out, his back to Diana.

"Liz?" Diana bit her lip, irritated with herself for not talking to David first. He was Chairman, after all.

He shook his head. "Try again. Brandon."

"Brandon?"

"Your other son. The one who actually works at Carruthers Medical. The useful one." Something flashed in David's eyes.

She paced the porch, considering. Perhaps it really *had* been time for her to step down. Not just for her, but for the company. If her own kids were upset, getting the approval of her company's Board and shareholders might be beyond her. She paused in the middle of the porch. "What did Brandon think? He didn't tell me."

David leaned back in his chair. "He doesn't want to run the company, but you didn't ask him. Did you ask Liz?"

"To run the company?"

The thought had never occurred to her. Liz lived in Washington, D.C. She had an excellent position in a good firm and had never been involved with the family business. She . . . wasn't one of Diana's sons.

"I'll take that as a no." David brushed past her on his way to the kitchen.

"I never—"

"Don't even say it." David whistled. "Want anything to drink?"

Numb, she shook her head.

"Sure? You might need it."

She followed him into the kitchen, where he poured a glass of some nasty chardonnay and handed it to her, then poured one for himself. He raised it in a toast. "To Diana Carruthers-Tanner. A brilliant woman and, most days, a great mom. Who just fucked up royally."

"David!"

He downed his entire glass in a single gulp and wiped his mouth with the back of his hand. "You're right about Suzy's wine. It sucks. So do the chairs on the porch, don't they?"

Her head spun. "I never—"

"Yeah, I think so, too." David propped himself on a stool at the kitchen counter.

Shaken, Diana turned to leave.

"Mom. Stop." David tapped a spoon on the edge of his empty wine glass, making it ring. He poured himself another glass.

"How much of that have you had?"

He shrugged. "This will be my second glass, since the first one went down so well."

"Because of me?"

"Because of life." He took a sip of wine, more controlled

this time. "I'm not angry—okay, maybe I am—but I'm still Chairman. Remember? You asked me not to leave. So here I am. Running the company."

"And you don't need my help."

"No offense, but you're not helping. You're taking over. And for once in your life, you're not doing a particularly good job."

She flinched. "I'm trying."

"Let's start over. What did you tell Liz?"

She relayed their conversation, ending with asking Liz's help in selling Carruthers Medical.

David rolled his eyes. "You didn't even ask her to help. You asked her to have someone else at her investment-banking firm help. Jesus."

"I didn't want to force Liz into anything."

"Mom . . ."

She held up a hand. "You're right. I never thought about involving Liz. She's been gone so long. I don't—"

"—think of her much at all."

"That's not true." She'd thought of Liz all summer. Every time Liz started another repair project the house didn't need, avoided her father, argued with David.

But Diana was beginning to understand why someone would argue with David.

He shook his head. "I'm not going to fight with you."

"Since when?"

"Now." He grabbed her by the elbow as he headed for the front door. "But if we're really going to consider selling the company, I want everyone involved. Starting with Liz."

She looked sideways at him. "Liz?"

"Yeah." Outside, he jammed his hands in his pockets and started down the steps. "Brandon may invent the fancy gizmos, and I can talk fast, but Liz is the brains of the operation. It's time you figured that out."

Reaching for his arm, she discovered a new appreciation for the instincts of the man she'd named Chairman.

SOME DRUNKEN ASSHOLE had just plugged the jukebox with several quarters' worth of Michael Jackson, prompting David to cover his ears. "Who the hell picked Pendulum?"

Brandon and Liz both pointed at Piper.

"Great place, huh?" Piper tapped her fingers to the ear-splitting beat. "Nothing like these fries!"

Liz dangled a few wilting fries from her fingers. "Greasy but true."

Brandon waved at the waitress, a punk-rock wannabe with a nose ring that didn't look comfortable, and ordered three more beers and a lemonade for Liz. As the waitress left, a tall, good-looking guy stopped by, and Liz and Piper waved at him.

Both of them looked way too pleased to see him.

He winked at both women. "I can't believe the people we let in here. But I guess it's a slow night."

Startled, Brandon glanced up, then leaped to his feet and shook the guy's hand. "Jake! Piper told me you owned this place. Nice."

"Thanks. It's going well." The guy nodded a hello to Piper, then looked curiously at Liz. "Liz Tanner? Wow, I thought you lived on the East coast somewhere. Nice to see you again. It's been too long."

Liz didn't have to blush like that. "Washington, D.C., but I'm here for the summer."

Still standing, Brandon glanced at David. "This is Jake

Trevor. We played football together at Southwest, but he was a year behind me. He graduated with the girls. Jake, this is my brother, David. He was four years ahead of you."

Liz might've stabbed David with a fork if he called her a girl, but she ignored Brandon's introduction and gave Jake an insipid smile. Okay, Liz was never insipid. But she didn't have to smile at the guy like that.

A minor skirmish broke out near the jukebox—probably started by someone who actually had decent taste in music— and Jake glanced from the jukebox to their table. "Gotta run, but I hope you'll stop back sometime when I can talk." He playfully punched Brandon in the shoulder. "The girls, at least."

David rolled his eyes as Jake hurried away.

Grabbing Piper's hand, Brandon leaned across the table, looking first at David, then Liz. "You guys are probably wondering why we asked you out tonight."

"So I could watch Piper and Liz bat their eyelashes at some random guy?" David laughed at his own joke, but no one else did. Liz slapped his hand. Their first physical contact since Saturday's kiss. His head buzzed, maybe from the first beer.

Piper turned to Brandon. "I can't believe you wanted this moron to be your best man."

He shrugged. "The first ten guys I asked were busy."

"Hey, don't worry. I've already thought up my toast."

The other three groaned.

"But seriously—" Piper, practically bouncing on her chair, leaned toward Liz. "We also wanted to ask you to be my maid of honor. Matron of honor. Best woman. Whatever." Piper stumbled over the words as she touched Liz's arm. "Would you?"

Liz had the funny little crease in her forehead that she

got on the rare occasions when something confused her. A moment later, she nodded without speaking, and David almost thought her eyes glistened. With tears?

"Then it's settled." Piper picked up Brandon's hand for the fortieth time since they'd arrived.

Brandon grinned like a man who'd just been crowned king of whatever. "We're gonna keep it small. Just the four of us in the wedding party, and not a lot of guests."

Piper cut in. "Forty or fifty, tops. We'll have it at the River, on the beach if it's a nice day."

Liz sat quietly, her burger and lemonade untouched. As David watched, Piper glanced worriedly at her a few times.

"What'll we wear? Tuxes and bare feet?" David tried to imagine a wedding at the River. Suzy would die. For their own wedding, she'd insisted on the biggest church and country club they could find. David had hated it.

Brandon shook his head. "We haven't figured out all the details yet, but it'll be pretty simple."

Piper turned to Liz. "What do you think?"

"It sounds nice." Her gaze met Piper's, offering a faint smile before she looked down at her lap. "Whatever you want me to wear is fine."

Piper exchanged a worried frown with Brandon, then pulled her chair closer to Liz. "What's the matter? Is it the beach wedding? We're doing it because of your dad—"

Liz wrapped her arms around herself. "It's not that. I just—"

Understanding dawned on Piper's face, and she gave Liz a quick hug. "I understand completely."

That made two of them. David caught Brandon's eye, and neither one had a clue. "I'll drink to that." David lifted his beer to his lips. "Whatever it is."

Turning to him, Liz sniffed. "You wouldn't get it."

"Try me."

Glancing over at the jukebox—which still cranked out Michael Jackson, although Jake was no longer in sight—Liz bit her lip. "It sounds silly, I know, but Piper and Tracy and I used to spend hours in our teens, late at night, planning our weddings. I always wanted to get married on the beach. To... the man of my dreams."

Piper nodded, and now only Brandon looked confused.

Feeling something burn inside of him, David took a long swig from his second bottle of Fat Tire. "It's never too late."

"It's not?" Brandon looked around the table. "What am I missing? Liz is already married."

Piper patted him on the arm. "I'll explain later. Maybe on our fortieth wedding anniversary."

David ransacked his brain for a different topic. "Should we talk about Mom wanting to sell the company?"

"Let's not." Brandon made a slashing motion. "Piper wanted to talk about the wedding. It's a month from tomorrow."

"Don't you want to talk about it, too? Is it only my wedding?" Frowning, Piper set down her bottle of Lonely Blonde.

David rubbed his hands together. "Oh, boy. A lovers' quarrel, and they're not even married yet."

Piper and Liz slapped him at the same moment. He grinned. "Even better—women attacking me!"

"You wish." Liz eyed him. "Watch it, or I'll pick out more Michael Jackson tunes. Anyone got a quarter?"

He put his hand over his heart. "Anything but that."

"Don't worry, you big baby. You're safe with me."

His heart felt anything but.

"Are you sure you're okay?"

Liz watched David miss a step as they reached the parking lot and his light-blue convertible. She was exhausted and would rather not drive. But she'd lost count after his first four beers, and *he* wasn't driving. No matter how much he argued.

He fished his keys from his pocket and dangled them in front of her. "Could you drive?"

As her jaw dropped, he opened the driver's door and held it for her. She slid past him and into the seat. A minute later, she headed out of downtown Minneapolis, aiming for Highway 94 and the River. She pulled into the marina half an hour later and stifled a yawn. Ten-thirty.

"You're tired?" David stretched his arms over his head. "It's a beautiful night. Perfect for a boat ride."

Liz walked toward their slip. "Way beyond tired." She also didn't need a moonlit cruise with a man who tempted her the way he did. She might not survive it.

"It's just a boat ride." David caught up with her and grabbed her hand. "Nothing more."

She yanked her hand away. "I can't do this, David." She pointed from him to her. "You. Me. The whole thing."

When they reached the slip, she brushed past him and climbed into the stern. Shrugging, he jumped into the bow, popped the cover on his hiding place for boat keys, and handed the key to her. She turned on the boat's lights, then backed out of the slip and chugged quietly through the no-wake zone, peering across the black water toward the other side of the River.

In the middle of the River, the boat's engine quit.

"What the—"

"Looking for this?" David dangled the key and a grin in front of her.

She snatched the key out of his hand. "What are you doing?"

"Trying to find some time alone with you. Time to talk."

"Right." With no boats in view, she put the key back in the ignition but didn't turn it. "You want to talk."

"I'd like to kiss you, too, but I didn't see that as an option."

"Smart man."

"Thanks." David leaned toward her, touching her thigh. "So. Wanna talk?"

She removed his hand. "Here? On a pitch-black night in the middle of the River—where I might not see another boat until it hits me?" She looked sideways at him as she fingered the key, debating whether to start the engine. "What is it you really want? More kisses? More . . . I don't know what? You're married, David. So am I."

He looked out over the bow, all traces of the beer he'd drunk suddenly gone. "Neither of us happily."

"Wait. Since when aren't you happy?" It'd been David-and-Suzy, almost as one word, as long as she could remember. The happy couple.

A horn blared, and they both jumped. David recovered first, turning the key in the ignition. Liz pushed down the throttle, zooming out of the way of a houseboat that appeared out of nowhere, and headed up the River. Past their beach houses.

When she reached the cove, she idled the boat again.

Standing up, David leaned against the engine cover behind Liz. "I don't know how long it's been. Five years? Ten? Suzy and I got married so young, and we never dated anyone else."

"No kidding."

"Look, it's not an excuse. And you're right—I'm not sure what I want. I do like you." He laughed. "Even when you torture me on hikes or make me bust a gut catching up with you. And, yeah, I'm attracted. But I don't really know you; Brandon knows you a helluva lot better than I do. Truth is, I don't even know myself at the moment."

Not exactly the bold declaration of love she'd always dreamed of.

And of course it couldn't be, definitely not now, even if they did get to know each other. They'd wasted so much time this summer playing hide-and-seek, and not just with Jenna.

"We both know that's not enough." Even if she weren't married, if he weren't married, it wouldn't be. "I have to think of Jenna and Paul, but I also don't know what I want right now any more than you do. It's crazy. It wouldn't exactly thrill Diana."

"Your dad wouldn't say anything." He grinned impishly.

Her lips twitched at his pathetic humor. "I'm serious."

"So am I, believe it or not." Bending down, he whispered in her ear. "Could I kiss you? Please?"

A quick shake of her head. "I can't. And you shouldn't, either."

He cupped her face in his hands, took a long look, and leaned closer. An inch from her face, he stopped. "Please?"

Sighing, she gazed out over the water, hating this. All of it. The realities of her life, the years she'd stupidly spent waiting for Paul, the unbelievable family battles she and David would face if this insanity went any further. So many dreams that had already died. So many regrets.

And David was right: they hardly even knew each other.

A minute later—or five minutes; she had no idea—she met his lips as if she'd known him forever. Loved him forever. A shudder raced through her as they kissed, touching each other with tentative hands that stopped short of going too far.

She caught his hands when they slipped under her shirt,

remembering with an embarrassed flush what she'd let him do last Saturday, but she heard her own shallow breathing and knew she'd worn a sheer lace bra tonight for a reason. As David tried to tempt her into a forbidden replay, her body ached with longing.

But her brain gave her a good hard slap.

She kissed him one last time, savoring the taste of him, before pulling away and restarting the boat. They'd gone far enough. Way too many steps toward hell.

CHAPTER 14

"What's the matter, Jenna?"

As she rocked on the porch Thursday afternoon, Diana glanced up from her beach book—the one pleasure that Frank's endless naps afforded her—and smiled at Jenna. The child wasn't nearly as riveted by *The Cat in the Hat*, since she tossed it on the floor.

"Nobody wants to play with me." Jenna's lower lip quivered. "I'm bored."

"You're too young to be bored, darling." Diana held out her arms, and Jenna climbed onto her lap. "Is your mom in the back house?"

"She's with David."

"Well, they can't be hiking. It's too hot." On a ninety-degree day with no clouds or breeze, even David didn't exercise. "Are they on the beach? Swimming? Waterskiing?"

"Dunno." Jenna curled up against Diana.

"Do you want me to help find them?" She ground her teeth, wishing she didn't have to go look for Liz. Talk about bad timing. The heroine of her book had just gotten locked in a closet with a homicidal sex maniac. "I'll bet they're on the beach."

"I don't wanna find them. I don't like David."

Diana laughed. "What did he do? Should I spank him?"

Jenna's eyes widened at the exact moment Diana realized what she'd said—and shouldn't have said, even in jest.

"Would you, Gram? Spank him?"

"No, dear." She hugged Jenna, then lifted her off her lap, and they both headed outside. "I'm just teasing."

"I want my daddy. I wanna go home."

Diana's eyebrows rose. "Don't you like the River?"

Jenna reached for the railing, heading down the steps to the beach without taking Diana's hand. A first? "Uh-huh. But I miss Daddy, an' David doesn't like me."

Diana caught up to Jenna, then bent down and looked her in the eye. "Of course you miss your daddy. He's coming to see you next weekend for the Fourth of July. But David loves you, too. He loves playing with you."

"He's not my daddy."

"Of course not, dear. But he's your friend."

And uncle, loosely speaking. Diana frowned. Liz must be writing, or fixing yet another room that didn't need fixing, and David must be ignoring Jenna. Or Jenna really missed Paul.

She'd speak to David and Liz. Two more items for her to-do list.

"Suzy."

"David." Suzy stepped onto the dock promptly at eight o'clock Friday evening, a small purse slung over her shoulder but no other bags in sight. "Is that how you greet your wife after she's been gone two weeks?"

"Twelve days." David waited in the driver's seat, not

bothering to get up to help Suzy into the speedboat, but he silently berated himself for his answer. But what was he supposed to say? That he wished she'd leave for another two weeks? "You never called."

"I called several times." She dropped her purse onto the back seat and shouted for Billy, who hadn't yet appeared. "At least twice, and you didn't answer. You could've called me back. Too busy carousing, no doubt."

She looked tanned, rested, and loaded for bear.

She also hadn't called once, let alone twice. At least he'd texted her when Pete got the job at the marina. He'd also called Billy on his brand-new cell phone a few times.

"Right. Carousing." He pressed a hand against his gut. Telling Suzy what he wanted—when he wasn't even sure himself—would be a nightmare. Life-threatening, if he knew Suzy.

Billy appeared at the top of the steps down to the slips, dragging his bags and Suzy's. David sprang out of the boat to help him.

"Billy!" Heedless of his son's cargo, he wrapped Billy in a bear hug. "No fair going away so long, kid. I missed you."

"Yeah." Billy pulled away, looking embarrassed. "You, too, Dad."

"Well? How'd it go?" He ran a hand through Billy's shaggy hair, hoping he hadn't bombed out too early or too badly.

"I, uh, won. Like, first place."

"What?" He picked up Billy in another hug, swinging him around in the air. All of the bags went flying. "I can't believe it!"

"Dad!" Back on his feet, Billy brushed himself off. "That is, like, so not cool."

David ruffled his hair, earning a swat. "You sound like Pete. What did they teach you at that tennis camp?"

"The usual. Forehand, backhand, how to pick up girls." Billy gave a sly grin. Eleven years old. Had David talked that way? Probably not until twelve.

"You'll have to give me pointers." He picked up two of the bags with one hand and wrapped his other arm around Billy's shoulder. "C'mon, sport. Your mom's waiting."

They reached the boat, where Suzy perched in the passenger seat, gritting her teeth. "You didn't hug *me* like that."

"You didn't win a tennis tournament this week." David stepped onto the driver's seat and winked at Billy.

"Cute. So what's new? Has Liz left yet?"

He expected it every moment. He'd spent most of yesterday trying to change her mind. Not to mention trying to get her alone, in his arms—even if just for a hug.

He'd gotten one button unfastened. On his own shirt.

"She's here for the summer." David backed out of the slip and inched through the marina's still waters. "She's been working hard on the big house. The back house finally looks inhabited, and she's even cleaned up the basement."

Suzy pursed her lips to reapply her lipstick. Unevenly, which was unusual for her. "I'm not surprised. When Frank dies, she'll try to boot Diana out of the house. Just wait."

Jolted, David looked back at Billy before frowning at Suzy.

She flipped a hand through her hair. "Billy might as well know. He's old enough. Liz has her own agenda."

David caught Billy's wide-eyed gaze. "She's kidding, Billy. Don't pay any attention."

"Mom says it a lot, Dad. I don't think she likes Liz."

"Well, I do, and so does everyone else. Liz is part of our

family, ever since her dad married Gram. Your mom's just, you know, probably tired." And pissed and jealous and, unfortunately, right on the mark about Liz's crush on him. Thank God she didn't know about his own crush. He hoped.

Billy nodded and stood up. "Can I drive?"

"You bet, sport." David stepped aside as Billy slid past him into the driver's seat. "Try not to hit any cruisers. Aim for something smaller."

"Funny." As Billy grinned, the boat lurched forward.

Suzy flew back against her seat. "Is this safe?"

This summer, nothing was.

A HAND CARESSED Liz's shoulder in the middle of an extremely vivid dream about David. Skin against skin, the pad of his thumb brushing oh-so-close to her breast . . .

"Up and at 'em."

David. Here. In her bedroom. Sitting on the edge of her bed, his hip pressed against hers. His thumb *was* brushing close to her breast. She sucked in a breath, panicking, as her gaze shot past him.

He'd closed the door.

She let go of the breath and arched her back, wanting him and too sleepy to say no.

"Shhh." He touched a finger to her lips, then leaned down and pressed light kisses on her forehead. His left hand slid under her camisole and closed around her breast.

Oh. My. God.

"Sorry." His lips moved to her ear. "Not sorry. I've wanted to do that for a week. Probably more like a month." Still close, he nibbled her ear. "I'd like to do more."

"You'd be good at it." Her voice sounded too husky, and

she didn't want to give him the wrong impression. As if she wanted him or something. Which she did. "What time is it?"

"Six."

His hand moved to her other breast, drawing a whimper as she wriggled. "Ohhh."

"Ohhh, it's six? Or ohhh, you like that?"

Smiling, she closed her eyes. "Just ohhh."

"Good." His hand moved to her waist. "Sounds like you're ready to hike."

Her eyes flew open, and he grinned. "Just wanted to make sure you were awake."

"I'm awake, all right." Her nipples were standing at attention, and she'd started tingling below the waist. "I'm—"

The doorknob rattled, and David's hand flew off her an instant before Jenna's sleepy head poked inside. "Mom?"

Rising to one elbow, Liz glanced down at her camisole. In place. Whew. "Right here, sweetie. David was just waking me up for a hike."

Jenna frowned at David. "Did you sleep in my mom's bed?"

He shot off the bed and ambled toward the door. "Nope. I have my own house, remember? I just wanted your mom to go hiking with me." Bending down, he winked at Jenna. "She's tough to wake up."

Jenna nodded soberly, then turned to Liz. "Can I hike, too?"

"It's a tough climb, sweetie." Liz tugged the sheet up to her neck. "I'm not sure you'd really want to."

Jenna's head drooped. "You never wanna hike with me. I even got up early. You like David better 'n me."

"Never in a million years." Liz shot David a helpless look. "It's just—"

"It's a beautiful morning for a hike. C'mon, kid. Let's get

you dressed while we wait for your mom." He grabbed Jenna by the hand and led her out of the room. "I'll bet you're faster than she is."

The door clicked shut, and Liz sank back into her pillow. Her resolve not to do anything more with David needed a swift kick in the pants. Leave it to a five-year-old to deliver it.

"SUZY? BILLY? ANYBODY HERE?"

Wet from an unexpected plunge into the River after Jenna tumbled into it from the boat, David dripped onto the porch around lunchtime Saturday and debated whether to dry off before trekking downstairs for dry clothes.

Suzy appeared from around a corner, glaring. "Finally decided to grace us with your presence? When did you slip out this morning?" Her gaze narrowed. "Or was it sometime during the night?"

He kept his face blank. "Six. I usually hike early. Then Brandon showed up, and we waterskied." With Liz, Piper, Jenna—and Pete, until he had to leave for work. "Where's Billy?"

"Playing tennis. I couldn't find you, so Diana had to give him a ride across at nine."

Suzy probably hadn't bothered looking for him, and now he'd have to make it up to Mom. Damn. He blew out an exasperated breath. "You need to learn how to drive a boat, Suz." It'd only been twenty-five years. "But why's Billy playing tennis? Isn't he sick of it?"

"No more than you are of waterskiing." She walked stiffly into the kitchen, obviously expecting him to follow. "But you've been skiing all this time?" She pointed at the clock on the stove. "It's almost twelve-thirty."

They'd stopped at ten, when the cruisers started running up and down the River, creating wakes they didn't want to jump.

"We quit a while ago." He opened the fridge and leaned down for an early beer. "Then we swam, jumped on the trampoline down at the Lees' house, hung out. Talked about the wedding."

"Like you ever gave a rip about a wedding."

"I'm in it." He downed a third of the bottle in one gulp. "It's coming up. July twenty-six."

"Piper must be pregnant." Suzy's mouth twisted. "Poor Diana."

What the hell? "Piper's not pregnant. They're getting married so soon, here at the River, because of Frank." And maybe for Liz, too, but he didn't mention that.

With jerky hands, Suzy rearranged the papers on the counter. "Still, it looks trashy."

"I hope you're talking about those papers." Toting his bottle, David headed for the stairs. "Piper is one of the last people I'd ever call trashy. Or were you including Brandon, too? Or my mom?" He snorted. "I'm getting tired of all this shit. Tired of a lot of things."

"Oh? And what are you going to do? Make me stop?"

She followed him, breathing hard right behind him. At the bottom of the stairs, he whirled. "No. If you want to look horrible in front of everyone, go for it. I just don't want—" He sucked in a breath and blurted out the words he needed to say. "I don't want to be married to someone like that."

"What?" She stumbled, and he grabbed her arm.

"It's time we talked. About everything."

Her eyes narrowed. "Is this about Liz?"

He shook his head but mentally thanked Liz for the wake-up call he'd needed for too many years. For the courage she'd unknowingly given him. Even so, it wasn't about Liz. "It's about you and me."

"What's the matter, Jenn?" Liz bent down to help Jenna out of her wetsuit. "Did you want to ski again?"

A quick head shake. Jenna's legs must be rubber after their hike, several waterski runs, swimming, and a half hour on the water trampoline, but it didn't mean she'd admit it.

"Do you want to take a nap?"

A fierce head shake.

"Go for a paddle in a kayak or canoe?"

Jenna looked past Liz to the canoe, hauled up on the beach. The two-person kayak was right next to it. "Is David gonna go?"

"He's not here." Liz glanced up at David's house. She hadn't seen him since lunch. "Maybe he's napping."

Diana, who'd joined them on the beach after getting Dad settled for his afternoon nap, looked up from her book.

Jenna wriggled in Liz's arms as she tugged on the wetsuit. "Is he napping in your bed?"

Eyes wide and avoiding Diana's too-sharp gaze, Liz laughed. "Of course not. He's probably at his own house."

"He was in your bed this morning."

Hearing Diana's book snap shut, Liz blew out a breath. "No, he wasn't. He has his own bed in his own house. He just came over to wake me up to go hiking, like he always does."

"You didn't want me to go."

"But I let you, didn't I?" Jenna's wetsuit got stuck at her knees, and Liz peeled it the rest of the way. "I thought you might not be able to hike that far. It's a steep climb even for grown-ups. Just ask Brandon." Carrying the wetsuit to the edge of the beach, she rinsed it in the water. "But David thought you could do it, and you did a great job."

Jenna stubbed her toe in the sand.

"I was proud of you." Even more proud of David. He'd carried Jenna halfway up the hill.

"He's always around."

"Who? David?" Out of the corner of her eye, Liz caught Diana listening in total absorption. "He lives here, Jenn. Just like Gram and Pete and Billy." And Dad and Suzy. "Of course he's around."

"But I want Daddy."

"Jenna?" Diana waved her over. "I left my favorite hat upstairs. The straw one on the glider. Could you get it?"

"Sure, Gram." Jenna took off at a run.

Diana waited until Jenna was halfway up the steps, then motioned to Liz. Liz trudged closer, picturing a guillotine in her future.

"I had the same conversation the other day with Jenna." Diana patted the arm of the chair next to her. "About Paul. Not about—" She coughed into her hand. "David being in your bed."

Flushing, Liz sat down. "He was *not* in my bed. He was waking me up, and I was dead asleep. You know he likes to hike at the crack of dawn."

Diana smiled. "He likes to hike with *you* at the crack of dawn, certainly."

"What are you saying?"

"Nothing, dear." Diana picked up her book but didn't open it. "Jenna misses her dad. It's understandable."

Jenna spent a lot of time missing Paul, and not just at the River.

"You haven't said much about Paul, but I've caught snippets of your phone conversations." Diana took a sip from the tall glass at her elbow. "Anything you care to share? Or is that what you do with David?"

"I— He's—" An explanation she couldn't possibly share with Diana lodged in her throat. "I haven't said much about Paul to anyone. Except maybe Piper."

Diana nodded thoughtfully. "No matter what issues you have with Paul, he's still Jenna's dad, and she misses him. I'm sure he misses her, too."

Liz chewed on her lip, wondering. "He says he does, but he doesn't make time for Jenna and me in Washington, and it's been that way for years. His whole life is work."

"I think you'd be surprised, dear." Diana flipped open her book to the page where she'd left off. "Nothing is ever exactly as it seems."

"I guess I shouldn't have expected you to understand."

"I *do* understand. Paul is your husband, and divorce is never easy."

Turning away, Liz tried not to feel the sting of finally being honest about Paul and getting shot down. She shouldn't be surprised, and it was her own fault. She'd made too many excuses over the years for Paul's nearly complete absence from her life, and now Jenna's. She worked hard, too, but it didn't stop her from spending time with her daughter.

She got up from her chair as Jenna skipped down the steps with two of Diana's hats.

"Oh, and Liz?" Diana called out as Liz headed toward Jenna.

Liz turned back to her. "Yes?"

"I'm a little worried about those hikes." She raised her eyebrows. "The path can sometimes be dangerous."

Liz tilted her head. "I'm always careful."

"Good." Diana nodded. "I hope David is, too."

"I ADMIT IT. I'm not David." Way too early on Sunday morning, Piper tugged a dawdling Liz up the hill. Even with Liz here all summer, they hadn't spent much time together, just the two of them, talking. At the moment, she wondered why she'd left Brandon's bed at dawn. Talking might be overrated.

"No question." Liz sped up a fraction. "You're not Brandon, either, or *with* him. Anything wrong?"

"I'm just working on maintaining a separate identity."

"Try saying that with a straight face." Passing Piper, Liz grinned. "Actually, I think he'll have more trouble than you will. The guy hangs all over you."

"I don't know." Piper raced past Liz and turned, jogging backward. "He's even insisting on keeping his last name."

Liz shook her head as she stopped to catch her breath. "What's this world coming to?"

Whistling, Piper walked back to Liz. The sun barely broke through the canopy of leaves above them, but it was a gorgeous morning. Even without Brandon.

Liz bent to tie her shoelace, then started out again. "So where's Brandon? Didn't he want to hike?"

"Naaa. Too satisfied at the moment." Striding alongside Liz, Piper grinned as Liz covered her ears. "Anyway, I wanted a chance to talk. Without David or Brandon around."

They walked in silence for a few minutes.

"Are you still thinking about going back to D.C.? Or has Diana talked you out of it?"

Liz shook her head. "She wants my firm to help sell the company, and David tried to get me involved, but I think she'd rather have someone else at my firm handle it. Besides, I should go home."

"Can't you at least wait until the wedding?"

Liz slowed her steps, and Piper matched them. "You've got it all planned, but I'll be back in plenty of time. I have the whole summer off."

"Then why are you leaving?"

"Jenna misses Paul. And I—"

"—miss Paul, too?" Liz hadn't mentioned him since the day Piper found her curled up in a ball in the back house. She knew Liz wasn't happy, but she also wanted to believe most things were fixable.

Biting her lip, Liz glanced sideways at Piper. "Things with Paul aren't good, so I'd be going back to D.C. to deal with that. Leaving the River would also give me a break from David. I'm starting to like him more than I should, and . . . you know. Trouble."

"It must be a nightmare, especially with Suzy back in town." At the top of the hill, Piper took the path leading to the dirt road. "She treats you even worse now than she did in high school, if that's possible."

"She just ignored me then." Liz stopped in the middle of the path. "I think she suspects something."

"She's always suspected something." Piper started back toward Liz, who looked surprisingly upset. "Has anything else happened?"

"Not much." She lifted a shoulder when Piper whistled. "A few kisses. Maybe a little more than that. Nothing, uh, below the waist."

"Ooh. I love it when you get clinical."

Liz ran a hand through her short hair. "It's hard to even admit it. I always wanted David, but not like this."

"When you're both married."

"I never planned it." A tear caught the corner of Liz's eye. "When I decided to come here this summer, I hated the thought that he'd be here. But I'm actually getting to know him."

"So don't run away. You want my advice?" When Liz didn't answer, she gave it anyway. "Stick around. Maybe you and David can figure it out."

"With Suzy's help?" Liz started hiking again. "Or should I ask Paul to join us, too?"

"It'd be quite a foursome. You know, Suzy and Paul wouldn't . . ."

"No." Liz laughed, flashing her first genuine smile of the morning. "Whatever it is—no. Anyway, Paul is coming out next weekend, for the Fourth. Maybe we'll all fly back together."

"Does Diana know?"

"About any of this?" Liz rolled her eyes. "I tried to talk to her—really talk—about how things actually are with Paul, and she brushed me off."

Piper hauled up short. "No way."

"She thinks divorce is out of the question." Her lower lip quivered, reminding Piper of Jenna. "I'm not saying Paul is a horrible person. He doesn't drink or hit or even swear much—" She broke off, startling Piper with a grin. "Except when he's watching football on TV."

They both laughed, then started hiking again. Brandon swore at TV sets, too, but the Vikings usually deserved it. Just another flaw in the dreaded Y chromosome.

Piper touched Liz's arm. "Are you sure you're done with him?"

"He works and sleeps and eats, and that's all it's been for a long time. No sex, no romance, no talking. Nothing. I don't think he's even attracted to me anymore."

"Oh, come on." David was so hot on Liz, she might as well be kindling. Didn't Paul see her the same way?

Liz gave a wry smile. "Yeah, yeah, you're engaged and madly in love. Not exactly what you want to hear. But I think I deserve more in life than a husband who doesn't hit me."

The dark look in Liz's eyes hinted at something, as if she'd actually *worry* about a guy hitting her. Piper laughed, but it sounded hollow in her throat. "I'd pay good money to see anyone try to hit you. You'd smash his face in."

"You'd be surprised." Liz stared at the ground, her mouth a flat line. "But that might be a subject for another day. Maybe."

Seriously? No way.

Liz stumbled on the path, which wasn't like her. "The thing is, I want and need more than I have right now, and so does Jenna. I didn't come home this summer just to see my dad. I need to decide what to do about my marriage." As they walked past a barking dog, Liz flinched. "I also think Diana suspects something about David and me."

"Diana's a smart woman."

"Sometimes." Liz kicked her shoe against a mailbox. "She's also David's mom."

"You'll figure it out." She put an arm around Liz. "I have every confidence."

"WHO'S HIDING THE SALAD?" David picked up Billy's plate, drawing a surprised laugh when he pretended to search under it for the large salad bowl, then looked around the table. He wagged a finger at Jenna, seated across from him. "Is it in your lap, young lady?"

"Nope." Jenna covered a giggle with her hand.

Diana produced the bowl from the small table in the corner. "Sorry. There wasn't enough room." Amused, she lifted one eyebrow. "But this is a little surprising, David. When did you start eating green, leafy things?"

"When Pete got old enough to realize I didn't."

At the other end of the table, Pete rolled his eyes. "When was that? Last week?"

David had almost forgotten Suzy, who hadn't uttered a word during dinner until she suddenly clutched his forearm. He jumped.

"Speaking of last week . . ." She cleared her throat, drawing everyone's attention. "I started to wonder, and I confirmed it today." She turned to David, her smile brittle. "We're going to have a baby."

Liz's glass slipped out of her hand, bouncing once on the table before falling onto the floor and shattering.

Everyone else stopped eating and stared.

"Good joke, Suzy." David peeled away her hand, which now clutched his arm in a death grip. "Especially from a woman who's been looking forward to Billy's high-school graduation for the last eleven years."

He put his glass to his mouth but couldn't swallow. They hadn't had sex in ages. A few months? He refused to do the math. The only woman he wanted sat across from him, face drawn, gazing at her lap.

Suzy giggled, totally fake. "Oh, you. Stop teasing. We've talked about this for ages."

He frowned. "Not in five years. Maybe ten." Just yesterday, they'd talked about a divorce. Okay, he'd talked and she'd stormed from the room.

"It's not gonna be a girl, is it?" Billy's mouth curled up in disgust.

Jenna stuck out her tongue. "What'sa matter with girls?"

David looked from one to the other, then at Pete, who

leaned back in his chair, arms crossed. "It's not going to be anything." He ruffled Billy's hair. "Your mom is kidding."

"I'm not kidding. We're having a baby." Pushing back her chair, Suzy threw her napkin on the table. "David, you're such a jerk."

She hurried across the porch and out the door, slamming it behind her.

David sat back, stunned.

"I don't know, Dad." Pete shook his head, looking smug. "She might be pregnant. She's sure got the hormones for it."

Billy tugged on his sleeve. "What're hormones?"

"Ask your brother. He knows everything." Standing up, David headed for the door.

Behind him, Mom spoke softly. "This doesn't call for champagne?"

"Not exactly."

He let the door close softly before he walked down the steps to the beach. Everyone had already heard enough loud bangs for one night.

LIZ STRUGGLED through three inane books that Jenna insisted on hearing for the fifth time that day. Finally, after a long snuggle and a kiss goodnight, she shut off the light in the sleeping porch and closed the door.

Glancing into her own room, she debated what to do. Her throat tightened. Air. She needed fresh air to breathe and water to dip her feet in. Sand to bury herself in, maybe until she suffocated. She padded down the stairs, crossed the great room, tiptoed through the porch and out into the night. The house was silent.

After Suzy's abrupt departure, then David's, everyone

else had stayed behind in a stupor. Diana, rattled for the first time in Liz's memory, had offered Pete wine.

Outside, crickets chirped and the tangy, smoky scent of a barbecue floated to her on the breeze. She swatted at a mosquito and almost went back for something with long sleeves. A door slammed in the big house, and she froze, then kept heading to the beach. Looking down, she almost didn't notice the solitary figure on the sand until she ran into him. Literally.

David.

"Small world." He kept his hands in his pockets and took a step sideways. "I'm probably the last guy you wanted to see. Liz, I have to tell you—"

"Don't. Please." She kicked at the sand. "The whole thing was stupid. It's not just that we're married. It's—" She shook her head. "It's everything."

"Yeah. I don't get it, though."

"How she got pregnant?" Liz choked on a harsh laugh. It was easy to get pregnant. For everyone but her. "We learned that one in sixth grade. Did you skip that class?"

David grabbed her hand and pulled her along the beach toward the point. As they walked, they passed several cruisers rammed up against the sand.

"She's not pregnant. Unless she's—I don't know—four months along. Three, minimum. That's not why she—"

"You don't have to justify anything to me." They reached the end of the point. Liz stared, mesmerized, at the dim outline of the red buoy marking the near side of the channel. Finally she blinked, returning to reality. "What you do with Suzy isn't my—"

"Stop it." David sat on the sand, tugging her hand until she joined him. "I never would've if— I asked her for a divorce." He buried his head against his knees. "I can't believe this."

"I can." She nudged him with her shoulder, feeling a strange relief. At least he'd asked Suzy for a divorce, even if it wasn't going to happen now. Even if Liz wouldn't have known what to do if it did happen. "But it still wouldn't have worked. At least—"

She broke off, unable to finish.

"What?"

After a pause, the words flew out in a rush. "Suzy can get pregnant. Jenna was our one miracle in ten years of trying." The memories tasted bitter as she swallowed hard.

"She can't get pregnant without sex." David shook his head, still denying the obvious. "The thing is, she hates being pregnant and never liked having kids. She had Pete just to make sure she wouldn't have to work."

"Is that why you had Pete, too?"

"Funny." He leaned back on his hands and actually laughed. "Yeah, we have money, but I've always wanted to find my passion. Something I care about as much as I do about the boys. A job that consumes me." He looked sideways at her. "A woman who'll share my life."

"I hope you find them someday. In the meantime, it looks like you and Suzy—"

She shivered against the wind blowing across the point, and he put his arm around her. She ought to pull away. Instead, she laid her head on his shoulder.

One last moment together. One last regret.

"I wanted something better." David drew her closer. "Everything felt different with you. More mature."

Thinking of all the water fights, the tackles on the beach, and the childish taunts when they played *any* sports together, she laughed. "Right."

He elbowed her in the ribs. "Good line, huh?"

She shoved him, and he fell sideways into the sand, pulling her with him. Laughing, they collapsed together, then grew serious as their lips drew closer.

"We shouldn't do this." Liz rested a hand on his cheek, staring into eyes that looked black in the night.

"Nothing has changed, and we can still talk. I want to see where this goes with you." Reaching up, David played with the ends of her hair.

She touched her lips to his, tasting salt, then drew back. "But you can't. You have a—"

"Wife." Appearing out of nowhere, Suzy flew at Liz, trying in vain to kick or slap her or worse. Liz leaped to her feet and darted to safety, but not before Suzy threw a sandal, clipping her hard in the arm. David grabbed Suzy, who fell onto her knees on the sand.

Breathing hard, she gave Liz a thin smile. "A wife who plans to keep him."

CHAPTER 15

"I don't wanna go home! Daddy's coming!"
Pausing in the hall outside the sleeping porch as the battle unfolded within, Diana watched Jenna race in circles, trying to elude Liz's reach as she held out Jenna's traveling clothes.

Liz stopped in the middle of the room. "He's not coming, Jenna. We're flying home to see him this afternoon."

Diana had heard the screaming from David's house and the quiet sobbing from Liz's room last night, and she knew a thing or two about math. She poked her head inside the sleeping porch. "Hi, girls. Can I help?"

Jenna threw her arms around Diana's thighs.

"Mom's making me go home. I don't hafta, do I, Gram?" Her wide eyes brimmed with tears. "Please can I stay?"

Diana rubbed Jenna's back. "Don't cry, dear. You can come back and visit. Every summer, I hope." She looked over at Liz. "Are you really leaving today? Why?"

Liz shuddered, visibly working to hold it all in, and Diana noticed the dark circles and streaks of dried tears.

"It's time. I have to go home."

"So you're running." Diana rested her hands on her hips.

"Just as you did when you were eighteen. Nothing's changed."

Liz blinked. "Everything's changed."

"Not from where I stand." Diana narrowed her gaze on Liz while disentangling Jenna's sticky hands from her own legs. "The circumstances might be different, but you're still running. Last time, from your father. This time, David?"

Liz kept packing. Her wooden movements made Diana ache for the defiant little girl who still held all her hurts inside.

"Gram, I don't wanna leave." Jenna sat cross-legged on the floor now, her thumb in her mouth and a tattered bear snuggled in her other arm. "Can you make her stay? Can you?"

"Not exactly." She hadn't succeeded nineteen years ago, and the Liz she knew now was even more difficult to break. She turned to Liz. "Can we talk? Privately?"

Liz bit her lip, looking little different from the nine-year-old girl she'd been when they first met. "There's not much point. You wouldn't like it. Or even understand."

"Try me." Leaving Jenna in the sleeping porch, the two women moved to Liz's room. Diana sat next to an open suitcase and silently prayed for a second chance with Liz. She'd bungled their conversation on the beach two days ago, out of foolish concerns for Liz's marriage. She should've saved her worries, and empathy, for Liz. And David. "I'm a fairly smart woman, or so I've been told." She winked at Liz, who didn't crack a smile. "And I'm your mom."

"Stepmom."

"I wish you'd get over that." Diana inched backward and leaned against the wall. "I care about you as much as my boys."

"You'll take David's side—or Suzy's."

"I'm not foolish enough to take sides in an argument between you and David." And Suzy was beyond her grasp in more ways than one. "What did you fight about?"

Liz blew out a breath. "We didn't, exactly."

As she suspected. "Then what's the problem?"

"David and I got too close."

"I've always wanted you two to be close."

"Not this close." Liz glanced over at Jenna, who quietly sat on the hallway floor outside Liz's room, rocking while she sang a song to herself. "Diana, I'm really sorry. If you don't— Well, you will."

"Grasping the meaning of fractured sentences was never my strong suit." Diana patted the bed, and Liz curled up next to her. "You and David—"

Liz nodded.

"Okay."

Jerking upright, Liz stared at her. "Okay?"

Diana smiled. "Well, not necessarily at the moment, due to circumstances, but I'm not judging, Liz. I'm just listening."

Liz closed her eyes. "We were just— It wasn't— And Suzy saw us— And I have to go home."

"Your sentences aren't improving, but I think I understand."

"You do?" Liz raised one eyebrow.

"More than I can say at the moment." Diana tilted her head at Jenna. "But I don't think you should leave."

Liz's jaw hung open, and Diana tipped it shut. "We have a business to sell, a wedding to plan, and—" Diana gazed at Liz, seeing Frank's kind eyes in hers. "You still need to speak to your father."

"He sleeps most of the time, and he can't talk."

"We both know you're making excuses. You've been here a month, and you haven't even tried." Diana squeezed Liz's arm to ease the sting of her words. "At a minimum, he can listen."

"I'm not sure I know what to say."

"Just start talking and see what happens." Diana moved toward the edge of the bed, trying not to worry about exactly what Liz might say to Frank. But she had to learn to trust Liz. Starting now. "Then you should talk to David."

"What about Suzy?"

Diana arched a brow. "My advice? Stay away from her."

Liz sighed. "She's going to be here all the time now, and I think it'd be easier for everyone if we left. I checked on flights—"

"No!" Jumping up, Jenna screeched the word as she raced to Diana. "I wanna stay here an' see Daddy. An' be with you, Gram!"

Liz reached for her. "Jenna, I was just talking to Gram."

"No! I hate you. Go away!"

Shrieking, Jenna ran from the room. Her feet scampered down the stairs and, moments later, the screen door banged.

"I'm so sorry." Liz started to get up. "I'll go find her."

Diana stopped her with a hand on her shoulder. "No, I will. Unpack. I do want you to stay, even if it's difficult with Suzy and, for that matter, with David. I don't know what's happening in your marriages, but I'm here for both of you. I love you, you know, and always have." She smiled, realizing the truth of her words. Liz was a challenge, yes, but also a gem. They just needed to get to know each other better. "No matter *how* much trouble you get into."

Liz gazed into Diana's eyes for a long moment before nodding.

Diana tapped her on the nose. "I'd better find Jenna. I don't think anyone is on the beach."

She hurried down the hall, calling for Jenna. At the top of

the stairs, her heart lurched unexpectedly, and she skidded in her stocking feet. As she clutched her hand to her pounding chest, she turned and missed the banister for the wooden stairs—and tripped, tumbling downward. Ankles, knees, hips, arms, and head hit the steps and wall, over and over in painful horror, as she fell in slow motion.

When she hit the bottom, everything went gray. Then black.

"Mom? Mom? Can you hear me?"

David pressed harder on his mom's shoulder as she stirred, her eyelids fluttering.

After a moment, her eyes opened. "You're crushing my shoulder, if that's your intention."

His hand flew off her, and he gripped the metal railing on her bed. "Are you okay?"

Blinking, she looked slowly around the stark white hospital room at the beeping monitors and her elevated, bandaged foot. She touched the oxygen tube sticking out of her nose. "I hate these. Help me take it off."

When he hesitated, she removed the tube herself.

"Are you sure you should be doing that?" He glanced quickly at the door. Any second now, a doctor or nurse would probably accuse him of crimes against his mother.

"Positive." Her hand—thinner and more bony than he remembered—reached for his, heedless of the tube protruding from it. "Where's Liz? Did she leave? Who's with Frank? And Jenna?"

A young male nurse with a buzz cut and a clipboard walked in, and Diana shooed him away.

"It's all good." David touched the tips of his mom's fingers. "Liz is taking care of both of them."

At the news, Mom looked as worried as Liz had been when she'd appeared at his door, frantic and shouting.

He shrugged. "Hey, someone had to take you to the hospital, and there aren't a lot of ambulances at the River, remember?" Grinning, he caught a slight smile in return. "And I'm the best driver. Or at least the fastest."

He'd also had to carry Mom, after they'd called 9-1-1 and confirmed that she could be moved. Liz couldn't lift her. Sobbing and choking on her words, Liz hadn't been able to do much of anything.

When Mom reached for his hand, he realized he'd withdrawn it. "I'm sorry, Mom."

"Why are you sorry?" She wriggled in bed, looking uncomfortable. "It's no one's fault."

"Liz said it was hers."

"And you believed her?" Mom rolled her eyes. "Liz thinks she's at fault for being born—and almost everything that's happened in the world ever since."

Unfortunately, Suzy would agree. "What happened?"

"My heart suddenly felt odd, and I reached for it instead of the bannister. I kept falling and falling. Oh, it hurt so much. Finally, I couldn't feel anything anymore."

"You blacked out. Liz ran and got me, and you were still unconscious when I reached you." Seeing her bloody and bruised and out cold, he'd lost ten years off his life. "You started to come to when I carried you to the boat."

"Did I have a heart attack?"

"All the tests are negative so far." He expected a grilling from a woman who knew more about medical devices than most physicians. When it didn't come, he pointed at her foot.

"Your worst damage seems to be a bad sprain on your right ankle."

When she tried to move it, she grimaced.

"You're right." She closed her eyes, then opened them. "Where's Suzy?"

David blinked at the unexpected question. "Uh, at home."

"At the River?"

"She went into town this morning." After calling him every name in the book and threatening him with everything but divorce, the one thing he wanted. "I think she'll be back this afternoon. I called her after I brought you here."

"Good." His mom closed her eyes again. "Liz told me what happened." She opened one eye. "In a manner of speaking."

He clenched his jaw. "It's not what you—"

She gave his hand a faint squeeze. "We don't need to discuss it now. I asked Liz to stay and help work things out. I trust you two, and I want you to be happy."

"Not easily done."

Wincing, he rubbed the sore spot on his arm where Suzy had slapped and scratched him when she couldn't reach his face.

Mom groaned as she shifted onto one side. "Life isn't easy, David. It's time you learned that."

"Don't worry." He adjusted her pillow, then stood back as an older, female nurse walked in and moved to her side. "I've known that forever."

———

"Wow. You look great, Diana."

Liz bent to plant a kiss on Diana's cheek, then looked

around the small hospital room. Flowers filled every nook and cranny, and one colorful basket rested precariously on top of a softly beeping monitor next to Diana's bed.

Her stepmom rolled her eyes. "All things considered."

"True." Liz pulled a bag of Ghirardelli white-chocolate caramel squares out of her beach bag and laid it on Diana's tray. "Here. Contraband."

Diana's eyes lit up as she immediately pried open the bag and unwrapped one of the squares. "Ooh, my favorite. No wonder I like you so much."

"I would've brought more, but David swiped the other bag." Grinning, Liz pulled out a second, torn Ghirardelli bag. "But I fought for you. Anyway, how are you feeling?"

"Sore. Embarrassed." Diana shot her a wry grimace. "I have a sprained ankle and too many bruises to count, and it turns out that I also have trouble descending stairs with grace."

Guilt ate a hole in Liz's stomach. "You were chasing Jenna. I should've."

"So you could lie here instead?" Shaking her head, Diana smiled gently. "I've nearly fallen many times on those awful stairs. I knew better. They're too slippery."

"You slipped because of me."

"Technically, dear, I slipped because of Jenna." Diana looked out the door. "Where is she? Did you bring her?"

Liz busied herself unwrapping a chocolate, unable to admit that Jenna was too traumatized to visit her beloved Gram. "I, uh, wasn't sure if she was old enough. To visit."

"That's fine. Jenna doesn't need to spend her life in hospitals." She wrinkled her nose. "I don't like them, either, except that they buy so many of our medical devices. In any case, they're going to release me tomorrow."

"That's good. But—"

"Have a seat, dear." Diana pointed to a chair in the corner and waited while Liz dragged it next to her bed. "Tell me what's happening. Is Frank okay? Is he worried?"

Liz wasn't sure whether Dad understood enough to worry. She'd glossed over Diana's situation with him and guessed David had done the same, only more smoothly. Not that she knew exactly what David had told Dad, since she'd spent most of her time since Sunday night avoiding David. "Dad is fine. David is taking care of him. And Jenna."

Diana's brow wrinkled. "Jenna's helping take care of Frank, or David's taking care of Jenna?"

"A little of both."

Liz twisted her hands in her lap, replaying in her mind the hours she'd spent yesterday while David had been at the hospital. Frantic for news about Diana. Trying to find Jenna, who'd hidden from her at David's house until Suzy returned to the River and kicked Jenna out. Periodically checking on Dad, in bed, always silent.

Diana had told her to talk to him. What was she supposed to say? *Sorry, Dad, but I almost killed Diana this morning.*

"Liz? Is something wrong?"

"Off the top of my head? Everything." She rested her cheek on the bed railing. "I'm so sorry. I tried. But I can't talk to Dad, Suzy hates me, David won't look at me, and—" She finally met Diana's worried gaze as tears welled in her eyes. "I almost killed you."

"Stress."

"No kidding. I'm more stressed than I was when I got here." She dabbed a wet eye on Diana's sheet. "That's another reason why I should go home."

Diana spoke again, her voice soft. "I meant my own stress. That's what the doctors said. My heart felt funny because of the stress. That's why I fell. It wasn't because of you."

"I gave you the stress."

Diana shrugged. "You gave it, Frank gave it, David gave it, Suzy gave it. I gave it to myself. It's been a difficult summer. You can't carry all the blame, Liz, no matter how strong you think those shoulders are."

"They're not strong enough for this."

"But I need you." Diana held out a hand, waiting until Liz took it. "Now more than ever. I know what you're going through, Liz, but I'm asking you. Stay. Help me."

Bitter disappointment clogged Liz's throat. "You could hire a nurse. David's here. And Suzy. Maybe even Brandon." She hung her head, knowing too well the harsh truth. "Almost anyone would be better than me."

Diana's serene face didn't mask the steel in her voice. "Frank doesn't want a nurse, and neither do I. Brandon isn't here during the week, and he's busy with the wedding. David can't do everything. And Suzy—"

Diana paused, considering.

"See? Suzy can do everything I can, and better." Like getting pregnant. Like holding onto David. Not that Liz was trying to hold onto him, but she'd actually started to think about it, and the guilt was eating her alive. "She can cook, clean, you name it."

And she might even be willing to do all of that if it meant that Liz left.

"She can't sell the company, and she's not my daughter." She waved a hand, cutting off Liz's protest. "It's also not her house."

"It's not mine, either."

"Oh?"

Liz bit her lip, not about to discuss her nonexistent claim

on the River house with the woman she'd sent to the hospital. "I can't do this. At least, I can't seem to do it right."

"It's not always about you, Liz."

Liz's gaze flew to Diana's calm but determined face. She wanted—needed—to go back home, even if it meant never resolving her lifelong issues with Dad or her extremely new issues with David.

Even if it meant disappointing a woman in a hospital bed with a sprained ankle and a stressed heart. A terrific woman who'd worked so hard, since the moment she'd met Liz, to love her and ease her struggles.

"Well, if it's not about me—" She gave Diana a half-hearted smile. "It certainly should be."

"I need you, Liz. I'll deal with Suzy if you'll—"

Liz held up a hand. "You win. I'll stay."

MOM WAS home from the hospital.

As David scurried from room to room in his beach house, emptying wastebaskets before Suzy arrived—so she couldn't claim he did nothing at home and spent all his time next door—he wondered why the news didn't make him feel better.

He'd see more of Liz, which was good and bad and, more than anything, a huge mess.

Every time he spoke to her, even to coordinate schedules, Suzy punished him again. He'd spent the last three nights on the couch, and even Pete and Billy were starting to feel sorry for him. He couldn't explain his conduct to them, let alone defend it, but he'd breathed a sigh of relief when both boys finally spoke to him yesterday. Sure, Pete just wanted to borrow his car and Billy needed money, but it was a start.

Liz was another story. She still sported a large, Suzy-inflicted bruise on one arm from Sunday night, and she looked skittish every time they spoke. He couldn't blame her. Liz was tough, but Suzy had at least forty pounds on her and knew how to get ugly.

The porch door banged. "Suzy? Is that you?"

No answer. David left the bathroom and its full wastebasket and poked his head into the hall. Jenna, dripping wet, stood just inside the door.

"Jenn? What's up?" He grabbed a towel from a freshly-washed pile and wrapped it around her shivering body.

Jenna looked all around her, silent.

"Suzy's not here."

She shivered under the towel, her teeth chattering. "Can you teach me how to canoe? I want to pick up my daddy tomorrow."

Damn. In the flurry of activity, he'd forgotten that Paul arrived tomorrow night. Talk about fireworks for the Fourth.

He wrapped the towel tighter around Jenna. "I can canoe with you in a minute, Jenn, but I'm not sure you can pick up your dad."

Her lower lip shot out, right on schedule.

"Not in a canoe, at least. We'll pick him up in the speedboat, but it might be past your bedtime."

"I wanna show him how good I swim."

"If you try picking him up in a canoe, you might have to." He grinned as he tousled her short, wet hair.

"Can I pick him up in the speedboat?"

She'd ignored the bedtime part. "Ask your mom."

"I can't find my mom."

"You don't have to ask her this minute. We'll find her later. In the meantime, we've got some canoeing to do." As she brightened, he headed back to the bathroom, calling over his shoulder. "Hang on. Two wastebaskets to go."

Humming, he picked up the trash bag where he'd dropped it on the floor, then moved to the wastebasket under the sink. He tipped it upside-down into the trash bag and spotted a balled-up, slightly bloody bundle that landed on top. Curious, especially with Pete on the prowl these days, he unfolded it.

Well, well, well.

David whistled. A blood-soaked tampon.

As Liz gave the kitchen counter a final wipe, she heard the screen door bang, followed by footsteps thundering up the stairs and, moments later, back down again, through the great room, and finally into the kitchen. A breathless David hauled up short at the sight of her. Jenna followed him and peeked at Liz from behind his legs.

"She's not pregnant, Liz." Arms waving, David heaved the words at her, then gulped in a huge breath.

"I sure hope not." Pointing at Jenna, she watched David jump. "She's only five. Not even dating."

"Not Jenna. Suzy. Suzy's not pregnant."

Head bent, Liz scrubbed another spot on the counter.

"Did you hear me?" David took a step closer.

She held up a hand, stopping him. "Yes. So did Jenna, Diana, and most of the people on this side of the River." After lunch, she'd helped Diana up to her bedroom, but she doubted anyone could nap through David's slamming, pounding, and top-of-the-lungs announcement. "What's your point?"

Speechless, David stared at her.

"So she's not pregnant. Why does that matter?" Her throat went dry as she worked not to think about it. It didn't fix anything. Suzy was in constant attack mode now, and Paul soon would be, the minute he arrived tomorrow and met Suzy.

"You're not gonna have a baby?"

Jenna's voice jarred Liz back to reality. Walking over to her, Liz bent down and ran a hand through her wet hair. "How do you know about babies?"

"Billy told me." She scrunched her nose. "They're inside your tummy."

"It's not so bad. You were inside my tummy."

Her eyes widened. "I don't remember that."

"It was a while ago." She turned Jenna's shoulders toward the kitchen door and propelled her forward. "So what did you want to do? Gram and Gramps are both taking a nap." She hoped. "We could go waterskiing, or swimming, or whatever you'd like."

To her mild irritation and equal pleasure, David followed them outside. "Jenn wants to learn to canoe so she can pick up Paul tomorrow night. In the canoe."

"Paul? In the canoe?" She gripped Jenna's hand as they walked down the concrete steps. "He'll want a bigger boat, sweetie. And it'll be late . . ."

"I wanna go. I wanna see Daddy." Jenna's defiance had grown over the summer, turning her shy, fearful little girl into something else. She told herself it was a good thing. And it was, mostly. "I can drive the speedboat."

Paul's flight arrived around eight. Maybe that wasn't too late. Just this once.

"I'm big enough and I wanna see him and—"

"Okay, Jenn. You can go."

Squealing, Jenna dashed ahead of Liz down the steps and headed for the canoe. David drew alongside Liz.

"I thought you'd be happy that she's not pregnant."

She watched as Jenna put on a life jacket, struggling determinedly with the buckles. She was growing up so quickly.

Liz grabbed her own life jacket and headed for the canoe. "It doesn't matter whether she's pregnant. She's your wife. Paul's my husband." For now, at least.

"But we have a chance now." David climbed into the stern of the canoe after dragging it to the edge of the beach. Jenna sat in front of the middle bar, clutching a small paddle, as Liz waded out to the bow. "Suzy doesn't want kids. All she wants is to keep her lifestyle. I told her I wanted a divorce, and I think that's why she—"

Shaking her head, she tried not to think about it. "Let's not discuss it right now." Turning, Liz frowned at David over the top of Jenna's head. "Okay?"

He nodded and pushed off from shore.

The trio paddled for half an hour, until Jenna's head began to bob in the bright sun. In tandem, David and Liz headed back toward the beach—where Suzy awaited them.

"Christ."

"Yep." Liz considered turning and heading south—toward the Gulf of Mexico. "What does she want?"

"The usual. To slit our throats."

Involuntarily, Liz touched a hand to her neck. She did like David, yes, and they'd stolen a few not-so-smart kisses, but she hadn't meant to ruin anyone's life.

Including hers.

DIANA AWOKE to shouts emanating from the direction of the beach. Goodness. Suzy must be home.

She pushed herself to a sitting position, swinging her legs

over the side of the bed. Ouch. A painfully swollen ankle protested. After a few deep breaths, she stood up anyway.

And nearly collapsed. The doctor had said the ankle should start feeling better by today, and she could walk without crutches by the end of the week, but her painkillers weren't doing their job. Pursing her lips, she bent to pick up her crutches from the end of the bed, then moved toward the door.

Ten painful minutes later, she reached the bottom step to the beach, where Suzy's tirade continued.

David stood between Liz and his wife, and Liz sat cross-legged in the sand at the base of a beach chair, holding Jenna protectively. Jenna cowered in her mother's arms.

"Suzy." Diana gripped the metal railing, having given up on the crutches halfway down. "Is something wrong?"

"Your son—" Suzy wagged a shaky finger at David, then Liz. "And that . . . that woman were out in the canoe. Together."

"You mean Liz. My daughter."

"Exactly. Isn't that disgusting?"

Diana lifted one shoulder. "I haven't seen them canoeing together, but, offhand, no."

"You've never supported me, Diana, but this is too much." Kicking at the sand, Suzy stubbed her toe and started cursing as she hopped on one foot. "I hate this place."

"Then perhaps you should leave."

"I live here, too." Dropping into a beach chair to examine her foot, Suzy nodded toward her beach house. Thankfully, her boys weren't here to see this. "I can do whatever I want."

Diana limped over to Suzy. David rushed to help her, but she waved her hand, sending him down the beach in the opposite direction from Liz and Jenna. He didn't go far. After a minute, she reached Suzy and dropped with little grace into a battered beach chair next to her.

"I care about you, Suzy." She lowered her voice. Out of the corner of her eye, she caught Liz leaning forward to listen and frowned at her. "I always have."

"You care more about David. And—" She grimaced. "Liz. That pig."

"She's not a pig." In fact, she hardly ate. "And, yes, I care about her, too. Very much."

"You know what they're doing, don't you?"

"Not really." She actually didn't know much and had learned long ago not to leap to conclusions. "And I doubt that you do, either."

"It's disgusting." Suzy shuddered, more than a little dramatically. "I'm gone a couple weeks, and look what happens."

"Only David and Liz know what has happened, if anything." She studied David, then Liz, and tried to read their faces. She also gazed at poor Jenna, who was curled up in Liz's lap and sucking her thumb. Her wide eyes said she was clearly taking it all in. Diana gritted her teeth. "In any case, it's not my business, and it's certainly not Jenna's. I just want peace. And quiet."

A string of loud and inventive curses spilled out of Suzy, startling Diana.

"That's an excellent example. I don't appreciate yelling or swearing." She brushed off Suzy's sputtered response. "Frank is quite ill, as you know. I'll speak to David and Liz, but you have to stop, Suzy. You're screaming in front of a child and upsetting everyone."

"I'm not losing David to that bitch."

"Don't ever use that word again." Diana tried to stand up but fell back onto the chair. She motioned to David, who ran to her side. Finally she stood, leaning heavily on David, and met Suzy's livid gaze. "But if your tantrums continue, I'm afraid that's what people might be forced to call *you*."

She hobbled away on David's arm, and Liz trailed while struggling to carry Jenna. At the top of the steps, Diana looked at David and Liz in turn. "This isn't the end, you know. I still need to talk to each of you. Separately."

David leaned forward and whispered in her ear. "She's not pregnant."

"Everyone on the beach knows, David. Suzy isn't the only person disturbing my naps." Her eyebrows rose. "But I fail to see the relevance. Perhaps you can explain."

Head bowed, David held the screen door for her, and she made it to the nearest glider before collapsing. Jenna put a pillow under her foot, Liz rushed to pour a glass of wine, and a shaken David stood watch over her.

Leaning back against a pillow, Diana closed her eyes. She should've stayed in the hospital and let them continue to test her heart. After a confrontation with Suzy that she'd expected for years, it throbbed as badly as her ankle.

The wine arrived. Too quickly, she asked for a refill.

CHAPTER 16

David fished a quarter out of the front pocket of his beach shorts and tossed it in the air. "Heads or tails?"

"Whichever one has you taking care of Dad."

He caught the coin, flipped it onto the back of his other hand, and peeked at it. "Well?"

"I'm serious, David." Crossing her arms, Liz tapped one foot on the kitchen floor. "I'm fixing up the house and taking care of Diana. I can't even lift Dad."

"You could talk to him." David shoved the quarter back in his pocket. "I don't have much to say to the guy."

"And I do?" Liz frowned, wondering what might spew from her mouth if she ever really spoke to Dad. "You guys were so tight when I arrived this summer. Enough to make me—"

"Children!"

A book slammed shut, and a minute later Diana hobbled into the kitchen.

"Diana." "Mom." Both grinned sheepishly.

"You're both being selfish, you know. I do understand how you feel about the past, Liz, but Frank isn't who he once was." She gave Liz a warning look, possibly because Liz rolled her eyes. "Is this how I raised you? I asked you to talk to your father. In any case, he needs your help, and so do I."

"Not from the looks of it." David pointed at Diana's ankle. "You'll be out dancing in no time."

"With whom?" Diana looked down, and tears glistened in the corner of one eye. "I'm sorry. I don't usually . . ."

"Oh, Diana." Liz hugged her at the same moment David did—and they sprang apart at each other's touch.

"Honestly." Diana wagged a finger at them. "You need to quit jumping. Regardless of your present issues, you *do* know each other, so you might as well admit it. Meanwhile, Suzy still isn't speaking to me, and the two of you spend most of your time hiding from her and acting like a couple of middle-school kids. Oh, and Paul arrives tonight. Did I mention that I wanted a nice summer?"

Talk about a pipe dream. But they both nodded.

"Good. Give me one." She looked at each of them in turn. "David can take care of Frank until I'm a little steadier on my feet."

When Liz stuck her tongue out at David, probably looking somewhere around Jenna's age, Diana whirled on her. "You're not in the clear. You need to talk to Frank, and for your sake I hope you'll talk soon. I'm counting on you."

"To do what?"

Diana smiled and caught Liz's hand. "You'll figure it out."

A conversation with a brick wall. Oh, boy. It was better than a conversation with a fist or a belt, she supposed, but not by much. Liz gave Diana a fake smile. She could hardly wait.

"One other thing." As Diana reached for a notepad on the counter, David and Liz both groaned. "I need help with a few things on my to-do list."

David snatched the list from her and howled as he read it.

"The fourth item says 'Save the world.' You're asking a lot, Mom."

Retrieving the notepad, she swatted him with it. "That's what you get for fighting with each other."

"Daddy! You're here!"

Jenna's squeals filled the air as Paul opened the door of his rental car and stepped onto the sandy gravel lot. Grinning, he crouched down and held out his arms. Jenna hurtled into them, almost tipping him over. "Wow! Who's this girl?"

Brown and taller than he remembered, she'd changed so much in a month. Even her demeanor. He hardly recognized his little girl. Blinking back unexpected tears, he squeezed her tight.

"It's me, Daddy! Jenna!"

"Are you sure?" He tilted his head as he held her at arm's length. "I bet you're just teasing."

Jenna's grin stretched the width of her face as she grabbed his hand and tugged. "Mom's waiting in the boat. She drove it all by herself. I helped."

"Excellent." He hoped Liz didn't let five-year-olds drive boats, but at this point he wouldn't put it past her. "Let me get my bag, and we'll go see Mom."

He reached into the back seat, retrieved his briefcase and weekend bag, and shut the doors, locking them.

Jenna held out her tiny hands. "I can carry it, Daddy. I'm big now."

"I see that." He set his briefcase on the ground and watched her strain to lift it. "But it's pretty heavy. Do you mind if I carry it?"

Crestfallen for an instant, she quickly brightened and

reached again for his hand. "I'll show you the boat, Daddy. An' the dock. An' the River."

"And your grandparents' house? Where is it?" He couldn't picture it and didn't understand why they had to take a boat to get there. The place must be some ramshackle old cabin in the middle of nowhere.

Halfway down the rickety steps, Jenna let go of his hand and pointed vaguely across the River. All Paul saw were trees, sand, and water. No houses or other signs of civilization. Below them, Liz waited in the boat. He raised a hand in a hesitant wave. She smiled—or didn't. He couldn't quite tell. She looked tan but thinner than he remembered.

He hurried down the steps, impatient to see Liz. They'd lost so much this summer, but he finally had it all again. Within his lucky grasp.

"Liz. It's great to see you." He leaned down just as she turned, so his kiss landed awkwardly on her cheek.

"Glad you made it, Paul." As she said it, she touched her cheek, looking thoughtful. A good sign? Or a bad sign? "It's all Jenna could talk about today. Hop in."

He tossed his bags on the floor of the boat, lifted Jenna over the side, and settled her on his lap in the passenger seat. As they cruised slowly through the marina and across the River, he glanced around, taking in the boats and landscape as the day's final rays of sun shimmered on the water.

"This is beautiful. I had no idea." He finally understood why she might want to spend a summer here. He wondered only why they hadn't visited sooner. "I wish you'd told me about this place."

She glanced sideways at him before returning her gaze to the water ahead of them. "I did tell you."

Faint memories teased his brain, of talks they'd had when they were dating. He missed those talks. He even missed dating, but Liz would laugh if he suggested going out on dates again. She'd tell him he didn't do that. He sighed, knowing she was probably right. "You said you couldn't wait to leave and never wanted to come back." Until this summer.

She swept the steering wheel wide of a fishing boat in the middle of the channel, where an old man was teaching a small boy how to cast. Liz glanced at Jenna, curled up on Paul's lap. "Life with Dad was complicated at best. Everything is different now."

He nodded. Different didn't have to mean worse. In fact, life was good. As of tonight, they had a fresh start.

He'd had better dreams.

David groaned, the dream that shook him awake still fresh in his mind. Starring solid, upstanding-citizen Paul, nobly slaying a dragon to win the heart of Liz, who looked a bit pissed. Hell. She probably wanted to slay the dragon herself, especially since the dream dragon had been David. He swore he could still feel that damn sword in his gut.

And Paul was actually here. He'd met the pasty-faced guy on the dock last night and shook his clammy hand, then wiped his own hand on his shorts and headed upstairs. To Suzy. To a different kind of hell.

He stretched his arms over his head, lay back on the sofa, and wondered what Liz was doing with Paul right now. He closed his eyes and felt his fists curl. Bit down on his lip so hard he tasted blood. Finally, he glanced at his sports watch. Six-thirty. Time to hike.

Rolling off the couch, he slipped off the shorts he'd worn to bed last night and put on a fresh pair, then added socks and running shoes. Rubbing a kink in his neck, he paused at his front door. Maybe he should wake up Pete and Billy and drag them along. The exercise would do them good, and he needed time with them. Suzy's propaganda efforts weren't working as well as she hoped, but enough to create distance with his sons.

Maybe he couldn't have Liz, but he'd never give up his boys. Even if, after his half-assed behavior, neither one looked him in the eye anymore.

He sighed. He wouldn't risk waking Suzy. Closing the door softly behind him, he paused a moment on the top step, then skipped down a couple of steps to the path and headed up the hill. He breathed in the dewy, early-morning air, expanding his lungs with it. Ahh, the Fourth of July. After Suzy met Paul, he hoped he survived it.

He upped his pace and was soon gulping harsh breaths. Ten minutes later, he reached the top of the hill. He started onto the road, then retraced his steps and followed the path to the overlook bench. The River would be quiet now, flat with an occasional ripple. In two or three hours, boats would take over for the entire three-day weekend.

Maybe he could get one of them to haul Suzy away.

Head down as he approached the bench, he studied the faint tire tracks on the path. Tomorrow he'd talk Brandon and Piper into an early-morning ski. If Liz could bear to leave Paul, maybe she'd even join them.

He kicked at a rock and swore. Damn it all to hell.

"David?" The soft voice floated to him as if in a dream. "Is that you?"

As he rounded a bend in the path, he saw Liz. In his dreams, she always wore something filmy that draped itself over her slim curves—if she wore anything at all. He grinned. The woman before him had on sweats, ratty sneakers, and a ripped tank top she must've stolen from Brandon's stash.

"Hey."

After a moment's glance, she turned back to the River. He couldn't blame her. He probably looked like hell, too.

"Where's Paul?"

"In bed." She started to say something more, then apparently changed her mind. "Suzy?"

"Ditto. I've been booted for the duration."

She stared at her hands as he took a seat on the bench, but not too close to her. "I'm sorry. I didn't mean to—"

"No more apologies, okay?" He barked out a short laugh. "I've made enough of them in the last few days for a lifetime."

"Did any of them help?"

"I'm still on the couch, aren't I?"

She fell silent, and he watched the wind dance in her hair. He longed to touch it, to hold the silk he'd felt so briefly. Looking more closely, he grinned. Her hair was tangled, just as it always looked at this hour of the morning. His fantasy woman was flesh and blood and, sometimes, a mess. He liked her that way.

"So . . . does Paul hike?"

"Not unless he can bill a client for it. No." She smiled briefly, barely meeting his gaze, then looked away. "He used to run but gave that up long before Jenna arrived."

"What do you guys do together?"

She ran a hand through her hair, her fingers catching on a snarl. "He works, mostly. When we do spend time together, it's probably like you and Suzy. Go to movies. Read books. Just so we don't have to talk."

"Suzy doesn't even read books except for—"

"—cookbooks." They ended his sentence in unison, their gazes tangling, then both burst out laughing.

Liz stood up, stretching for a moment before walking over to the split-rail fence that marked the edge of the cliff. "Sorry.

Believe it or not, I'm not usually the type to pick on someone like Suzy. I was picked on enough as a child. I don't like it."

David felt a twinge of shame, and something else. Respect. He liked Liz. Not just her kissable lips, or a waist he liked to grab, or legs that outran him, or breasts that—

His face heated up as he watched her. Beneath all that shit she'd given him throughout her teens and most of the last month, she was pretty cool. Someone he'd want to pursue if he were single.

But he wasn't.

"Come on." He joined her at the railing but didn't touch her. "Let's take a run along the road. It's the only exercise I'm going to get today."

She hesitated a second before catching up to him, matching his stride, then burning past him. Laughing, he grabbed her hand. He didn't want to lose her. Not again.

JENNA JUMPED UP AND DOWN, begging Paul for a shoulder ride. "Daddy, I wanna see the parade."

Surprisingly, Paul hoisted her on his shoulders and didn't even complain when she left gooey chocolate in his hair. Liz watched them from behind the safety of her sunglasses as the first parade float motored past, followed by a sewage truck painted pink. There was nothing like the Afton Fourth of July parade. That might be a good thing.

A little dog sailed by, a red bow around its neck, as it perched precariously in the basket on the handlebars of a little girl's bike. It was amazing that Afton could rustle up even a few hundred spectators for its parade. Everyone in town seemed to be marching in it.

Jenna twisted on Paul's shoulders just as the king and

queen of the parade drove by in a baby-blue vintage convertible. The king had to be pushing eighty; the queen was barely out of her teens. "Where's Gram? Is she coming?"

Liz shook her head. "Gram stayed back with Gramps. If you're going to get her some candy, it'll be tough to do that from on top of Daddy."

Wide eyed, Jenna scrambled down from Paul's shoulders as he mouthed a silent "thank you" to Liz. She nodded. Carrying Jenna for any long stretch was a load.

Jenna scurried into the street and grabbed several suckers from the asphalt. Every float gave away candy—too often with kids on the floats flinging it in the faces of the spectators. A Tootsie Roll landed at Liz's feet, and she bent to pick it up. Paul's eyebrows rose.

She grinned as she unwrapped it. "Get your own."

"I intend to." Stepping closer, he drew an arm around Liz as she tried not to flinch. Or to lean into him. She had no idea what to do around Paul anymore.

"Does that mean you've done some thinking?" She held her breath, waiting for an answer that might not matter anymore.

He held out his cupped hands when Jenna scampered up and dumped her candy haul, then ran back into the street. Turning, he looked at Liz over the tops of his sunglasses. "I want you, Liz. Same as always."

Her breath whooshed out. "Same as always" didn't cut it. Even before spending a complicated month with David, she wanted more.

"THERE'S NOTHING LIKE A BONFIRE." As the face of her hot-pink Swatch inched closer to ten o'clock, Piper warmed her hands over the flaming pile of driftwood and observed the glowing faces around her.

Jenna, holding a marshmallow on a stick about ten inches from the flames after torching her last one. Brandon, licking his fingers after scarfing down Jenna's blackened marshmallow. Liz, looking awkward and unsure next to Paul, who looked both happy and utterly clueless. David, pretending to help Billy with his s'more, over Billy's protests. The kid must've realized his dad just wanted to steal his marshmallow. The slime.

Piper grinned, enjoying the show. Diana had opted out, preferring the comfort of a book over Brandon's homemade fireworks and semi-stale marshmallows that kept dropping in the sand. Pete had stopped by earlier with his girlfriend, Nicole, but escaped the first chance they got. Suzy hadn't shown.

In fact, Piper hadn't seen Suzy all day, which was weird. Not at the parade or the big lunch afterward or for drinks on the beach before dinner. Not for dinner. Even Diana had hobbled down the steps for drinks.

Liz glanced at Piper and bit her lip on a smile. "Did you get a fire permit? I swear it's going to scorch the trees."

Piper made a face at her. Any self-respecting Fourth of July bonfire ought to flame upward as high as the fireworks. Of course, Brandon's fireworks usually fizzled or landed on David's speedboat.

"Hand me another one, will ya, Piper?" Brandon wiped his hands on his shorts and held out his long stick.

"Such endearments from the groom-to-be." She pulled a marshmallow out of the bag and held it toward Brandon—then popped it in her mouth.

"Hey!"

"I was waiting for 'pretty please.' Sorry." Talking around the marshmallow in her mouth, Piper shook a finger at him.

"We were roasting those, in case you forgot." Brandon reached into the bag and grabbed two, then dropped a kiss on her cheek before whispering in her ear. "Wanna sneak out of here?"

Laughing, she whispered back. "You have to do fireworks." She blew in his ear, making him shiver. "The ones on the beach."

"Hey." David grinned as he covered Billy's eyes. "There are kids present. Cut out the heavy breathing, will you?"

Billy broke away from him with an "Oh, Dad."

Paul chuckled while Liz just stared at the fire.

"Funny you should say that, David."

As Suzy appeared from out of the shadows, Piper jumped. The others clustered around the bonfire did the same. Suzy flicked her tongue over her lips as she looked from David to Liz, then ran her gaze the length of Paul, head to toe. Piper shivered. Despite the bonfire, the night air took on a sudden chill.

Brandon, dear soul, stepped forward. "Hey, Suzy. Have you met Paul? Liz's husband?"

Leaping to his feet, Paul smiled and moved toward Suzy as he thrust out his hand. Suzy ignored him. "Did you hear me, David?"

"Couldn't miss it." David mumbled under his breath, but the breeze picked up his words and floated them to Piper.

Suzy brushed past Paul, pushing his still-outstretched hand away as she marched up to David and stood in front of him.

"Please, Mom. Don't."

She shot Billy a sharp glance. "This doesn't involve you." Her words slurred slightly.

Billy moved closer to David. "Then don't shout in front of me, or anybody else."

"I'm not shouting."

"You're gonna." Billy stepped behind David, trembling as if seeking protection from his mom. Wow.

David caught Suzy by the hand. "Cut it out, Suz, before you do something you regret."

She yanked her hand away and took a step backward, a little too close to the fire, then lurched toward David again. She pushed him in the chest, but he maintained his balance and didn't push back. "A little late for regrets, isn't it, David?"

"Never too late." David glanced around the group as everyone stood silent, watching him. He shrugged an apology and pulled an arm around Billy.

Even Paul lost the giddy smile he'd sported all day. He blinked as he watched the verbal ping-pong match between David and Suzy. "Am I missing something?"

Piper grabbed Paul's arm as he took a step toward Suzy. He hesitated and looked at Liz, who shook her head and walked away from the bonfire, headed toward the point.

Suzy glared at Paul. "Maybe you can keep your *wife*—" She spat the word. "Away from us. Take her back to Washington and keep her there. She's done enough damage."

Paul bristled. "I know it's tough for Liz—"

Her back to the group, Liz halted in her escape.

Suzy hooted. "Tough for Liz? She's spent the summer trying to steal my husband."

"I . . . don't think so." He looked from Suzy to others in the crowd. His gaze landed on David, who met it, then returned to Suzy. "You're wrong. Liz wouldn't do that."

Jenna ran up to Paul and threw her arms around his thighs. "Daddy, she's a big ol' meanie." She pointed at Suzy, her finger quivering. "Make her stop."

Mouth open, Suzy stumbled toward Jenna until Paul's arm shot out, stopping her. "I don't know what your problem is, but get away from Jenna, and stay away from Liz. From all of us." He took Jenna's hand and led her down the beach toward Liz, who'd started walking again.

Suzy called after Paul. "You fool. She's a slut!"

"Stop it!" David grabbed her shoulders and shook her, stunning himself as much or more than Suzy, who screamed as she tried to claw him. He held her wrists, protecting his face, until she finally broke loose and stumbled away, up toward their house.

Dropping to the sand, he buried his head in his hands. "I can't believe this is happening. I'm so sorry, Billy."

Billy sat beside him, quiet and obviously upset. Brandon went to David, clapped a hand on his shoulder, then walked to the edge of the beach and stared out over the water.

Piper, alone with her bonfire and the two sad figures on the sand, blew out the breath she felt like she'd been holding for the last ten minutes. David had always been so casually hurtful to Liz, and he'd never had a clue, but he didn't deserve this. Not in front of a crowd. Definitely not in front of the kids. Crouching beside him, she put an arm around the man who'd soon be her brother-in-law.

Family stuck together.

"You're staying? Not coming home with me?" Sunday afternoon, Paul stared at Liz as he packed his weekend bag, deepening her guilt and anguish. "But you promised."

"I didn't promise. I thought so, a couple weeks ago, before Diana had her accident and asked me to stay."

"But . . . Suzy . . ."

"Suzy's an idiot." Sure, she might not be entirely wrong about David and Liz—except for the "slut" part, which still rankled—but she *was* an idiot. And she'd been nasty several times to Jenna, who definitely didn't deserve it.

"I need you, Liz." Paul's hands ceased their robotic packing, but he stared at the small pile of clothes on the bed. "I want to make you happy."

She shook her head. "I'm not sure anyone can do that." Maybe least of all Paul, who hadn't accomplished it in the last eleven years. Not that this was all on Paul. It took two people to make a relationship work. "But you never tried. You spent three days here and didn't really say anything."

"We talked."

"About baseball and politics and everything you could think of except us. Our marriage. What each of us wants."

"That counts." Paul balled up a shirt and threw it at his bag. It bounced off and landed on the floor. "Geez, Liz. Guys don't talk about relationships. Even to themselves."

"They do if they have to."

"I'm trying." He bent down and picked up the shirt, folding it neatly and setting it in the bag. "You used to say I didn't talk. I talked a lot this weekend."

"Not about us, and that's what I need right now."

Paul gazed at the bed. "Suzy said you're . . . involved with David."

They'd never discussed Suzy's outburst. After it, Paul and Jenna had caught up to Liz as she wandered along the beach, and they'd walked hand-in-hand, Jenna between Paul and her, to the point and back.

"Suzy has issues." That was true enough, so the guilt didn't stab Liz the way it often did. "David and I don't even do much together. He takes care of Dad, and I take care of Diana and fix up the house."

Paul threw his shoes on top of his sunglasses in the bag, and they both flinched at the sound of cracking plastic.

"Why are you fixing up the house? I mean, anyone could do it. You haven't even set foot here since you were a teenager."

"It's something to do." Something lasting. An attempt, however futile, to make the house feel more like hers. "I'm also helping Diana sell the company."

"Isn't David, too?"

She frowned. Despite David's title as Chairman, he hadn't joined in any of their conversations. In fact, he'd left the room whenever the topic came up. "No. He's not involved in the sale, for some reason."

"Which law firm is going to handle it?"

With Paul, it always came back to business.

"I don't know. Probably someone here in Minneapolis." Diana hadn't gotten that far yet. "The company's usual law firm, or maybe even Piper's firm, although I'm not sure her firm is equipped to handle such a big transaction."

"Hmmm."

"Look, Paul, the summer's not over yet." Maybe it was, in some ways, but she wouldn't rule out anything at this point. "I mean it. Start thinking about what you want—"

"I already know."

She waved a hand, cutting off his automatic response. "And articulate it to me. It's all about our relationship, Paul, and whether it should survive."

Paul sat on the bed and looked up at her, a pair of swim trunks clutched in his hands. "Do you already know the answer?"

It didn't lean in his direction, but she fought to keep an open mind and heart. For Jenna's sake, if nothing else. "No. But by the end of the summer, I will."

"Frank? Are you awake?"

David nudged his stepfather, tamping down the anger he'd felt toward him most of the summer. Frank was finding out, finally, what it felt to be helpless. At the mercy of others. The way Liz must've felt as a kid.

Frank's eyelids fluttered, then closed again. His mouth hung open, and mottled skin sagged on his thin frame. Labored, sour breaths gurgled out of his throat.

David wondered again how he'd gotten stuck with this.

It took Frank longer these days to wake up from his naps, and it took David a while to get him out of bed, settled in his wheelchair, and ready for polite society. "Frank?"

The eyelids squeezed shut once more before opening. Frank blinked at him. "Diana?"

"She's doing better, but she still has trouble walking around on her ankle." David ran a washcloth over Frank's face, then pulled back the light covers. "She's on the porch right now, waiting to have lunch with us."

They wouldn't see Suzy, who'd stayed away from everyone, even the boys, since her outburst on the Fourth. Paul had left two days ago, Billy was playing tennis with a friend, and Pete was working. That left Liz and Jenna joining the lunch gang.

He wondered why Suzy didn't try to forbid even that limited interaction, but maybe she'd stopped caring. Mom had wanted peace and quiet all summer. Now, with Liz and him both on edge, Mom got what she'd asked for. Mind-numbing silence at every meal.

"Liz?"

David blinked. Frank didn't often mention her—at least

not without looking worried or upset. David might think more highly of him if he at least looked regretful.

"Uh, Liz is pulling lunch together. Sandwiches and stuff. With Jenna." Jenna's assistance meant they'd have chocolate on the table. He had no clue where the kid kept finding it.

A slight nod from Frank. "She's . . . a good girl."

David tried not to frown, but he hadn't heard a complete sentence out of Frank—or one that made sense—in months. "Liz?"

"Good . . . girl. Shouldn't . . . hit her. So . . . small."

David felt tears in his eyes. He didn't want to hear this. Didn't want to know more than he had to.

"I . . . love her. So . . . much."

He'd have trouble convincing Liz. David gripped Frank around the waist and lifted him into his wheelchair. "Yeah, well, maybe you should tell her that."

"So . . . proud."

David swiped a hand over his damp eyes, then adjusted the foot braces on the wheelchair and set Frank's feet on them.

"Want her . . . to know."

"Then tell her, Frank."

Frank's shaking fingers touched David's wrist, trying to grip it, as he stared up at David and blinked. "Liz?"

CHAPTER 17

"Check it out, kids." At the foot of the stairs, Diana peeked around the corner into the great room, where Liz and David huddled over a stack of papers. "I'm a new woman."

She was finally walking without crutches for the first time in over a week. Her ankle felt stiff, sore, and . . . wonderful.

"Woo hoo, Diana!" Liz clapped her hands as she got up to offer a quick hug.

David waited until Liz had moved a safe distance away before hugging his mother. Diana's head swiveled as she looked for Suzy.

"It's just us, Mom." David offered his arm, leading her over to the old brown sofa strewn with wildly colored afghans. He took a seat next to her and pointed at the papers on the coffee table. "We're going over Liz's strategies for selling the company. They're good."

"Hey!" Liz, who'd moved to the rocking chair, shook a finger at him. "Better than good. They're brilliant."

David flipped to a page in the middle of the stack. "Except for the part about giving up my first-born child."

"I didn't think you'd mind. You hardly see Pete anyway."

Leaning back against the cushions, Diana enjoyed the friendly banter as the two jabbed each other about their progeny and general inability to do anything right. So different from how David and Liz had spoken a month ago. Even a week ago.

"What do you think, Diana?"

Somehow she'd missed the moment they'd stopped teasing and started working again. The seamless transition reminded her of the early days with Frank—after he'd proved himself in the company and they'd grown comfortable with each other.

Their romance had started soon thereafter.

Liz ran a yellow highlighter over a few lines on the top page. "See this? Your profit margin is incredible."

Diana clasped her hands and smiled. "I'm quite aware of that, dear."

When David chuckled, Liz blushed but tapped the page. "I mean, sure, but my point is that you can attract higher multiples."

"I love it when you talk dirty like that." David grinned—until Diana elbowed him.

Ignoring him, Liz looked at Diana. "The company is clean, profitable, and generates huge cash flows."

"Isn't that what we're supposed to do?"

"Of course. But most don't."

Diana knew that, of course, from all the ramshackle little companies she'd considered acquiring over the years, a few of which she had. "How do you propose to capitalize on that?"

"Well, my thought is . . ." And Liz proceeded to share her thoughts, one after another, for fifteen solid minutes.

When she finished, Diana's mind spun with the possibilities. She also couldn't help being impressed by Liz, who practically bounced in the rocking chair as her excitement grew. Liz knew what she was talking about.

"Can you explain that to our board of directors?"

Liz shrugged. "It's what I do for a living. Sure."

Reaching across the table, where papers now flew in every direction, Diana grasped Liz's hand. "Thank you, dear. It sounds . . . wonderful."

But also, if she were being honest, heartbreaking.

Liz watched her carefully. "Of course, this assumes you want to sell. The company is so strong, you could also consider going public. Or just hanging onto it."

Diana shook her head. "I don't think we have any options."

"You have a world of options." Liz pointed to a highly sophisticated cash-flow analysis that had surprised even Diana. "And, yes, one option is keeping the company."

"But David doesn't want to stay."

"True, but you've got a great CEO. Technically, that's enough. If you want family involved, you can find a way to make that happen, even without David."

"I can't do it, dear." Diana pushed a hand through hair that badly needed an expensive and time-consuming trip to her hairdresser. "Frank is so sick, and I'm getting older. That's why I retired."

Liz started to speak, then caught herself.

"What? Brandon? I don't think so." She'd considered him, several times, but he'd followed his heart to her research-and-development division. "No one else knows the company." Diana watched Liz avert her gaze. "No one who lives here."

"I . . ."

"You'd be wonderful, dear. You obviously understand the company, but isn't your life in Washington?" She felt David fidget next to her. "With Paul and Jenna and your own work?"

"You're right." Liz stared at her hands. "It was just another stupid idea."

"It was an excellent *option*, as you called it." Diana patted Liz's hand. "Please, keep going on your sale strategy. I want to hear more."

David stood up, rested his hand on Diana's shoulder for a long moment, then left the room. Biting her lip, Liz straightened the documents into an obsessively neat pile and didn't say another word.

Diana sighed. She suspected she'd done it again.

———

"WHAT DO you think of Brandon running the company?" Liz shot David a quick glance as they dropped onto opposite ends of the bench after a fast hike up the hill early Friday morning.

"Brandon? Not much." David stretched his legs and tried not to notice the trim sleekness of Liz's legs in white shorts. "Great inventor. Lousy at public relations. He also hates it."

"Public relations?"

"Management, human resources, auditors, bullshit."

"He has to deal with regulators." Liz stood up, arching her back in a stretch that turned David on more than he wanted. "They must be a pain."

"A pain he's familiar with."

As he watched Liz bend at the waist, revealing more skin than he'd seen or touched in what felt like forever, David almost stopped breathing. He raised his arms over his head, filling his lungs. Liz's were already . . . full.

He sounded like he was Pete's age. Or maybe Billy's.

"But Brandon is smart. He can learn."

"Remember, Liz, he went to med school. In college, he double-majored in biology and chemistry. The guy's brilliant, but he's a science geek. He likes it that way."

"But—" She twisted as she talked, and David couldn't help watching her shirt creep high on her stomach.

She was totally oblivious to what he was thinking, which was both good and bad.

He wiped his palm over his mouth. "Shouldn't we talk about a more viable possibility? Like you?"

"Me?" She froze in place.

"It's what you want, isn't it?" Giving up his struggle, he left the bench and walked toward her, stopping a foot away. "Admit it. The company excites you."

"Any great company excites me. That's why I—" She looked away, at a fallen log or dirt or something other than him. "I love my job."

"You can't stand it." He moved closer. "You don't want to go back."

"I don't—"

"Admit it, Liz." He touched a hand to her waist, and she shivered but didn't stop him. "You want to stay here and run the company. Maybe even—"

He broke off, unable to articulate the fragile hope he'd nurtured for weeks. He and Suzy were through, even though Suzy avoided the subject and he hadn't pressed it. He hadn't even confronted her on the fake pregnancy. But Suzy would do anything—maybe even try to *get* pregnant, no matter how much she'd hate it—to stop him from exploring a relationship with Liz. Who lived in Washington. With Paul.

He rolled his eyes. Hope? It felt more like lunacy.

"Be with you?" Head down, kicking at rocks, she walked over to the rail at the edge of the cliff. "You don't even know what you want."

"Fine." He joined her at the rough wooden rail. "Forget about me, but don't deny everything else. I see how giddy you get when you talk about the company. You're like a kid in a candy store."

"Please." She glanced at him before gazing out at the River. "I'm not a kid. I don't think I ever was."

"Maybe not." At age nine, she'd sure seemed like a kid. A tough, defiant one, yeah, but a kid. "So come back and do what you always wanted to do."

"I didn't always want to run a company."

"No, but you wanted to be part of a family. Joining the company would pretty much seal it." He inched closer to her and hugged her from behind. "You're part of our family, whether you like it or not."

She pushed him away, but without making any real effort, and he felt her heart hammer. "I . . . don't always like it."

"Who does?" He dropped his chin to her shoulder, nuzzling as she wriggled, alternately resisting him and letting herself relax. He wasn't the only mixed-up person around here. "Families yell. We argue. We steal marshmallows."

She laughed softly. "From little kids. That was pathetic."

"Everyone else is too quick for me, and you wouldn't share."

"Piper was holding the bag." She twisted slightly in his arms to smirk at him. "You're lucky you got any."

"Hell. I'm lucky she's letting me come to her wedding." He pulled Liz a little tighter, and she sighed, leaning back against him. "Are you going to dance with me at the reception?"

Her spine went rigid. "On the beach? In front of God and Suzy and everyone? Doubtful."

"Maybe she won't show up."

"She'll show up. Trust me."

"What about Paul?" He didn't know why he even bothered asking. Paul wasn't going anywhere. And except for a few quick hugs at the farthest point of their hikes, he and Liz had stayed away from each other. David wondered whether she felt as lousy as he did.

"No."

"Do you want to—"

"I can't." She pulled away and started back toward the path. "I'm still married."

Still married. Interesting?

He kept up with her on the descent, exchanging one sore topic for another. "And the company? What about that?"

"Diana wants to sell it. End of story."

He tugged on her elbow, feeling about twelve years old. "What if we give it a different ending?"

"Like what?"

"I leave and you take my place. Happily ever after."

Liz pointed out a fallen log he hadn't noticed. Progress. "Diana obviously doesn't consider me a suitable candidate, and I don't beg."

"That's not—"

Liz held up a hand. "It's true, and you know it. But it doesn't matter. Life's not a fairy tale, especially not mine."

He planted a quick kiss on her cheek before they caught sight of the first house on the path. "I don't know, Princess. Maybe you'll get your company . . . and Prince Charming too."

As she broke into a run, her snort didn't do much for his ego.

———

A WEEK FLEW BY, filled with sale strategies, house repairs and clean-up, waterskiing, hiking . . . and wedding preparations. Friday afternoon, as she poked a pin in Piper's wedding dress, Liz shook her head at the hubbub of activity.

Piper spun in front of the mirror, swirling the skirt of her dress. Soft ivory silk and stunning—and, knowing Piper, picked out in ten minutes on an afternoon break from work.

"I can't believe you're getting married. To Brandon." Sticking a few pins in her mouth, Liz tried not to choke as she helped Diana with the slight alteration.

"What's that supposed to mean?" Piper blew out a breath, sending a few pins flying.

"Nothing, I'm sure." Diana fiddled with the tea-length hem. "It just happened so fast. Another week and my baby boy is getting married."

"Eight days."

"Nervous, huh?" Grinning, Liz almost swallowed a pin.

Piper's hands shook slightly. "Not at all. I'm just—"

"—getting married!" Diana clapped her hands.

"Remember, Diana, it's Piper's wedding." Liz bent to adjust a pin that had fallen off the hem. She didn't know much about sewing, and Diana didn't either, but Diana had insisted on this. She should've stuck to ordering the food. "She's the bride. You know, the hysterical one."

"Hey!"

Diana ducked as more pins flew off the dress. "But I'm the groom's mother." She rose to give Piper a spontaneous hug, at least the tenth in fifteen minutes. No wonder they kept losing pins. "And for all practical purposes, Piper's."

"Oh, Diana." Piper hugged her back as Liz turned away.

"I'm yours, too, kiddo. Don't think you can escape me." Diana pulled away from Piper and bent down to Liz, bestowing an awkward hug. "Even if it kills me."

Feeling a sting in the general vicinity of her heart, Liz broke away. "I have to go wallpaper a room."

Peals of laughter followed her as she went in search of a task that wouldn't spill tears down the front of her, or make her ache for something she couldn't have.

WHISTLING, David returned to his house a little after seven on Sunday morning, easing the porch door open and shutting it softly behind him. He didn't want to wake everyone up.

He'd caught Liz for another hike in the middle of all the wedding preparations. They'd also shared a long, totally unexpected but heart-stopping kiss at the end of the road, with no houses or people in sight. Liz had protested, of course, even as she wrapped her arms around him and buried her face in his chest. Thinking about it, he grinned, happy with the world.

As he stepped into the kitchen for a glass of juice and a muffin, Suzy materialized in front of him.

"Where were you, David? Out with *her* again?"

He headed for the fridge. "It's seven in the morning, Suz. I went for a hike and a run."

"With *her*?"

Hands on her hips, Suzy's robe gapped apart, revealing a filmy black negligee she hadn't worn in forever. David turned and peered into the fridge, debating between pineapple-orange-banana juice or strawberry-mango. He grabbed the carton of strawberry-mango and poured a tall glass.

"Admit it. You were with her."

"Her name's Liz." He swallowed half the glass. "Yeah, she went running, too. I also invited Brandon and Piper."

They hadn't gone, opting to stay in bed to do exactly

what he'd wanted to do with Liz every morning for the last few weeks. But he'd take it one question at a time.

And Liz was right: this wasn't the time.

It might never be the time.

"Hmpf." She pulled her robe together, tightening the belt. "I suppose you're going to the wedding."

"I'm in it. Yeah, that seems like a definite."

"And she'll be hanging all over you." Suzy dragged a hand through her hair, looking oddly vulnerable, and David felt a tug of guilt.

He shook his head. "We're both in the wedding, but it'll be Brandon hanging all over Piper." He suppressed a grin as he bit into a raspberry muffin. Suzy wouldn't grasp the humor of his shy, studious, almost monkish brother falling in love. Liz did.

"If you dance with her, I'll—" Picking up a rolling pin, Suzy slapped it a few times against her open palm.

"I'll dance with anyone I want." Crap. He probably sounded like Pete or Billy, or even Jenna, and might as well stick out his tongue while he was at it. "But aren't you coming to the wedding? It's on the beach."

"So I heard." Suzy rolled her eyes. "How incredibly tacky. I can't believe Diana tolerates it."

David tried hard not to grin. "Mom suggested it."

Suzy tapped her fingers on the counter in a frenetic rhythm. "I hope, for her sake, that's all Diana is suggesting."

David popped the last of the muffin in his mouth, chewed slowly, and swallowed. He licked the few remaining crumbs off his palm, making Suzy cringe. Finally, he wiped his hands on his gym shorts. "Okay, I'll bite. What did you mean, Suz? Is this another threat?"

Her gaze narrowed. "I'm your wife, David. If you do anything with Liz, I'll stop you."

"Yeah?" For the first time, his anger overwhelmed his guilt. "How? By claiming to be pregnant? Was that your way of avoiding a divorce? Lying?"

She'd spent two weeks complaining of morning sickness, eating pickles, and going to bed by seven. He hadn't said a word, even though she hadn't done any of those things when she'd actually been pregnant with the boys.

Clutching her stomach, she stumbled back against a stool. "What do you mean?"

"You're no more pregnant than I am."

A crease split the middle of her forehead. "I've already been to my doctor, and she confirmed it. If you're not willing to accept your responsibility for this new life—"

He rolled his eyes. "I found a bloody tampon. Unless Pete or Billy has started using them, you're out of luck. Nice try." Leaning against the counter, he crossed his arms. "Now maybe we can get back to discussing a divorce."

She tried to speak but choked on her words. Turning his back on her, David set his glass in the sink and headed downstairs to shower.

He'd never imagined a victory could feel so hollow.

WITH DIANA RUNNING ERRANDS, David picking up Billy from a tennis match, and Dad and Jenna down for afternoon naps, Liz had a free moment—and the house to herself. She tiptoed past the open door of her dad's bedroom, hoping not to wake him.

"Liz?"

She took a step farther, past the door, and peeked at her watch. Damn. David had just left, and Diana wouldn't be back for at least another hour.

Turning, she tilted her head toward the open door. Dad lay in bed, eyes open and more alert than usual, crumpling the end of his sheet in his right hand. Over and over.

She stepped into the room. "Need something, Dad?"

His hand quavering, he reached for the lidded plastic cup that Diana had left on his bedside table. Liz picked it up, holding a straw to his parched lips. He nodded after a shaky sip and pushed the cup away.

"Anything else you want?"

Dad stared at her, his pale blue eyes blinking. She stood in place, crossing and uncrossing her arms. Fidgeting.

"Want . . . to talk." His words came out on a wheeze, and he drew in a long, hacking breath.

"Diana's not here right now." She fluffed his pillows behind his head, feeling useless.

He whispered something she didn't catch, so she leaned closer. "Want . . . to talk . . . to you."

Stumbling, she almost fell onto the bed, slamming a hand against the bedside table at the last moment to catch herself. His cup bounced off the table and onto the floor. She bent down to pick it up, praying for a way to escape and hide somewhere until David or Diana returned.

But Diana had asked her to talk to Dad, and the part of her that didn't feel like a terrified five-year-old wanted closure. She glanced around the spartan room. Flowers everywhere, and photos, but little else except the bed. Spotting an old folding chair in one corner, she dragged it over to the side of the bed.

"What do you want to talk about?" She scoured her brain for neutral topics and brightened as she thought of one. "Brandon's getting married in three days. To Piper."

He might not know who Brandon was at this point, and he sure wouldn't know Piper. Liz reached for an old photo of

Piper, Liz, and Tracy standing on the dock. She held it up to her dad's face and pointed. "See? There's Piper. Brandon's marrying her on Saturday, here at the River. Isn't that great?"

Her dad touched the picture, his shaky finger landing on Liz.

"Nope. That's me." She pointed again. "That's Piper. The one who's marrying Brandon."

His finger didn't move. "You."

"Uh, yes. That's me around age sixteen. I'm with Piper and Tracy. Tracy will be here for the wedding, too."

Dad frowned at the photo. "You were . . . on dock. You . . . fell."

Liz turned the photo in her hands, staring at it, trying to remember the day it was taken. They'd had a hundred days just like it in high school. Sunny skies and three bright smiles. "Um, no, Dad. I'm pretty sure I didn't fall in the water."

Unless Piper or Brandon pushed her, but they wouldn't. Piper knew swimming terrified Liz, even though she'd never admitted it in so many words and couldn't explain it even to herself. In fact, she'd always done a pretty good job—of both swimming and faking it.

"Your mother . . . jumped in. After you."

Liz held up a shaking hand. Dad's brain was gone, but she still couldn't believe he'd have the gall to mention Mom after everything he'd done to her. She sucked in a breath. "No. Mom was dead by then." Long before then, on a night Liz would never forget. She'd also never forgive Dad for it.

"Baby . . . died."

Startled, Liz snorted the breath out her nose. Mom and Dad had produced only one kid—her—and she definitely hadn't died. A miscarriage? She shook her head, but it was possible. *She'd* certainly had more than one. Another connection she had with Mom; another unhappy one. "What are you talking about?"

Her dad wet his lips and held out a shaky hand for his cup. It took forever before he pushed it back at her. "Important. Want to ... talk ... about you."

He'd apparently given up on the baby. Fine. She sat back and crossed one leg over her knee. "It was important a long time ago, Dad." Praying to God that she didn't cry in front of him, she crossed her arms. "I'm not sure it is anymore."

She held his pained gaze and refused to budge.

"Must ... talk."

"Why? 'Cause you can't hit me anymore?"

He flinched, and his hand kneaded the top of his sheet in a frenetic rhythm. "I ... hurt you."

"Yeah." As tears started to fall, Liz lurched to her feet. Finding a Kleenex, she blew her nose and tried to stem the torrent. Turning back to her dad, she squared her shoulders. "Why? I was a little kid, for God's sake. Why did you hit me? Why did you let Mom die?"

Dad's hand ceased its movement, and he stared at her, through her, his eyes fading back into the zone where he hardly knew her name, let alone the hell he'd once inflicted on her. As tears filled her eyes, she stumbled out of the room, blindly, knocking over the folding chair and slamming into the doorjamb on the way out. She'd never learn the truth. At this point, it might be too late.

"ALL READY FOR THE BIG DAY?" Liz handed Piper a glass of champagne as she sipped her own lemonade. "It's not too late, you know, to dump the loser and run off with me for a week canoeing in the Boundary Waters."

Brandon, casual in khakis and a polo shirt, stood talking to David and Pete across the porch. Next to the guys, Billy stared out the window, probably calculating his odds of escaping. Piper couldn't help laughing. Liz would go camping in the Boundary Waters the same day Tracy would. Never.

Jenna walked up with her own glass of lemonade. "You look pretty, Piper." Wearing a red sundress with a minimum of bows, she touched Piper's light-blue silk skirt.

"So do you, Jenn." Piper bent down to admire Jenna's dress at closer range. "You look so grown up."

Giggling, Jenna ran over to David and Brandon, who both whistled as she drew near. David picked her up in his arms.

Liz touched Piper's arm. "You do look good, Piper. But so dressed up for the River!" She put a hand over her heart. "I'm not sure I can handle it."

"Is that why you wore capris and a tank top?" Piper leaned closer to Liz. "Trying to make me look good?"

Liz grinned. "Not an easy task."

"Why, you—"

Laughing, Piper and Liz took off, champagne sloshing on the floor as Piper chased Liz around the porch and into the great room, where some of the guests had gathered for the rehearsal dinner. When Liz hauled up short, Piper ran into her. They'd almost tripped right over Frank in his wheelchair as Diana pushed him through the great room and toward the porch.

"Sorry! We were just, uh, running around the room." Piper glanced from a horrified Liz to a smiling Diana, feeling stupid. "Just like old times."

Frank stared at Liz and didn't say anything.

Diana started pushing the chair again. "No harm done,

girls." She winked as she moved past. "But try not to hurt our other guests. They might sue."

Piper laughed. "Good advice."

Diana glanced around the great room and into the porch. "By the way, has anyone seen Suzy?"

Piper shook her head as Diana frowned and kept moving. On edge now, Liz looked as if she might be contemplating her escape route if Suzy appeared. Piper grabbed her arm. "Hey, let's go talk to the guys. I'll be so busy mingling with wedding guests tomorrow, I probably won't even have a chance to speak to my new husband."

"That's what it's like when you're married."

Piper started to laugh until she saw the haunted look in Liz's eyes. Liz shook her head, looking horrified, before she forced a smile. "I'm sorry. I do think it'll be wonderful for you."

"I sure hope so. I must've paid a hundred bucks for that wedding dress." She dragged Liz back out to the porch. "C'mon. Let's flirt with our boyfriends. Just like in high school."

Liz nearly spewed her lemonade. "*Your* boyfriend. And we never flirted with those guys in high school."

"I flirted with Brandon when you weren't looking."

"Tell that to Brandon." Liz lowered her voice as they drew within a few feet of the two brothers, who were busy regaling Jenna, Pete, and Billy with their youthful escapades. "I don't think he was looking, either."

Piper slugged her in the arm.

As they stepped up to the group, Brandon whistled at Piper and David watched Liz over the top of his drink. After a moment's silence, David grabbed a bottle of champagne from the table next to him and topped off Piper's glass.

"Thanks, but I probably shouldn't—"

"Chase Liz around the house with a glass of champagne in your hands?" David grinned at Piper, then started to tilt the bottle toward Liz's glass before he spotted her lemonade. "Sorry. I forgot."

"Not everyone drinks as much as you do, David." Suzy, poured into a glittery black cocktail dress that no one else would wear at the River, shoved a path between David and Liz as she moved to David's side. Her face in her lemonade, Liz took a step backward, then slipped across the room to Diana.

Piper wished she could do the same.

Suzy rubbed up against David and purred. "Here you are."

His eyebrows rose. "At the party? Yeah. Have been since it started an hour ago. You said you weren't coming."

"Am I late?" Tittering, Suzy didn't bother to refute him. Even Brandon stared at her. "I was just getting ready." She scanned the porch, her gaze landing on Liz. "Too bad Liz didn't have time to change."

David glanced across the porch. "She looks fine to—"

"David!" Piper cut him off with a hand on his arm as Suzy scowled. "Would you mind pouring me more champagne?"

"No prob." Picking up the bottle while Piper quickly drained her glass, David waited, then poured, ignoring Suzy's outstretched hand.

"Thanks. Shoot, I just remembered I have to talk to, uh, Diana." Piper shot a desperate look at Brandon, then took Jenna's hand. "Let's go, Jenn. I think Gram wants to . . ." Her voice trailed off as they left the group.

"Wants to what?" Jenna looked up at her, an adorable smudge of blue frosting on the corner of her mouth.

Piper snatched a napkin from a nearby table and wiped it off. "She, uh, wants to see your pretty dress."

Jenna giggled as they walked up to Diana, who was talking quietly with Liz and Frank.

Diana tilted her head in the direction of the group Piper had just escaped. "Anything I want to know?"

Piper wrinkled her nose. "More of the same." Pictures of a ruined wedding flashed through her mind. "I hope she doesn't—" Her voice caught.

Diana patted her shoulder. "She won't. Your wedding will be perfect. I guarantee it."

Liz wrapped one arm around Diana, the other around Piper. "I don't think they give guaranties like that. But don't worry. We've always got the water hose."

All three women laughed. Not wanting to be left out, Jenna giggled, too.

CHAPTER 18

Saturday dawned bright and clear. A little after nine, David crisscrossed the beach with Brandon and two grumbling boys, picking up stray sticks and raking the sand. He stared wistfully at his speedboat. They could sneak in a few ski runs and—

"Don't even think about it."

David whipped his head around. Leaning on his rake, Brandon wagged a finger.

"They'd kill us. We're supposed to be cleaning up the beach. The wedding starts at eleven, in case you forgot."

"Plenty of time."

Pete edged closer to the water and eyed the boat. "I don't see why the girls don't have to help."

David tousled Pete's spiked hair, sending it up even higher than usual. "They don't clean up beaches for parties. They're upstairs getting dolled up."

Billy stopped raking the same yard of sand he'd stared at for the last fifteen minutes. "Is Mom coming?"

"I think so. Unless she changes her mind."

Billy and Pete started raking in earnest, heads down, as David caught a sympathetic glance from Brandon. He didn't need sympathy. People with much less money struggled through divorces and somehow pulled their kids through. He could, too.

"Dad?"

"Yeah?" Buried in his thoughts, David kept raking aimlessly.

"Dad?"

He finally looked up to see both Pete and Billy staring at him. Brandon had moved farther down the beach, toward David's property, probably to avoid getting caught in the crossfire.

Pete's gaze drilled him. "Are you gonna leave Mom and hook up with Liz?"

Startled, David fumbled with his rake, and he watched it hit the sand.

Arms crossed, Pete glared at him. "It really sucks, you know?"

Billy, still raking the same patch, kept his head down but peered at David through his long bangs.

David drew in a ragged breath. "I'm not hooking up with anyone. Liz is married, as you know, and she's not hooking up with anyone, either." He almost wished Suzy were. "Your mom and I are working on some tough issues right now, and she'd rather blame it on Liz."

"Or you?" Pete jabbed his rake in David's direction.

He nodded. "All of this is between your mom and me. Liz and I—"

"—are just friends. And family." Brandon stepped to David's side. "If you guys keep coming up with lame excuses to avoid raking, then get outta here. It looks good enough."

Pete stood his ground, glaring but unsure, while Billy raced up the stairs before Brandon changed his mind. After a minute, Pete dropped his rake and went upstairs, too.

David turned to Brandon. "That's not totally—"

"—true?" Brandon threw an arm around David's shoulders. "I figured. But they're kids, David. Whatever you do, you've gotta keep them out of it. It'll just hurt them."

"But I've always been straight with them." Straight, maybe, if not entirely open. Thinking about all the times he'd told Pete to be honest with him left knots in his stomach.

Fists on his hips, Brandon surveyed the beach before glancing again at David. "You're a good dad. You're there for them. That's what counts."

"I've really messed it up. With Suzy *and* Liz."

"You'll figure it out. Hopefully, while I'm on my honeymoon." Brandon grinned as he gathered the rakes and headed for the stairs.

David followed a few steps behind, hands in his pockets, considering everything.

And finding no solutions.

He shook his head at Brandon. "I hope it's a long one."

A FEW MINUTES PAST ELEVEN, guests milled about in the great room as the minister stood with Liz, David, and a nervous Brandon in front of the hearth. Frank sat propped up in his wheelchair to one side of David. The children circled around him. Separate from the rest of the family, Suzy leaned against a table at the far end of the room, sipping a drink.

Diana stood in the hall just outside the great room, at the foot of the stairs, as she listened for Piper's entrance. A skirt swished and heels clattered down the stairs. Suddenly nervous, she prayed Piper didn't trip.

With more calm than Diana felt, Piper reached the bottom step, eyes bright, her wedding dress dazzling.

Leaning forward, Diana whispered. "You look beautiful, dear. I'm so happy for you. And proud." Piper blushed, and Diana whispered again. "I also have no idea exactly how I'm supposed to do this."

Catching a tear on the tip of one finger, Piper whispered in Diana's ear. "Try not to screw it up."

As they both laughed, she escorted Piper to the group gathered at the hearth. When they reached Brandon, he stepped forward, gave Diana a peck on the cheek, then grabbed Piper's hand and turned with her toward the minister. Diana took a chair next to Frank and reached for his hand, squeezing it.

In ten minutes, it was over. Brandon and Piper, husband and wife. The sweat stopped trickling down Brandon's face halfway through his vows, and he beamed at his new wife before the happy couple turned to greet her and Frank. Diana smiled as she brushed a tear from one eye, then gave them each a hug, followed by a hug for David and Liz, who each stood to one side, eying each other nervously.

"Mingle, everyone." She could still direct the troops as well as a field general, and did. "Brandon and Piper, you have a plane to catch this evening, so you don't need to spend the whole afternoon kissing."

"Mom!" Brandon choked on the champagne the caterer had just handed him.

"And try to handle your liquor." She tweaked Brandon's rosy cheek. "David and Liz—" She pulled them both to her, then leaned in close. "Have fun. You're family, you know, so you can talk to each other."

Liz shot a wary glance at Suzy, still at the far end of the room, watching them sullenly as she continued to sip her drink.

Diana touched Liz's arm. "She's not your problem. She

and David have issues to resolve, yes, but they were present long before you arrived this summer."

Liz gazed at the floor. "I don't think she realizes that."

"Most people don't." Diana touched Liz's chin until she looked up again. "Remember, this is Piper's and Brandon's day. Let's not spoil it for them."

"I wouldn't do that."

Jenna appeared at Liz's elbow, demanding attention. Diana bent to hug her, then turned back to Liz. "I know, but I need your help making sure no one else does."

After a meaningful glance in Suzy's direction, Diana watched as David strode across the room to Suzy.

She returned to Frank's side, offering him a sip of lemonade while she watched the guests wander down to the beach, where the reception festivities would soon be underway.

So far, a beautiful day. She hoped it lasted.

APPROACHING SUZY, decked out in yards of something pink and swirly, David contemplated the differences between talking to his wife and attending his own funeral. He couldn't count many.

She stood alone in the corner of the room, not talking to anyone, not smiling, nursing a drink that didn't leave her hand. Looking as happy as he felt. He clinked his champagne flute against her tumbler. "Nice dress." As she shrugged and looked past him, he eyed her over the top of his glass. "What are you drinking?"

"Diet Coke."

He caught a whiff of something that didn't smell like Diet Coke. "Anything else?"

She touched the glass to her lips. "Anything to get me though the day."

He glanced around the great room, mostly empty now except for Liz, holding hands with Jenna while she chatted up her pal Tracy and the guy Tracy brought with her. "I thought the ceremony went well. Nice and short."

"I'm not too fond of weddings." A tear glimmered in Suzy's eye. "They only lead to marriage."

"True." He ran a finger inside the collar of his dress shirt, which felt snug. "Some marriages are happy. Ours was, in the beginning."

"How long ago?" She took another sip, a bigger one, then hiccupped into her hand. "I'm not sure I remember anymore."

"It's been a while."

"Now you want to toss me aside." She pointed a shaking finger at Liz, whose back was to them. Hopefully, she couldn't hear this. "Just because *she* shows up for the summer."

He glanced at Liz, admiring her lithe figure—in a simple but sleek blue dress instead of her usual shorts or sweats—without letting it register on his face. "You and I both know our marriage hasn't worked in years, and it has nothing to do with Liz. It's about you and me." He took a sip of champagne, swallowing hard. "And I'm not running to Liz. She's become a friend this summer, someone I talk to."

"You also kiss her, and God knows what else." A look of revulsion soured Suzy's face.

"Nothing else." They shouldn't have this conversation here, even though most of the guests had already headed down to the beach. "We were horsing around on the beach, joking, and . . . it just happened. By accident."

"Just that once?" Suzy's brows shot skyward.

He took another sip as he pondered his answer. Whatever his flaws, he'd always been honest with Suzy. Silent, maybe, but honest when it came right down to it.

The champagne, swirling on his tongue, tasted bitter.

"Like I said, Liz and I are friends. Nothing more."

Suzy set down her empty glass and beckoned a twenty-something waiter, who quickly brought a fresh one. David exchanged his champagne for bourbon, straight up.

"You can't have her, David."

He nodded absently, numb to her threats and tantrums. Her eyes glimmered again, and a tear rolled down one cheek. Without thinking, he reached over and brushed it away.

"It's just that—" She buried her nose in her drink. "I tried. All those years I tried. I'm not happy, but I don't want to lose you."

"Why? What do we have left?"

She drained her glass in two gulps. Jesus. When the waiter approached again, he waved the guy away. Reaching out, Suzy grabbed the waiter and asked for another drink.

"Take it easy, Suz. The reception is just beginning."

Her eyes already looked slightly out of focus. One ankle twisted beneath her, sending her stumbling backward against the table.

"How many drinks have you had?"

"Not enough." She batted her eyelashes at the waiter as he handed her another drink, then followed him with her gaze as he crossed the room. Right. The guy had a man-bun and could use a shower. David rolled his eyes.

"Drink up." She tilted his glass against his mouth, sloshing liquid over the rim and down the front of his shirt, and smirked when he jumped. "I don't plan to lose you, David."

He grabbed a napkin and mopped up his shirt, half-tempted to pour something down the front of Suzy. Damn. He'd stay drier and halfway sane if he postponed this conversation, but the words popped out of his mouth. "And I'm asking why. Since you're not happy, either, why should we stay together?"

"We have two boys." She poked at the ice cubes in her glass. "We're married and I stayed home, and . . . and I don't want to go back out there."

"Money would never be an issue." But it always had been to Suzy, for reasons he'd never understood. "Whether we're together or apart, you don't have to work."

"You say that like we've already signed the papers." She set down her drink. "I'm a big girl, David. I know I wouldn't be welcome in the Carruthers family anymore. Everything would be cut off."

He frowned at her. "You know that's not true, but this isn't the time or place. I'm sorry I even mentioned it."

Suzy rubbed up against him, giving him a close-up view of breasts that strained at their leash. He wished he felt something other than embarrassment.

"I want you." She reached for his hand, pulling it around her waist. "I want to keep you."

Letting go of her, he backed away. Her words made him feel even less like a husband and more like a prize bull.

"You haven't wanted me in years. We're way past that." And Suzy was way past reason. "I'm headed down to the beach. For the reception." He set down his drink before his eyes got as glassy as Suzy's already were. "Want to join me?"

She waved at the air. "You go ahead. I'll stay here and . . . have another drink."

At least she wouldn't have to drive home.

Stuffing his hands in his pockets, David walked through the porch and outside, frowning as he trotted down the steps.

LIZ HUMMED to herself as the jazz quartet started playing on a makeshift platform of plywood and strategically placed cement blocks, cables running in every direction. She spotted Piper and Brandon, hand in hand, talking to Tracy and her boyfriend, Kevin, a cute guy who kept his eyes locked on Tracy and his arm around her waist.

Biting her lip, Liz tried not to feel sorry for herself. She had someone, too. Paul. He hadn't wanted to fly back for the wedding, and she'd agreed that he didn't need to.

She couldn't help watching David as he traipsed down the stairs, no Suzy in sight. Turning her back on him, she concentrated on the music. When her hips started to sway to the rhythm, she abruptly froze. She didn't need to send any signals to David, intended or not, and Suzy didn't need another excuse to jump on her.

Her silk dress felt hot and sticky under the midday sun. Piper and Brandon wanted everyone comfortable at their wedding, but the invitations hadn't mentioned swimsuits. She wouldn't exactly relish wearing one in front of fifty people, but the water looked cool and inviting.

A few wedding guests she didn't recognize—like most people here—had similar thoughts, pulling off their shoes and dipping their feet in the water. Liz started toward them.

"Wait up." With a hand on her shoulder, David twirled Liz in place. "Isn't it time for the first dance?"

She glanced at the stretch of beach they'd set aside for dancing. Brandon and Piper were chatting with their guests, and Tracy and Kevin stood apart, probably whispering sweet nothings to each other. No one danced.

"That's for Piper and Brandon." She saw her reflection in

his wire-rim aviators, which he'd had since high school. Yes, she'd even asked. "And Suzy would throw a fit."

"She's pretty mellow." He grinned at her over the top of his sunglasses. "Alcohol will do that to you."

"I wouldn't know." Turning, she kicked off her sandals and headed for the water.

He kept pace with her. "Is that because of your dad? He doesn't drink, either."

Her steps slowed as they reached the water's edge. "He drank when I was a kid, believe me. So did my mom." She never thought that way about her mom, but of course it was true. She suddenly realized that David must not know. "She died because she drank so much."

"I'm sorry."

Silent, they stood next to each other, not touching, as they gazed out at the water. Despite the heavy waves rolling in from the constant parade of boats, Liz dipped her toes in the water, lifting the bottom of her dress up to her knees. David stayed on the beach. For the first time, she noticed that he wore a pair of old, decrepit boat shoes with his suit and tie.

David. Rebel without a cause.

She waded in another step, the water splashing her shins, as she laughed at David over her shoulder. "Want to join me?"

He pointed at his feet. "Can't. I have to preserve my footwear, such as it is, not to mention a little decorum."

Rolling her eyes, she took another step. The water had receded from its peak warmth and felt cool against her legs. She hitched up her dress a little more, trying to keep it dry.

"Watch it. There are laws against nude bathing." David chuckled behind her when she barely managed to keep the hem of her dress above the water.

Turning, she started to say something just as a wave

caught her knees, knocking her off balance. "Oh!" She danced an impromptu jig to stay upright. Hop, hop... down. With a splash, she landed on her butt, soaked to her chest.

"Are you okay?" David kicked off his shoes and waded in.

"Not at the moment." She reached for his outstretched hand but, halfway out of the water, her own wet hand slipped out of his grasp. She fell back in, even worse this time, and was so mortified that she started laughing hysterically.

The crowd noticed, of course, and some started toward the water, which only fueled her embarrassment. Piper was going to kill her. David reached down again and yanked her up so hard that she tumbled against him, grabbing him for a moment to get steady before stumbling back onto the beach.

"I'm so sorry, David. I—"

"I can't believe you!" Suzy swooped in, slapping Liz's hand away, even though she'd already let go of David. "Embarrassing me like this."

Suzy was embarrassed? On what planet?

David backed away from Liz, trying to calm Suzy, whose voice kept rising. Horrified and shivering, Liz wrapped her arms around herself, frantically trying to cover the wet fabric of her dress. Tracy rushed over, quickly handing her a sandy beach towel. Farther up the beach, Diana and two upset newlyweds circled the crowd, trying to steer everyone away from the water.

So much for a cool dip on a hot day.

Liz bent to pick up her discarded sandals, then tiptoed across the sand to Piper, shaking violently as she mouthed an apology that would never make up for what had just happened.

With the towel draped around her, she headed up the steps amid whistles and laughter that almost drowned out Suzy's high-pitched shrieks and David's lower, placating words. A speedboat roared off—probably David, which would only irritate Brandon and Piper even more. Without looking back, she walked though the screen door and into the porch, then trudged through the great room and upstairs to her bedroom.

She wouldn't show her face again today. Or maybe ever.

"SHE CAN'T EVEN DRIVE that boat, let alone drunk." David stalked up and down the beach, running his hands through his hair as he watched his speedboat streak through the no-wake zone. "I hope the sheriff stops her before she hits another boat."

His mom appeared and rested a hand on David's lower back, calming him. Her other hand shielded her eyes against the sun as she peered at the River. "Couldn't you stop her?"

"Try to stop Suzy when she's that pissed? She would've killed me." David shook his head, wishing he'd realized sooner what she planned to do. Wishing he hadn't left the keys in the ignition. Wishing she hadn't rammed the dock as she took off. "Shit."

He kicked his foot against the sand, sending a spray of it flying. "You're right. I should've gone after her. She just—"

He broke off when he noticed Pete and Billy standing nearby, looking upset.

His mom patted his arm. "She'll be back soon. Probably towed by the sheriff."

Herding David and several guests to the large tent on the beach, where two linen-topped tables overflowed with food, Diana kept a hand on David's arm.

He grimaced. "I'm sorry I wrecked the party."

"It's not my party." She tilted her head at Brandon and Piper, who both approached.

"I'm really sorry, guys." He shook his head at Piper and slugged Brandon's arm. "I guess I really blew it this time."

Piper touched his arm. "I saw the whole thing. Liz doesn't know enough to stay out of the water, but it's not your fault. Or hers. Suzy was just—"

"Yeah. I know." David glanced at the meats, salads, and sweets lining the table next to him and felt his gut clench. "I think I'll take a walk and blow off some steam."

"Become respectable again." Brandon grinned.

"Or try." Turning, David spotted Pete and Billy headed for the water now, anxiously watching the boats. He went to them, draping an arm over their shoulders, and the silent trio walked together to the point. No sheriff's sirens. Nothing to calm his nerves.

Pete patted him awkwardly on the shoulder. "Mom shouldn't drive the boat. She always tells *me* not to drink and drive."

David tweaked Pete's nose. "You're sixteen. You're not supposed to be drinking, period."

"Is she gonna be all right?" As they reached the end of the point and turned to head back, Billy gazed over his shoulder at the channel. "Mom looked kinda scary."

"She'll be fine."

"Yeah, squirt. Even Mom must be able to drive the boat better than *you* drive it." Pete took off at a run, Billy hard on his heels, as David headed slowly back to the party.

He reached the crowd just as the beach phone rang. His mom picked it up, pressing the receiver to one ear and covering her other ear with her hand.

"Who's calling? What? I can't hear you." She shook her head and frowned. "I'm sorry. What did you say?" As she listened, a deep crease ran down the middle of her forehead. David stopped a few feet from her. Maybe Suzy had actually come to her senses and realized she couldn't drive her car, but wouldn't she have called his cell phone? No, not in her current mood. She'd want to talk to anyone *but* him. Still, Mom shouldn't have to deal with placating Suzy, especially today. She was his issue, but he'd fix it. He moved closer, trying to get his mom's attention.

Before he could, she dropped the phone, falling to the sand next to the dangling receiver. David snatched up the phone and held it to his ear. The caller had hung up.

"Mom? Who was that?" He dropped to the sand, too, wrapping an arm around her as she rocked back and forth, her hands covering her eyes, shuddering uncontrollably.

What the hell?

Mom's rocking stopped, then started again. "I'm . . . so sorry, David. Suzy . . . had an accident. At an incredibly high speed." Her head swiveled, taking in the crowd gathered around them, before turning to face him. "They're afraid she might not make it."

Crumpling into her arms, he sobbed.

CHAPTER 19

She was alive. But dear God, she looked like hell.

David stepped gingerly into the ICU, his quick gaze taking in the jangle of wires and tubes and beeping monitors. Suzy lay propped up on pillows, eyes closed, her bruised and bandaged head unnaturally tilted to one side and supported by a hideous white neck brace. The glare from the overhead lights illuminated the puffy swelling of her face and the ugly gash across her forehead that even the best plastic surgeon, which she'd had, couldn't completely fix.

He took a deep breath, wishing he didn't have to see her like this, remembering his terrified but entirely different visit to his mom a few short weeks ago. He'd worried about Mom. A horrible part of him that he loathed had actually wished—for an ugly moment—that Suzy had died in the car crash. That she wasn't here, utterly broken after almost losing her life.

Her eyelids fluttered open.

"Suzy, I'm so sorry." Sorry for everything, including maybe marrying her, but once he'd married her he should've stuck it out. At least until a more natural end to his marriage.

Her eyes blinked, and a teardrop stabbed one corner. He sprang forward, desperate to do something. Anything. Her hand, tethered in all those tubes, brushed him away.

"I'm just trying—"

She started to shake her head, stopping abruptly when she choked on the tube in her throat. The ugly slash of stitches sliced across her forehead, and he winced at the deep purple welts on her cheeks. "No."

"No what? You don't want me to help?" If he'd helped her sooner, she might not be here. He'd always harped on her wild driving—

No, he hadn't. He'd silently fumed and spent his only worries on the boys not being in her car when she raced off after an argument. How many arguments had they had this summer? And how many *before* this summer?

Groggy, she kept struggling to talk, kept choking on the tube in her throat and scaring the crap out of him.

"Suz, don't try to talk. I'm just relieved that you—" He broke off, not knowing how much Suzy knew of the miracle she'd received after the EMTs almost gave up on her.

Her eyes closed again, probably thanks to the boatload of morphine they'd given her. "I . . . don't want you to stay." A few more tears appeared, but he caught himself before he reached out to wipe them away.

Frank had spoken almost the same words to Liz after he'd fallen this summer, nearly sending her packing. David had hated Frank for it, but now he understood *exactly* how Liz must've felt. Like shit. He took a deep breath, seeking courage, silently begging for answers to the questions racing through his mind. Guilt overwhelmed everything else. "I'm not a complete jerk, Suz. I'm . . . willing to make this work."

"Not now." Suzy tried to turn her head again, slowly,

away from him, but was stopped by all the tubes and wires. "Are the boys here?"

Crestfallen, David headed for the door, opened it, and let Pete and Billy inside. Billy grabbed David's sleeve, so many questions in his eyes, but he shook his head and nudged him closer to the bed. After making sure Billy seemed okay, he waited out in the hall. Suzy didn't want to see him. He'd wanted the same thing just a few short hours, days, weeks ago. Now he just wanted peace. With Suzy?

He hung his head and softly cried.

———

"DAVID WON'T SPEAK to me. Or even look at me."

Tuesday morning, Liz sat cross-legged on the end of Diana's bed, staring in disgust at the nails she'd spent the last few days chewing down to the nub. Diana had invited her in for "girl talk"—something neither of them was exactly in the habit of doing—but now she seemed to be fixated on examining the slew of expensive earrings in her jewelry box.

"Here. Something to match your eyes." Diana held out a stunning pair of sapphire earrings circled with diamonds, pressing them into Liz's hand when she resisted. "He's hardly here at all, dear, and doesn't say much to anyone except his boys, and perhaps Suzy. She's getting a lot of sedatives and pain relief, so I'm not sure how . . ."

Diana trailed off, probably as unsure about Suzy's lucidity as she was about how much to tell Liz. She might be Diana's stepdaughter, but she'd also been thrust into the role of the Other Woman.

"How are they all doing? Including Suzy?"

"As well as can be expected." Diana's hand fluttered over

a strand of pearls, even though she'd already tried to give Liz half of the jewelry collection she kept at the River, for reasons Liz couldn't begin to fathom. "It sounds like Suzy will have a few scars but will otherwise be okay. David is a wreck, to put it mildly, and his boys are trying to manage without a functioning mom or dad. It's a difficult proposition when you're sixteen and eleven."

Liz hadn't seen Pete or Billy since Saturday, or David since Sunday. David shuttled back and forth to the hospital, sometimes spending entire nights there, and spent the rest of his time at his house in Edina, getting it ready for when Suzy left the hospital. She definitely wouldn't be coming back to the River. Brandon and Piper had postponed their honeymoon until tomorrow, but only Diana had been permitted to visit David and his boys. And Suzy.

"What can I do to help?" Liz's hands shook as she shifted the earrings from one hand to the other, then gently set them back in the jewelry box.

"Nothing at this point, dear. Wait. Be patient."

"Patience was never my strong suit."

"I think I knew that." Diana's eyes twinkled. "Consider it a chance to practice. You can also pray for them."

"Do you think it's, uh, my—"

She choked, unable to finish the sentence.

"Fault?" Closing her eyes for a moment, Diana wrapped her arms around Liz. "It's no one's fault. Or it's my own."

"How could it be yours?" She bowed her head, feeling so small next to Diana. "You're . . . perfect. You do everything right. I ruined David's life and my life, and Suzy's."

Tears bubbled to the surface, claiming the mascara she'd already reapplied twice. No wonder she hardly ever wore it this summer.

"Stop." Diana reached for a tissue and dabbed Liz's eyes. "No one's life is ruined, although a few lives—and Suzy's body—might be a bit banged up at the moment. I'm not perfect, and you're thirty-seven. When you hit my age, we'll talk about perfect."

"But Suzy hated me."

"Since you were teenagers. Perhaps you gave her something to be jealous about this summer—" Diana tilted her head as she continued to dab at tears. "But this started long before you came back home. You were just unlucky enough to provoke the most recent dramas."

Her words didn't bring the comfort Liz craved. Nothing would. For the rest of her life.

Paul had sent flowers. Not to Suzy, still in intensive care and still in Paul's mind the woman who'd tried to terrorize him at the bonfire on the Fourth, but to Liz. A dozen long-stemmed roses, a fragrant mix of pink and yellow. Liz's favorite. He wasn't entirely clueless, or forgetful, or faded into memory, no matter how much Liz tried to rewrite the story of their marriage.

Paul still wanted her. David *didn't* want her anymore. In the course of the summer, after zigzagging in completely opposite directions, everything had returned to its starting point from all those years ago.

Sighing, Liz finally understood why people drank.

———

"Sure you're ready to go back to work?" Friday morning, back at the River but not feeling a shred of its usual comfort, David eyed Pete as he pulled his neon-orange T-shirt over his head. "I'm sure they'll cut you some slack if you ask. Or I can ask for you."

"Don't." Pete held up a hand. "I kinda need a break, if you know what I mean."

"Yeah. I guess I do." He straightened a couple of pillows on one of Suzy's butt-ugly chairs. Did staying together mean he had to keep this crap? Probably. "I'm sorry."

"Sorry won't erase her accident, or what she looks like." Pete grabbed his backpack and headed for the door, pausing on the threshold to glance back at David. "Nothing will."

"Her scars and bruises will heal." Mostly.

"How can you be so sure? And what about ours?" Pete's hand balled into a fist at his side. "Shit, Dad. We thought she was dead."

"But she made it." David told himself it was a blessing, but he still remembered the moments after that first phone call, when he'd selfishly wondered whether Suzy's death might be a hell of a lot easier than a painful divorce. He still hated himself for that. "She'll be fine. We'll all be fine. Eventually."

Pete didn't exactly look reassured. "Because you've still got us? And . . . we've got you?"

David felt his first glimmer of hope in six long days. "Yeah. Bad news, huh?"

"Sucks." Winking, Pete stepped outside.

His chest easing slightly, David turned in the direction he'd seen Billy disappear earlier. He found him curled up in a chair in the master bedroom, flipping through an old photo album Suzy had brought out to the River last summer when a few of her high-school girlfriends visited.

"Any good ones?" David dropped onto the carved wooden armrest of Billy's chair and glanced at the photos.

The kids at the River. Learning to waterski. Waving sparklers on the Fourth of July. Grinning as they hugged their dad. Suzy, seldom smiling and often standing to one side.

"Did Mom ever like the River?" Billy focused on the pictures, entranced by a rare one showing the four of them together on the beach when Billy was five or six.

"Yeah, when we were teenagers. We spent all summer out here." David shook his head, remembering how it had changed soon after Suzy got pregnant with Pete. She'd always wrinkled her nose at what she called the rustic uncleanliness of the River. Even when they bought the McIntyre house, after years of Suzy's complaints, she hadn't been happy, despite having a dream kitchen and modern bathroom.

Billy kept flipping pages.

"It's a gorgeous day, sport." For big chunks of the last six days, Billy and Pete had stayed cooped up inside with him, mostly at the hospital or their Edina house, all of them miserable. "Want to go waterskiing before the crowds come out for the weekend?"

Billy shook his head.

"Or we could sail or kayak. Or walk down to the Lees' trampoline. Or just hang out on the beach. I'm not going back to the hospital until this afternoon." He told himself that Billy needed some air that didn't smell like a hospital, but so did he.

The pages kept flipping. "You go, Dad. I'll stay here."

David ruffled Billy's hair as he stood up. "You should get some sunshine. We've stayed inside too long."

The album snapped shut. "So you're done then? Pete went to work and you're gonna waterski? What happened to worrying about Mom, huh? She almost died." He wiped the back of his hand across his nose. "And you don't give a shit."

"Billy! Don't talk like that."

"You and Pete do. And Mom's still in the hospital, and she still looks scary, and you don't—" He paused. "You don't *care*, and I can say whatever I wanna say."

"I do care." David perched again on the arm of the chair, which dug a painful groove into his butt. "Things with your mom and me aren't perfect—"

"No lie."

David brushed past Billy's interruption, which reminded him of Pete. "But I care about her." He stood up, refusing to consider what he and Suzy might do after she healed. When he first saw her in the ICU, he'd offered to stay with her forever, and she hadn't exactly leaped for joy. Forever was already starting to look like a long time. "And I love you and Pete more than anything. We're sticking together."

"Yeah? Says who?"

"Says your dad, who'll hang you upside-down from your ankles if you don't come outside with me."

Billy slid out of the chair and to his feet, grumbling all the way to his room, where he changed into a swimsuit while David waited in the hall. After a minute, they walked upstairs together and headed outside.

Billy peered up at David. "After waterskiing, do you think we could go to Selma's?"

David grinned as he hoisted Billy in the air. "You bet, sport. Anything for you."

DAVID AND BILLY ran around on the beach, tossing a Frisbee and acting as if no one else existed. They even ignored Jenna, who kept waving at them, too shy to walk right up and join in their game.

When Liz finally caught David looking at her, she approached, Jenna in tow. "David? And Billy. I'm so sorry."

"You should be." Billy spat on the ground and scowled,

and David didn't bother to correct him. It told Liz everything she needed to know.

Her stomach lurched as she clutched Jenna's hand. Billy stared at his bare feet. David gave Jenna a tight smile, then looked away.

Diana joined Liz, softly touching her back, before walking over to David and Billy. She hugged each of them. Even Billy—sullen and ready to kill someone, preferably Liz—hugged her back. "How are you boys holding up?"

David shrugged and said nothing, and Billy followed suit.

"Remember, we're here for you. All of us."

As far as Liz could tell, David wished one of them—Liz—would just go home.

"HELLO?" Liz peered through the screen door at David's house after rapping again, hard, and wiping her sweaty palms on her shorts. Her stomach rumbled, telling her it was almost time for Sunday dinner, but she also felt queasy. "Anyone home?"

"The door's open." David's voice called out, but she couldn't see him in the gloomy interior.

She took a few steps inside and poked her head into the empty living room. She finally found David in the kitchen. He didn't look up from the newspaper.

She wet her lips and fidgeted and tried to think of what to say to a guy who still wasn't speaking to her, a guy who spent most of his waking time at the hospital. With his wife. "Diana was, uh, wondering if she could borrow a bottle of wine."

The newspaper rattled in his hands, but he still didn't look at her. "Haven't you tried that once before?"

"Yes, but it worked. I always like to run with a winning formula."

She caught a hint of a smile as he pulled the newspaper closer to his face.

"Speaking of running—" Her mind searched for a topic that might actually generate a nonlethal response. "I miss our morning hikes."

"Huh. I haven't seen you taking any."

So he'd been watching for her. Interesting. She vowed to take one tomorrow, if only to get a reaction from him. She walked over to the counter and rattled the newspaper. "Hey, I know what you're—"

"Feeling? No, you don't." He tugged the newspaper from her hand and tossed it aside. "My wife nearly died. Pete and Billy don't know what hit them, and I fucking caused it. What a selfish fucking asshole of a jerk I am!"

He slammed a hand on the counter so hard, he winced.

Her breath caught in her throat. "But I was part of it. I was talking to you. And . . . whatever."

"Whatever is right." He ran a hand through his hair, sending it in every direction. "I kept telling myself it was harmless, and I— Fuck."

She longed to touch him, comfort him, do something, but she didn't dare. "Is there anything I can do to help?"

"Yeah." After lurching to his feet, he walked her to the door. "Make sure I don't come near you. I fucked everything up the last time, but I won't do it again."

Biting her knuckles as she held her hand over her mouth, Liz brushed past him and slipped outside.

He didn't need to ask twice.

———

"WELCOME HOME." Echoing the words on the banner the boys had painted and hung over the front door, David pushed Suzy's wheelchair over the threshold of their Edina house. Her right-leg cast stuck straight out in front of her, a constant reminder to David of what she'd gone through a week ago, and every day since.

As if he could forget.

The purple bruises had faded to greenish-yellow, but the white neck brace stood out in harsh contrast to the blue blouse a male nurse had buttoned her into this morning after she'd turned down David's repeated offers to help. She hadn't let him see her undressed since the night she caught him kissing Liz at the point. Sure, he hadn't been too interested in seeing her undressed, and frankly still wasn't—not in that way—but everything else had changed.

They'd gotten married for better or worse, and it couldn't possibly get much worse than this, but he deserved it. The fires of hell. He saw them glowing in Suzy's eyes.

"Quit looking at me like that."

He blew out a breath. "How am I looking at you?" She kept telling him what *not* to do, but he didn't have a clue what he *should* do. How he should feel. He mostly just felt like shit.

"Like that." Her nose wrinkled, as if a rotten odor had hit it. "As if you pity me. I don't need your pity."

"I don't—" He broke off before the lie slid off his tongue. It might not be pity, exactly, but he also wasn't sure what it was. Duty? A habit of twenty-five years? She just sat there, unable to move. Utterly unable to slug or scratch him or do any of the other things she'd tried so often since that night with Liz on the beach. "What is it you want from me?"

She sighed. "Time. Patience. And maybe a little cooking." Her eyes twinkled at the end, surprising him.

"I think I can manage that."

Suzy slumped in her wheelchair. "I don't know how I'm going to handle stairs, even with help."

"You're not. I'm way ahead of you." For once. He wheeled her into the dining room, the only room available on the first floor of their house. He and Brandon and the boys had moved the huge mahogany table just yesterday, stashing it in the garage. "Voilà."

He'd rented a hospital bed from the place where Mom had found Frank's, and it sat in the middle of the dining room. It had expensive, freshly washed, bright-yellow bedding and was surrounded by flowers and every comfort he could think of. Okay, Mom had suggested most of it, but Suzy didn't need to know that.

Her gaze went around the room, the expression on her face going from doubt to surprise to maybe even a hint of happiness. No, not happiness. Her neck was in a brace, her leg in a cast, and her butt in a wheelchair. But a slight smile curved the corners of her mouth. She hadn't smiled at him in forever, since long before Liz had entered their lives this summer.

"Thank you." She sighed as if searching for something else to say—a question or an insult or *something*—but nothing came. He wondered when they'd last talked about anything other than their kids or how much she hated Liz.

He remembered his halting, awkward conversations with Liz at the start of the summer and of the longer, deeper talks they'd evolved into. Or had they? In truth, his conversations with Liz were still often difficult because of the issues they both had, the things they couldn't really talk about with each other. But he and Suzy could discuss anything—except Liz—and they didn't. Hadn't, in too many years to count.

"Are there any books I can get you? Movies?"

"You've . . . done so much."

Of course he had. He wasn't in a wheelchair, and he felt unending guilt for what had happened. A shopping spree and his massive cleaning, moving, and redecorating project weren't much. He'd only begun to do his penance.

Suzy gazed at him, silent. She probably wasn't eager to ask what he was thinking. He was usually thinking about Liz, who must hate him now. "Maybe a movie?"

He went to the stack of DVDs he'd collected. A dozen of her favorites, which meant romances, mostly, and a few musicals. He blinked, realizing how inappropriate a romance might be at this point.

He almost grabbed *Gidget*, a teenage beach romance with no guaranty that Moondoggie would stick with her for the long haul. Jesus. What an idiot. Instead, he helped her into bed, then brought the whole stack of DVDs to her bedside table. She'd have to pick her own movie, one in which the hero didn't call it quits at age forty-one.

Suzy needed a happy ending. And he didn't deserve one.

"How's IT GOING?" Pausing on the threshold to the porch, Diana watched Liz rock back and forth on the glider, Jenna asleep in her arms.

"Hi, Gram!" The sleeping child bolted upright.

"Hi, cutie." Diana sat down on the other glider, Jenna quickly joining her. "Did you take a nap?"

"I'm too big for naps, Gram." Jenna nodded solemnly. "I was playing with Mom 'cause David is being mean."

"He's not mean." She said it to Jenna but intended it for Liz's ears. "He's just busy. And very sad."

"I know. Suzy got hurt really bad an' almost died an' went to the hospital."

"That's right, but she's home now, at their house in town." One arm around Jenna, Diana gazed at Liz, who looked nearly as depressed as David. At least his boys were showing signs of recovery. "How would you like to take a boat ride? We could go to one of those restaurants on the water."

Liz looked sharply at her. "With Dad?"

Diana flinched. Until this moment, she hadn't forgotten his condition in months. After all, how could she? "Sorry. I was just trying to cheer you up."

"I'm fine."

"I'm not a fool, dear. You and David are both suffering, and the best cure for that is talking. To each other. Yes, even though he's also busy taking care of Suzy." Diana studied Liz over the top of Jenna's head. "One good thing has come from this summer, you know."

"Oh?"

"You and David have become friends. Good friends. It's what I've always wanted for you."

Liz frowned. "You're kidding, right? Our so-called friendship sent Suzy to the hospital." She held up a hand when Diana started to shake her head. "Don't deny it. It also isn't much of a friendship if one friend stops speaking to the other."

"He's hurting, Liz, and preoccupied with everything he needs to do. Give him time."

"It's been ten days. We'll be leaving in a few weeks, if not sooner."

Diana shivered, thinking of everything Liz had done for the house and for her. Tending to her, even if not to Frank. Working on the sale of the company, which had been put on hold since Suzy's accident. Drawing Brandon and Piper back more often to the summer house. With Jenna, keeping the house . . . alive.

"How's your novel?" Maybe that would keep Liz here longer, although she could write a novel in Washington as well as at the River. "You haven't mentioned it in a while."

Liz's eyes went wide, almost as if she were a young girl again, caught in a rare fib. "That's because it's, uh, well, I'm not sure what you'd call it, exactly."

"You don't have to explain." Diana nodded, pondering other projects. Something other than selling the company, which might drive Liz away rather than keep her here. "I've heard that many writers don't like discussing their work before they've finished it."

In Liz's silence, Diana let the subject drop. She watched as Liz stared at her lap.

"I changed my mind." Diana patted Liz's hand. "Don't give David any more time. Make him talk to you. Get him to do something. Go hiking."

"I tried."

"Try something new. Tell him you miss him. Tell him what you want . . . whatever that is."

"He's not exactly in the mood for deep conversations with me. Besides, he's not here."

Obstacles, indeed, but not insurmountable. Thinking of the haunted look that hadn't left David's face since the accident, and the low odds of his usual grin reappearing after Liz returned to Washington, Diana made a decision. "Tell him his mother insists."

"Seriously? But what should I say?"

"Whatever you want. Confide in him. Be friends again. Above all else—" She squeezed Jenna, who jumped off her lap and ran outside. "Be honest."

Liz twisted her hands in her lap. "About everything?"

Diana paused, wondering whether she was prodding Liz in the right direction or into deeper troubles. Eventually, Suzy would be back on her feet and likely back on the attack. "Yes. As soon as you decide what 'everything' is."

CHAPTER 20

David propped up his feet and relaxed in the comfy leather recliner he'd finally dragged into the dining room—Suzy's temporary bedroom. The late-afternoon sunlight filtered through the gauzy drapes, and he tried not to think about how beautiful the River must be right now, how much he'd rather be waterskiing or sailing, or how he was basically stuck.

He'd promised Suzy he'd stay, and he meant it, but the hell she'd put him through in the weeks before Brandon's wedding had just been a warm-up act. At least then he'd had the River. Now he had sappy movies and Suzy 24/7, but not even. Suzy wasn't the same Suzy she'd been before the accident, and he wasn't sure the new, passive version was an improvement.

Glancing at the big-screen TV, he rolled his eyes. Jack Nicholson and Diane Keaton were in Paris in a movie he couldn't remember the name of but which Suzy had watched at least three times already. Diane had just sent Keanu Reeves off in a taxi, choosing the old geezer over the buff young stud. Ahh. Hope for the future.

Suzy's gaze was glued to the screen as a tear trickled

down her cheek. Weird. She'd shed more tears today than in all of last week. Why? Because they'd never gotten around to traveling to Paris like she'd always wanted? But they had plenty of time. In fact, the future stretched before David like an endless chasm.

Something else he'd rather not think about.

When the movie ended, he reached for the remote, but Suzy stopped him.

What had he done wrong now? He tensed, searching her face, trying to guess her latest accusation or demand. "Want to watch another movie, or should I start dinner? Or both?"

She shook her head as the credits rolled. "I think it's time."

Frowning, he glanced at his watch. "Time? For what?"

The tears flowed faster now, and he jumped up to hand her the box of Kleenex. She daintily plucked out one tissue, which wasn't going to cut it.

She wadded up that one, unused, in her hand. "I've given it a lot of thought, and you were right. About us. That maybe we shouldn't be together anymore."

Her words hit him like a punch to the gut, and the elation he'd expected to feel if Suzy ever agreed to a divorce didn't come. "Because we never went to Paris? Because Diane dumped Keanu?" He glanced at her bedside table, wondering how many pain pills she'd taken today. She might be too drugged to think straight. "Maybe we should talk when you feel better."

"I feel fine."

Highly doubtful. Nearly two weeks after the accident, she was still basically immobile, and her face reminded him of a patchwork quilt. Not that he'd ever say that to her.

"Seriously." She held out her hand for the remote and,

when he handed it to her, clicked off the TV. "I don't think we should postpone this any longer."

Even though she'd deep-sixed any discussion of divorce every time *he'd* brought it up this summer. "I told you I'd stay with you. The moment I saw you in the hospital."

She blew out a soft breath. "I remember." She closed her eyes for a few moments, and more tears trickled down. Damn. "I knew something was wrong when you never lectured me for taking a boat I didn't know how to drive, let alone while drunk, and running my car off the road."

"Of course not." He waved a hand. Only the biggest jerk in the world would've chewed her out right after she almost died. "You were upset, and I would never—"

"—yell at a person lying helpless in the ICU? I know. And you wouldn't have asked for a divorce at that moment, either, or done anything different from what you did. I appreciate it."

"I'm not being noble." Hell. Like Suzy, he was just trying to survive.

She shook her head, offering a slight smile. "I didn't accuse you of being noble. You were just being you: the man I married."

David frowned, totally confused. So now he was a knight in shining armor? The man she'd married had been little more than a boy, a boy who thought he loved the girl while also thinking he was getting married too young.

"But you're also *not* the man I married. I married someone who was madly in love with me, and you're not anymore."

He glanced over at the stack of DVDs, wishing they were watching another drippy movie instead of having this conversation. He couldn't tell if Suzy really wanted a divorce or was just being stoic. She didn't sound even remotely like herself.

"Madly in love is for kids." Okay, maybe he wasn't a romantic. But he'd once been, hadn't he? "We've been together twenty-five years, Suz. People change. We've both changed. But we can start over and get to know each other again."

"Would you marry me today?"

His breath caught as his mind raced for an answer, knowing he couldn't give her the one she wanted. Could anyone give that answer after twenty-five years?

She shook her head. "I didn't think so."

"That's not fair. I'm willing to—"

"—start over? I know, and I really do appreciate it. But you can't put wrapping paper on a broken marriage and make it tidy with a bow, and you can't really ever start over. We don't have a clean slate, David. As you said, we have a history. Twenty-five years."

"And two kids."

"Who've been living with two very unhappy parents for quite a while now." Suzy grabbed another tissue, but the tears had stopped. "The truth is that I hate the River, and you love it, but it's not just about the River."

"Then what's it about?" He braced himself, figuring the word "Liz" was coming soon.

"Liz." She paused on the word, studying him, and he tried not to flinch. "Your family. Your company. It's even about the boys. Pete will be in college in two years."

"But Billy has quite a ways to go."

"He'll still have two parents, no thanks to me." She cleared her throat as memories flooded back to him of the boys' horror—and his own—when she'd nearly died in the accident. "But we don't need to be together to raise him. And he'll be happier if *we're* happy."

"I'm happy." Occasionally. But more this summer than he'd been in years.

"I've never seen you more miserable." She rolled her eyes at his polite lie, but she didn't lash out at him, and he kept wondering who or what had possessed Suzy's body. "I'm not happy, either, and I refuse to spend the rest of my life drinking to get through the pain."

The pain of being married to him. Ouch. He felt even more like a jerk than all the times she'd ripped into him this summer, and she wasn't even raising her voice. She was right, at least about him, but he'd also made a promise. He opened his mouth to protest.

"No. You're being very sweet, but we're done."

———

"JENNA? WHERE ARE YOU?" Liz looked behind the large sofa in the great room and kept hunting. "We have to go. We're late for Selma's."

Not exactly true, but worth a try after fifteen minutes of searching. Liz moved to the porch. No Jenna. She'd already scoured the whole second floor, kitchen, basement, and back house, after first trying the beach. All she'd found had been Diana, trying to catch an afternoon nap.

Pausing on the threshold to the great room, she heard muffled giggles.

"Jenna?" The only room she hadn't checked was—

Dad's room.

The door stood ajar. As Liz approached, she heard Jenna's high-pitched giggle.

"Oh, Gramps!" A major giggle fit. "That's silly. I'm not Liz. Liz is my mom!"

A low murmur came from her dad that Liz couldn't quite hear.

"Don't be sorry. You didn't do anything wrong."

More murmurs, which made Liz's skin crawl. She poked her head into the room. Jenna sat on the edge of Dad's bed, showing him a few pictures she'd drawn this morning.

Her dad was actually smiling—in a forced, painful kind of way—and didn't look as tired as usual. "I'm . . . sorry, Liz." He spoke again in a voice less faint. Straining to listen, Liz almost fell into the room. Had he seen her? "I never . . . meant to . . . hurt you."

"You didn't hurt me, Gramps. Billy did when he bit my finger yesterday. See?" She proudly held up her bandaged finger as Dad strained forward to look. "I bit him back."

Dad sank into his pillow. "Billy?"

"David caught me biting him and told me to stop."

"David?"

Jenna nodded. "I told him Billy bit me, but he still didn't think I should bite."

"Don't . . . bite."

"I won't, Gramps. Cross my heart."

"Or . . . hit. Don't . . . hit. Like I . . . hit you."

Liz almost crashed through the door.

"Gramps, you never hit me!" Jenna giggled and patted his chest. "You just take naps, an' we talk an' stuff."

Liz frowned, concerned but also not. She'd always worried that Jenna might not tell her if someone hurt her, but Jenna was right. Dad was barely able to hold a cup, let alone hit anyone. Even someone as small as Jenna.

She stepped into the room. "Okay, Jenna. I think you've bothered Gramps long enough."

Jenna protested but scrambled off the bed, blowing kisses to Liz's dad. "Bye-bye!"

Dad's eyes followed Jenna out of the room before he stared up at Liz, frowning.

"Liz?"

———

Sunday morning, David yawned and stretched, then rolled over and looked at the clock. Six-twenty. Before this summer, if he hadn't set an alarm, he'd wake up around eight. Now his eyes popped open every morning between six and six-thirty.

Face down, he buried his head in the pillow, willing himself to go back to sleep. Five minutes later, he groaned as he stumbled out of bed, threw on workout clothes, and dragged himself out the door. If he had to hike, he may as well drag Liz along.

Liz, the woman he still wanted. He hated himself for it.

Pete and Billy had spent the night in town with Suzy, after an awkward dinner of takeout Chinese during which Suzy had calmly told the boys about the divorce and the boys had glared nonstop at David. As if it were completely David's fault. Great. After finally helping the boys work through the aftermath of Suzy's accident, he'd now spend the rest of his life trying to get his own sons to speak to him. Divorce was turning out to be a lousy proposition.

Inside the big house, he hesitated a dozen times as he made his way through the porch and great room, then up the stairs. Her door was ajar. Pushing it open, he tiptoed inside. Not wanting to wake her. Wanting to watch her chest rise and fall as she slept. Wanting to touch her hair. He felt like a stalker.

Instead of perching on the edge of her bed like he usually did, he cleared his throat. "Liz?"

Her head rolled on the pillow, then went still. He softly

called her name again. Her eyes flew open as she yanked the covers to her chin.

"Want to go for a hike?"

She blinked. "With you? Are you . . . kidding?"

"Nope." He jammed his hands in his pockets as he walked back to the door. "I'll wait outside while you get dressed. I could use some exercise." He took a deep breath. "And we need to talk."

"What time is it?"

He grinned, feeling more like himself. "The usual."

Groaning, she sat up and swung her bare legs over the side of the bed. "I'll be right there."

A few minutes later, she met him on the path in front of the house. They stretched in silence and, by unspoken agreement, set off up the path. Ten minutes later, they reached the top. Liz didn't stop or ask where they should go, just headed in the opposite direction from usual. Toward the old stone fireplace in the middle of nowhere.

She hiked faster now, almost jogging, and he struggled to keep up.

When she stopped abruptly in front of the fireplace, in a patch of grass that probably used to be the main room of a little cabin, he bumped into her.

"Sorry." He jumped back a foot. "I didn't see you stop."

Bending down, she touched a broken-off stone. "The cabin is gone."

He frowned at her back. "It's been gone forever. Even when we were kids." He'd come up here to the fireplace with Suzy when they first started dating. They'd shared their first kiss here.

He wouldn't mention that to Liz. Not because he couldn't—like so many things he'd never felt comfortable saying to Suzy—but because he'd already hurt her enough.

Standing up again, she caressed the smooth stone of the fireplace, which was remarkably intact. "But the fireplace is still here."

He rolled his eyes. "Yeah. Like it's always been."

"Exactly. Even after the cabin collapsed, the heart of it remained standing." Gazing at the fireplace, she locked her arms behind her back, one hand on her other elbow. "Like you."

"Uh, I'm not sure I know what you mean." But he would after he'd replayed their conversation a hundred times. Same as always. Still, he felt the comfort in her words wrap around him. Wait. She couldn't possibly know yet about the divorce, right? Did she think the accident had miraculously fixed his marriage?

His head spun. No one he knew was making any sense lately.

She turned to face him. "You're going to make it, David. I'm sorry about Suzy's accident, and for whatever part I played in it, but you'll both be okay. You're still standing."

"Yeah. Right here with you." Just how he liked it.

She gazed past him, but there was nothing up here except trees and trampled grasses and weeds. "School starts in a few weeks, and it's time for me to face work again. And Paul."

His heart dropped into his stomach. "What about me?"

"You've still got Suzy." She didn't look at him, and he struggled with how to tell her about the divorce just as her next words floated softly to him. "But I wanted to tell you, just this once, that I . . . love you."

"Yeah?" His yo-yo heart skipped a beat. "What I mean is, I'm, uh, starting to love you, too." Ugh. What a moron. But if he wasn't honest with her, why bother? Right now, the only thing he knew for sure was that he liked her and wanted to spend more time with her. Despite Suzy's accident and the promises he'd made to her in the ICU. Despite treating Liz like shit ever since.

She took one last look at the fireplace, then slowly headed back to the path. "I still have to go home."

He stayed right by her side. "But you said you loved me."

"That doesn't mean I can have you. Or, even if we weren't both married, that I'd be ready anytime soon to jump into another relationship." She kicked at a rock on the path but didn't seem unhappy. In fact, she looked much calmer than he felt. "And you're not ready, either."

He wouldn't deny it. Divorce wasn't a magic pill that would solve all the problems in his life, and he had to take care of Suzy. Divorce or no divorce, right now she needed him. But he didn't want Liz to leave anytime soon. His heart thumped wildly in his chest, and it hurt like hell. He brushed a leaf off her back. "What are your plans?"

"I need to figure myself out." Her eyes glimmered. With tears? He couldn't tell. "But I can't do that around you. And I need to talk to Paul."

It sounded like she'd already decided. She'd stay in D.C. and stay with Paul.

"Any chance of changing your mind?"

"About leaving?" She shook her head. "I can already feel the end of summer. It's time to go home."

They walked back in silence, David's heart thudding with each step. More than ever, he wanted Liz. He wished he'd told her when it might have made a difference.

"Liz."

Hearing Dad's faint call, Liz set down her book and eased

off the sofa in the great room, then glanced at the porch, where Diana rocked as she read a magazine.

She rubbed her knotted stomach as she padded in bare feet to Dad's room. August thirteen. Summer was quickly drawing to a close, and she'd avoided the unavoidable all summer. She and Dad still needed to talk. Pushing open the door, she found Jenna. For the fifth time this week, propped on Dad's bed, giggling in delight.

Liz leaned against the doorjamb. "You wanted me?"

Her dad continued talking in a low, halting voice with Jenna, as if Liz didn't exist. Like always. Tapping her foot, Liz waited.

"Jenna?" At Liz's voice, Jenna finally turned around. "Should you be bothering Gramps? You were in here this morning."

Jenna giggled. "Hi, Mom. We were just talkin'."

"About what?"

"About . . . Liz." Dad looked at Liz and frowned. "Liz . . . and I . . . were talking."

He'd touched a match to her already short fuse.

"She's not Liz." She jabbed a shaking finger at her own chest. "*I'm* Liz. *I'm* your daughter. You don't need to talk to Jenna about me. Jenna's *my* daughter."

"Mom, I—" Jenna's voice came out on a squeak. "I was just talking to Gramps. We were having fun."

"But I never did." To her annoyance, her voice shook. "Because of my dad, I had the most unbelievably horrible childhood, and I'm sick that he can't understand me now." She glared at Dad, who stared blankly. "And I'm sick of goddamn everything!"

She caught her breath at the end of her tirade, gazing in mute shock at her dad and Jenna, and slid down the wall to the floor. Burying her head on her upturned knees, she cried for every tear, every year, she should've let go three decades ago.

"You're not sick, Mom. Gramps is." Jenna's little voice quavered as she slid past her and out the door. "You're mean. You oughta be more nice."

A dull roar filled Liz's ears as embarrassment hit scabbed-over pain and hot tears flooded unchecked. After several long minutes, a hand touched her shoulder. Jenna. She had to apologize to her little girl. And then to Dad.

Looking up, she met Diana's sad gaze, not Jenna's. Diana walked over to Dad, fussing with his pillow as he lay staring at Liz.

Her back to Liz, Diana spoke. "What happened?"

"I . . . lost it." Liz wiped her soggy face on her arm and wished she could bury herself someplace. "Dad keeps saying Jenna is me and he talks to her and he won't talk to me and he never—"

She ended on another sob.

"Treated you half so well?" Diana held Dad's hand as she turned to face Liz. "I know. But have you talked to him this summer? Have you even tried?"

She whispered into her knees. "No."

"Then I suggest you start. Now." With a reassuring smile at Dad, Diana patted his arm before moving to Liz. She held out a hand, helping her up from the floor. "It's not too late, and you're a strong woman. Strong enough, if you choose, to forgive your father. He's a good man, and it's time you realized it."

Liz bowed her head. "I'm sorry, Diana."

"I'm not the person to tell." She squeezed Liz's hand, then stepped to the doorway. "I'll see if Jenna's all right while you talk to your father."

Liz started after her, but Diana whirled, holding Liz in

place. "You have to face him, Liz. It's time." She sighed. "It's long past time."

Swallowing against a dry throat, Liz bit her lip and nodded.

"Good girl." Diana patted her shoulder. "Now remember what Jenna said. Be nice."

CHAPTER 21

"Jenna? Jenna!" Diana's knees creaked as she peered under each of the beds in the sleeping porch upstairs. No luck.

She rose, rubbing her back, and glanced out the windows overlooking the River. In the past half hour, clouds had descended on their sunny day, dark green and angry, and winds howled through trees that bent over sideways. A limb banged against the window frame, startling her.

The weather eliminated the possibility that Jenna had gone down to the beach or up the path. She'd already searched the house from top to bottom. That left David's house. She'd check the basement one more time, then call him. Thank God Suzy's parents were spending the day with her, letting David and the boys take a mid-week break at the River.

Time for reinforcements.

LIZ APPROACHED her dad's bed as if it were the gallows. One. Step. After. Another.

He'd closed his eyes, but his hands gripped the sheet at his waist, his knuckles white against the spotted yellowish skin.

She watched a tear form in the corner of his eye and trickle down his cheek. Without thinking, she reached over and brushed it away. Looking at him, Liz felt a twinge of anger, a dollop of sadness, and a mountain of shame for shouting at a dying old man who lay in a darkened room while the rest of the family enjoyed a glorious if topsy-turvy summer.

She felt smaller than the terrified little girl she'd once been, scrunching herself into a ball as she hid from her dad and nursed the blows he'd already delivered. Wondering if she'd get out alive. Wondering, sometimes, if it mattered.

"Dad?" She stood at his side, awkward and uncomfortable.

His eyes blinked open. "Liz?"

"Yes." But, then, he called everyone Liz.

He patted the bed next to him. She gazed into his eyes as she remained frozen in place.

His hand stilled on the bed. "Jenna is . . . a good girl."

"I know." Her face felt pinched as she tried to smile. "She likes talking to you."

He blinked. "I . . . love you."

She bit her lip, not knowing how to respond.

"Always felt . . . bad. All my . . . life."

"Oh, Dad." The fragile dam burst in her eyes, and she sat down hard on the bed, fumbling for a Kleenex from the box on his table. "All those years. You never loved me and I always wanted you to and you kept hitting me and—" She blew her nose. "It never stopped."

A shaking hand clasped hers.

"Need you . . . forgive me."

"Tell me why." She waved her free hand in the air. "Why it all happened. Why you didn't love me."

"Always . . . loved you."

"But you hit me. I was so little. I couldn't stop you."

He shook his head as more tears pooled in his eyes. "Can't . . . forgive myself. No . . . excuses. Drank . . . to forget. To stop . . . pain."

Wheezing, he relaxed his grip and pointed at his cup. With shaky hands, she picked up the cup and held it close to his mouth. He took a long sip from the straw.

When he finished, she wiped the edge of his mouth with a napkin. "What pain? Mine?" She closed her eyes, reliving the days and nights of terror. How she'd slip and fall as she ran. Cowered behind her mom, who was often as drunk as Dad and either unable or unwilling to protect her. "Your drinking caused the pain. It made it worse."

"My . . . pain. Your . . . mother's pain. Baby . . . died."

Liz sat back, frowning. He'd mentioned a dead baby once before, and it still didn't make sense. The first time, she'd assumed it was a figment of his cancer-addled brain. "What do you mean, Dad? What baby?"

He closed his eyes, and her breath caught as she pleaded with the Universe not to let him fall asleep again. After a tense minute, his eyelids fluttered open to half mast.

"You . . . fell in water." His chest rose and fell as his breathing became more labored. "I was . . . at work. Your mother . . . was pregnant. She . . ."

His eyelids started to droop, and she touched his hand. "Mom what? Where were we? Here at the River?"

He blinked, looking as if he was seeing Liz from a different time. As a little girl? Like Jenna? "Here. You . . . couldn't swim. Your mother . . . jumped in. You . . . kicked her. Scared."

"Mom was scared, or I was?"

"You were . . . scared. Two years old." He wet his lips, the process taking an eternity. "Kicked and hit. Baby . . . died."

Oh. God. She'd nearly drowned, and Mom had saved her, but Liz had repaid her by causing a miscarriage?

"Couldn't . . . have another."

"Dad, I never—" Never what? She'd never known about this. Never meant to cause a miscarriage, obviously. Liz felt sick, ashamed of her two-year-old self—until she pictured Jenna at age two. No one could blame a two-year-old for much of anything except a lot of messes and the occasional tantrum.

Her mind raced, searching for even sketchy details and remembering none, as Dad stared at her, waiting for . . . she had no idea what. She tensed, remembering how much she'd always been terrified of the water. Had it started that day? Maybe. But no one had ever told her about the accident, or about the baby they'd lost as a result.

But it still hadn't been her fault. She'd been two years old, for God's sake.

"Is that why you hit me?"

Dad blinked once, twice, then slowly nodded. "No . . . excuses. When baby died, we . . . drank. No hope. Angry. I kept . . . hitting."

Liz screwed her eyes shut against the horrific pain. He'd drunk so much and hit Mom and her because he was upset about losing the baby, or because a two-year-old child had caused it? Mom drank, too, and never told her any of this. Maybe they'd loved her, but they'd never protected her. They'd cared more about an unknown baby who hadn't lived than a flesh-and-blood child right in their home. Her.

She thought of her own miscarriages, her own inability to have a second child, and wondered if she'd ever taken out her frustration on Jenna. Physically, never. But she'd upset and probably frightened Jenna just ten minutes ago when she'd been lashing out at her dad. She had to fix things with Jenna before it was too late.

"Oh, Dad." She bit her lip. Part of her understood, but she wished she'd known when she'd still had time. Seeing the stark pain in his eyes, she knew he'd struggled, even if not hard enough. "I don't know what to say." She leaned toward him and, on an impulse, hugged him. For the first time in memory.

Caught in an awkward embrace, hampered by her dad's hospital bed and wasted body and feelings neither of them could express, Liz felt his tears on her cheek. Pulling away, she wiped her arm across her face, then grabbed a tissue and dried his eyes.

He stared at her intently.

Gazing into his gaunt, pallid face, her heart opened. Maybe just a crack, but still. "It's okay, Dad." She patted his hand, sucking in a breath and letting it rush back out. "I forgive you."

A shadow of a smile lit his eyes as he touched her hand again. "Not too . . . late. Start . . . over."

She only wished they could. "I hope so."

"Talk more . . . tomorrow." His eyelids fluttered. "Need to . . . rest."

She watched his eyes close, heard his breathing deepen as his head tilted slightly to one side.

"Liz."

She whirled at Diana's voice, searching her face, wondering if she'd heard everything. Diana pursed her lips as David appeared at her back. Her words came out strangled. "We can't find Jenna."

Diana pointed at the window. Outside, lightning flashed,

and thunder shook the house seconds later. Rain lashed at the windows. Caught up in her own drama, Liz hadn't even noticed the sun leave the sky.

Brushing past Diana, David grabbed Liz's hand, pulling her to her feet. "We've already searched both houses, and I just checked the beach. I think she was down there."

As he hurried her out of the room, her brain registered his words. When they reached the porch, she froze. "She *was* there?"

"Yeah." He shot out the door ahead of her, Diana tripping behind them. "One of the canoes is missing."

AN INNER TUBE blew across the beach as David ran to Pete and Billy, who'd thankfully obeyed the quick orders he'd barked at them. Billy huddled on the dock, shivering against the cold northwest wind and buried under a pile of towels and life jackets. Pete had started the speedboat's engine and stood next to the driver's seat, arms crossed on his bare chest.

Pounding across the rainswept beach in bare feet, David reached the dock in seconds that felt like hours. Liz and Mom were behind him, Liz halfway across the beach, Mom at the bottom of the concrete steps. As he watched them, Mom fell, clutching her ankle, then struggled to her feet again and kept coming.

He silently urged them on. They couldn't lose Jenna.

David swallowed past a lump in his throat and turned toward his boys, then slipped and slid across the gangplank leading to the dock as waves washed across them.

"You guys ready?" Heart pumping, he took the towels from Billy, tossing them into the boat. He turned back to

Billy, shouting over the wind. "Give everyone a life jacket. Then go back upstairs and stay with Gramps."

Billy stayed put. "Dad—"

"I know you want to help, but Gramps needs someone to stay with him." David put a hand on his shoulder, looking him in the eye. "I need Gram to go with us. In case—"

Liz reached them, breathing hard, and David didn't say anything more. Dropping the life jackets on the dock, Billy took off like a streak, almost colliding with Mom at the end of the dock.

"What are we doing?" Liz's words came out so fast they ran together. "She's not in the water, is she? Jenna knows the rules. She wouldn't take— Oh, God."

David followed Liz's gaze as she turned, her hand shaking as she pointed at the canoe paddle floating near his dock next door.

Mom appeared at David's elbow, her lips pressed in a straight line as she noted the paddle, then climbed into the boat without saying a word. David guided Liz into the bow.

Tossing the life jackets into the boat, he cast off the mooring line and climbed into the driver's seat, nudging Pete aside. "I'll drive. Go to the bow and help Liz. And put on life jackets. In this storm, everyone needs one." But he didn't bother with one.

Pete leaped into the bow, hauling several towels with him, and draped one over Liz as she clung to the side railing.

David turned on the running lights and reached beneath his seat for the high-powered flashlight. As the raging storm turned afternoon into night, he couldn't see much in the inky darkness. He tossed the flashlight to Pete, who caught it and pointed it at the water.

Pulling away from the dock, David pushed the throttle down in slow increments, afraid of what—or who—he might hit. He shouted at Pete. "Keep sweeping the light back and forth in front of the boat, about fifteen feet out. Yeah, like that."

They moved out twenty feet, thirty, as fast as David allowed himself, heading directly into the whitecaps toward the point and the marina.

Pete shouted as his flashlight lit up something floating in the water. Another canoe paddle. Liz nearly fell over the side of the boat until Pete grabbed her life jacket with one hand, the other still holding the flashlight, and hauled her back in.

David felt his Mom's hands on his shoulders as he gripped the steering wheel harder.

"Keep going, dear." Her calm voice soothed his nerves. "But perhaps a little faster."

He pressed harder on the throttle, sending them forward in a spurt. No cruisers lined the yacht club beach near the point, no other boats dotted the River. Rain soaked them as huge waves crashed against the boat, pouring over the bow and rocking them from side to side.

"She can't— In this—"

"Keep driving, dear." Mom's hands pressed harder on his shoulders as his jaw clenched. "You can do this."

Watching the flashlight's beam arc across the water ahead of them, David saw the tiny yellow life jacket bobbing a moment before Pete shouted. Jenna's life jacket. Empty.

"Oh, God." Mom's voice faltered as her fingernails dug into David's shoulders, making him jump.

"We'll find her, Mom." David glanced back at his mom's stark face. "You promised."

Rain poured down, blending with her tears. "I still hope."

He pushed a little harder on the throttle, then pulled up, holding it steady as they nosed past the life jacket and Pete scooped it out of the water. Liz snatched it from him, burying her face in it, and Pete kept one hand on her back.

As they kept going, something large floated in the water ahead of the flashlight's beam.

"Over there, Pete! What's that?" David shouted over the wind's roar, and the flashlight beam shot out twenty feet, flickering over something long and gray and quite familiar.

Their canoe.

Liz struggled with Pete as she tried to jump into the water. The flashlight's beam bounced everywhere, then nowhere, as Pete lost his grip on the flashlight and it dropped to the floor.

"Stop it!" David shouted as he pulled back to neutral. "For God's sake, stay in the boat, Liz. Someone pick up the goddamned flashlight. I can't see a thing!"

Mute, Liz curled up in a ball, and within moments the flashlight's beam again swept the water. David pushed down on the throttle, slightly, inching toward the canoe. They drew alongside it. No Jenna in or near it.

"Dad, look!" The light bounced up and down as Pete jumped. "The buoy!"

"Hold the light steady!"

The flashlight's beam shot out ahead of them and held. There, just out from the point, the red buoy at the end of the point bobbed in the waves.

A tiny form clung to its base. Jenna.

David pressed down on the throttle and sped toward the buoy just as her head disappeared beneath the water. She returned to the surface, thrashing as her hands clawed at the narrow ledge on the base of the buoy—and missed, going under again.

David shot forward to within ten feet of the buoy and slammed into reverse, struggling to hold the boat in place as the water rushed and swirled around them. Without warning, Pete leaped out of the boat and dove at the buoy. Before anyone could stop her, Liz flung off her life jacket and jumped in after Pete.

"Pete! Liz! Jesus Christ!"

Pete's head and torso disappeared under the water, and waves crashed against the buoy. When he came back up, sputtering, Liz dove underwater as Pete clung to the buoy. Mom hurried into the bow, knelt on the seat, and started fastening a couple of life jackets to a ski rope. Finally, Liz came to the surface, sucked in air, and dove again.

David counted the seconds. Five, six, seven—

Liz came up a second time, spitting out water but holding Jenna, motionless in her arms.

"Liz! Jenna! Pete!" Mom threw the end of the ski rope, with the life jackets attached, toward the trio. "David, pull closer!"

As Jenna started to struggle, Liz held her tight against her chest with one arm and reached for Pete with her free hand. Pete held onto the two as he grabbed hold of the rope's handle. Somehow, Mom lifted Jenna, then Liz, into the rocking boat, and Liz hauled Pete in before grabbing Jenna, who coughed up water. Liz wrapped several towels around her and held on tight. Mom draped a soggy towel over Pete, then pulled him onto her lap.

"Aw, Gram!"

"Pete, my dear, dear boy." She choked against the sobs now wracking her body. "I'm so proud of you."

"I didn't do anything. Liz saved her."

Liz touched his arm over the top of Jenna's head. "I . . . I can never thank you enough. For trying. For giving me the courage to jump in after you. We both saved my baby." She held on tight to Jenna, who shuddered violently.

"M-M-Mom?" Jenna's teeth chattered. "I'm . . . safe now. An' I'm not a baby."

"You're *my* baby, Jenn. But, yes, you're safe." Liz clung to Jenna as they rocked together on the seat. "I have you back."

TURNING AWAY from the fireplace in the great room, David handed a golden-brown marshmallow to Jenna, who was curled up in Liz's arms on a rocking chair pulled close to the fire. An afghan was draped around her dry clothes.

"You forgot crackers and Hershey bars." Jenna wagged a little finger at David, who laughed and bowed before her.

"Sorry, Princess." He slapped his forehead in mock chagrin. "I keep forgetting your lack of appreciation for marshmallows."

Liz stretched her legs, letting the heat of the fire warm her toes. "Her mom appreciates them."

"Then her mom should get off her butt and roast some marshmallows." David tossed the marshmallow bag to Liz, hitting her in the face. "Oops. I missed?"

She flung the bag back at him. "I'm taking care of Jenna. Here. On my butt."

"I see that."

"Now, children." Diana looked over at them from the middle of the sofa, her hands curled around a steaming mug of cocoa. "Enough."

Billy and Pete, on either side of Diana, smirked.

"Jenna, dear, are you feeling better?" Leaning forward, Diana smiled at Jenna, who promptly shivered.

Everyone laughed, bringing out Jenna's lower lip.

"I was real cold! An' wet!"

Liz trembled, trying not to think about how close they'd

come to losing Jenna, how limp she'd felt in Liz's arms while David raced them all back home in the boat.

"An hour ago." Billy rolled his eyes. "You're fine now. Don't be such a baby."

"Billy..." Diana leaned toward him and tweaked his ear.

He turned bright red and crossed his arms. "Why'd she take the canoe out in a storm, huh? That was pretty dumb."

Burrowing into Liz's chest, Jenna sucked her thumb.

"It's okay, sweetie." Liz ran a hand through Jenna's baby-soft hair. After nearly bursting with relief, terror, joy, and gratitude at Jenna's miraculous rescue, she'd spent the last hour asking herself the question Billy had just voiced. "But why did you take a canoe? Alone? And in a storm?"

She shivered, unable to forget watching Jenna disappear under the water, or her own stark terror when she'd leaped in after Jenna. She wondered whether her mom had felt the same terror the day she'd jumped in to save two-year-old Liz.

"It wasn't raining when I left."

Crouching down next to Jenna, David handed Jenna a s'more. "But you took a canoe by yourself, without your life jacket on. You know the rules, Jenn."

Her lower lip quivered. "I put on my life jacket." Her chin dropped to her chest. "But I couldn't make the buckles go together."

He patted her shoulder. "Why did you go?"

"I... I wanted to see my daddy."

Liz looked from David to Diana and rocked harder.

"That's so—"

"Shhh." Diana squeezed Billy's hand and frowned.

Liz leaned forward to look at Jenna. "But Daddy's in Washington, Jenn. He's not anywhere near the River."

Jenna again sucked her thumb.

David tapped Jenna's nose. "You can tell us, kiddo. We need to understand."

Jenna pulled her thumb out of her mouth. "Mom yelled at Gramps an' made me feel bad. I didn't wanna ever come back. Daddy loves me."

"I—I'm sorry, sweetie." Liz stroked Jenna's hair as everyone's gaze landed on her and the last s'more she'd eaten tap-danced in her stomach. "I love you to the moon and back, but Gramps and I had to talk about . . . some things. And we did." Liz glanced at Diana, who nodded. "It took me a long time to find the courage to talk to him."

Jenna twisted in her lap, peering at Liz. "You were scared of Gramps? But you're so brave, and he's so nice."

"I know. I mean—" She faltered, not wanting to spoil Jenna's opinion of Dad. "It's complicated."

Jenna nodded wisely. "That's what grown-ups always say when they don't wanna tell me something."

Laughing, David tugged a lock of Jenna's hair. "You've got it all figured out, kid."

As the others laughed, too, Liz hugged Jenna and vowed not to lose her again. She also wouldn't waste another second of her life crying over the other babies she'd probably never have. Jenna, all by herself, was absolutely perfect.

———

"Liz? Wake up. Please."

The hand nudging her shoulder didn't feel like David's, and the voice didn't belong to David. Piper. No, Piper was still on her honeymoon. They were coming back Saturday and this was . . . was . . . Thursday.

The day after Wednesday. When she'd screamed at Dad, forgiven Dad, and almost lost Jenna. A painful, terrifying, and ultimately blessed day. She still had Jenna, and she'd finally faced her dad—and gotten a new chance with him. The chance she'd craved her whole life. Smiling, she rolled over and buried her face in the pillow.

"Liz." The hand pressed harder on her shoulder.

Her eyes flew open.

"Diana! What's going on? Is Jenna all right?" Terror gripped her, thrumming the length of her body. "Where is she?"

Diana's always-perfect hair stood on end, and lines bracketed her mouth. "She's fine. I'm sorry. I didn't mean to worry you." She sagged onto the bed next to Liz.

Liz whirled to check the clock. Six-thirty.

"Then what is it?" She pushed herself to a sitting position as Diana opened her mouth and closed it again.

Diana's hand found Liz's. "It's . . . your father. Something made me get up to check on him." Diana's head dropped as Liz held her breath, waiting. "He died. Sometime during the night."

"No!" A sob tore itself out of her throat. "He can't!"

"I'm so sorry. I . . . lost him, too."

They held each other and rocked, back and forth, as tears fell between them.

"He said we could start over." Liz shook her head, tasting salt on her lips. "I finally had a chance. He—"

"He loved you, Liz."

"But I . . . I never knew. Until yesterday. And now it's too late." Her hands balled into fists. "I still needed to understand why he hated me enough to hit me. He said he loved me, but—"

"And he did."

"But now it's too late. I'll never know. I might make the

same—" She fumbled blindly for a tissue and blew her nose. "The same mistakes with Jenna. I might hurt her."

"No, you won't." Diana brushed a hand through Liz's hair, then pulled her in tight. "You're much too strong. You would never hurt her."

"But I hurt her y-yesterday." Tears falling harder now, she rubbed her face against Diana's robe. "That's why she ran away."

Diana glanced down at her robe as she brushed her hand across the robe's lapel. "Who can blame the child? You wiped your nose all over my robe." She wrinkled her nose. "That's somewhat disgusting."

Liz laughed but kept crying. "Only somewhat?"

"I was being nice." Diana grasped her hand. "Come. We need to tell David. And perhaps the children." She tilted her head to one side as Liz helped her to the door. "Or perhaps we'll tell them after we call whomever it is we should call."

Liz drew her arm around Diana as they walked downstairs, thinking of all the things she wished she'd said to Dad. The things she wished he could've told her. The things she still needed to understand. Regret stabbed her, berating her.

Until she noticed Diana's bleak, faraway gaze.

"Oh, Diana." When they reached the bottom, Liz pulled Diana against her, holding on tight. "I'm so sorry. All I think about is me, and what I lost. You lost your husband."

She ached at the pain etched in Diana's eyes.

"Not just my husband, dear. My love."

CHAPTER 22

David pressed his nose against the screen door to the back house and peered inside. Liz, at her laptop. Like old times.

But she hadn't looked like this in over a month.

"Hey." He called out as he swung open the door, expecting her usual violent motions as she stabbed at the "save" button and slammed the damn thing closed. "I finally found you."

Twisting in her rickety old chair, she looked at him expectantly and left the laptop open. Surprised, he stepped inside. The screen held lots of words and a few wet smudges.

"Here." He grabbed a Kleenex from the box on the desk and handed it to her. "I'm getting good at this."

She blew her nose, wadded up the tissue, and tossed it at the wastebasket, which overflowed with more of the same.

"How's it going?" As if he needed to ask. Black streaks ran down her cheeks. "I mean, are you, uh, doing okay?"

She reached for another Kleenex. "Okay, I guess. I mean —" She stopped abruptly, rested her elbows on the desk, and held the palm of one hand to her forehead.

He dragged a chair a dozen feet across the room and sat next to her. "I'm sorry. I know it wasn't great timing."

She blew her nose. "Understatement."

"But he must've hated lying there, unable to do anything."

She studied her laptop screen for a long moment before sighing. "I know. But I needed more time."

She'd had all summer, hadn't she? "Mom said you talked to him yesterday."

"Finally." She held up a hand, as if she knew what he was thinking, even though he would never have said it. "It's my fault for waiting so long, but you can't imagine how angry I've been all these years."

Uh, yeah. He definitely could.

"And terrified. Even though I told myself he couldn't hurt me anymore." She shrugged, brushing the back of her hand across her eyes. "At least, not physically. And now I'll never get to understand what happened."

In silence, they both looked at everything in the room except each other. He finally cleared his throat. "I'm sorry he died. He was good to me after my own dad died." After David had loosened up enough to let Frank get anywhere near him. "We were . . . pretty close."

Liz slammed the laptop closed. "I'm so happy for you."

He shot to his feet, catching her as she tried to move past him. "Wait, I didn't mean it that way. I'm sorry, for God's sake. I know how it was—"

She pried his hand off her arm. "Like I said, no one knew. No one but Dad and me."

Tears splattered on the back of Diana's hand as she sat cross-legged on her bedroom floor and sorted through a box filled with memories. Report cards the kids had brought to the River on the last day of school. Boat repair bills. Ticket stubs from the hot-air balloon ride they'd taken, despite Diana's shrieks, on her sixtieth birthday. A weathered billfold.

Meaningless junk. Treasures. Often both.

Her knees creaked as she bent forward and reached for a stack of file folders. She smiled at Frank's scrawled handwriting. *Finances. House. Boat slip. Wills.* She shook her head, wondering why he'd kept these at the River. Knowing Frank, he had duplicates at their Wayzata house.

Her eyes caught the single word on the last file. *Liz.*

She held her breath as she opened the file. A sealed envelope, addressed to Liz in Frank's handwriting.

Shaking, she stumbled to her feet, clutching the envelope as she ran in search of Liz.

Liz trembled as she ran a finger inside the envelope, getting a paper cut for her impatience. Ouch. She sucked on her stinging finger, then shook open the letter.

Written the day she'd graduated from high school. She sank into the pillows on her bed, remembering. Everyone else had moved out to the River that day. She'd gone straight from her graduation ceremony to parties with friends, then took a cab the next morning to the airport. Alone. Diana had offered to drive her, but she'd claimed she had a ride with Piper.

Dad must've assumed he'd give her this letter at the River. But she'd never returned until this summer, when he couldn't possibly have remembered he'd written it. He could barely remember *her*. But why, in all these years, hadn't he just mailed it?

As she read the letter word by word, line by line, she grabbed the box of Kleenex.

My dear Lizzie—

You're a grown woman now, too big for "Lizzie," but still a little girl in my heart.

Not the little girl you remember. The one I do. Lizzie, a newborn in my arms, staring at me with wide eyes. Lizzie, a year old, taking your first step, tripping and falling down the basement stairs as I raced after you and made a heart-stopping trip to the emergency room. Lizzie, four years old, pigtails flying, riding your bike with training wheels. Lizzie, five years old, clutching your mother's hand as you walked to your first day of school. Lizzie, seven years old, singing in the Christmas pageant at church. Lizzie, eight years old, back straight and eyes bright as you watched your mother's casket roll silently past.

In some ways my memories ended that day. Seeing the anger and hatred in your eyes in the ten years since—all of which I deserved—I've always wished it had been my own casket.

Lizzie, I loved you more than anything. How can I ever explain what I did?

Diana has prodded me all these years to "fix" things with you. Weak man that I am, I turned away each time your eyes flashed, afraid of the accusations you'd rightly hurl. And so I write this letter, hoping you'll read it and try to understand, and let us try again to be close: father and daughter.

Tears streamed down Liz's face. Another reminder of her idiotic stubbornness—and of all the years she'd lost. She'd cost herself a relationship with her dad and, two days ago, almost lost Jenna, too. So Dad hadn't been able to forgive himself? It ran in the family.

The words blurred before her.

Your mother and I loved each other—in the beginning, at least. Alcohol changed us. We both grew up in alcoholic homes, hers the polite, don't-talk-about-it sort, mine more violent. We grew into adults who emulated our parents.

I know you adored your mother—as I did, in my own way—but we had problems. When she was pregnant with you, we both vowed to change. Your mother did, for the most part, not breaking down until I'd broken completely. My own vow lasted in earnest only a few months, but I soon convinced myself that I didn't have a problem. That I could drink again.

Then, when you were two, the worst happened, and I stopped pretending I was okay. Your mother was pregnant again, and we were thrilled. When I wasn't working, I was drinking to celebrate. One afternoon, when I was at work, your mother called, sobbing, barely understandable. You'd tried to swim by jumping off the dock without warning her, while her back was turned, and in saving you she lost the baby. She miscarried.

I never came home that night. When we learned that the complications from the miscarriage also meant that your mother could never again get pregnant, all I can say is that I lost it. In the process, I lost your mother and you. I kept trying to fight my way back, but the demons inside me only grew with time. Your mother started drinking again, too. We were both weak and blamed each other.

Lizzie, you were always my beacon. I tried so hard to stop, but I couldn't. Or didn't. I never found the courage until your mother died, when I knew she could no longer save you from me—I'd have to save you. My last drink came that night, several years too late for you, a lifetime too late for me.

My life with Diana is so much more than I ever deserved. You deserve everything, Lizzie—a life filled with love and happiness. Never settle for less. I did, for a few long years, and I hurt you. I pray every day and every night that you won't follow in my footsteps. You're a strong, smart, capable young woman. I expect and hope for you everything that this world has to offer.

I love you, Lizzie. Forever and always.

After she finished the last line, and the "Love, Dad" scrawled beneath it, Liz drew a long breath. Then she calmly folded the letter, slid it back into the envelope, and laid it next to the lamp on the shelf behind her. Letting out the breath, she curled up in a ball and rocked back and forth on the bed.

They'd both wasted so many years, but Dad had finally saved her. From herself.

"I CAME AS SOON as I could, Liz." After hauling his bag up the steps, Paul pressed a hand to his stomach, then pulled a handkerchief from his suitcoat and mopped his brow.

He'd run all day, scrambling to finish projects and racing to the airport for the last flight to Minneapolis on a Friday night. He'd made it with only minutes to spare, then was rewarded with an awkward boat ride across the River from David's son—Pete?—who'd told Paul only that the adults had been tied up most of the day.

Liz glanced up from the porch glider, where she held Jenna in her lap and read a book out loud. She looked tired. "Thanks. Sorry I didn't pick you up myself, but it's been a long day."

Jenna scooted off Liz's lap and ran to him. "Daddy!"

He dropped his bags and bent down, hugging her hard. "You must be a foot taller."

"You silly." She giggled in his arms. "Gramps died. An' Mom is real sad. An' I took a canoe and—"

Liz leaped to her feet. "Jenn, Daddy just got here."

"I don't mind." No one else here said much to him, and he hadn't discussed anything except mergers all week.

Jenna's lower lip trembled. "There was a big storm an'—"

"Jenn!" Liz rushed up and tapped Jenna's nose. "Let's not tell Daddy about big storms right now. I bet he'd like a nice big glass of—" She glanced at Paul, eyebrows raised.

He could use a cold beer. Maybe several. "Lemonade?"

Jenna scampered to the kitchen.

"I'm sorry about your dad, Liz. And I want to talk. I've given it a lot of thought, and I'm ready to fight for you. For us. For Jenna."

"No one has to fight for Jenna. She's ours." Liz returned to the glider. He sat next to her, reaching for her hand, but she clasped her hands in her lap.

"Of course we wouldn't fight. We've never fought." Or they hadn't until this summer, when they'd done little else. "I meant that I want to be with both of you. Happy again."

"Were we, Paul? Were we ever happy?"

He'd been happy every day of their marriage until the day she'd left this summer for the River. So had she. "We've had great times. Going out to restaurants—"

"I go with friends. You eat from vending machines."

"Movies, concerts—"

"DVDs and Netflix. CDs and the music on our phones. Or my phone, at least."

"Watching Jenna grow up—"

"I've watched her. You saw the pictures I took."

Frustrated, he ran his hand through his hair. He'd spent

the summer alone, groveling for a few damn scraps from Liz, and all he kept getting from her was ice. He didn't deserve it. Yeah, he worked hard. But they'd been together, a team. She'd stolen Jenna from him, but she'd also stolen the best of herself, and he was finally pissed. "You told me to think, Liz. I've done a lot of thinking."

"So have I."

They sat in awkward silence, Paul watching Liz, Liz gazing outside at the darkening sky, as Jenna sauntered into the room holding a tiny cup of lemonade.

Behind her, Diana carried a couple of tall glasses and offered a weary smile. "Paul. Welcome."

He jolted to his feet.

"Please, sit down." She handed him a glass and kept the other when Liz shook her head. After clinking her glass against his, Diana moved to the rocker. "It's been quite a summer."

She glanced from Paul to Liz and back again, obviously noticing the gaping void. After a few minutes' mindless chitchat, she reached for the notepad and reading glasses on the table next to her.

"The funeral is on Monday, Paul. Can you stay that long?"

"I'll stay as long as it takes." He glanced at Liz, who tensed. They couldn't have the conversation he needed right now, not with Diana and Jenna here, but they'd have it. He wouldn't get on another plane before they did.

"Good, good." Diana skimmed a finger down the notepad. "I've been wondering about the funeral, Liz. Would you like to do a reading? Or would that be too difficult?"

Liz stared outside. What in the quiet black night could possibly hold her gaze? He couldn't see a damn thing.

"I'd like to give the eulogy."

"If not, I could always—" Diana halted abruptly and peered at Liz over her reading glasses. "What did you say?"

When Liz repeated her request, Diana blinked a few times, then reached for her lemonade without responding.

Liz's shoulders drooped. "Unless you don't want me to."

"It's not that, dear." Diana took a sip of lemonade, pursing her lips as she swallowed. "It's just that—"

"I know." Pushing herself up off the glider, Liz trudged across the porch as Paul scrambled after her. "David would probably be better at it. I just thought I'd ask."

Paul glanced over his shoulder as he followed Liz. Diana's reading glasses had dropped onto her notepad, and her head rested on one hand.

He had a glimmer of an idea how Diana felt.

———

"We're home." Piper dropped her suitcase in the middle of the porch. "Don't everyone rush out to say hi or anything."

Diana padded toward her from the kitchen, then greeted her with a hug. "I'm so glad you're back. Where's Brandon?"

"David's helping him with the rest of our stuff." Piper stepped into the empty great room and saw, at the far side of it, the open door to Frank's room. Almost lunchtime and no one appeared. "Where's Liz? How's everybody doing?"

Diana took Piper's hand and walked back to the porch, where they sat next to each other on the glider. "Let's wait for Brandon, but how was your trip?"

"Great." Piper stretched out her legs, glad to be anywhere other than sandwiched in an airplane. "I loved the Riviera. And Brandon loved the topless beaches."

Diana shook her head, smiling. "You married him."

"I did indeed."

He and David appeared then, both weighed down with luggage and souvenirs.

"Geez, Piper. Didn't they have furniture in the hotels?" David grunted as he dropped two bags on the floor. "You had to bring it with you?"

"Anything to make you sweat, David." Laughing, she patted the seat next to her. "C'mon, Brandon. I want to hear all the news, but Diana wanted to wait for you."

Brandon exchanged a glance with David, then walked over to the glider, stopping to kneel in front of Diana. "I'm so sorry, Mom. I wish I'd been here."

"Why? What happened?" Piper's spine went rigid as Diana leaned forward to hug Brandon.

"Frank died, dear. On Thursday." Diana shook her head at Brandon. "There was nothing you could do, and I didn't want to spoil your trip. The funeral is Monday."

"How's Liz taking it?" Piper got up to hunt for her friend.

"Reasonably well." Diana gave a soft, faraway smile. "Quite a few things have happened in the past few days. She's giving the eulogy."

"You're kidding." Three voices joined in stunned unison.

"No." Diana pushed off from the glider to stand up. "She's in the back house now, trying to write it, I believe. Paul is upstairs with Jenna."

Piper watched as Diana moved slowly across the porch, head bowed as she returned to the kitchen. With a parting kiss for Brandon, Piper went to find Liz.

———

THE WORDS WOULDN'T FLOW, dammit. They hadn't flowed all summer. This time, though, she was writing a eulogy, not a novel without a plot and definitely not a bitter memoir.

Liz's fingers hovered over the keys, waiting for inspiration. A glimmer of an idea—an odd, possibly ridiculous idea—popped into her head just as she closed the document. Tilting her head, she considered the idea, unable to dismiss it. She'd attempted two doomed writing projects this summer. Would this be just another dead end?

Hmmm. No, a beginning. The new beginning she'd longed for with Dad.

But first she needed closure. Nodding to herself, she jotted a few notes, then opened another document file. Her memoir. Bracing herself as the words popped up on the screen, she scrunched her nose and hit "print." Thirty pages groaned from the ancient printer.

She gathered them just as Piper appeared at the door. After closing the document, she hit "delete." One blink and it was gone.

"Piper!" She set the papers on her desk and groaned to her feet. "I missed you."

Piper offered her condolences, and they hugged. But she felt fine, actually, and better every day. Thanks to Dad, the knot of pain she'd carried inside her for so many years was slowly dissolving, leaving something else in its place. Hope.

After Piper filled Liz in on the highlights of her trip, she pointed at the memoir pages on the desk. "Is that the infamous novel I keep hearing about but never get to read? It looks way too long to be a eulogy."

As she reached for it, Liz snatched it away.

"Hey, it can't be that bad."

"Worse." Liz flushed as she held on tight. "I never told anyone, but the novel tanked my first week here. I've, uh, actually been working on a memoir."

Piper's eyebrows rose, but for once in her life she didn't say a word.

"The memoir probably tanked my second week here, but I kept nursing it along, not sure what to do with it." She'd spent most of the last several weeks avoiding it entirely. "When Dad died, I realized that I should let the memoir die, too."

Piper shrugged. "Maybe writing isn't in your future."

"Or maybe it is." At Piper's puzzled look, Liz laughed. "It's too soon to say anything, but I just had an idea. I might write a children's book. Especially for fathers and daughters."

"Are you sure? You've never said much, but I was here this summer, you know. I don't exactly see you cranking out some syrupy picture book and calling it 'Daddy's Little Girl.'" Piper stared at Liz as if she was crazy. Which she might be. "Maybe it's time for you to go back to work."

"Maybe." Liz bit her lip. She probably shouldn't have mentioned an idea that was still elusive even to her. "I should definitely come up with a better title. But I can see it in my mind. It would be a book to help fathers get to know their daughters, and vice versa."

Piper still looked skeptical. To put it mildly. "Like . . . Paul and Jenna?"

Liz's breath caught. Exactly. But right this moment, she'd rather focus on her own dad. She'd wasted so much time this summer that she could've spent getting to know him. Maybe her book would help other dads and daughters before it was too late.

Her arm around Piper, they walked out the door. "Enough about me. Hey, let's celebrate your trip. How about a bonfire tonight on the beach?"

"Are you kidding?"

She laughed as Piper gaped at her. "All those pages from my ill-fated memoir are just the thing to burn."

Liz tripped, barely avoiding a fall, as she made her way to the podium for the eulogy. David held his mom's hand and put his other arm around Billy, who hunched over in the pew. Pete, looking stiff and biting back tears, sat next to Jenna and Paul. At the far end of the pew, Brandon and Piper held hands.

Suzy had decided not to come today. Despite the boys' disappointment and his mom's mild disapproval, David had selfishly breathed a sigh of relief. Their détente was holding, so far, but testing it against the raw emotions of a funeral probably wasn't a smart idea.

He glanced up as Liz's quavering voice began, faltering over her greeting to the assembled churchgoers. He caught her eye and winked.

She stumbled over her next sentence.

The church grew silent as people strained to hear her quiet, almost whispered words. She described Frank as the man who'd married Mom after their respective spouses died, helped build a successful company, helped raise Mom's sons. Next to him, his mom smiled faintly.

"Finally, he was my dad." She'd moved on while his mind wandered. "We . . . had a difficult relationship."

His mom pursed her lips, and he squeezed her hand.

"We both made mistakes. Dad made mistakes early in my life, ones he never forgot until, maybe, the brain cancer took away so many of his memories and so much of Dad." Her voice broke, and she fumbled with her notes. "We managed to talk, finally, the day before he died. We should have talked sooner. Dad always hoped we would."

She cleared her throat. "His stubborn, foolish daughter wouldn't let that happen until it was too late."

Mom gripped David's hand so hard, it ached.

"But it turned out that he'd written a letter to me, two decades ago, when I was eighteen and headstrong. As opposed to thirty-seven and headstrong, like I am today."

A few titters came from the rows behind David.

"I read the letter after he died. Dad didn't ask for forgiveness, although I've given it. He gave me his love and asked me to be strong. And I finally realize that I am. After all these years, thanks to my dad, I'm finally, today, discovering in myself the person he always hoped I'd become. I want to make sure that my own little girl, Jenna, can do the same." She smiled at Jenna, who squirmed in the pew. "I hope Dad will be proud of me. No, I think he already is."

Mom nodded as tears streamed down her face. Gazing at her, Liz smiled.

"But, most of all, Dad wanted me to be happy. His final gift was the letter he hoped I'd read when I broke down and came to my senses and returned to the River. It took me too long, but I finally did. Thanks, Dad. I . . . love you."

The moment Liz stopped speaking, Mom hurried to the podium, and the two women held each other in a tearful but somehow happy embrace.

Liz was going to be okay. Maybe with Paul, maybe alone, almost certainly not with David—but he grinned at her anyway.

CHAPTER 23

After the last of the stragglers finally left the church, Liz walked with Paul through the deserted church parking lot. Jenna had insisted on riding with Diana in the funeral director's black limousine, and everyone else scattered to their cars, headed for the cemetery.

Still drained, she barely listened as Paul praised her eulogy. She hardly knew what she'd said. But she'd done it. Dad was gone, soon to be buried, and she could finally move on.

Without Paul.

They reached their respective rental cars. She'd return hers tomorrow, then focus on building a new life. She doubted her convertible back in D.C. could survive a Minnesota winter. It sometimes couldn't even handle D.C.'s weather. Glancing at the side-by-side cars, Liz walked over to the bench just beyond them, near a bubbling fountain in a small garden.

"Aren't we going to the cemetery?" Paul sat beside her as she squinted up at the sun. "I have to get back to Washington, Liz. After the cemetery, I should catch my flight, but I can't leave before we talk."

His bags were packed and in the trunk of his car.

"You're right." She sighed. Paul had tried to talk all weekend, but the eulogy had consumed her time and energy. She'd also dreaded this talk almost as much as she'd dreaded talking to her dad all summer, but she'd learned the hard way the mistake of waiting. "I can skip the cemetery." For both their sakes, she couldn't postpone this talk another moment. "I'm sorry. I know what you want, but I—"

"You don't know how I feel." He grabbed her hand. "I know I screwed up. Really. I finally see how much I've blown it. But this has been a hard summer for me, too, and I love you. In some ways, more today than when we first married. More than when the summer began."

"But I—"

He squeezed her hand harder, relaxing his grip when she flinched. "We have Jenna, and I don't know what I'd do without you. Without either of you." A tear trickled down his cheek, and he squeezed his eyes shut. "I flew out here ready to fight for you—or, hell, fight *with* you—but we can start over. Start fresh." He swallowed hard. "I'll even move to Minnesota, if that's what you want."

The weight of his hopes was crushing. "Please, Paul, that's not the answer. I can't stay married to you. I don't . . . love you."

Pain, and a flash of anger, shot across his face. "That's not fair. You told me to think about what I wanted, and I've spent the entire summer doing it. You can't give me that chance and then just walk away. We have Jenna. We have our life together."

She reached for him, offering a quick hug before pulling away. "I never meant to hurt you, but I've changed this summer. I did ask you to think, but I've spent my summer thinking, too. I'm finally figuring things out." She kept replaying the words in her dad's letter. "Or I'm starting to, at least."

"Is it David? Do you want him?"

She glanced at Paul, not really seeing him. Part of her wanted David, yes, but despite her silly high-school crush, she wouldn't have even considered the possibility if her marriage hadn't already been over. "It's not about David. It's about you and me. We haven't been happy together in a long time. I'm not sure we ever really were."

"I was happy." Paul stared at their joined hands. "I wanted to spend the rest of my life with you."

"But I can't do it. I need to be happy. I owe that to myself, and we both owe it to Jenna."

"Jenna?"

Liz looked at the fountain, which sputtered for an odd moment before flowing again. A metaphor for her life? "I watched my parents struggle until the day my mom died. I didn't understand much, but I knew they weren't happy."

"That was different. They drank. He hurt you."

"Jenna doesn't have that, thankfully, but I want her to have two happy parents." She pictured bright, smiling Jenna, who'd blossomed this summer. "We're her role models, Paul. We owe it to her."

He let go of her hand. "I won't be happy without you."

"Believe it or not, you'll be happier." She touched his arm. "Not right away. But soon."

"Will you . . . come back to Washington?"

She tilted her head, considering. In some ways, that had been the hardest decision. She still wasn't sure she'd made the right one. "Only long enough to wrap things up at work and pack up some things. I haven't figured out what I'll do, but it feels like I'm home here. Finally."

"And Jenna?" His voice broke. "I can't lose her, Liz. She's all I'll have left."

She ached, thinking of the agonizing hours she'd spent trying to figure out how to divide their precious little girl's life between two parents who loved her. "You can't take care of her, Paul. Your work consumes you."

"I-I could try not to let it."

She watched his face, feeling every ounce of his anguish. He was a good man, and she knew he wanted to do the right thing. She also knew he wouldn't change. "I'd never keep Jenna from you. Weekends, vacations, whenever you want to spend time with her. Anything. I want her to know you, and I want you to know her more than you do right now."

He nodded, absorbing her words. "So it's over."

"In a way, I think life is just beginning." She touched his shoulder, wishing she could've spared each of them this pain. "For both of us."

TUESDAY MORNING, Diana blinked against the rays pouring in through the curtains she'd forgotten to close last night.

Frank was buried. She was alone. Again. This time, likely forever.

Her door banged open, and Jenna squealed as she slid across the wooden floor and flung herself at Diana's prone body. They both giggled.

"What are you doing up so early?"

"Gram! We're gonna stay here! Me and Mom, and maybe Daddy." Diana had heard rumblings yesterday, but she'd let most conversations float past her. "In different houses. Mom gets one, Daddy gets one, and I get one."

Diana tapped Jenna on the nose. "I don't think it works that way. You don't get a house to yourself."

"Then I can stay with you sometimes. 'Cause Gramps is in heaven, and I don't want you to be all alone."

Diana hugged her. "I'd like that very much."

"An' Mom and I can stay here with you at the River in the summer, can't we?"

"Yes, indeed." She hoped so. It would be up to Liz. "In fact, let's go wake up your mom." Diana swung her legs off the bed and crossed to her dresser, where she picked up the folder labeled "Wills." She didn't need to be the only victim of Jenna's internal alarm clock. "We can ask her."

A squealing Jenna raced into the hall and pushed open the door to Liz's room. By the time Diana entered, Jenna had landed on top of Liz's legs. Rather painfully, based on Liz's groans.

"Good morning." Diana cheerfully pointed at Jenna. "It's a little early, I know."

"And you're encouraging her?"

Diana smiled as she perched on the edge of the bed. "I'm afraid, in that regard, the child is past saving."

Laughing, Liz toppled Jenna onto the other side of the bed, provoking more shrieks and giggles from Jenna.

Diana gripped the folder in her hands. "So you're staying in Minnesota. And Paul?"

Liz shrugged. "We're getting a divorce. He wants to be near Jenna, but I can't imagine him actually moving here. He can't easily move his law practice. And I need to figure out what I'll do and where we'll live."

"In the summers, you'll live here, of course."

"Would that be . . . okay?"

"More than okay." Diana opened the folder, which held copies of the wills Frank and she had signed so many years ago. "In fact, that's something I need to ask you. Would you mind if I still stay here in the summer?"

Liz blinked. "What do you mean?"

"You now own this house. When Frank and I wrote our wills, he insisted that you have this house when he died." She smiled as Liz's jaw dropped. "And I agreed. Happily. It's yours, Liz."

"I don't understand. You're—"

"His widow?" Diana tapped the first page of Frank's will. "Yes, but this house belonged to your mother. More important, Frank felt it belonged to you. He kept it for you, always hoping you'd return someday."

Liz covered her mouth as tears fell onto her hand.

"So . . . would you mind if I stayed here, too?" She tilted her head. "Of course, if Brandon and Piper decide to buy the Seltzer house up the path, I could always stay with them, or perhaps with David sometimes."

Bolting upright, Liz threw her arms around Diana. "You're staying right here. Nothing could make me happier."

"Nothing? That's unfortunate." Diana pulled back from Liz. "I'd so hoped that you'd help me with something else." She paused, her lips twitching, when Liz looked utterly confused. "You see, I have this little company to run, and I—"

Liz frowned. "But you're selling the company. And it's not exactly little."

"That's my point, dear. I've decided to keep it, but only if I can find the right person to take the helm." She clasped Liz's hands in her own. "Will you do it?"

"Are you joking?"

"I never joke about business." Diana arched one brow. "I would've thought you'd realized that by now."

Liz snorted. "I'm beginning to think I do."

DAVID RUMMAGED through boxes of books as Pete sauntered into the porch of their summer house.

"I'm heading over to Nicole's house." He reached for the keys on the hook near the door. "Okay if I take the boat?"

"And my car, I take it?"

Pete grinned. He'd shot up a couple of inches over the summer. Before too long, he might catch David or even wind up taller.

"Can we talk a minute?" David walked to where Pete slouched against the door, his hands in his pockets.

Pete eyed him cautiously. "I guess."

"Good. Have a seat." He pointed at Suzy's flowery chairs at the far end of the porch.

Pete stared at him for a long moment before shuffling to a chair, and David took the chair next to him. "I've made some decisions, and I wanted to talk to you about them."

"You mean you want to announce them." Pete's lip curled as he looked out the window. "Like you're gonna marry Liz. Geez, Dad. You and Mom aren't even divorced yet, and Mom's still laid up, and you're already in deep. That blows."

David clenched a fist at his side. "Sorry to burst your bubble, but I've got news for you. I'm not marrying Liz. I'm also not 'in deep' with her, as you say, or anyone else."

"You're not? But you guys—"

"Became good friends this summer, yeah. But she's not staying here for me. She's staying for herself." Mom broke all the news this morning before he'd even had breakfast. "She's also going to run Carruthers Medical."

"No way, Dad. You run it."

"Nope. I've already turned in my resignation."

David caught Pete's eye a moment before his son almost

slammed a hand down on Suzy's ridiculously fragile coffee table, which was barely strong enough to hold a bottle of wine. Pete swallowed, hard.

"I talked to Gram about it earlier this summer. The thing is, I've never liked running the business. Medical devices don't do it for me."

Pete sneered. "But Liz does?"

"Stop it." David slammed his own hand on the table. One of its legs broke, and it went down for the count. "I don't want to hear that again. Ever. Like I said, I'm doing this for me. And, actually, for you and Billy."

Pete's eyes looked wary. "Doing what?"

"I'm going back to school. I'd like to be a teacher before I'm too old to remember how kids think."

"Too late." Pete smirked. "You passed old several years ago."

"Ha ha." David rolled his eyes. "I've given it a lot of thought, and teaching sounds good to me. Probably high school."

"Poor Billy. You'll be teaching by the time he hits high school. There goes his rep."

"I'll aim for a different school." David cleared his throat as he pictured Billy's reaction, but it couldn't be worse than Pete's. "But that's not the point. Your mom and I are both making changes in our lives right now, changes that are pretty tough, but I want you guys to be happy. I did some things I've regretted in my life—"

"I don't wanna hear about Mom. That sucks, Dad."

"So I won't talk about her. But I got married too young—and so did your mom, I think. Then I went to work for my own mom because she asked me to. No other reason."

"Isn't that a good enough reason?"

Restless, David stood up and paced. "No. See, that's the

thing. It didn't do either Gram or me a favor. I wasn't happy, so I avoided work as much as I could and spent as much time as I could with you and Billy. Because that's what I really enjoyed."

Pete, whose face was turning red, didn't say anything.

"But now you guys are growing up, and I don't want to waste any more time. I think teaching is what I want. If it's not, I'll keep searching until I find it."

"How does that help Billy and me?"

"I love you guys. I don't want you to make the same mistakes I did." He grinned as Pete stared back in confusion. "So go hang out with Nicole. Just don't marry her."

"Ever?"

"Maybe when you're thirty. We'll talk then."

HEAD DOWN, oblivious to the world, Liz walked along the beach, headed for the point. She finally had a spare moment to absorb everything that had happened. Paul was back in D.C., although he'd fought it more than she'd anticipated, and she was here. Perhaps forever.

She hoped she'd done the right thing.

"Hey." David drew alongside her, startling her. "Mind if I join you?"

They strolled together in silence until they reached the point. On a Wednesday afternoon, no boats were anchored. A few sailboats and cruisers passed slowly through the channel. Across the River at the marina, Liz's brand-new Jeep was parked and waiting. She needed to make a trip back to D.C. before school started, but not today.

She sank into the sand, next to David on the deserted strip of beach, and tried not to think about the insane kisses they'd stolen this summer. They were actually free to kiss now, she supposed, but life had gotten more complicated for both of them. They'd both suffered losses. In a way, they'd both grown up.

She glanced sideways at him. Despite her hard-won wisdom, David was still hot.

He wrapped his arms around his upturned knees. "It's been quite a summer. Pretty hard."

"But good, too." She'd lost Dad, but she'd also found him. Diana and Suzy had both had terrifying accidents, and they'd nearly lost Jenna, but they'd all survived. Liz and David were both ending their marriages, but—

Okay, she wasn't sure how that one came out. She'd had a rollercoaster of a summer with David, filled with pain and surprising joy. Despite all the trauma, she loved being with him.

"Good? How do you figure?" David's eyebrows shot up. "The whole summer was tough on you. But you hung in there."

"I didn't have much choice." She picked up a stick and traced words in the sand. "I lost Dad, but you nearly lost Suzy. No matter how things were with her, that's not how you'd want your marriage to end."

"No." David grabbed another stick and tapped it against Liz's. "But she's alive, and it did end. So did yours, I hear."

She nodded, thinking of Paul, who'd looked so sad when he'd left for the airport. He'd sounded even more sad this morning when he called to talk to Jenna.

David dropped his stick. "Is there a chance for us?"

"As a couple?" She watched the waves ripple toward the shore, then looked sideways at David, who stared at the sand. "I need time. Time to think, time to heal." She touched his arm, feeling the sparks of electricity shooting between them. As always. "So do you."

"How long?"

Six months? A year? Longer? "The truth? I like you and want to be with you, but I won't rush it. Dad said—" She choked up every time she thought of his letter, and she thought of it often. "He wanted me to be happy. I need to be happy with myself first."

"Yeah. Me, too."

She blinked. "Really?"

"I talked to Pete yesterday. I'm getting a second shot and won't make the same damn mistakes twice. I just wanted—"

"What?"

He shrugged. "To be with you."

"I thought you just agreed we should wait."

"We did." He grinned. "But I'm a selfish bastard."

She slugged him. "Not to mention impatient."

He moved closer, and she sighed as he drew his arm around her, tempting her with the warmth of his body. She took a deep breath, wanting him despite her words, despite knowing it was the wrong thing. Or the wrong thing right now. Frankly, the guy was a little too sexy for her own good, and he always had been. Something else she liked about him.

He touched the ends of her hair, his fingertips brushing her cheek, making her shiver. "And I always get my way."

"If you're really lucky, I have a feeling you just might. " She leaned into him, feeling safe and content, even if certain parts of her were moving toward hot and bothered.

He dropped a kiss on her forehead as she closed her eyes. "And when might that be?"

"Next summer?" She envisioned the year ahead. Finding a house, starting Jenna in school, learning the family business. And working through the end of her marriage with Paul.

"After Memorial Day. Surprise me." She thought back to all those silly dreams she'd had about David in high school. How he'd sweep her off her feet. How he'd love her forever and never let her go. Twenty years later, maybe the dreams weren't quite so silly. "Right here."

"Here? At the River?"

"No." She shook her head as he brushed a kiss on her cheek and boldly headed for her lips. She pressed her fingers against his lips, even though she probably wouldn't try to avoid his kisses forever. "Here at the point. Some starry night when you can't think of anything but me."

"And you'll say yes?"

Her eyes twinkled as she imagined life with the golden boy. Kisses and lovemaking and ridiculous arguments and stupid hikes and—oh, yes—laughter. She hoped she'd be ready for him in a year. She wondered whether she could wait that long.

Guessing the answer already, she smiled at him. "It's a definite possibility."

A NOTE FROM MARY

Thank you for reading *Sunsets on Catfish Bar!* The summer house is almost identical (in my mind, at least) to the summer house that has been in my husband's family since the 1950s and now belongs to my husband and me. (But I made changes to the floor plan of the house next door, David's house in this book, to make it suit my author whims!) The beach, the boats, the waterskiing, the hikes: very much the same as ours. I've always thought that someone in a hurry could take quite a nasty fall down the slippery wooden steps in the house . . . but hopefully that fall will remain only in these pages.

If you enjoyed this book, I would really appreciate it if you could leave a review wherever you buy or talk about books. Whether super short or longer, all reviews are good, and they help other readers discover my books. Thank you so much!

I also love to hear from my readers! Please stay in touch by signing up for my newsletter. You can also connect with me on Facebook, Twitter, Instagram, or through my website. For links, check out my bio on the next page.

Happy reading!
Mary

ABOUT THE AUTHOR

Mary Strand practiced law in a large Minneapolis firm until the day she set aside her pointy-toed shoes (or most of them) and escaped the land of mergers and acquisitions to write novels. The first manuscript she wrote, *Cooper's Folly*, a romantic comedy, won RWA's Golden Heart award and was her debut novel. Her love of Jane Austen prompted her four-book YA series, The Bennet Sisters.

Mary lives on a lake in Minneapolis with her family, too many Converse Chucks, and a stuffed monkey named Philip. When not writing books or songs, she lives for sports, travel, rocking out on guitar, dancing (badly), and ill-advised adventures (including dancing) that offer a high probability of injury to herself and others. She writes YA, romantic comedy, and women's fiction novels.

Sunsets on Catfish Bar is the first novel in The Pendulum Trilogy.

You can find Mary at www.marystrand.com, follow her on Twitter or Instagram, or "like" her on Facebook.

ALSO BY MARY STRAND

Cooper's Folly

THE BENNET SISTERS

Book 1 - *Pride, Prejudice, and Push-ups Bras*
Book 2 - *Being Mary Bennet Blows*
Book 3 - *Cat Bennet, Queen of Nothing*
Book 4 - *Livin' La Vida Bennet*
The Bennet Sisters four-book set

THE PENDULUM TRILOGY

Book 1 - *Sunsets on Catfish Bar*
Book 2 - *Driving with the Top Down*
Book 3 - *Seemingly Perfect* - COMING SOON

ALSO BY MARY STRAND

Cooper's Folly

THE BENNET SISTERS

Book 1 - Pride, Prejudice, and Push-up Bras
Book 2 - Being Mary Bennet Blows
Book 3 - Cat Bennet, Queen of Nothing
Book 4 - I Nifer't Vant Boxter
The Bennet Sisters four-book set

THE PENDULUM TRILOGY

Book 1 - Sunsets on Catfish Bay
Book 2 - Playing with the Toy Boxer
Book 3 - Seemingly Perfect - COMING SOON